Birdie —
Here it is! Like it.
Hope you
like it.
Kathi
11-2-12

LILY'S WAR, A NOVEL

By Kathi Jackson

DEDICATION

To all those who had faith in LILY, especially The Lunch Ladies.

Love, as always, to William.

Lily's War, A Novel

ACKNOWLEDGMENTS

Thanks, as always, to Cheryl.

CHAPTER 1

The sky was black and the temperature bitterly cold, but the fashionable Louisville house was alive with tinkling piano music and rowdy laughter when two young men in sleek gray military uniforms came to the door and asked to see Polly's best girl, Lily. The statuesque madam with the upswept honey-blonde hair had barely opened the door when Lily entered the foyer and stopped dead in her tracks. Standing on tiptoe, she peered over one of her mentor's regal shoulders then whispered, "Oh my."

The usually confident woman curiously studied her favorite and most valued employee, opened her mouth to speak, then shut it and blinked rapidly as she shook her head. A keen businesswoman, Polly had a good eye for people—taking in Lily proved it. Who else would have seen the potential in the thirteen-year-old who had appeared from out of nowhere dressed as a filthy and ragged boy and obviously hiding from someone? And she was certainly accustomed to young cadets as customers, but still she hesitated.

And Lily couldn't understand why. She'd never seen Polly waver about any decision, large or small, and everything about these two reeked of money . . . Lily looked into the older woman's eyes and mouthed, "Please. . . ."

Again the woman started to speak but instead thrust out her hand and let one of the youths fill her palm. With pursed lips, she stared at Lily as she made a fist around the coins and walked away.

The three young people stood silent, suddenly shy and embarrassed about the reason that brought them together. But the moment of innocence quickly passed and the cadet who had done all the talking winked at Lily and she nodded in silent appreciation. Handsome. Impeccably attired. Slender build. Wavy blond hair. Exquisite profile. Sparkling blue eyes. Very nice.

2

They smiled at each other.

But even as Lily aimed her winning smile in his direction, her attention was captured—as it had been the moment she'd peered out the front door—by his companion, the one who hadn't uttered a sound and was so inebriated that he could barely stand. Mussed brown hair. Jacket buttons in the wrong holes. Droopy collar and tie. Glassy brown eyes that stared aimlessly around the room. Lily found it impossible to take her eyes off of him.

She also found it hard to breathe.

"I'm sure glad she decided to let us in." The blond rubbed his arms. "It was getting a little chilly standing out there."

Lily laughed. "Yes, I was about to find a shawl myself."

He smiled intimately as he made an elaborate gesture of kissing her hand, purposely letting his lips linger. "I'm sure you remember me, don't you? Saul. Remember?"

How many times had she heard that question? But it was the easiest of the two to satisfy, easier than the more common, "Why are you in such a business?" And she could laugh at this question. In fact, the ladies spent many an hour laughing about it. "Nothing about you to remember" was often their favorite quip—the response they wished they could give to these pompous men who thought themselves a stand-out in a sea of men. But because men were their business, the women always smiled demurely and responded . . .

"Of course I do." Lily patted his arm even as her attention returned to his friend.

"I thought you would. We had a good time, didn't we?" He winked again.

"You bet." Lily was starting to remember him, how he'd bragged during sex, boasted of bedding so many women and being told he was their best. Well, he hadn't been her best but she'd made sure he left thinking he was. It was the trademark of a good prostitute. It was Lily's trademark. Every man felt confident when he left Lily.

"I'm sorry I'll have to forego the pleasure tonight. I brought the *general* here to celebrate his graduation. He needs to be initiated—if you know what I mean." He winked again then patted his friend on the back. "David, ole' man, this is Lily, the lovely little flower I told you about, the Lily of the West. You know, like the song?"

David hiccuped and swayed and almost fell down.

Lily laughed. "A general, huh?" She looked up at him, but he continued to stare blindly around the room.

Saul spoke again and Lily began to wonder if David was mute. "Yes, ma'am. I told him about you and he was curious but too much of a

3

momma's boy to come here by himself. Even had to get him drunk first and he doesn't drink—never touched a drop before tonight—so I had to spike his punch." He laughed. "Yeh, he'll probably be sick as a dog before the night's over and should have one hell of a hangover in the morning."

The look Saul gave his friend chilled her, and she quickly returned her attention to the boy/man beside her, the pup who had no idea where he was. She laughed at his innocence and knew that Saul was telling the truth: She had a teetotalling virgin on her hands.

But he wouldn't look at her and being ignored was something Lily wasn't used to and couldn't stand. Oh, she knew she wasn't the prettiest girl at Polly's, but she knew she was the most popular and the most attractive in all the ways that counted. She'd once been described by a customer as having "hair the color of a setting sun, a mouth made for lovemaking, and a voice that hardened a man's tool." Not a romantic description, perhaps, but then Lily wasn't in the romance business, she was in the man-pleasing business. And she knew how to make the most of her assets—she'd certainly spent enough time thinking about them.

And why not? Her appearance and ability to please were her tickets to the independent future she had planned—running her own house. She'd learned early in life not to depend on anyone or allow herself to become involved in complicated emotions—people desert you and love doesn't last—so Lily was learning the business, honing her skills, and exploiting her youth.

She didn't blame Mama Rose, the madam in Lexington who'd raised her. She knew it wasn't the old lady's fault that her death had set the self-righteous townspeople on a clean-up campaign that closed down the house and sent the ladies to jail. It wasn't Mama Rose's fault that little Flora lost her virginity through rape by two policemen then had to change her name and appearance to escape. No, Mama Rose hadn't purposely deserted her.

But she couldn't say the same for her parents.

After all these years, her curiosity about them was as strong as ever. Had they loved each other? Had they loved her? No, they must not have. Would you desert a child you loved? And who did she look like? Was the dimple in her chin from her father? What about the gray eyes? And the deep throaty voice? And where had that bump on the bridge of her nose come from? And those damned freckles that covered it?

Well, they may not have given her love but they'd given her what she needed to attract men, and she hadn't found a man who could resist her—until now. She put herself in David's line of vision. "So, you don't drink?" "No ma'am." He hiccuped again. "Not a drop."

At least he wasn't mute.

Lily smiled at the liquor-coated mumble then laughed nervously. "Well, *General*, it looks like you could do with some rest. Want to go upstairs?" She put his arm around her shoulders then shivered at how he felt against her.

But his size and condition made it a struggle to get up each step, and just as they got to her room, he halted and almost fell on her when he poked her nose with his finger and slurred, "Who hit you?"

Lily gritted her teeth and pushed him onto the bed. "Damn rich boy."

He was asleep as soon as he landed.

She tugged off his boots and dropped them on the floor then yanked his arms out of the gray coat and tossed the heavy garment on a chair. Standing back, she folded her arms across her chest and stared at him—then realized she was smiling. How different he was. Most men were down to their drawers before the door was even shut.

Again she removed articles of his clothing—vest, tie, collar, sash—but this time she did so gently and placed them, carefully, on the chair—after she brushed off the coat and positioned it on the chair's back and after she stood the boots side by side between the chair's legs. With considerable effort, she maneuvered his six-foot frame to a more comfortable position on top of the covers then walked to her dressing table, shaking her head in amazement at how soundly he slept, how oblivious he was to everything she'd just done.

But she also shook her head to get rid of the warnings that ran rampant there. Warnings that ran wildly inside her stomach and her rapidly beating heart. Warnings that screamed out to her from the mirror's reflection even as she took the silky white gown out of the bottom drawer and let it flow down her arms and over her head.

As she admired the delicate lace gown that covered her breasts, she smiled at the memory of the night she'd received it—one of the last nights of her innocence, the day she'd had her first menses. Was it really just a year ago?

How the ladies had teased her as they'd showered her with soaps, combs, powders and perfumes! And the seductive gown . . . It had been her favorite gift and she'd been so anxious to wear it on the night she learned what it was like to make love. . . .

Well, she'd had sex many times since that night—but she'd never worn the gown.

She brushed her hair and finally looked into the eyes in the mirror, the admonishing eyes that filled with tears, the lovesick eyes of a vulnerable girl.

No! She jumped to her feet and ran away from the mirror and toward the bed. She was Lily, *the* Lily of the West, a well-known purveyor of pleasure, and there was nothing special about this man in her bed. No, tonight was no different than any other night.

But just as she started to blow out the light, she stopped.

And was, again, hypnotized by the sight of him.

Snoring. Brown lashes against tanned cheeks. Thick dark eyebrows that furrowed even as he slept. What was he dreaming about? Unruly dark brown waves that fell onto his forehead and onto the top of his shirt at the back of his neck.

Lily lowered the suspenders from his shoulders, covered him with a blanket, then got under the covers, all the while watching him, finding it impossible not to. When he snorted in his sleep, she laughed.

Then burst into tears.

There had been so many men but never one like this, never one whose face so captivated her, whose features she felt compelled to touch. "Who are you?" She whispered. "What are you doing to me?" She restrained her fingers from touching him then scolded herself. Why not? It was her job after all. She'd never been shy before—well, not since her first time—but that had been a year and countless men ago.

Surely this desire to touch him was because she had a weakness for men in uniform, a trait she'd inherited from her two favorite ladies at Mama Rose's, Stella and Gladys. Or perhaps it was simply because he hadn't touched her and her pride was hurt. Surely these were the reasons for this fascination. Surely after they had sex she'd feel differently.

But the warnings wouldn't go away and she was afraid, more afraid of the sleeping form on her bed than of anything else in her life. More than the rape. More than the slave auction she'd witnessed in Frankfort.

Afraid because every hair on her body and every drop of her blood needed to be a part of him, needed him inside her. How foolish, she thought, that a body that had known so many men could yearn for one so desperately.

"Wake up, soldier," she whispered. "Let's get this over with so this yearning will leave me. Let's get this over with so you can leave me."

But leaving was the last thing she wanted him to do and she fell asleep watching him.

CHAPTER 2

Then woke during the night.

And sat up to savor the peace of the predawn hours and the nocturnal sounds of nature—the neighing and stomping of restless tethered horses, the barking of dogs, the screeching and hissing of cats enjoying their amorous ceremony. Then there were the human sounds that penetrated the rose-patterned paper-thin walls—snores and giggles, feminine shrieks and squeals, deep-throated male laughter.

But his sounds were all that mattered—his grunts and snorts, his wetting of lips—and Lily nestled closer to him. What was it about him? What was this almost primitive connection she felt, this deep-rooted nurturing instinct made stronger with each slumbering breath that fell on her bare shoulders?

She could wait no longer and put her lips on his. Soft. She kissed him again, allowed the tip of her tongue to taste him. Was her mouth the first to claim his?

He grew restless and tossed onto his side away from her then back again. He licked his lips, opened his eyes, frowned, then blinked and forced himself awake. His eyes looked into hers and widened. "Where am I?" His voice was a hoarse whisper. He blinked again. "Who are you?"

Lily stayed silent, mesmerized by his struggle to wake from the alcohol-induced sleep. He sat up, groaned, and put his hands to his head, then slid back down onto the pillow and slept again.

The next time he opened his eyes, he looked at her, frowned, then raised himself onto his elbows and slowly glanced around the room. As Lily watched, she saw his expression turn from puzzlement to panic, and suddenly he bolted upright and swung his legs to the side of the bed before the pain in his head made him groan again. Stationary for a moment, his hands on his head, he took a deep breath then again surveyed his surroundings. His eyes blinked and his head shook and Lily saw panic rise in him again as he mumbled, "I shouldn't be here. How could I have been so stupid to go with him? I should have known better. What have I done?"

She inched toward him and put a hand on his shoulder.

He flinched and jumped to his feet, his hands forming fists at his sides.

"What's wrong, soldier?"

He brushed his fingers through his brown hair, mussed even more by sleep. "I shouldn't be here, can't be here."

"Then why are you?"

He stopped his nervous gesturing and looked at her but said nothing then scanned the room until he saw the chair with his things. A lump swelled in Lily's throat as he walked toward the chair, but just as he started to pick up his boots, he stopped.

She held her breath and restrained the urge to beg him to stay that filled her lungs, an urge she'd never felt before. Finally able to speak, she managed a calm whisper. "Please tell me what's wrong. Have I done something to anger you?"

"No, of course not. It's not your fault." He stared hard into her eyes. "Have we met before?"

An icy chill ran down her spine and she heard the nervousness in her voice. "I don't know." She had to make him stay . . . "It's still awhile 'til daylight. Why don't you come back to bed? Your head's bound to hurt."

He nodded then put a hand to his stomach. "Actually . . . "

Lily hurried to the chamber set and wet a cloth then reached up to pat his face. He smiled halfheartedly then took her hand. "You don't understand, do you?"

"No. I don't. You talk in riddles."

He shook his head as he stared at her then suddenly dropped her hand and almost ran to the window. Lily stared at his back and willed herself not to throw her arms around him, kiss his back, put her fingers in his hair. She stood, instead, with a wet cloth in her hand, more lovesick child than experienced prostitute.

He turned around, slowly, and walked past her and sat on the edge of the bed.

She had never felt such conflicting emotions—anger at herself for wanting him and anger at him for not wanting her. Why wasn't he grabbing at her?

But he was watching her, and Lily—well aware that the moon's light outlined her body through the sheer gown—purposely stood still, expecting—hoping—for a reaction from him. But his eyes were on her eyes, not her body, and she saw no longing in them, only confusion and sadness.

Bewildered, she got back under the covers and leaned against the headboard.

His eyes still on her, he coughed nervously. "I'm sorry, but I don't remember your name."

"Lily."

He nodded then looked uneasily around the room.

Was someone after him?

He extended his hand. "I'm David."

As her hand fit snugly into his large calloused one, Lily felt the same secure warm feeling that she'd felt when he'd leaned on her coming up the stairs.

He looked down at the top of her hand as his thumb rubbed it nervously, and when he again looked at her face, Lily saw that his eyes were shining, almost glistening, in the moonlight. He whispered, "You're beautiful."

"That's not what you said earlier."

"What?"

She pointed to her nose and repeated his comment then watched him turn red and stammer, "I'm truly sorry. I can't believe I'd . . ." He touched her nose and whispered, "I think it's a fine nose." His finger touched the curl by her cheek then grazed her lips as it left her face.

Lily closed her eyes.

"Saul called you something. It was . . . that song, 'The Lily of the West.' Why are you called that?" She opened her eyes to see his eyebrows furrow and his eyes turn dark. "Do you cause men to kill each other then betray them?"

Other men had asked the question but laughed when doing so. This one didn't laugh.

She quickly turned her face toward the window. "Of course not." Shrugging her shoulders, she barely spoke. "It's just a name." She coughed then turned back to find him watching her. "Don't soldiers give each other names? I think yours is 'general'."

He rolled his eyes. "That's just Dundee's way of giving me a hard time, but I do feel that I was born to be a soldier, born to train men, to turn them into gentlemen warriors and lead them into battle."

His intensity made her smile.

He jumped to his feet. "I will not be mocked."

Startled by his reaction, she reached toward him. "I'm sorry. I wasn't mocking you." *Come here, my soldier. Come love me.* "Sit down, please. I didn't mean to offend you. I'd never do such a thing."

He sat down and muttered, "I shouldn't be here anyway."

"Yes, you've said that. Why?"

"Because it's not fitting, not responsible, not moral. It's probably the last place on earth I should be."

"Well, no one's forcing you to stay."

His face turned meek. "I know."

"Well?"

He walked to the window again. With his back to her, he tucked in his shirt and raised his suspenders then spoke. Although just a whisper, Lily heard every syllable. "I don't mean to confuse you. It's not your fault. It's mine, all mine. I was weak but . . ." He turned to face her and leaned against the sill. "You don't know how things are. I've been reared a certain way and . . ." He ran his fingers through his hair. "Never mind." His head fell to his chest.

Lily patted the bed, silently begging him to stay. "Tell me how things are. Tell me about yourself."

He looked up, surprise on his face, then returned to the bed and sat down. She fluffed his pillow and helped him get comfortable then positioned herself so she could watch him. And how soon she fell into his patterns. The way his eyes moistened and his speech drawled when he seemed cautious then widened and rushed animatedly when he forgot himself. An open book, she thought. I can see your brain sorting out the do's and don'ts, the rights and wrongs. But she especially loved watching the small dimple by the left corner of his mouth deepen when he smiled or frowned.

His family had lived in South Carolina for decades. One of his grandfathers had been an eloquent speaker and a giant of a man who stood six inches over six feet and had served in the Continental Army. Another grandfather had been a member of the state senate and a doctor in Washington's army. Every uncle had a lustrous past, and even his older brother, Richard, was accomplished and had married well. Both sisters were also older and had married well. David was the baby, and the love he felt for his siblings and they for him was obvious. It was also obvious that he adored his mother.

When he began to speak of his deceased father, he hesitated then continued in an almost reverent whisper. The man, who'd been dead for six years, was not only the perfect gentleman and land baron, he was intelligent, witty, charming, and handsome. In other words, David thought him a god.

"My." Almost breathless, Lily wondered how many times he had recited this litany.

He was frowning. "What are you thinking?"

She shrugged her shoulders and touched the dimple with a fingertip. "Nothing."

"Yes you are. I feel you're judging my family, judging me."

So sensitive. She put a hand on his cheek and he closed his eyes and leaned into her palm. She let her thumb touch the full lips. "No, David. I'm not judging, certainly not you."

He opened his eyes. "Then what?"

Her hand still on his face, Lily gazed at his melancholy features. "I'm thinking of how proud your family must be of *you*. I'm thinking that *you* carry a heavy load." She dropped her hand and sighed then looked toward the ceiling. "I used to think that a heavy load was being deserted by your parents and raised by whores, of having only yourself to depend on." She turned her gaze back to him and let her eyes admire his broad shoulders, his dark brown hair, his sad eyes. "But you've had a much heavier load than I."

He coughed, his eyes moist, his brows knitted. "I don't know what you mean."

"I mean that you just told me about almost everyone in your family but you. What's *your* background? You said something earlier about training men. What do *you* want out of life?" She scooted down into the covers and lay on her side, propping herself up on her elbow. She wanted to memorize everything about him.

He spoke hesitantly as if sharing secret information. "Well . . . what I really want to do is open a military school. That's what I *want* to do but my family doesn't think teaching's suitable."

"How can they not? What could be more suitable than molding young minds?"

His eyes brightened and he nodded eagerly. "You think so too? I knew I was right. It is a fine profession, isn't it?" He frowned again. "But it's not profitable, not to their standards. They approve of soldiering but there's not much call for that right now. I thought I'd combine teaching and soldiering by training future soldiers. You do think it's an honorable goal, don't you?"

Lily wanted to look into his shining brown eyes forever. And did he really care about her opinion? "Yes, I truly do."

His eyes brightened again. "Oh Lily, you should see the piece of land we've bought."

Her name had never sounded so sweet, but "we"? She shivered and dreaded his next words. But what had she expected? Someone like him was bound to have been betrothed since childhood to an old family connection.

"We?" How she hated the quiver in her voice.

"My best friend, Jonathan. We're partners. You'd like him, everyone does."

Lily smiled again.

He turned somber and almost whispered, "He's the only person I can truly be myself with." But the bright eyes and smile returned and Lily savored his excitement, even if she found it a little hard to understand the words as they flew out of his mouth so quickly as if trying to catch up with his thoughts, dropping "r's" along the way. "The land is beautiful. It's a long way from home but just perfect otherwise."

a long way from home . . . "It sounds wonderful. You're smart and ambitious, David. I'm sure you'll establish a fine school *and* make it profitable. I can't imagine what your family does that can be better than teaching."

"We raise cotton."

Again the familial pride, the use of "we" even though he'd planned his future elsewhere. "Cotton, huh?"

"Yes."

Her stomach churned. "Do you use slaves?" *No, please, no* . . .

"Of course."

"How can you say that so casually?"

"Why not?"

"Because slavery's so cruel and unjust." She put her arms around her raised knees and shuddered then noticed that his eyes had darkened and she feared he'd leave. But slaves . . . The idea so horrified her that she couldn't restrain herself. "You do realize that, don't you?"

"No. I don't." He turned toward the edge of the bed then looked back at her. "And I don't need to be lectured by yet another Yankee who doesn't know what they're talking about."

"I am not a Yankee, sir, but I most certainly know what I'm talking about." Memories of a young black girl on an auction block made Lily nauseous. She blinked away tears. "How can you justify such a barbarous lifestyle?"

"Barbarous. . . ." He closed his eyes then opened them and spoke slowly and deliberately. Masking anger? "Because the manpower is necessary for an agrarian way of life. I know you've heard horror stories, but we treat our people very well. My mother sees to their care and we don't allow our overseers to beat them."

"Oh, well, I guess that makes it okay. I mean if you don't *beat* them. . . ."

"Well, we don't, and I resent your mockery. We care about the people we own."

"Don't you hear yourself, you 'own' people? Doesn't that word bother you?"

He seemed genuinely perplexed. "No, why should it? We do own them."

Lily shook her head and heard her voice rise. "Why? Because they're human beings and one human should not own another. It seems very simple to me."

"That's typical Yankee talk, easy for people to say who resent our way of life. I'm sorry, but I don't see why this should concern you."

She stared at him, her posture stiff. "And why's that? Because I'm a stupid whore or just an ignorant female?"

He winced. "I'm sorry, ma'am, but I find such language offensive."

She folded her arms across her chest. "In case you've forgotten, you're in a whore house."

Female squeals came through the walls and David looked startled then bounded off the bed. "Yes." He glowered at her even as he grabbed his boots and shoved his feet into them. "Thank you for reminding me." He yanked his coat off the chair and thrust his arms through the sleeves then grabbed the remaining items with one hand and grasped the door knob with the other.

Lily panicked. She hated his belief in the abominable institution and hated herself for wanting him in spite of it. But she did want him, wanted him desperately. She couldn't let him leave. She knew she'd never see him again. She'd known that from the first moment. David was a "good" boy, the type to marry and settle down. This night, this moment, was the only chance she would ever have to hold him, feel his arms around her, feel his mouth on hers, feel him inside her—and she felt she'd die if she couldn't feel him—all of him—just once.

He stood at the door, his hand on the knob, his face down.

"Saul gave Polly a lot of money for me to entertain you. Don't you want to get his money's worth?"

13

CHAPTER 3

He looked at her, his brows knitted, his eyes moist.

Please stay, please.

The dark eyes bore into hers and he opened his mouth then shut it and looked back at the door. His eyes were closed, his jaw clinched.

Lily wanted to scream his name, pull at him, beg him to stay. But she did none of those things, just sat on the bed and stared at him, silently trying to make him want her as much as she wanted him.

He looked at her again then sighed, his voice cracking. "You just don't understand."

"Yes, David, I think I do." She raised open arms to him. If he denied her, she'd be humiliated but it was a chance she had to take. Their eyes met and she nodded.

The wanton Eve tempting the good and noble Adam?

He removed his hand from the door knob and walked toward her as if a doomed man going to his execution.

But he entered her arms the aggressor.

And kissed her with the force of a novice, so hard that she pulled away slightly and whispered, "Shh, slow down." Seeing confusion in his eyes, Lily brushed her fingers through his hair and traced his features with a fingertip then kissed his eyes and cheeks. When she again put her lips to his, she opened his mouth and felt his frustration escape as their tongues met.

Her heart had never beat so fast.

His mouth fixed on hers as his inexperienced hands groped and pawed until she guided them to the straps of her gown and he slid the silky garment off her shoulders. But when the gown fell to her waist, his brows furrowed and he blinked glistening eyes. Was he such an innocent that she was not only his first sexual partner but the first woman he'd seen unclothed?

But she savored his innocence as she lowered his suspenders and unbuttoned his shirt.

She would be his first. He would always remember her.

But if he was the novice, why were *her* fingers shaking as they caressed the soft brown curls on his chest? Why were *her* lips trembling as she tasted him? And when he lowered his mouth to her breasts, why did *she* bite her lips to restrain the words that she'd never spoken and never planned to speak, words that she now wanted to scream again and again?

Tom had been Lily's first lover and he'd taught her well, taught her not only how to make a man satisfied but how to have fun during sex, make the time something special that left both partners happy and fulfilled. As Lily now taught David how to please a woman, she remembered how scared she'd been that first night until Tom's tenderness had relaxed her as hers now relaxed David.

They laughed, sighed, and moaned. They stared into each other's eyes and grasped each other with hands and mouths. And no matter how close Lily came to losing herself, she wouldn't allow it. This would be their only time together. This would be the one time in her life that she truly made love, and she wanted to memorize every detail.

And it wasn't hard because every detail was precious. His taste. His smell. The very way he breathed. The way he felt inside her, how her legs felt circled around his waist, how his chest hair tickled her, how their mouths moved in a harmony that normally would have taken weeks to perfect, how his mouth lingered on her breasts, how his hands grasped her buttocks to push their bodies closer, closer . . . how his tongue explored her, how his breathing accelerated and his eyes squinted when he came inside her, how he grinned and his eyes twinkled afterward.

He had no idea how endearing she found his inexperience, how she treasured his mistakes, how she would cherish the bruises from the times he nibbled a little too hard or grasped a little too tightly. He had no idea that the feel of him inside her was the most exquisite sensation her body had ever known. But even as she savored him, her mind screamed: How will I live when he's gone?

To her great delight and relief, he seemed in no hurry to leave.

On the contrary.

He seemed enchanted with his new discovery like a child with a new toy. That's what I am to him, she thought, this toy called the female body. And he seemed quite pleased with it—smiling as he hugged and tickled and continued to explore her with his hands and mouth. Even when they rested, their arms and legs were so woven together that it was hard to tell whose were whose.

Lily had never been happier. She looked at the boy soldier and he looked at her and they both grinned. He nibbled on her shoulder and licked her ear then fell backward onto the pillows and shouted, "I've never felt so free!"

15

She stroked his face and kissed the dimple by his mouth. "I'm glad, David, very glad."

He sighed deeply then chuckled.

"What's so funny?"

"Me."

Propped onto an elbow so she could look at him, Lily stroked his face with its slight stubble then fingered his mussed hair. "What do you mean?"

"I'm such a pompous . . ."

"Shh, no you're not." She touched his lips with a fingertip. "I admire your intentions. They're honorable and fine, like you."

He put her fingertips to his lips and sucked them then kissed her palm and held it to his chest. "Really? You think I'm 'fine'?"

"Yes I do."

"Why?"

"Why shouldn't I?"

"There's no reason you shouldn't, except that you don't know me."

She ignored his arrogance as a sign of immaturity, but his words "you don't know me" reminded her of their stations in life and of their relationship—reminded her that there *was* no relationship. *You're a fool, Lily, thinking that you're lovers. Treat him like all the other customers and keep your feelings out of it.* She wanted to bury her head in the pillow and cry but took a deep breath instead. "You're right, of course."

"I am a fine person, Lily, but I've had to work at it, and it's been terribly hard. Like now . . . My family would be horrified to find me here." He looked at her. "They expect so much of me."

"You don't tell them everything, do you?"

"No, of course not, but I know what I'm doing is wrong."

Feeling a knife twist in her heart, Lily sat up, pulling the sheet over her chest. "I'm sorry, sir, but I don't know what you expect of me. Do you want me to be your whore *and* your priest? Do you want me to fulfill your carnal needs then absolve you of them? I can do it, but I don't think it would mean very much."

He sat up and kissed her shoulder, whispered, "I'm sorry," then turned her toward him. He looked at the curls by her cheeks and blew lightly on one to make it bounce. "My life's just so complicated."

"Just follow your heart, David. You have a good heart and a good mind. You'll do the right thing."

He looked into her eyes and frowned.

"What's wrong?"

He shook his head. "No one's ever said such a thing to me."

She touched his cheek. "Maybe they should."

"But you're paid to say such things, aren't you?"

Was he deliberately cruel? She turned to get out of bed but he grabbed her arm.

"It's true, isn't it?"

"I tell you I'm a whore and you cover your delicate ears. I speak from my heart and you call me a whore. What do you want from me?"

He closed his eyes and shook his head.

"Yes, I'm paid to please men, but that doesn't mean I don't care about them."

"But is any *one* man ever special to you?"

You, David! You and only you. "Yes."

He looked down and traced the blanket's pattern then looked back at her. "Why do you do . . . this?"

There it was. She straightened her shoulders and raised her chin. "What difference does it make?"

His eyes downcast, he said nothing.

"Damn you and all like you who wonder why we do this."

He flinched. "Is it for the money?"

"Of course." She stared at him. "Isn't that what everything's about?"

He continued to frown and take hesitant glances at her.

"Think about it. Try to imagine yourself a woman and wonder what you'd do for a living."

He shrugged and casually said, "I suppose I'd get married."

She held her arms across her chest to keep from slapping him. "You men are so damned hypocritical. Once a woman's lost her virginity she's no longer marriage material. You wouldn't marry me, would you?" Her insides twisted at his closed eyes and guilty face. "Besides, wives aren't much better off. They have no lives of their own, no money of their own. They're whores too, but they whore for respectability, a house, food, and clothing. Their husbands can beat them, cheat on them, get them pregnant constantly, and if the husband chooses to leave, she has no recourse. Hell, a man can kill his wife if she's unfaithful. Don't you see? Women have few options, precious few options."

"But surely this should be the last resort."

"Of course. I could do laundry or clean spittoons. I could serve drinks in a saloon—pitiful jobs that pay pitifully." She laughed. "Oh David, you have no idea what the real world is like." She remembered the women who'd raised her and the way the "good" women of the town had spit at them, torn their clothing, shouted vile names at them. "The 'nice' women I've known haven't been very nice. I'd rather be an honest whore than a hypocritical 'good' woman." She stared at him, almost daring him to argue with her.

"I could tell you my story but I don't want your sympathy. I don't want anyone's sympathy, and I don't need it. I'm doing very well, thank you, and

I'm quite satisfied with my life. I enjoy sleeping late, dressing in pretty clothes, and taking scented baths in tubs made of porcelain instead of steel. I enjoy living in a house of red velvet and polished woods, gleaming crystal and brass, good food and drink.

"I'm not looking for a husband but neither am I planning to lie on my back for the rest of my life. A woman's worth is her looks and we all know that looks don't last. I'll soon have enough money to buy my own house and be my own boss, and then I'll have all that matters—independence."

She'd not meant to berate him, but the question always raised her dander. And she particularly hated discussing it with him because for the first time she wanted to forget what she was. Until tonight she had enjoyed her life, had never apologized for it or regretted it, had even prided herself in not caring about love.

Oh, there had been moments when she'd fantasized about love, had wondered what it would be like to feel silly and moody about just one man, but then she would remember the tears and bruises that she'd seen other women endure and decide that she was better off staying away from such a distracting and demeaning persuasion.

So why had she allowed herself to fall in love with this rich slave-holder sitting beside her, this boy soldier who looked quite worn down by her tirade? Lily touched his shoulder. "I'm sorry."

"No." He touched her lips with his fingers. "You have nothing to be sorry for." He stared into her eyes.

Her heart was breaking but she couldn't let him see. "I really can't imagine why you're asking such questions. After tonight, we'll never see each other again." She circled her bent knees to hold herself together even as she looked hopefully into his eyes. *Tell me I'm wrong, David, please.*

His eyes widened then he turned his face away. "You're right, of course."

Sounds of lovemaking came through the walls and they looked at each other before nervously turning toward the window at the traces of early morning in the sky.

"I should go."

NO! She couldn't let him leave. "Listen," she said as casually as her rapidly beating heart would permit, "You have a few more hours . . . unless you want to leave."

He shook his head and put a hand on her cheek. "No. I don't want to leave."

I love you, David. No, she mustn't think such words. Such words were forbidden, useless.

He kissed her lips softly then pulled her close and whispered, "God forgive me, I don't want to leave."

She pushed her body against his. "Then don't, David, don't."

CHAPTER 4

The days and nights that followed were meaningless. Lily did what she had to do but inside she cried and begged for David. Her love for David—was it something tangible? Was that why she had trembled in his presence? Was he in the very blood that kept her alive? If she bled herself, could she release him? Such a tempting thought . . .

Now she knew the wretched withdrawal that addicts suffered and she despised herself for needing him so. How had she allowed such weakness to ruin her life—she who had planned her future so thoroughly? And where was that determination, that strength and self-assurance that earned her the reputation that was going to buy her her own business and make sure she never had to depend on anyone?

Why, oh why, had he walked in that night? How could such a short time with one stranger affect her so? How come he already filled her every waking thought? She could still see and feel his eyes, his lips . . .

This wasn't supposed to happen.

Tom had showed up the night David left. Sweet Tom with his curly graying hair, pale blue eyes, and sentimental soul. An honest smile shone from a face darkened and lined from years of farming, and a faint scar that stretched from his left eye across his nose only added to his vulnerability and rough handsomeness. For the past three years he'd struggled to keep his farm afloat and raise his son and daughter from his marriage to a Shawnee woman. Tom was a good man, a genuine and dependable man.

Had she wanted to fall in love, she would have with Tom.

She should have with Tom.

But instead she used him, selfishly pawing and biting, desperately riding and manipulating, all in frantic search for release.

But it was release from David that she searched. It was release from the craving for David that she couldn't satisfy, even after climaxing with Tom. As she lay in his arms, Lily turned away to hide her tears.

"What's wrong, Lil?" He was behind her, his gentle hand on her shoulder, his loving lips on her neck. "I've never seen you cry. Something must be horribly wrong. Please tell me."

She turned toward him and wiped her eyes with a corner of the sheet then searched the sweet face that conveyed so much love. She shrugged her shoulders then let him cradle her.

He whispered and placed kisses on her face and shoulders. "You know I love you. I've loved you from the first moment I saw you. I know that sounds like some hackneyed expression but it's true." He raised her chin and looked into her eyes. "And you know it."

Oh yes, sweet Tom. I, too, now believe in love at first sight. And I hate it. And now I know how you suffer because of me. Lily sat up and covered her breasts with the sheet.

He sat too then took her hands in his and traced her palms with his finger as he spoke tenderly. "I know all the things you're going to say so I won't bother asking you to marry me again, but you know I want you to, desperately." His voice tightened. "I'm so lonely without you."

Lily touched his cheek with her fingertips.

Tom kissed them then coughed nervously. "Tonight was . . . unbelievable." He smiled in his familiar endearing way then shook his head. "Whew . . . I knew something was different, but I hoped, pretended, that it was because you'd finally fallen in love—with me."

But the truth was in her eyes.

And his eyes filled with tears as he pulled her to him. "Oh, Lily . . ."

Lily did everything she could think of to rid herself of the uninvited destructive being that had taken over her body and mind. She helped Polly with the bookkeeping and took as many clients as she could squeeze into the days and nights. Surely one of them could make her feel as David had. As she had sex with each of them, her heart and mind screamed, Make me want you. Make me want to kiss your lips as I want to kiss his. She hated David for changing her, hated him for staying in her mind. Why wouldn't he go away?

Even in a parlor full of laughter and clicking piano keys, even while flirting outrageously with a customer, it was David's face she saw, his face she sought each time the door opened. But the worst moments were during the midnight hours when the moonlight spread its taunting magic into her bedroom. That's when she could see him lying next to her, his feathery lashes on his tanned cheeks, his disarrayed dark hair on the pillow, that dimple by those soft lips. That's when she could hear the murmurs and groans he made as his broad shoulders rose and fell with sleep.

But even as Lily's soul remained in endless winter, the rest of the world turned to spring. How it mocks me, she thought, this season of renewal and rebirth. Had nature come alive again just to taunt her, to tell her that this relentless ache she carried meant nothing in life's cycle? She was jealous. She wanted a fresh start too.

Although David had been gone four months already, the cut was just as fresh and painful as the morning he'd left. He'd been sweet that morning, kissing her so gently and genuinely acting as if he cared for her. Well, perhaps he was as good an actor as she, for wasn't the secret to her success making men feel that they stood out from the rest? But act he must have done, for he hadn't come back. She hadn't expected him to. But she'd hoped. Oh, how she'd hoped. . . .

She began spending most of her free time in the garden. Not only did the weeding, hoeing, and watering help tire her and enable her to sleep, she found the survival of struggling plants an optimistic sign that she, too, might survive.

And that's where she was one particularly bright early spring day, squatting between rows of newly planted peas and singing as she tugged at weeds and dropped them into her apron. "Buffalo gals won't cha' come out tonight and . . ."

" . . . dance by the light of the moon."

Her head jerked around.

And her heart stopped.

He was leaning next to the willow tree that shaded a white wrought-iron bench but began walking toward her as he whistled the tune. Her eyes followed him, squinting because the sun shone on him in such a way that she could barely see him. But was it really him or a ghost? Perhaps not even a ghost. Perhaps her mind was playing tricks, a sure sign of how he'd bedeviled her. But he walked out of the sun's glare and in a moment was squatting next to her.

And though the sight of him made her catch her breath, there was something different . . . The mussed and unkempt appearance that had so enchanted her was replaced by elegance and perfection. His face was smooth of any stubble, his uniform was spotless, his hat well creased, and his boots so shiny she bet she could have seen her reflection in them. No, this time there was no denying his wealthy upbringing. Lily tried not to stare but couldn't stop her eyes from examining every inch of him—and she smiled when she found a wisp of hair that refused to cooperate with the rest and at the dark waves that defiantly brushed the back collar of his coat.

As she admired him—this man she loved with her mind, body, and soul—her mind raced. Why had he come back? Funny, she'd never asked that question of any other client. They were supposed to come back. The women encouraged them to come back.

Lily had prayed every day that David would come back.

Then hoped her prayers were never answered.

21

How she wished he'd do something to purge her of this torture.

Kneeling beside her, he picked up a handful of soil and closed his fingers around it then spoke almost reverently. "You know, this is the most valuable thing there is besides family and honor." Lily watched his eyes as they stared at the soil and wished it were she he admired so fervently. "It takes hold of you and won't let go." He brushed the dirt from his hands then rested his elbows on his knees and looked at her. "Much like a woman."

She gulped then stood up, dropping the corners of her apron and the gathered weeds. David's eyes followed the weeds as they fell then he laughed quietly. "I didn't mean to startle you." His hand gestured toward the garden. "Or interrupt your work." He squinted at the sun then looked back at her. "Where are your bonnet and gloves? Aren't you afraid the sun will spoil your complexion?" He touched the freckles on her nose and smiled. "I see it's kissed you already."

"You've commented on my nose before, I believe." She enjoyed seeing his boyish embarrassment return despite his sophisticated countenance. "Actually, sir, I'd be wearing breeches if I had my way."

His eyes widened in surprise then he nodded and studied her, a knowing smile on his lips. "I dare say you would."

Inwardly shaking and fearing an onslaught of delirious tears, Lily wiped her hands on the apron and hurriedly walked out of the garden, leaving the weeds where they'd fallen.

But David motioned toward the bench and called to her. "May we sit for a moment?"

Too nervous to speak, she walked to the bench and sat down, demure and proper like a chaste schoolgirl.

Why did he do this to her? Why, when he was around, did she lose the wit and sarcasm she was known for? What happened to the Lily of the West?

But that was Lily.

This was the innocent Flora, the naive young girl from Lexington who was head over heels in love with this boy soldier who stood in the sun and looked down at her. Lily knew better. Lily knew that Flora was asking for trouble.

Flora knew it was too late.

David put a foot on the bench then leaned on it, his hat in his hands. (She could, indeed, see her reflection in the boot and smiled to herself.) His fingers inched nervously around the hat's brim again and again. "I came by today to apologize for . . .before."

Her heart sank. Was he sorry for making love to her? Was he doing penance? "I don't understand."

"Well, I was quite . . . inebriated, and I'm afraid my conduct wasn't that of a gentleman. I just want you to know that it's not my true persona.

Normally I'm as you see me today. I just don't want anyone to think otherwise."

"Even a whore?"

His foot dropped off the bench and he turned around then back. "I find that language offensive, particularly coming from a lady."

"I'm sure you do, but I'm no lady, and the rest of my clients aren't so easily offended. Besides, that word's not so bad compared to many of the others." *Why are you challenging him? Do you want him to leave again?*

He stared at her. "How old are you?"

"Why?"

"Because you appear very . . . young. I mean you're lovely and quite . . . but something tells me you're not old enough to . . ."

Now she knew why he was back. He was worried. How much would he offer for her silence? Her heart was tearing, ripping, wrenching, but she defiantly lifted her chin. "I'm plenty old enough so don't worry yourself about it." She stood and straightened her skirts. "I really must get back to work. I accept your apology though there's absolutely no need for it. Good day Mr. Evans."

He caught her arm. "How'd you know my last name?"

Lily's face went red. Most customers don't give last names and Saul had been no exception when he'd introduced David, but she'd found out on her own. "I . . . I heard it somewhere."

He released her arm and stood still, looking at the ground.

She almost ran to the house, her heart beating much too fast, her tears flowing much too freely.

CHAPTER 5

Polly was on the porch of the luxurious house. How long had she been watching?

"Why is he here?" Her arms were folded across her chest, her chin high.

"He came to . . . what difference does it make?"

"A lot of difference. You've been almost worthless since he was here before and I don't want you getting any schoolgirl moon-eyed notions about him."

"Schoolgirl notions? I've never been a schoolgirl. What would I know of such things? Besides, he's leaving. I doubt he'll ever come back."

But Polly's gaze caused Lily to turn around. David had followed her.

"Wipe your face," Polly whispered. "Don't let him see you cry." She called out to David, her voice cracking. "Sir, my ladies are not here to sit in the sun for free."

Humiliated, Lily aimed her eyes at the porch floor.

"How much for a full night?"

"One hundred dollars." The madam walked down the steps to meet him.

"Polly!"

David stared at Lily for a moment then patted his pockets as he walked toward Polly and pressed three coins into her palm.

"That's only fifty."

"It's all I have. I'll spend the afternoon and evening then leave at midnight."

Polly clinched her fingers around the coins. "Midnight, not a moment later." As she passed Lily on her way into the house, the girl saw tears in her eyes. Lily had never seen Polly cry.

What was happening? The situation was so odd. Had David really paid to spend time with her? The notion filled her with a lightheadedness that she thought would surely lift her right off the ground yet he looked perplexed and uncertain and his eyes were moist. Did he already regret his decision? *Smile, damn you. Be happy that you did this.* When his lips finally curved upward, Lily could tell the smile was forced but it was warm and filled her with thoughts of loving him. "Shall we go to my room?"

He looked at the house then shook his head and nodded toward the yard. "Let's walk a little."

They strolled through the well-manicured lawns, Lily nervously describing every plant and flower while pretending they were a married couple inspecting the grounds of their home. See, dear, how the gardener has planted the wrong flowers. What shall we do with him, David? And the children are just ruining my rose garden. We simply must make them a separate play area.

How totally absurd he would think her dreams. *How totally absurd for a woman like me to even fantasize about someone like him.* She looked up at him and wondered who he would choose to mother his children. Who would that most lucky of women be? Did he already know her? The idea was too painful, much too painful. *You mustn't think of those things, Lil. Not now. Not ever. You're only hurting yourself.*

"Polly's very proud of her landscaping." Lily pointed at the sculptured shrubs. "She tries to have some color year round." They stopped by a birdbath and laughed at the finches and sparrows shaking water off their feathers and chattering animatedly to each other.

David stood with his hands behind his back. "What do you think they're saying?"

Was it possible that he, too, was pretending that they were a real couple? Lily tried to calm the rapid beating of her heart. "Oh, I don't know. What do you think they're saying? You seem to understand their language."

"Actually, I do." He smiled broadly then leaned toward the birdbath. After a moment, he returned to her side, a mischievous smile on his lips and in his bright eyes. "Just as I thought."

"What?"

"I believe their exact words were: 'That certainly is a a a lovely young lady you're walking with'."

Could he really feel something for her? Was it possible? Lily felt her face redden and she walked away quickly, but David caught up with her and assumed her pace.

His face was almost in hers. "Am I wrong? Isn't that what they were saying?" He smiled again.

"I doubt it."

He tossed his hat in his hands as they walked. "Oh, I think I'm right. You know why?"

Please don't tease me. "No, why?"

He stopped walking.

She turned to face him.

"Because it's true."

Why was he doing this?

"I think you've been drinking again."

He shook his head adamantly and walked toward her. "No ma'am." His face was just inches from hers as he smiled devilishly. "Want to smell my breath?"

She looked at his lips, stared at his lips, then turned around and walked again, quickly, quickly . . . chattering even more nervously than before. "So, what do you think of our gardens? Don't you think Polly has exquisite taste?"

He stopped again. "I don't think she likes me."

Lily laughed as she turned toward him. "Well, that's not what I asked, but what makes you say such a thing?" They strolled again. "You've certainly given her reason to like you—the amount of money you've spent here, I mean."

He shrugged his shoulders. "Well, she has an odd way of showing it. The way she hovers over you—almost as if she were jealous. I don't see how that could be good for business."

"Really? Well, I think she's an excellent businesswoman and truly the most beautiful woman I've ever seen. She's so regal, even the way she wears her hair. No other woman could get away with wearing it up like that, but it just accentuates Polly's neck. Everything about her is elegant. I've never met anyone with such confidence and polish. Even her manner of speaking. Haven't you noticed? She pronounces each word as if she's practiced it. From the first moment I saw Polly, I knew that my life's goal was to be just like her."

"That's quite a testimony, but I think you're wrong."

Lily stopped. "Wrong? In what way, sir?"

He put his hand on her cheek then touched the ringlet of hair that fell there before gliding his thumb back and forth across her mouth and whispering, "You're much prettier than she is."

Lily closed her eyes and wished time would stop so she could live forever in the moment, but his silence made her open her eyes. He was staring at her, his brows furrowed, and he quickly removed his hand and began walking again.

She caught up with him and resumed her mindless chatter, hoping he couldn't hear the choking in her voice. "What's really funny is the difference between Polly and Mama Rose." She saw his confusion. "The woman who raised me. She couldn't have been more different than Polly." Lily smiled as she remembered the sweet lady who'd given her her last name and left her the small fortune she kept safely hidden. "Sweet Mama Rose. She wore so much rice powder that her face was white and she never quite got the solution right for her hair so it was usually some shade of orange and always brittle and frizzy." Lily laughed. "And she was so short and pudgy that she always reminded me of a wad of dough." Lily put her hands under her own breasts to illustrate as she laughed. "Her breasts like rising loaves."

David stopped and slapped his hat against his thigh. "My, but you have a cruel streak."

"Do I? I don't think so." She smiled wickedly. "Just a good imagination."

She didn't like the judgmental look in his eyes. "I'll have you know, sir, that I loved Mama Rose. She and the other ladies were the only mothers I ever knew. Hell, if it hadn't been for Nellie, I wouldn't be alive today."

His brows furrowed as he stared at her.

She started walking again. "I never knew my parents, don't even know who they were. I used to fantasize that Mama Rose was my mother but I don't think she was. I still think that one of the ladies knew who my mother was but no one ever told me. I'm sure she was a whore." Lily looked him in the eye. Why did she always challenge him? "Like mother, like daughter, you know."

He winced. "Who's Nellie and how did she save your life?"

She shrugged her shoulders. "I don't want to talk about it, not now."

They reached the lacy jasmine-covered gazebo and sat together on the narrow bench. Lily inhaled him—fresh air, soap, wintergreen—and found herself so nervous she could barely breathe. "I must tell you, Mr. Evans, that I am surprised to see you again." She pretended to look around. "I don't see Saul with you so I assume you weren't brought here by force—or deception as before."

He nervously tossed his hat between his spread legs then stopped when his leg bumped hers. He cleared his throat. "As I told you, I came back to apologize." His smile was bashful, sweet.

"But that's absurd. No one apologizes to a whore, especially for being drunk. Many if not most of our clients are drunk, either at the beginning or at the end of the evening."

"I really wish you wouldn't use that word."

"You . . ." She jumped up, put her hands on her hips, and stared down at him. "I am what I am and most men are glad of it. Men don't visit me for my words."

He squinted his eyes shut.

She paced for a moment then sat back down. "Is it the word that offends you or the fact that you're with me? Since you said I wasn't moral, I guess it's me. I guess the word's too much of a reminder."

"I said no such thing."

"Oh, yes sir, you did. You seemed quite distraught and kept mumbling that you shouldn't be here. I believe your exact words were, 'Because it's not fitting, not responsible, not moral. It's probably the last place on earth I should be'."

Suddenly he grabbed her hands and kissed each palm and fingertip with such tenderness that Lily felt she'd either fall to the ground or burst into flames. *Make love to me, please.* Then she wondered as she had before: Why wasn't she taking the initiative?

But everything was different with David and all she could do was watch his face and stare into the glistening eyes as they came toward hers. "Oh, Lily . . ."

Shaking, Lily closed her eyes and waited, waited . . .

But he pulled away and she opened her eyes to see fear in his face. "What's wrong?"

He jumped up and coughed nervously as he straightened his uniform. "I'm sorry. I don't know what possessed me to do that." He laughed nervously and turned away.

"What possessed you?" She stomped over to him and stopped just inches from his back. "I don't appreciate that very much, sir. In fact, I find it quite insulting."

He turned around. "I didn't mean it like that, and you know I didn't."

She was too angry to speak, too afraid that she'd cry, and she couldn't afford such a sappy luxury, such an unbecoming and manipulative maidenly gesture. What must it be like, she wondered, to be sheltered, cared for, to expect such a man as David to court you and wed you? What must it be like to be weak and fragile, to behave as Lily never could? It was tiring being strong. But it was her fate, so she folded her arms across her chest and said nothing.

David smelled the tiny white flowers that stuck their heads through the gazebo's latticework. After pinching off several blossoms, he looked at Lily. "This is jasmine, isn't it?"

The man was dumbfounding, completely unsettling.

He sat beside her and put the delicate flowers in her hair as he whispered, "It has a wonderful scent, don't you think?"

She felt his breath on her ear and stared at his mouth just inches away. But he pulled back and she could tell he was weighing his words.

Her stomach churned.

"I know this is hard to understand but I've been reared in a very certain way, a very religious deliberate way." He lifted her chin.

As his eyes probed hers, Lily wondered how his eyes and words could contradict each other. It was as if he made love with his eyes and used his words for contraception. They'd been intimate, as intimate as two people could be. Had he forgotten or had he, indeed, come back for some sort of payoff or contrition?

Lily remembered every detail of their lovemaking and had to hold her hands in her lap to keep from touching him, had to bite her lip to keep from screaming her love for him.

"I've been trained to be a gentleman. Every time I open my mouth, my family's honor is at stake. We take such responsibilities very seriously." He lowered his eyes as he took one of her hands in his. "That means I'm not to drink, gamble, curse, or . . ." He rubbed the top of her hand with his thumb and took a deep breath. "When I marry, I'm to be a faithful and loving husband to my wife. When I have children, I'm to teach them proper values and set a good example." Lily tried to pull her hand away but he grasped it tighter, his eyes on the union. In a strained almost breaking voice, he said, "Do you understand what I'm saying?"

"Of course." In an icy voice, she added, "What does that have to do with me?"

He looked up, startled.

She deliberately jerked her hand from his and stood up. "I don't know why you're telling me these things. I didn't force you to return here today, much less spend fifty dollars to spend time with me. You're free to leave any time—just don't blame me for your downfall, your moral decline, or your guilty conscience."

Pacing, she held her arms firmly against her chest, her insides aching from wanting him. "Or perhaps you're excited by the naughtiness of it all. I've serviced men like you before, you know. You're raised to marry good girls but it's the forbidden fruit that really excites you. Or is it the guilt that excites you? Which it, Mr. Evans?" She stood in front of him. "Just tell me. I've serviced every type of male fantasy and weakness. I can certainly handle yours. Does pretending we're a couple add to your fantasy or do you just need a lot of talking to get yourself going? Are garden walks and listening to birds part of the game?" She leaned toward him seductively then blew in his ear and put her hand on his crotch before speaking in her huskiest whisper. "Do you want me to spank you because you've been bad?"

He jumped up and walked past her so quickly that she almost fell, and it wasn't until his long legs had traversed the gazebo's length several times that he stopped. Lily watched as he took a deep breath, his brown eyes almost black, his hands balled into fists. "How dare you speak to me in such a manner! If you were a man I'd challenge you for such offensive verbiage."

He stood over her like judgment day, his eyes boring down into hers making her feel trapped, but Lily wasn't about to give in and she maintained eye contact and spoke quietly and calmly, coldly. "Then tell me, sir, what do you want to do with the remainder of your time? I'm yours until midnight. Should you choose to leave now, however, it's all the same to me."

His eyes softened and she saw his fists relax. "You don't mean that, do you?"

"Mean what?"

"That it's all the same to you."

Damn his puppy-dog look. Damn his game playing. If he expected her to declare her love, if leaving a trail of broken hearts was his game, he could rot in hell before she'd play it. She'd be damned before she'd satisfy his ego with her broken heart.

When he reached for her and she stepped away, he raised his chin defiantly. "I thought you said you were mine until midnight."

She stepped back into his reach but purposely remained stiff and aloof.

He didn't hesitate this time, didn't change his mind and pull away.

They groped with hands and mouths, their faces flush and their breathing heavy. And even though David showed no trace of affection as he used her body, Lily clung to him and gave herself completely to him.

Then felt tears stream down her cheeks when he stood and straightened his clothing as soon as he was through.

CHAPTER 6

"I'm sorry."

Her back to him, she straightened her clothes and wiped away tears. Sorry? He'd barely finished using her and was already repenting. So it was the guilt that excited him. Why else would he keep hurting her?

Because you're just a piece of purchased merchandise to him. After all, he is an owner of slaves, a man who thinks human beings are property to be bartered with. What do you think you are if not a piece of merchandise?

Hesitantly, she turned around and watched him straighten his uniform and comb his hair. "That was . . ." He took a deep breath. "It wasn't very romantic, was it?"

She shrugged. "It's your money, your time, your fantasy."

"Don't!" He pulled her to his chest. "I came here today to tell you of my better nature but proved just the opposite." He held her at arm's length and looked down at her, his eyes moist and warm. "What is it about you, Lily? Why can't I control myself around you?"

She shrugged her shoulders again, too confused to speak.

He kissed her forehead then whispered, "Let's go to your room."

This time they smiled, kissed, and explored. This time they held each other afterward. This time David traced circles on the tops of her hands, kissed her palms, toyed with her hair, kissed and caressed the hills and valleys that shaped her. This time he lingered and showed no regrets, and Lily's soul was in the bliss she thought she'd never feel again.

But their time was short, so very short, and she had so many questions. She wanted to know everything about him so that when he was gone she could try to imagine what he was doing. Her head on his shoulder, she wove her fingers through the soft chest hair and whispered, "Did you open your school?"

"Yes, in January."

"Is that the reason for the new uniform?"

"I wondered if you'd noticed it. Do you like it? By the way, I'm a captain now."

His childish need for recognition and approval matched hers, and she could picture the two of them as children sharing toys and vying for attention. No, she would have fought for attention with other children, but not with him. With him she would have been proud. She would have pointed to his sand castle and cried out, "Look, Mommy, look at David's!" She knew she had no right to feel proud of him, but she did.

She nuzzled his neck and kissed his mouth. "Of course I noticed it and find it quite handsome. Captain, huh? Congratulations." She snuggled deeper into the covers next to him, smelled him, placed her hand on his warm belly.

He grinned again then seemed to distance himself. "It's not been easy but I'm sure we'll succeed. It's just a matter of time."

"Well you have plenty of that." She kissed his chest and pushed herself even closer against him, fitting her legs around one of his and moving gently against it. Lulled by his nearness and soft manner of speaking, Lily felt the foggy blanket of sleep as she murmured, "It's not like you have a family to support."

His body grew still and cold, and Lily felt her blood turn to ice.

Shaking, she sat up and forced herself to look at him, only to see him turn his face away. "Or do you?"

"Soon."

Soon. Her head reeled and her stomach churned. Soon. "May I ask a question?"

"Of course."

"Why are you here?"

Silence.

"Being here is totally against everything you believe in and now you say you plan to . . ." she almost choked, ". . . get married. You must have a particular young lady in mind?"

He sat up and leaned forward on drawn knees. "Yes."

"And you love her very much?"

"Yes."

Hurt clawed and tore her insides, shredded them until she felt raw. He didn't say it. Please don't let him have said it. She stared at him, willed him to look at her, willed him to take the words away. But he wouldn't look at her and she wanted to slap him, beat him, hurt him as she'd never wanted to hurt anyone before. But no amount of physical pain could match the nauseating heart-ripping pain that filled her, pain she wished would kill her. "What's her name?"

"Mary Anne."

Lily bit her lip and closed her eyes. "And she's accomplished, I'm sure. Intelligent and very beautiful?" She looked at him through a maze of tears, cracked glass, a broken mirror that would bring her eternal bad luck.

He looked into her eyes and nodded. "Yes, very accomplished, very intelligent, and very beautiful." With the fingers of one hand tangled painfully in her hair forcing her to look at him, the fingers of his other hand traced her features as he described Mary Anne's, his voice low and almost cruel, each word and feathery touch ripping her heart. "Her hair is black and her features . . . so delicate." When his fingers touched her lips, Lily closed her eyes and learned of Mary Anne's pink rosebud mouth. When his shaking fingers touched her shoulders and his wavering voice described Mary Anne's tiny proportions, Lily's tears flowed freely down her cheeks.

As David kissed the wet cheeks and lay her back onto the pillows, Lily clung to him and greedily affixed her mouth to his. But even as she tasted her own salt, her brain taunted her with visions of David loving a petite woman with black hair and rosebud lips.

This time there were no smiles, no giggles, no sighs of happy relief. And this time when they were sated, they lay still, his arm around her shoulders, her face on his chest.

Did he feel her tears that fell there?

"Whe . . . when?" She damned the weakness in her voice.

"I don't know. Right now we're having problems with our families. Everyone thinks I'm too young and not financially secure enough."

"So, how does Mar . . . she feel? Is she ready to go against her family's wishes?" *Please tell me she's a wealthy shrew who's interested in only status and wealth.* Surely there was something wrong with this woman.

"Not just yet. She's very close to her parents and can usually get her way, so it's just a matter of time. Mary Anne usually gets what she wants."

Lily sat up, covered her breasts with the sheet, then leaned against the bed's wrought-iron headboard. Her head hurt. Her stomach hurt. Her palms hurt where her fingernails had brought blood. She took a deep breath. "And she wants you . . . Isn't she concerned with your future?"

He sat up and shrugged his shoulders. "She's confident the school will succeed. Why shouldn't it?"

Lily laughed quietly.

"What's so funny?"

"The idea that you expect success. You expect it because you've always had everything you've ever wanted or needed. You can't imagine what it's like to really want anything, as for really needing something . . ." She shook her head. "A hardship for you is not getting your boots polished to the right sheen. You can't begin to imagine being scared, cold, lonely . . . I suspect your young lady is the same way."

His eyes were clouded. "I . . ." He cleared his throat and raised his chin arrogantly. "There may be some truth in what you say but Mary Anne loves me and will support me. She'll be the perfect wife and mother."

"Of course she will!" Lily threw off the sheet and stomped to the wash stand. She tightened the belt of her kimono then splashed water on her face, knowing he was watching. Damn this spoiled rich . . . slave holder! *Why do you love him? You have nothing in common with him. You have no future with him. If it weren't Mary Anne it would soon be someone else—never you. Even if he somehow fell in love with you, he would never marry you. But he'll never allow himself to fall in love with you. Unlike you, he has control of his life. Hear him. His life is planned. And you're not a part of his plans, never will be.*

Lily yanked a brush through her hair then turned to him. "Then I guess it's just a matter of time. Congratulations."

"Why are you upset?"

"What makes you think I'm upset?"

"Your demeanor and your less than sincere congratulations. Does it bother you that I'm getting married?"

She laughed and squeezed the brush as she glared at him. "Bother me? Why the hell should it? You're just a customer to me, David Evans, a novice who pays well."

"And a clumsy one, right?" He was pacing, holding his pants but not stopping to put them on. "An inexperienced, bumbling . . ." He shook the pants in his hand as he pointed at her. "You said you cared about your clients, and I'd assumed from your lofty title that you were the best, but I find you quite immature."

The hairbrush had barely hit the wall and fallen to the floor before his fingers gripped her arms. "No one treats me with such disrespect."

"Then get out. You don't belong here. You've made that perfectly clear. Immature? You're a fine one to talk. I've been with more men than years you've been alive, real men who know what they want and aren't ashamed of it. Men who know what to do with a woman. I'm not here to babysit toy soldiers."

"How dare you!" The walls banged with irritated clients as David shook her.

They stared into each other's eyes until she asked again, "Why are you here?"

"You know why."

"Using a whore so you can save your precious Mary Anne for marriage?"

He grimaced. "You really think that?"

"Why not? Many boys come to us for that reason."

"I am not one of many—and I am not a boy."

"But you love her very much. You just said so."

"And I do, very much."

"Then why?"

"Why do you make me say it?"

"Why can't you?"

"You know why."

"Just go, damn you. Just get out." She got down on her hands and knees to find the hairbrush and hide her tears. "Where is that damn thing?"

As she silently cursed him and herself for loving him, she felt the length of his body spooning hers from behind. His lips were on her neck. His voice shaky, pleading. "Please Lily, let's don't waste time quarreling."

CHAPTER 7

Tears ran down her cheeks as Lily raised herself so she could watch David sleep. The hour was late, their time together running out. *Oh, my sweetheart. How can I tell you good bye? You're getting married. I'll never see you again. How will I live?*

But if he was so much in love with Mary Anne, why had he come back? But the answer was simple, wasn't it? He came for the sex he couldn't get before his wedding night. What other reason could there be? Despite all his good intentions, even David was a man with needs he couldn't ignore. Despite the fact that she thought him a god, he was an ordinary man.

She touched the hair on his forehead then kissed the spot. How lovely it was to kiss him openly, to be kissed by him . . . so different from that first night when she'd kissed his lips hesitantly and secretively. But now she had to take advantage of the moment for she'd never see him again. Never.

"Wake up." She leaned down and kissed his mouth then nuzzled his neck.

"Wha . . .?" He smiled. "What time is it?"

"Almost time for you to go."

He kissed her fully then his eyes grew dark.

"What's wrong?"

He stared at her, probed her with his eyes until she turned away. "I'm sorry." He turned her face toward his and kissed her nose. "I didn't mean to make you uncomfortable. I was just . . ."

"What?"

"Nothing. I just feel . . . " He continued to stare. "Did you cast a spell on me?"

She laughed then saw the earnestness in his face. "You think I'm a witch?"

His laugh sounded half hearted and forced. "Just bewitching." He gave her mouth a quick kiss. "Forget it."

Lily leaned on her elbow and traced his face with her fingers. His eyes were closed but he was smiling, and he playfully sucked her fingers when they touched his lips.

Suddenly the grandfather clock in the hall chimed and silently they counted the cruel bongs, then breathed sighs of relief when only eleven were heard.

"One more hour," he whispered as he kissed her then cuddled closer, wrapping his arms and legs around her, spinning his web around a very compliant fly. He nibbled her ear and was soon snoring softly again.

And again she watched him, smelled him, listened to him, touched him, knew she'd never tire of him.

Eleven-thirty.

"David, you've got to get up." *Sweetheart.*

He finally woke up enough to sit on the edge of the bed but was still dozing off, so Lily got a wet cloth then knelt in front of him and patted his face. He laughed quietly and kissed her nose as he touched her hand. "I think I can do that."

Embarrassed, she whispered, "I'm sorry," and started to rise.

But he put his hands on her shoulders to stop her. "I'm not."

"You're not?" She found it hard to breathe.

"No."

She crawled into his lap and wrapped his arms around her then held his face with her hands and kissed his lips.

He returned the kiss then sat her on the bed and began putting on his clothes. She watched him tuck the striped shirt into his pants and raise each red suspender then pull on his brown boots. He leaned down to look in the mirror and comb his hair then brushed off his coat and put it on. She watched the time he spent tying his magenta sash, straightening the magenta stripe that ran down each pants leg, wiping his boots.

But her heart broke. She'd never see him again.

When he was dressed, he walked to the door and pulled her to him then kissed her forehead and looked into her eyes. "I don't know if . . . "

"There's so much I wanted to ask you."

"I know." His eyes traveled her face as he brushed hair off her forehead and caressed her cheek then teased the ringlet of hair. "Oh, Lily."

As he held her against his chest, Lily felt his heart race even through the heavy coat. Could he really care enough about her that he didn't want to leave? Her nose memorized the fresh air embedded in the coat as her hand memorized the rough texture.

Suddenly he kissed her hard on the mouth and ran out.

Her fingers touching her lips, Lily ran to the window and peered at the porch below, craned her neck to see David step off of it. She watched him mount Samson, the stately bay, then grinned when he looked up at her and waved. Lily waved back then felt her stomach lurch when he turned the animal around and rode away.

The next weeks did nothing to cure the ache. Lily tried to tell herself that he didn't return because he was busy with his school but she knew the real reason. She also knew that he would never return. Never.

And since she spent most of her time leaning against the window, staring into the darkness, clawing at the cold glass, and shaking uncontrollably, it didn't take long to lose clients. Even Tom, the ever gentle and loving Tom. Lily could tell he was tiring of her giving him nothing but tears and talk of David. She knew she was hurting him. She knew she was hurting everyone, hurting people who genuinely loved her and cared about her, but she couldn't help it, couldn't shake David out of her system. He'd come back and she'd not expected it. Would he come back a third time? If she stared out the window long enough, would he come back?

"You must get yourself back to normal, Lily."

She stared out the window.

"Do you hear me?" Polly walked to the window and forced the girl to turn around then raised her chin. "Lily, please snap out of this. You're my best girl here—or were. Our business is dropping because of this tragedy you're performing. I can't afford it. Do you understand me?"

Lily nodded and drifted to the sofa and plopped down. Polly sat back in her chair. "Can I do anything to help you?"

She shook her head.

"Then what are you going to do?"

She shrugged her shoulders.

"I was afraid this was going to happen. I should have known it wasn't safe to hire someone who hadn't experienced love and heartbreak yet." Under her breath, she added, "I knew he was trouble." She spoke firmly. "You must know that a boy like that would never be serious about a girl like you. You do know that, don't you?"

The young eyes jerked up and toward her mentor, stared a moment, then sobbed hysterically.

"Oh, Lily." Polly rushed to her side and nestled the young girl's face in her bosom. "Men are callous and cruel. I wanted to warn you but what could I say? Why must we all suffer before we realize that men can't give us the love we need?"

Lily barely heard the words. Nothing penetrated the wall of David that surrounded her.

As the girl's tears ranged from sobs to whimpers, Polly cooed and whispered as she rocked her. "Poor baby, sweet baby." Polly's graceful hands stroked Lily's hair and face as the girl sniffed and fell into the timeless maternal rocking. Polly moved the red hair away from the young forehead and kissed the furrowed brow, kissed the wet cheeks, kissed the trembling lips. "Lily, oh my sweet Lily."

The girl jerked away and jumped up.

"What's wrong my pet?"

"I am not your pet. Why did you kiss me?"

Polly stood and tried to retrieve her charge but Lily stepped back.

The noble chin was raised and the regal shoulders thrown back. "I thought it was perfectly clear. Now that you've seen how disgusting men can be, how little they care for your feelings, you can treat them as a business. You can get over this schoolgirl crush and let me give you the love and affection you need. Believe me, you won't miss him and I won't leave you."

"What's going on?" Rosemary stood at the doorway, hands on hips, anger and hurt in her eyes.

Lily rushed up the stairs to her room.

Then spent the next hours contemplating her future.

Although surprised at Polly's affections, she wished with all her heart that she could return them. How she'd welcome relief from the constant ache for David. But while she knew there was no such relief, she also knew that it was time for her to move on. She'd saved a lot of money and still had Mama Rose's cache, and she knew that the other ladies, especially Rosemary, would welcome her departure. Polly had always been her only ally.

At long last Lily could once again relate to the outside world. Polly's show of affection had done that, had made her awaken to her surroundings, and for that she was grateful. Yes, it was time to move on, to get serious about building her own business. But to be successful she needed clients, so that very night she decided to get them back. That very night she forced herself to reclaim her title and become, once again, the Lily of the West. The Lily before David.

But it was hard, so hard. She was tired, so tired, and she couldn't keep food in her stomach. Perhaps she was dying. The peace of death . . . She welcomed it.

But when she missed her second menses, she realized that she wasn't dying after all and cursed her luck. She couldn't be pregnant, not now. Not that any time was good for an unwed woman, especially a prostitute, but Lily was trying to start a new life.

Then she realized that she had already started a new life. Touching her stomach gently, she smiled.

David's child.

What better life could there be?

The first three months of the pregnancy ended and Lily was grateful to feel her energy return. Now she could really concentrate on reacquainting herself with her clients, remembering their eccentricities, and enjoying each one for the differences he brought, the distractions. She apologized to them for her "slow" spell, blamed it on illness, then made them forget their troubles as they helped make her forget hers.

And instead of focusing on her hurt, Lily focused on the quickly accumulating pile of money. She went the extra mile with her customers to receive gifts and tips. It's all for the baby, she told herself again and again. For his baby. David's child deserved the very best, and Lily focused her life on obtaining just that. She was looking for a house, *the* house.

Although David was always on her mind and in her heart, Lily had just to pat her stomach to remind herself that she had part of David, would always have a part of him. It was almost enough. Almost.

Time began to pass quickly now, and it wasn't long before the young woman was established with a fine house and plenty of ladies to bring in plenty of customers.

And what a house! A black wrought-iron gate opened onto a long walkway that led to a red brick house that was tall, straight, proud, and regal. Its massive white arched door was topped with a glistening fanlight and flanked by two tall narrow windows. Two rows of the same windows were above the door, all with their own wrought-iron balcony. The flat roof was accented by a white cornice.

Lily loved the simple elegance of the house but chose it for three specific reasons.

One was the floor plan. As you entered the front foyer, there were double doors to the left and right. Directly in the center was a spectacular flying staircase. The double doors to the left led to Lily's private living quarters that included a parlor, dining room, and kitchen downstairs, and two bedrooms upstairs. The rest of the house was for business. The main parlor was through the double doors on the right and the staircase led to the ladies' bedrooms. Lily's cook, Edith, prepared all the meals in the main kitchen that adjoined the ladies' dining room, which was located behind their parlor.

Second was the landscape—extensive gardens and wooded areas that would provide a sense of normalcy and privacy for David's child. Lily wanted the child to pick flowers, run and turn somersaults, climb trees.

But there was one feature that told Lily that the house was meant for her and only her: the stained-glass skylight of a white lily entwined with the letter "D."

December sixth was moving day—and David's birthday. Her ever faithful and loving Tom was there with his kids, TJ and Ruthie, who were running up and down the stairs with the ladies, all of them giggling as they admired the place.

"You know I respect you for accomplishing so much, Lil, but I wish you'd give it all up and move to the farm with me."

"I know." She patted her belly. "But you deserve better than a woman with another man's child."

"I told you I'd love the child as my own. You know I could."

She shook her head. "But it wouldn't be fair. I wouldn't be fair. I don't think I could ever let it be yours. This child is all I have of him."

Sudden sharp pains made her wince and Tom rushed her to the couch. "I'll get the doctor."

"No." She took a deep breath. "Not yet."

"Are you sure?"

She could only nod, putting a hand on Tom's worried face. "Oh, Tom, why are you so good to me?"

He kissed her palm. "Because I love you, Lil. Always have, always will."

Another pain sent Tom for the doctor and left Lily listening to the happy sounds in the house and laughing at herself. What should have been the happiest day of her life, the day she achieved her goal—at the ripe old age of fifteen—left her empty. Oh, David, you're all I want. Only you can make me truly happy. The child kicked. "I'm sorry little one. Forgive your melancholy mother. I'm sure you'll enchant me as much as your father."

What are you doing, David? Are you surrounded by family and friends and about to cut an enormous birthday cake? Is she with you? Of course she is.

Suddenly a strange sensation forced Lily to her feet just in time to save her new couch from the warm rush of water that spewed from between her legs.

CHAPTER 8

Calls for war escalated over the next five years until they seemed to become the cry of the land. But Lily couldn't understand it. How could American citizens fight each other? The very idea was unbelievable. It hadn't been that long since men had fought to keep the hard-won independence. What would happen to the country? Would it dissolve and be easy pickings for England again? Perhaps even another country? Lily read the papers every day and hoped it wouldn't happen.

Yet the idea of freeing the slaves was an honorable and justifiable reason to fight if that's what it took, but what would happen to David if war came? Lily knew he'd be anxious to fight and knew on which side he'd fight.

But why should I care about him when he obviously cares nothing for me?

It had been almost six years. How she wished she could forget him.

But she knew she never would, especially now that she had his daughter.

But she knew he'd forgotten her. She knew that he was married, having children, running his school, living the life he'd always planned. A life that never included a woman like her.

And certainly not an illegitimate daughter.

But if only he could see her.

That was Lily's thought each time she looked at her daughter—*their* daughter, their beautiful Grace. If only, if only. . . .

Lily knew he'd adore her, for she was truly a beautiful child, truly David's child. Yes, David's child. A pair of eyes was all it took to know the child's paternity. Yes, many men have brown hair and brown eyes, but Grace had David's brown hair and eyes. When Lily looked at her daughter, she saw the same soulful puppy-dog eyes that had captured her the first moment she'd seen David. The child's features—even the dimple—and many of her habits were carbon copies of her father's. She looked nothing like Lily.

Did I look like my father? Had my mother once looked upon me with such thoughts? Had her heart ached when she looked upon the product of their love? Grace's birth made

Lily feel closer to her mother. Perhaps her mother had been in a similar situation. But what did it matter? She knew only that she wanted and needed the woman's guidance now more than ever. All the anger she'd placed toward her parents all her life now diminished. She thought she'd needed them while growing up, but that was nothing compared to how she needed them now.

Lily had taken no more clients since Grace's birth and had made sure to hire the best women so she'd never have to work again. Tom was still there—sweet wonderful Tom who'd watched Grace enter the world, who'd taught Lily how to care for a child, who'd walked the child hour after hour when it had colic or trouble teething—who still helped with the child's frequent nightmares, and who never complained when the child crawled into their bed when he spent the night.

It was December 6, 1860 and, as Lily had every year, she prepared for her daughter's birthday with constant thoughts of David also growing another year older. Was he happy?

The night was cold but Lily's part of the house was cozy with fires, mistletoe, and candles and, as she had every December 6th, she left the doors open to the private apartment so everyone could hear the piano being played in the parlor. As Lily supervised Edith's decorating of the table in the small dining room, she glanced toward Tom and the children and felt a warm melancholy at the sight of them roasting marshmallows over the fire. She adored Tom and his children and they were all so perfect together. She and Tom were open and honest and accepting of each other for who and what they were. And it was because of that honesty that Lily had told him about loving David and about David being Grace's father. But still he stayed and still he loved her.

Edith soon had the highly polished rosewood table piled high with goodies, including two giant bowls of punch—one for adults and one for children—then whispered to Lily that the cake was ready. Everyone clapped as Edith brought out the pink and white cake and Grace blew out the candles.

"Thank you, Momma." She hugged her mother's neck then stepped off the chair and walked to Edith and hugged her neck. "Thank you. Is it chocolate inside?"

Edith nodded. "Of course. And Tom made ice cream."

"Thank you, Tom," she said as she ran to him and hugged his neck.

"You're welcome, princess." He hugged her and kissed her cheek. As always, the scene broke Lily's heart. Why couldn't he fill the void David left? Why couldn't she let him?

After a few toasts, the ladies retired to their rooms with their gentlemen and Lily shut her apartment's doors. She and Tom lounged on the sofa while TJ attempted to teach the girls a new game.

"This has been a nice night, very nice." Tom put down his coffee and pulled the woman he loved next to him. "You look beautiful in the firelight." He kissed her. "Of course you look beautiful all the time, but with your hair down and that gown . . ." But just as he began nibbling Lily's neck, Gracie started crying.

"I think it's past someone's bedtime," Lily said as she pushed Tom's lips away with a fingertip. "But remember what you were doing."

He motioned for her to stay put. "I'll get her." As he picked up the little girl, she whimpered then dropped her head on his shoulder.

"Out already?" Lily stood on tiptoe to kiss her daughter's head now settled heavily on Tom's shoulder. "Good night sweet Birthday Girl. Sweet dreams."

"Come on, kids," Tom whispered to TJ and Ruthie to follow him upstairs.

Just as Lily bent down to stoke the fire, she heard a knock at the door. "Go away," she mumbled to herself. The perfect evening and a little too much punch had left her feeling drowsy and anxious to be alone with Tom, and she certainly didn't feel like telling a horny—and probably drunk—customer that all the ladies were busy. But whoever it was was persistent and knocked again.

"Okay!" She threw a lap blanket around her shoulders and headed for the front door. The foyer floor tile was cold under her bare feet and she shivered as the door knocker clanked once again. "Okay, okay!" Her speech was started before she opened the door. "I'm sorry, all the ladies are . . . David."

"Hi." His smile was broad—and charming. His eyes twinkled in the lamplight, his uniform's brass buttons sparkled.

And Lily went mute.

"May I come in?"

Her mouth dry and her mind jumbled, she moved aside so he could enter, then shut the door behind him. The foyer was lit by only one wall sconce so his image was shaded, but even in the dim light she could see the face she loved, the face she still saw in her dreams, the face made only more handsome by the years. As she examined his features her heart raced. Why had he come back?

"I'm sorry it's so late." His voice was a whisper. "I can't see much at night, of course, but it looks like a nice place." He shivered and folded his arms across his chest. "Cold night."

"Yes." She pulled the blanket tighter around her shoulders. "How . . . how'd you find me?"

"Oh, it seems everyone still knows 'the Lily of the West'." He smiled again. "Polly wasn't happy to see me. I told you she didn't like me."

How dare he speak as if they'd just seen each other! She looked down at the floor, trying to avoid his eyes.

And his smile disappeared. "I see that you're not either." His fingers were cold when they raised her chin. "Lily?"

"Excuse me." She brushed his hand away. "It's quite late and I've had a long day. How may I help you?"

He looked startled and Lily found it almost impossible not to throw her arms around his neck and kiss the lips she'd adored for six years.

"I . . . I wanted to see you." He reached in a pocket. "I'll pay." He was looking at his money. "How much?"

How dare he? And why was he back now after so long? Was his marriage in trouble? Was his wife too big with child to make love? Lily took a deep breath and folded her arms across her chest to keep from shaking. "You can't afford me."

His brows furrowed.

"I don't service customers anymore."

"Oh. Oh? That's good." He smiled. "Really good. How come? This is . . . isn't it?"

"Yes it is. You had your plans and I had mine. This is my establishment. I hope yours is as successful."

"Congratulations. I guess."

"You guess?"

"Yes. If this is what you want."

"It's exactly what I want." She maintained a steady unemotional glare.

He turned toward the door then back to her. "I guess I shouldn't have come. I thought you might be glad to see me."

"Really? Well, yes, I do enjoy seeing old customers."

His eyes grew hard.

"Most return a little sooner, however. Since you hadn't, I'd assumed you'd not been satisfied with my performance and were taking your business elsewhere." She hoped he couldn't see that she was trembling.

He squinted. "I think you know better."

"And how would I?"

"Who is it, Lil?" Tom put an arm around Lily's shoulders.

"An old customer." She started to introduce them but knew that one look at David would identify Grace's father.

Tom whispered into her ear. "Are you all right?"

She nodded. "I'm just trying to find out what this gentleman wants."

Obviously confused, David stuttered, "I guess I'd better go," and turned to leave.

No! Her mind raced. How could she stop him without appearing needy?

He turned back toward her. "I am sorry I bothered you so late, but it's important that I speak to you. May I call on you tomorrow?"

Tom looked defeated. "You might as well stay since you're here. I'll go on home."

"Don't go, Tom." Lily looked at David. "Tell me."

"I'd rather speak to you in private."

"There's nothing Tom can't hear, *nothing* he doesn't know."

David's eyes widened, his brows raised.

Tom kissed her cheek. "I'll go."

"No, Tom, he's interrupting *our* evening. Why should you go? Besides, the kids will be disappointed." She saw that her words confused David even more and she enjoyed his confusion.

"I'll come back in the morning." Tom leaned toward her and whispered, "Watch your heart and remember that I've always loved you and always will." He kissed her again then walked out. Lily stood at the open door and waved as he rode away.

But as she closed the door, she panicked. *What am I doing? Am I making things worse for myself? But if I turn him away without knowing what he has to say, I'll go crazy. Who are you fooling? You'll never be able to turn him away.*

David followed her into her private quarters and sat down on the sofa while she closed the double doors and nervously stoked the fire. "So, what's this you need to say that's so important?"

He was silent until she looked at him. But the fire in his eyes was too much for her to bear and she swallowed and looked away.

"Why are you being so . . ."

She faced him. "How, Mr. Evans? How am I being?"

"Unfriendly. I thought you might be glad to see me."

"Well, I'm sorry my welcome isn't what you'd hoped but, as I told you, I don't service customers anymore. If you'll come back in a few hours, one of the other ladies might be free and a little more friendly."

His eyes winced then hardened. "What's Tom then?"

She lifted her chin. "*Not* a customer." With folded arms, she paced prissily. "After all your high-toned words of morality, I *am* curious as to why you're here." She stopped in front of him. "What's wrong, soldier, isn't that perfect wife giving you enough?"

He jumped to his feet, his eyes cold and cruel, his jaw clinched, his hands balled into fists. "I'm sorry I bothered you." He marched to the doors then stopped, his hand on the knob. "It seems I misunderstood our relationship." He looked at her, his eyes moist. "I'd remembered you being more . . . compassionate." His eyes grew hard again. "I guess compassion has a price."

She dug her fingernails into her arms to keep from slapping him. "So 'compassion' is what it's called now? Leave it to you to label sex in such a way.

Okay. I'll rephrase my question. Isn't your perfect wife giving you enough 'compassion'?"

"That is enough!" His knuckles were white, his eyes closed. He mumbled to himself, "Why did I come here?"

"You seemed very sure of a reason when you arrived."

He turned the door knob but didn't open the door. He looked at her again.

And she looked at him, at the handsome but tortured face, and she searched her brain for the words that would make him stay without making her look weak. She motioned toward the couch. "Well, since you're here, you might as well stay—at least until you tell me your important news."

He almost ran to the sofa then watched Lily as she sat on the other end and tucked her bare feet under her.

"So, what is it?"

He grinned. "I've been chosen as a delegate to the convention this month. South Carolina's going to secede!"

"Secede? That's crazy!"

He jumped up and frowned. "Crazy? We're crazy for not leaving sooner. We've been pushed into this. Our needs have been ignored for too long. We've been punished for too long. We've got to stand up for ourselves and get the Feds out of our hair. We don't want them telling us what to do any more."

"But you can't possibly want to dissolve the Union."

"Oh, yes, I can. And we will. We're hoping Lincoln will let us go peaceably but I doubt that that will happen." He looked directly into her eyes. "I'm sure we'll have to fight. I've been training a group of militia for a year now."

She shivered at the thought of him in battle, getting hurt, getting killed? No, she couldn't bear it. She blinked back tears and turned away from his searching stare. "Let's talk of something else. You must have more pleasant news to share."

He sat down again, his excitement deflated.

Where was his enthusiasm for the school that had been so important before? Was he that excited about war, or had the burdens of building a school, a militia, and a family worn him down? She smiled her brightest. "How's your school?"

"Good. Good instructors, about a hundred students."

She patted his shoulder. "That's wonderful. Is Saul working with you?"

His face grew stony. "Why do you ask about him?"

"Because you're friends. You are, aren't you?"

"No. We are not friends." Cold and crisp.

"I'm sorry. I thought you were. What happened?"

"I'd rather not talk about it. Let's just say I don't trust him." His dark brows furrowed. "You didn't really like him, did you?"

She shrugged. "As a lover?"

"Lily . . ."

"Well, that's the only way I knew him."

He looked hard in her eyes then continued. "I bought some more land."

"For the school?"

"No, for us."

Her heart twisted. "Us?"

He turned his face away and cleared his throat. "Yes. My family."

Although she knew it had surely come to pass, hearing David confirm the reality of a family was like a knife piercing her heart. Had she really thought he would marry and not make love, not produce children? *Be strong, Lily. You can get through this.* "Ah, ha. I thought so. Tell me about them." She tucked her feet more tightly under her and hugged her knees.

Hanging on?

He stared at her as he spoke. "Richie's three, Franklin's a year and a half, and William's eight months. They're really a handful but I enjoy them."

Lily playfully kicked him with a bare foot. "They sound wonderful, and I would think that they would be the first thing you'd tell an old friend about."

His brows furrowed. "Friend?"

She giggled seductively and rubbed his thigh with her foot. She knew she was acting the harlot, but it was either that or bawl like a baby. She'd missed him desperately and news of his family was more than she could stand. And though she damned herself, she wanted him and knew she'd take him under any circumstances. The very idea of making love to him made her lightheaded. And besides, in her business, what difference did it make that he was married?

Just don't hope for more, Lily. If he loved you, he would have been back much sooner than this. He's just come for the sex his wife won't or can't give him. Don't expect more. Take what you can when you can.

She forced a wicked smile. "I'm sorry. I guess 'friend' isn't the appropriate word. You said you'd misunderstood our relationship; I guess I did too. But 'friend' sounds so much nicer than whore, don't you think? And I know you don't like that word." *Tell me I'm wrong, David. Tell me you love me.*

Suddenly he grabbed her feet and jerked her toward him, his face in hers, his eyes dark. "Tell me, Lily, if you're not servicing clients, why this teasing?" He yanked off his coat and threw it on the floor. "Perhaps you'll make an exception for old time's sake." He was jerking at his shirttail and fumbling with his pants. "Wouldn't you like to see how well you taught me? You once called me a novice, an immature boy soldier, remember? Well, I've had a lot of practice since then. Wouldn't you like to see how much progress your student has made?" With Lily penned under him, he raised to his knees and dug into his pocket. "I'll even pay. That's more than you can say for Tom, I'll bet." He pressed coins into her palm. "Is this enough or has your price increased now that you own the place?"

"How dare you!" She flailed at him until he released her, then threw the coins at him as she stumbled to her feet.

He towered over her, his hands on his hips. "Come on, Lily. This is what you want, what you expect. You talk such a big game and have always delighted in reminding me of what you are. I can do that too. I'm a client; you're a whore. I pay; you service."

She slapped him. "Get out of my house, now!"

CHAPTER 9

But he didn't.

But when they came together they didn't make love.

They had sex. Coldly. Cruelly. Selfishly.

Then sat with legs wrapped around waists as hands and mouths caressed and sleepy eyes communicated. Lily leaned into his chest as his fingers trailed up and down her back and stroked her hair, his husky voice whispering her name. Her arms tightened around him. He kissed the top of her head. She looked into his smiling eyes. He played with the curls that fell on her cheeks then inhaled deeply and smiled. "Jasmine?"

"Of course."

"I had to see you before the war starts . . . in case I don't . . . can't get back."

Was he planning—wanting—to come back? Though thrilled by the words, Lily dared not get her hopes up. He was hers for the moment and he was holding her tightly against him. She could feel the movement of his chin and the vibrations of his voice and she grew drowsy and lethargic, a butterfly dormant in its safe cocoon, a child inside the womb. She tasted his chest and buried her face in the soft curls, played with them with her fingers.

"I am sorry I haven't been back. I really am." He pulled her even closer and whispered, "I've thought of you so often." He lifted her chin and looked down into her eyes. "You know that, don't you? You know why I haven't been back, don't you? You understand, don't you?" He hugged her again. "I've missed you so much, so very much."

Lily looked into the eyes she loved so dearly, the eyes she saw in her dreams every night, the eyes of their daughter.

Grace!

"Get up!" She almost knocked him over.

"What's wrong?"

"I just remembered something."

"What?"

"Never mind, just get dressed."

He laughed and put his arms around her but she pushed him away. "Lily?"

"Just get dressed, please."

She watched as he started to dress but found herself wanting to love him again, so she forced herself to walk away. "I'll get coffee."

When she returned, he was inspecting his coat, brushing it off and admonishing himself for throwing it so carelessly on the floor. Lily smiled as she watched him look around the room, find a corner chair, and carefully drape the garment over its back. He was adjusting his suspenders when he saw her watching him. "I'm dressed."

His obedient tone and puppy-dog smile reminded her of Grace's when the child sought approval, and she smiled as she set down a tray with coffee and cake. "I thought you might have worked up an appetite."

David blushed as he sat down. Pointing to the cake, he asked, "Special occasion?"

Lily was about to answer when she noticed the amount of sugar he was putting in his coffee. Was that four teaspoons or five? She winced.

"Momma? I had a bad dream, heard noises."

David spilled his coffee then dabbed at the moisture with a napkin as Lily pulled her daughter into her lap and kissed the top of her head. "It's okay angel. It was just a dream." The child immediately fell back to sleep, her face against her mother's bosom.

David stared at the mother and child. "I guess I'm not the only one keeping secrets."

"Secrets? Is that what you call your children? Grace is no secret."

His lips pursed and he spoke coldly. "I'm very proud of my family, extremely proud."

"Then why didn't you tell me about them right away? Your militia and your precious South Carolina were at the top of your priority list." She whispered to keep from waking Grace who'd stretched out on the sofa.

"I didn't think you'd want to hear about them." He set aside his uneaten cake then stood and paced, thrusting his hands deep into his pockets. "And now I'm ashamed of myself. Not only should I not be here, but I'm denying my family." He came close. ". . . my very important loving family. Yes, I have a family. I have a beautiful and loving wife and three handsome sons. I couldn't be prouder or happier." He plopped back down into the chair and glared at Lily, showing yet another expression she'd seen on their daughter's face.

Grace stirred and Lily patted her while frowning at David then whispered, "I can't imagine why you'd hesitate to tell me such wonderful news. Didn't you think I'd be happy for you? I wish all my clients well."

"Aw, Lily . . ."

"So . . . how is she?"

"Don't start that again." He lightly pounded a fist on the chair's arm. "I shouldn't even mention her name in such a place. She's a true lady, you know. An angel. Perfect in every way. She's sweet, a wonderful mother, good helpmate . . . and perfect lover."

"My, my. When you have such a wife, why on earth would you visit a whore?"

"Damn you."

She smiled teasingly, her eyes twinkling. "I'm sorry, Mr. Evans, but I'll have to ask you to leave if you're going to curse around my daughter. I thought profanity, like alcohol, didn't cross your lips. You've certainly slipped down that ladder of perfection, haven't you?"

He jumped out of his chair and and walked toward his coat. "Good night, madam." He took a few steps and turned back. "And I use that term in the truest sense."

"Mommy, I can't sleep." Grace sat up and rubbed her eyes then blinked and looked at David. And he looked at her.

And his reaction was priceless.

"Oh, my . . ." He knelt in front of the sofa and took Grace's hand in his. "I'm sorry, little one. I couldn't keep my mouth shut. Will you forgive me?" He let go of her hand but continued to look into her face. "I can't believe it." He looked at Lily and she nodded. "Why didn't you tell me?"

She shrugged.

Grace leaned against her mother then saw David's cake and perked up. "Cake? Mommy, can I eat cake for breakfast too?"

"May I."

"May I?"

"Just this once."

She jumped off the sofa, plopped into the chair, and quickly dove into the cake. After the first bite, she pulled her feet underneath her and smiled at David. "This is my birthday cake."

David couldn't quit staring at her as he sat down on the opposite end of the sofa from Lily. "Today's your birthday?"

"Huh-uh." She held up her hand and spread her fingers. "I'm five."

David almost stuttered. "Today's my birthday too."

"How old are you?"

"Twenty-five."

"Twenty-five? That's old. How old are you, Momma?"

"Twenty."

David's eyes widened and his face turned white. "That means you were only . . . My God, Lily, why . . . ?"

"What difference would it have made?"

52

He shook his head.

Lily smiled at him then looked at their child and felt a contentment she'd never known, a contentment she'd never dared wish. The man she loved and their child were with her. The three of them were together. For one breathtaking moment, they were a family. Lily's heart almost burst with happiness as she savored the moment.

The little girl licked the last crumbs off the fork and wiped her mouth then put down the plate. "Where's Tom, Mommy?"

"He went home but he'll be back soon." Lily felt David's gaze as she faced her daughter. "Go on upstairs and tell TJ and Ruthie that their daddy will come after them later this morning. If you kids want breakfast, find some biscuits, okay?"

"Okay." Grace jumped out of the chair then hugged her mother. Lily watched David watch Grace as the little girl skipped away.

"I can't believe it, Lily. She looks . . ."

"Just like you?"

He nodded. "It's like looking into a mirror but with a sweet feminine face staring back. I just wish I'd known. I could have . . ."

"What, David? It wasn't, isn't, your place to help with her. You have your own family, your reputation, your career." She leaned back against the sofa arm and added, "Besides, getting pregnant is one of the hazards of the job."

"Stop it! Why do you speak as you do?"

"I speak the truth, that's all. You just never want to hear it."

"Does she think Tom's her father?"

"No."

"What have you told her?"

"Not much." She shrugged her shoulders and blinked back tears. "I just told her that her father was a handsome man I once knew."

"I want to be a part of her life."

"I don't think that's a good idea, even if it were possible."

"But I can't bear the thought of never seeing her again."

"But she's not worth the risk of losing everything, is she?"

He looked away.

"I didn't think so. Don't worry about Grace. Tom's a good father to her. He's here all the time. He loves her. She loves him. We may not be a 'proper' family, but we're a happy one. Grace just happened—for me a very fortunate 'accident'. She's no concern of yours."

"Go ahead. Treat me like I don't matter to you, like I'm just a regular customer off the street. I may not matter, but Grace does. She's my daughter and I care about what happens to her."

"Well, that's too bad because you really have no claim on her." She forced a laugh and slapped his shoulder playfully. "Oh, David. Don't let your conscience bother you so. Grace and I have been fine without you and will continue to be."

He grabbed her hands and rubbed them then looked into her eyes and touched the hair by her cheek. His voice was a whisper. "Why must you be so tough?"

Tough? She was anything but and so weary of pretending to be. Couldn't he tell how much she loved him? *If you'd tell me you love me, David, I'd do anything, say anything.* But such thoughts and wishes were useless and his touch just made it harder to say good bye, so she pulled her hands from his and looked down at her lap.

He stammered and cleared his throat as he stood up. "Well, I guess I don't have to worry about you mourning me if I die in battle."

She turned away in horror, a hand to her stomach. "Why would you say such a thing?"

"Because it's obvious I mean nothing to you."

Damn him! Can't he see me shaking? Can't he see my love? "Nonsense. I wish all my clients good health."

"Then I guess I'll be one of hundreds." His voice was cruel and cold but it wavered and cracked. "I don't know what possessed me to come here tonight. I love my wife, adore her. I don't deserve her and she certainly doesn't deserve to share me with a . . . a . . . . Good day, madam."

CHAPTER 10

Still shaking, Lily stared out the window and watched David leave, watched him pull at the reins so forcefully that he almost choked his horse. Damn him! After all these years, why had he come back? He loved his wife and children and his life was running so smoothly. . . .Why had he risked it all?

Lily was desperate to believe that he loved her, but even as she stared into the pink sky of early morning, she berated herself, for if he had returned because of love, she'd just chased him away, and now he'd *never* come back. Why should he? If a man can't get compassion from a prostitute, why bother? *Are you happy now? If he'd had any doubts, your pride and tough words just convinced him that he made the right choice with Mary Anne.*

She turned from the window and dragged herself toward the stairs. Sleep. Yes. Sleep was what she needed. She was tired, so very tired. She could crawl into bed and sleep. Forever.

But as she neared her bed, she remembered that David had taken her to this point before and she'd almost died from it, had survived only because she was carrying his child. Well, David's child still needed a mother, didn't she? Besides, the way David had looked at Grace and his words of concern for her . . .

Hope surged inside her breast and a smile rose to her lips as she threw open the curtains and welcomed the new day. Yes, he'd be back.

God, please bring him back.

Clinging to that hope, Lily walked downstairs to the kitchen and found the children eating biscuits and jam. She kissed the top of Gracie's head. "Honey, you're going to get sick from so many sweets."

"I told TJ and Ruthie that you let me eat birthday cake for breakfast."

"Did you really let her, Lily?"

"Yes, I'm afraid I did. Well, your birthday comes only once a year." Lily touched the tip of her daughter's nose. "Remember that, okay?"

Gracie nodded her head in the heavy exaggerated way she did so often that caused her barley-sugar curls to bounce. The child loved attention and was often quite demanding and Lily was thankful for TJ and Ruthie to bring her down to earth.

"Gracie says there was a handsome soldier here last night." Ruthie's grin exposed missing teeth. "Was there really? Was he very, very handsome?"

Gracie nodded again, this time even goofier than before, then giggled.

Lily laughed. "Yes, Ruthie, there was a handsome soldier here last night, and yes, he is very, very handsome."

"Daddy!" Ruthie was off her chair and hugging her father. Gracie followed suit while TJ simply said, "Hi, Dad."

Gracie squealed, "You missed the handsome soldier! He said it was his birthday too, just like me."

Lily squeezed Tom's hand.

He looked at her coldly. "When did he leave?"

"Just now."

Lily had never seen anything but love and kindness in Tom's face, but at this moment there was neither. As he pulled her toward the stairs, he spoke to his son. "Take the girls outside for awhile, okay?"

The bedroom door had barely shut before Tom pushed Lily onto the bed and began taking off his clothes. As one heavy boot then the other hit the floor, Lily backed up against the headboard. "What's going on?"

"Just how much do you think I can take?"

"What do you mean?"

"Come on, Lily, you know exactly what I mean. We have something so good here yet you pine away for some sad-eyed clunk who wouldn't know a good thing if it bit him." His pants hit the floor. "I know I'm not as young as he is and my body's not as lean, but I love you, damn it, and I'm the one who's always been here for you, not him. I'm tired of being made a fool. I cursed myself all night for walking out of here instead of knocking that guy's block off."

He positioned himself over her, pushed up her gown, then forced himself inside her. And though she made no effort to stop him, neither did she participate. Instead, she lay there, her mind racing as Tom plunged into her again and again. He was right. She'd hurt him too much for too long. Perhaps it was time to end their relationship. Perhaps it was time for her to survive on her own, completely on her own.

"Love me, Lily. Love me the way you love him. Love me the way you did that night six years ago, remember? You were so filled with passion for him that night. Why not today?" He became angrier with each thrust. His eyes filled with tears, his voice choked. "Or did you make love to him so many times last night that you're actually full of him?" He stopped and stared into her defiant face. "He's still in you, isn't he? Damn you." He rolled off. "Get him out of your system, Lily. Please, I beg you." He lay with an arm over his face but his weeping was impossible to hide.

Lily said nothing as she walked to the washstand.

"He's probably married with kids, isn't he?"

"Yes." She held a cool cloth to her neck.

He shook his head in disgust as he sat up and reached for his clothes. "Why did he come back after so long?"

"To tell me that South Carolina's going to secede."

"Really? Well I'm not surprised. Those SOBs have been whining for a long time now." He watched her. "Oh, Lil, can't you see what kind of man he is? He owns slaves, cheats on his wife, and now he's going to be a traitor to his country. He doesn't deserve your love and you know it."

"You're right." She studied the limp cloth in her hand.

"I am?"

She nodded and looked hesitantly at him. "I know what you say is partly true."

"Partly?"

"Oh, Tom, he wants to be a good man. He tries so hard."

Tom jumped to his feet. "Ah, hell, Lily! You'll never see this guy for what he is. I don't understand it and guess I never will." He folded his arms across his chest and took a deep breath. "What do you want me to do then?"

"What do you mean?"

"Stay, leave, what?"

She panicked. Her brave idea of living alone had already come back to haunt her. Tom leave? But she couldn't appear needy. She shrugged her shoulders and said nothing.

He bent down to look her in the eye. "I mean that little to you then?"

She bit her lip but said nothing.

His voice cracked. "Then I guess it's good bye."

In a few seconds she was alone.

She stared at the door, tears in her eyes, then stomped around the room. "To hell with him. To hell with both of them." A bath, she needed a bath. Everything would be better after a hot scented bath. That was one of the first lessons she'd learned at Mama Rose's. She bounded down the stairs toward the kitchen to get water.

But the room was silent, a silence that brought her to her senses. Did she really want Tom and his children out of her life? Did she really want them out of Grace's life?

No.

No! She couldn't let him leave. She had to stop him, apologize to him. Tell him she'd forget David. Of course she knew she couldn't, but she had to try. She had to. For Tom's sake.

She searched the apartment but it was quiet, too quiet—and too empty. Desperation rose inside her as she opened the back door. Outside . . . Tom had sent the children outside . . . Surely they're there. *Please God, let them be there—all of them.* Her walk sped to a fast pace as she headed toward Grace's favorite spot—a shady glen with a pond and gazebo that the little girl swore was inhabited by fairies. And it did seem a magical place with its posted sentry of tall pines. Surely that's where Tom and the children were. He wouldn't leave Grace by herself so he must still be there. He had to be. Unless he were so angry that . . . Lily held her breath and walked faster down the flagstone path, pulling the thin robe more tightly around her.

And soon she heard voices.

Then witnessed the effect of her arrogance.

Tom was telling Grace good bye, and though it was obvious that he was trying to make the farewell seem ordinary so as not to alarm the children, Lily could see the difference. He adored Grace and would miss her. Grace would miss him. And what about TJ and Ruthie? They'd miss Grace. She'd miss them. As for Lily, she'd miss all of them. They were family. She must make him stay. "Tom?"

He looked up defensively. "Just tellin' my little girl good bye."

"*Your* little girl?"

All heads turned to see David standing at the end of the sentry line, his eyes darting from Lily to Grace to Tom, his jaw tightening and his eyes flashing as he approached them. "Lily, may I have a word with you?"

Grace pointed toward him. "There he is, Ruthie. There's the handsome soldier!" Not the least afraid of a man she'd met just hours earlier, Grace ran to David and threw her arms around his legs. "I'm so glad you came back." She grinned at Ruthie. "He and I have the same birthday!"

David knelt in front of her. "We do, don't we, sweetheart?"

Tom turned red and shouted, "Keep your hands off of her, you piece of . . . you secessionist traitor!"

David's shocked and pain-filled eyes darted toward Lily and his head shook in disbelief at her betrayal of his confidence. He gently skirted around Grace then grabbed Lily's arm so hard that she winced even as he mumbled, "Don't worry, I don't hurt women."

"Get your hands off her."

"Mommy?" Grace tugged at her mother's gown.

"It's okay, sweetheart." Lily jerked away from David's loosened grip then pulled her daughter close and kissed the top of her head. "TJ, please take the girls back to the house. And keep them inside, okay?"

TJ looked at his father. "Dad, I want to help you and Lily."

"No, son. Do as Lily says and take the girls inside. Better yet," he gave his son some coins, "take them to town for breakfast."

Tom and Lily kissed all three of the children then stared at David as he stared at them, all three listening until they were sure the children were gone.

58

"Well, you've scared the children." She spit the words at him. "Are you happy now?"

"I am sorry to upset them, but I . . . Did you tell Grace about me?"

The veins in Tom's neck protruded as he rolled up his shirt sleeves. "Just leave, you bastard."

"I demand an answer."

"You don't demand anything around here. This isn't your plantation and we're not your slaves."

David's jaw clinched and unclinched as he walked toward Lily, his eyes for her and her alone, his voice soft when he whispered, "I'd like to talk to the lady, alone." His breath fell on her cheek.

But Tom stepped between them. "I said get out of here. The lady's through with you."

David's hands formed fists but he took a deep breath. "Please. I just want some answers about the girl." He looked again at Lily. "She is mine, isn't she?"

Lily walked around Tom—to David. "Why do you care?"

"You know why."

"But a few hours ago you left, ready to forget her. Your precious wife was more important, remember?"

"Yes, but the child's future is also important and I want to help her."

Her robe open, Lily folded her arms under her breasts then watched David's gaze travel the length of her barely hidden body. She smiled seductively and raised her chin. "Don't worry about her future. I have the means to take care of her."

His eyes squinted as he nodded toward the house. "In this place? I can put her in the best schools and keep her away from the scum who come here."

"Like you?"

His nod was solemn and penitent and she started to weaken but steeled herself, more determined than ever to hurt him, and as she moved past him to stand next to Tom, she purposely brushed her body against his then rubbed Tom's shoulder with familiarity as she spoke haughtily. "Well, Tom, I guess the *general* needs to scourge his conscience and plans to do so by protecting my daughter from the likes of you and me."

David's eyes focused on hers. "I can certainly see now how you earned your nickname . . ."

Tom's fists clinched and he leaned forward but Lily pulled him back.

". . . and I've certainly enjoyed today's performance, but . . ." David took Lily's hand and rubbed it with his thumbs. His voice was low and it cracked when he spoke. "Since you won't let me speak to you alone . . ."

His touch made her shiver and she gazed into his eyes.

"I just want what's best for her."

Tom watched David's touch pacify the woman he loved, watched as the two drew together like magnet and steel.

David continued to act as if Tom weren't there. "But I need to know if she's mine. She is, isn't she?"

Tom stepped between them. "And if she's not? If she's not the offspring of your rich pampered loins, you don't care if she has a good future or not, do you? Let the child grow up any way she can. Isn't that right?"

David dropped Lily's hands as his hands formed fists and his face turned red. "Damn the both of you! I just want a simple answer! Give it to me and I'll gladly leave." He took a deep breath. "And you can both go to hell."

Tom's large fist hit David's cheek and the two men became a tangled mass. Lily cried out for them to stop but their cursing and scuffling made her inaudible. Their anger made her invisible.

They finally separated and Tom taunted his rival. "What right do you have to claim either of them? I'm the one who was here when Grace was born. I'm the one who's been here when they've both been sick. I've been with Lily hundreds of times. I was her first." Although his words addressed David, his voice turned tender and his eyes fastened to Lily's. "You probably don't know that she was raped when she was thirteen, that I've loved her since the first night I saw her, that I've begged her to marry me." He looked again at David and sneered, "Because *I'm* free to marry her. *I'm* free to publicly acknowledge Gracie. You can't do either, can you, you adulterous son of a bi . . . "

"Damn you!" David's eyes glistened as he moved toward Tom, poor loving Tom who didn't see the knife in David's hand until it was embedded in his stomach. His eyes widened and he looked from David to Lily, question in his eyes. "Lily?"

With a groan, he hit the ground.

David stood over him, stared at him, then looked at Lily with red eyes and blanched face. "Oh my God, Lil, I . . . "

"Tom!" She fell to the round and brought the dying man's hands to her lips.

"Lil?" Ashen and barely audible, he mumbled, "Kids . . . watch them, please?"

Her tears and kisses covered his face and hands. "Of course. Hang on, please. Don't leave me, Tom. I'm sorry for everything, so sorry."

"I love you, Lil. Always have, always will."

"I know, I know. I love you too, Tom. You know it, don't you?"

He nodded then closed his eyes.

As she held Tom's body tightly to hers, she cried and mumbled softly, "I'm so sorry, Tom, so sorry." She rocked his body then looked up at David, her eyes wet and dark. "Look at what you've done! Why did you have to come, ever? Damn you! Damn you . . ." She held Tom and cried.

David didn't run away.

Lily barely knew what was happening around her, barely realized that the sheriff was cuffing David. Through the fog in her head, she heard cruel words, something about hanging, then looked up to see David staring at her as he was taken away.

It was Ruthie's piercing scream that woke her, made her look at the innocent victims—now orphans—who fell to their knees beside their father's body. TJ quieted Ruthie's screams and held her to his chest where she sobbed. While Lily continued to hold Tom's head in her lap, she held Gracie against her side, the child's small fingers clawing at her mother's shoulder, her dark eyes wide with fear, her chest heaving.

Look what you've done, Lily. Look what your love for David has done.

And what of the three boys in South Carolina? What of the beautiful loving wife? What of the fine reputation?

CHAPTER 11

"May I see the prisoner?"

The young deputy looked at her with fright and curiosity. But Lily was used to it. Like everyone else in town, he knew who and what she was, but because his youth made him easily manipulated, Lily had purposely waited to visit David until she knew the boy was alone. She didn't have the stomach for the vulgar things she knew the sheriff would say. Funny how former clients were always the rudest.

The first thing she noticed was that David had folded his beloved jacket to use for a pillow—and to hide the stains of Tom's blood? With his shirt sleeves rolled up, the neck of his shirt open, and his hair mussed, he almost looked like the boy she'd first met. But his eyes were those of an older man, a much older man, and although Lily wanted to hate him, she couldn't. She tried to look at a killer but all she could see was the face she loved more than life itself, and it broke her heart to see him caged and helpless.

He reached through the bars and grabbed her hands and kissed them. "I'm so glad you came. I was afraid you wouldn't."

She squeezed the fingers of the rough hands then stroked his sad face with its slight stubble. "Are you okay?"

He turned his mouth into her palm and kissed it then shrugged. "It's not too bad when I'm alone, but the sheriff's using me as a trophy. He brings his friends in here to show them 'a real toy soldier rich-boy slave holder'." The string of words made them giggle in spite of their danger, but the amusement was short-lived, and David whispered through clinched teeth, "The sooner we leave the Union, the better. Kentucky can do what it wants." He took a deep breath to calm down. "I'm sorry." He peered into her eyes. "Are you okay? And Grace?" He squeezed her hands. "And his children . . . are they okay?"

"As good as can be expected. Grace doesn't understand what's going on. The funeral's tomorrow." She looked at their joined hands. "I'll take care of TJ and Ruthie. It's the least I can do, the very least. Besides, they're like my own children and I love them deeply." She took a deep breath and shook her head. "It's all my fault, everything's my fault."

"No." David squeezed her hands then touched her cheek. "It's my fault. I should never have come here. I should never have met you. You were so happy then, such a carefree spirit. No, it's all my fault. I've betrayed everyone, especially my family." He looked away and spoke as if to himself. "I just hope Mary Anne doesn't find out about any of this."

Lily pulled her hands from his and felt the all too familiar knot in her stomach, the knot that tightened each time she heard "Mary Anne." How dare he speak of her? But she tried to stay calm. "So . . . you regret it all?"

"Yes . . . No . . . I don't know. Don't you see, Lily? If I'd not given into temptation, we'd both be happy."

"And Grace?"

His voice softened. "There'd be no Grace."

"Then I would never have known the happiness she's given me. It's all right for you to have your family yet you'd deny me mine, is that it?"

He shook his head. "Oh, Lily, you know I don't mean it like that. Why must you twist what I say?"

"Because it always comes back to you and your family, your honor . . . your precious Mary Anne."

His face reddened. "Is she the reason you haven't told the sheriff it was self defense? Do you want me to hang?"

She raised her chin. "I haven't told him it was self defense because it wasn't, not exactly."

"But Tom swung first. I . . ."

"You pulled your knife first. Besides, I don't think they'd believe me. I don't think they'd believe a prostitute's word that a rich slave holder killed a local man in self defense, and it's your knife and clothes that were covered with blood. Do you really think they'd listen? David, for many of us you stand for everything that's evil."

"Us?"

"Yes, us."

He spun away and walked the length of his cell then back. He ran his fingers through his hair and emitted a frustrated defeated sigh. "I don't believe this." He came back to the bars and curled his fingers around them. "How can you say such things? Do you really believe I'm evil?"

"You own slaves. There's nothing that can excuse that. It's the vilest, cruelest thing I can think of. Have you seen the way slaves are mauled when they're auctioned? Have you seen those families when they're ripped apart? Have you heard their screams?"

"No, but . . ."

"I have, David. I have, and it's something I will never forget, never!"

As far as Lily knew, David Evans hadn't a mean bone in his entire body. He was proud and ambitious, yes, and he had a relationship with her that went against his moral beliefs, but he wasn't mean or cruel, and it was because he was such a good man, and because she loved him so much, that she felt obligated to make him see how abhorrent it was to own slaves.

And she had a captive audience, did she not?

So, feeling like a preacher at a revival meeting, she took a deep breath and began. "I once saw a girl, just about my age, pushed onto a platform, her wrists and ankles in shackles. I remember thinking how ridiculous the precautions. She was so frail that I wondered how she could walk, much less escape." As Lily sat down on the cold floor, she was Morgan again, a frightened thirteen-year-old "boy" running away from Lexington who mingled into a crowd near the train station in Frankfort.

She avoided David's eyes as she described the auctioneer, a short round man with a third chin of white whiskers and a face so red that it looked as if his tight black boots were pushing all the blood to his face and he might explode. His eyes beamed with disgusting enthusiasm as he eyed his newest piece of merchandise, and Lily remembered thinking that the words he used could just as easily have described her. "'Now here's a fine looking girl. Another good breeder'." Lily stared into her memories and hypnotically touched her shoulders as she described how the auctioneer ripped away the gunny sack that covered the girl's frail body, how the girl's eyes widened and her bony fingers clutched at the falling burlap, how the man slapped those fingers and made them fall limp. He'd tamed her body—but not her eyes. "Those eyes . . ." Lily shook her head. "I can see them so clearly."

David had quietly paced his cell and now leaned against the bars, his back to her. She stood and walked to within inches of him. Her hand stretched out to caress the thick unruly brown waves that touched the neck of his shirt, but she pulled it back then cleared her throat and continued her story.

"I think what was even more frightening than the girl's expression was the coldness in the man, for his face clouded with rage then cleared so quickly that his verbal barrage didn't skip a beat. 'Just coming into breeding age,' he said as he lifted one of her breasts—so casually, as if it weren't connected to her body. 'She'll make a fine wet nurse'. "

Lily watched David's head shake slowly from side to side. She hated hurting him but knew it was for the better good. He had to see what she'd seen, what she still saw. The auctioneer's eyes beaming with sickening enthusiasm, the lack of outrage in the faces of the onlookers, the finely-dressed woman walking onto the platform and opening the girl's mouth to examine her teeth. "I couldn't believe my eyes, David. I'd seen men examine horses exactly that way and I wondered, were Negroes equivalent to animals?

Didn't they cry and laugh, have babies and die? Nellie cried and laughed. Nellie had a kind heart, a very human heart. Nellie saved my life."

Lily laughed. "Hell, if it hadn't been for Nellie forcing me to learn my letters and numbers, I wouldn't be able to read and write. If it hadn't been for Nellie, I would have gotten pregnant a long time ago." She almost pitied David's seemingly permanent state of confusion. "Yes, Nellie was a Negro. She was our maid and cook. But she was also my teacher. I called her 'No Nonsense Nellie' because she wouldn't let me get away with anything. It was Nellie who jumped all over me when she caught me doing 'unladylike' things like climbing trees and smoking. I'll never forget the way she ranted at me when I came home after swimming in the creek with the local boys. 'I can't believe you'd let those varmints see you in your underdrawers! You scat upstairs and get dressed! '" Lily laughed as she remembered Nellie's scoldings then saw that David was smiling and nodding. Was he remembering similar words from his mammy whom he lovingly called Mauma Hattie?

"Anyhow, I knew Nellie was every bit as human as I was which meant that all Negroes were just as human. That's why I can't justify the theory that they're less than we are. That's why people who deal in slavery treat the slaves as nothing more than cattle—they can't afford to know them as human beings."

David looked into her eyes then frowned and turned away.

"As the bids rose, the girl's eyes searched the crowd looking for . . . help? Sympathy? Understanding? At one point her eyes linked with mine and I swear . . ." Lily bit her lip, ". . . I swear she was asking me for help, pleading with me for help. I think she saw through my boy's disguise and straight to my female heart. I'm ashamed to admit it, but I tore my eyes from hers. I couldn't bear her sadness and my lack of courage."

Tears flowed freely as Lily told the rest of the story. How the girl howled when the auctioneer pushed her toward her new owner. How a high-pitched wrenching wail came from an elderly gray-haired blue-black woman as she pushed her way through the other slaves, her unintelligible screeching mingling with the clanking chains that weighed down her skeletal outstretched arms. As Lily described the scene, she could feel the same sickness in the pit of her stomach that she'd felt that day, that very moment when she'd realized that the women were mother and daughter.

"The round man's face grew redder and sweat ran off in sheets as he yelled for order—and help. He was frightened. *He* was frightened!" Lily shook her head. "I remember thinking how ludicrous it was that he was frightened by two frail women in chains.

"The girl was yanked through the crowd and put in a wagon that immediately pulled away. And though the old woman's screams were quickly muffled, the old eyes followed her screaming daughter's face. I could tell the

65

exact moment that the girl was out of sight because the mother's eyes glazed over and her head fell forward onto her chest." Lily wrapped her fingers around the cell bars. "I knew that her soul had left her body just as sure as if she'd died." She looked into David's red eyes. How she loved this man with his good heart, his idealism and childhood lessons. She knew he was battling demons, but he *was* battling, he *was* trying.

"Oh, David, I wanted to cry out and curse all those people for their participation in such barbarism, but I dared not. I feared for my life because I was escaping the horrors in Lexington, escaping a probable jail sentence. I couldn't afford to forget my disguise or bring attention to myself. But that was a handy excuse. The truth was that I didn't have the courage to speak my mind, and that made me feel dirty. How could I witness such obscenity and do nothing?"

She took a deep breath and wiped away tears. "But I learned many lessons that day. One was that had our cultures been different, had I been living in another time or place, it could have been me stripped to the waist, me being handled like an animal.

"But then I realized that my future wouldn't be much different. Yes, I'd get paid but I'd get paid to be pawed on and to please others."

She saw him wince and knew how much he hated being reminded of who she was, what she was, and it took all her courage to continue. Did he care about her past? Would her words make a difference?

"You asked me once why I made my living as I do . . . At one time I'd assumed I'd be a prostitute because it was all I knew, but then I was raped by two local policemen. Then I saw the ladies who raised me marched to jail while the nice townspeople spit at them and ripped their gowns. Then I saw a girl my age sold like a farm animal. That's when I learned what being a prostitute meant. That's when I learned that all women are slaves, even the finely-dressed woman who bought the girl."

David grabbed her hands and kissed them, rubbed the tops of them with his thumbs and whispered, "My poor girl, my poor, poor girl."

My poor girl? Did he mean it?

"Now you know why I was dressed as a boy." Her eyes twinkled. "Except for the auction, I enjoyed my life as Morgan and could scratch, spit, and belch with the best of them."

David laughed, his eyes shining as he touched her cheek. "Now I know why you said you'd wear breeches if you could."

Her heart raced from his touch, his words, his bright eyes, and his memory of their meeting in Polly's garden. "Well, now you know." She intertwined her fingers with his. "But there's something else you must know." She took a deep breath. "You asked before how Nellie saved my life. It was Nellie who shot the two policemen who raped me. It was Nellie who helped me escape." She stared at him coolly. "Now you see just why I owe her so much."

He looked at their fingers then nodded as he spoke softly and slowly, his drawl hypnotic. "Yes, I do understand." He took a deep breath then sighed. "But you still don't see the entire picture."

Lily jerked her hands from his. "I don't believe you! I don't believe. . . ."

"Listen to me!" He reached out and grabbed her hand. "I don't like what you've described and I'm sorry. . . ."

Again she pulled her hand away then began to pace, gritting her teeth to keep from shrieking, but he'd listened to her so it was only fair that she listen to him. She folded her arms across her chest and glared at him.

"Perhaps the time to end slavery is almost here, but we're fighting for much more than keeping slaves. We believe in freedom from a government that's growing bigger all the time, a government that believes it can dictate its will to the states, can tax the states when and for what it wants. How can a bureaucrat in Washington understand what we need when he doesn't live where we live, how we live? The Yankees have always been jealous of us and our way of life. They've always wanted a reason and opportunity to ruin us. We don't tell them what to do, why should they tell us? We just want to make our own decisions—the way our founding fathers believed we should."

Lily shrugged her shoulders. "Whatever you say."

His eyes darkened. "No Lily, I want you to understand."

"Why, David? I don't live in your world and never will. Let Mary Anne understand."

His eyes flashed before he paced again, pounding a fist into an open palm again and again as he walked. She saw the sweat beading on his forehead when he spun around and stared at her. "So you're going to let me hang because I own slaves? Do I really mean that little to you?" He grabbed her hand again and held it to his trembling lips. "I'm scared, Lil. I'm a soldier. I shouldn't be scared. I . . ." He pulled her head to his and kissed her almost cruelly. But his lips lingered and softened and Lily put her arms around his neck. He leaned his forehead against the bars. "Oh, Lily."

She kissed and caressed his face, her tears mingling with his. But loud voices entered the anteroom and they knew the sheriff was back.

He clutched her hands. "Will you do me a favor? Will you get a suit for me? My uniform's . . ." He looked at his cot then back at her. "I don't want my uniform disgraced or have it used against me at the trial. It's tomorrow, you know."

She panicked. "So soon?"

"Yes. But that's good because if I'm found innocent, I can get back home in time for the convention."

Home . . . She answered coldly. "Of course. I'll be back in the morning."

He nodded and kissed her hands then let them go and quickly wiped away his tears with the heels of his hands.

The booming voices grew louder. "Come on, Sam. Come look at this rich soldier boy we've got back here."

Lily turned and looked at David and they shared the unspoken truth: David didn't have a chance. Although there were many pro-slavers in Kentucky, there were too many abolitionists shouting for satisfaction. David would be an excellent scapegoat.

And Lily knew that his fear wasn't for himself. She knew that he believed he deserved to be punished for betraying his values. No, it wasn't for himself that he feared but for those he would leave behind, those who would suffer from the revelation of his actions—the mother, siblings, wife, children—all those who would suffer when they learned that this grand son of South Carolina had killed a man because of a trollop and a bastard child.

And though his words of home hurt her, a last glance at David's worn and worried face convinced her to return with the suit as soon as she could and not wait until morning.

Tonight might be their last time together.

CHAPTER 12

Last time? No! She couldn't let David hang!

Why hadn't she told the sheriff it was self defense? Was David right? Had she wanted him to hang because he was married? Because he owned slaves?

But was it too late? Would it look suspicious for her to come forward now? Would her testimony be taken seriously?

Her ego had already killed Tom; would it kill David too?

She ran into the house and rushed a client home to get his best suit and a straight razor then huddled her children around her. They were suffering yet she'd not been with them and the next day was Tom's funeral. Lily tried to quit thinking of David for their sakes then laughed inwardly at the absurd notion—how could she forget David now when she'd not been able to for six years?

"They'll hang him, won't they?" TJ asked Lily while the girls played with their dolls. "I can't wait. I hope the rope burns his neck and he twists and wriggles for a long slow time. I . . ."

"Stop it!" She nodded toward the girls. "Not in front of them, please."

He nodded and frowned then whispered, "But why'd he do it? Why'd he kill my dad?"

Lily put her arms around his shoulders and pulled him close. "Grown-ups do stupid things sometimes, TJ. I won't even attempt to explain them. Your dad and David . . ."

"You mean that damn traitor?"

"Don't use language like that. You know your dad didn't like it."

The boy stared at her then nodded and looked down.

"David and your dad had some disagreements and they lost their tempers. I don't think either one of them really wanted to seriously harm the other, but once weapons are drawn men get killed. That's why your dad always wanted you to control your temper. Now you can see how disastrous it can be if you don't." Tom, sweet Tom. "Once someone's been killed, it can't be undone."

TJ's eyebrows furrowed and she feared her words had been too strong. "Were they fighting over you?"

The girls looked up and Lily knew they'd been listening all along. Taken aback by the forthrightness of his question, she considered her words carefully. "In a way, yes."

"Why? What did you do? Did you make them mad?"

"Oh, TJ. Men and women are strange. You'll soon learn it on your own."

"Dad loved you."

She looked into the eyes of the boy and saw the quickly maturing man. She also saw Tom. TJ knew what was going on. He just wanted an adult to confirm it. And he didn't hate David. He was just filled with so much pain and anger that he needed to vent it. "I know, TJ. And I loved him, just not in the way he wanted me to."

"Did you love . . . ?"

She nodded and sighed. "I wish I hadn't, didn't, but I did and still do."

"Does he love you?"

"That I don't know, but he's a good man, TJ. He's a noble man, like your dad. He doesn't deserve to die."

"Then you can't let him. I don't think Dad would have wanted it."

She swallowed hard. "What?"

"Besides, I kinda saw what happened."

"You did?" He nodded and she pulled him closer. "Oh, sweetheart. How awful. I'm so sorry." She kissed the top of his head then whispered, "Did the girls?"

"No. We were on our way back when I saw Dad hit David, so I threw something, a rock I think, and made the girls go find it." He sniffed and looked through fearful eyes.

"Did you see . . . ?"

He nodded again. "I should have stopped them."

"Shh. No, don't think that way. I don't think anyone or anything could have stopped them, not by then. If either of us had come between them, we'd be dead now too." She wiped his eyes with her handkerchief. "Your dad was proud of you, you know. And he's smiling right now because of the way you took care of the girls. And he's probably the proudest that you're man enough to accept David's innocence under the circumstances."

TJ smiled sheepishly.

"And I love you and am proud of you too."

His bright smile lit her heart and she hugged him again.

They spent the next several hours talking and comforting, crying and venting their anger. As soon as Max came back with the suit and razor, Lily left TJ in charge and rushed back to town then waited until the sheriff was out to go inside the jail.

David jumped up and pulled her close then kissed her hard on the mouth. His eyes traveled over her. "I'm so glad you came back tonight. I was hoping you would. I didn't think I could wait until the morning to see you again."

She loved his words and hoped he would be just as happy to see her if he hadn't been in jail. She handed him the suit. "I hope it fits. I also brought a razor but the deputy said he'll have to supervise your shave in the morning."

"Thanks." He laid the suit neatly on his cot.

"They inspected it." She nodded toward the suit.

He tried to smile. "So I shouldn't look for hidden weapons?"

She shook her head and returned his smile. How his eyes sparkled when he smiled! *Oh, David, is locking you up the only way I can keep you?* What a crazy idea.

Their lips met again then they sat down on the cold floor, their hands locked between the bars. David rubbed the back of her hands and she smiled as she looked at the connection.

"I'm going to ask to testify."

"Really?"

"Yes. I'll tell them I saw the whole thing and it was self-defense. I mean, I did see it and it was almost self-defense. I just don't know if they'll believe me. My defending you won't settle well with these people."

"I don't want you or Grace hurt."

She squeezed his hands. "Thank you. There's something else. TJ wants to help you. He saw the whole thing and knows you didn't mean to kill his dad. He knows you two just lost control."

David's eyes widened and his face turned white. "You mean he saw me kill his father?" He swallowed hard and blinked. "Oh, Lily, how can I ever . . . Maybe I deserve to die for . . . everything."

She grabbed his face and held it between her hands. "No! You do not deserve to die. TJ will be okay. He's a mature boy who seems to understand that there was a male-female 'situation' going on." She eagerly scanned his eyes for acknowledgment that he and Tom had fought over her, but there was none.

Instead, his mind seemed to be elsewhere. "Listen," he coughed nervously as he took a folded envelope from a pocket and handed it to her. "Just in case I don't make it home again, would you see that Mary Anne gets this? I don't know if you can, but please try."

She took the note with shaky hands and put it in her skirt pocket. Was he deliberately cruel? Unfeeling? Dim-witted? How could he not know how such a gesture would hurt her?

Her hands were still shaking when he clasped them firmly in his. "I've been doing a lot of thinking. If I get out of here, I want to take Grace home with me."

She jerked her hands from his and jumped to her feet. "What?"

He stood. "Listen, Lil, please. I can give her the best of everything. I can make sure she learns what she needs to know so she can marry well. I want to help her—and you too. I want to do the right thing for both of you. I'm sorry I've . . ."

She covered her ears and shook her head. "I can't believe what I'm hearing!" She took a few steps and deep breaths. "How dare you even imagine I'd give my daughter to you or anyone else. How dare you!" She was crying and hated the weakness, but she had never been so angry or so scared. His family had power and money—could he take Grace from her? "I will not, do you hear me, WILL NOT allow my child to be raised by anyone except me, especially slave owners! Do you really think I'd allow such selfish cruel minds to inflict their diseased ideas on my child?" She paced the same few steps again and again.

"She's my daughter too!"

She stopped in front of him, dumbfounded.

"Or is she?"

Lily flung herself at the cell bars and gripped them so tightly that her fingers turned white. "How I wish I could make you pay for your insults!"

"Well, how am I supposed to believe that she's not Tom's, or someone else's for that matter? How many men could be her father, Lily? And why do you say she's mine?"

She glared at him and calmly responded. "Because you know she's yours."

He was silent.

"Why do you want her? Isn't your quiver full yet? Or do you need a daughter to worship you? What if your next child's a girl? Would you send Grace off somewhere? And how would you introduce her to everyone? How would you explain her very existence? No, David Evans, you will not use my daughter for your high-minded selfish needs. You rich people think you can buy anything, especially people. Never, do you hear me? Never!"

"Lily, I . . ."

"No!" She covered her ears again. "I have the financial ability to give my daughter the best of everything. If you had any decency at all, your words would sound as offensive to your ears as they do to mine. Do you hear yourself?" She gritted her teeth and took a deep breath then folded shaky arms across her chest.

In a calm but icy voice, she added, "I think, Mr. Evans, that our relationship has come to an end, and I see no reason why either of us should seek out the other ever again. That is especially true for my daughter. Don't you ever come near her again. Do you hear me? Ever. You have your family and I have mine. Mine may not be deemed as respectable as yours, but my beliefs are much more respectable. Good day, sir." She took a few steps then turned around. "Oh, I hope you and your maker have made peace because you'll be seeing Him soon."

Lily stomped out of the jail and bumped into the sheriff coming back from supper. He grabbed one of her arms and spun her around. "I understand you want to testify on behalf of that piece of shit. Is that true?"

"No, sir. You have been misinformed. I'll see you in court tomorrow morning all right, but it will be to help you hang the traitorous bastard."

CHAPTER 13

The courtroom was packed as she knew it would be. TJ wanted to go but Lily made him stay at home with the girls. She didn't want him to hear a dramatized account of his father's death, details taken out of context and sensationalized. The main reason, of course, was that she didn't want him to hear her testimony. She was determined that David be found guilty. It was the only way she could keep Grace.

And then there was that note for Mary Anne . . . Of course Lily had read it, then read it again and again, each time wishing the words were for her—"No matter what you might hear of me, I love you"—but the words weren't for her and each time she read them she grew angrier at him for asking her to deliver such a note.

Now all she wanted to do was hurt him. He had everything and wanted more, and what he wanted was all she had—Grace.

But could she really say the words that would hang him?

She didn't sleep at all that night. She cried, walked the floor, looked out the window, visualized David sitting alone in that cold cell.

When Gracie woke from a bad dream, Lily held her, held the only part of David that she would ever have. When the little girl slept, Lily paced again.

And debated with herself.

Just as she would decide to help him, she would re-read the note for Mary Anne and look at her daughter and be overcome with a renewed determination to hurt him. Then she would think of how much Grace adored him, and he *was* her father . . . Wouldn't Grace hate a mother who had purposely killed her father? When Grace found out that her father had offered a wealthy and respectable lifestyle, wouldn't she not only hate her mother for killing him but for denying her the rich and full family he could have provided?

No! These people, David's people, owned slaves and Lily wasn't about to let Grace think that such a lifestyle was okay. Besides, how could David possibly think that Mary Anne would accept Grace? What woman could accept her husband's bastard child?

Right or wrong, Lily vowed that she—and she alone—would rear her daughter.

Lily had never seen David in civilian clothes. And though he was as handsome as ever, he seemed vulnerable, as though the uniform had been his shield. And though he stood tall and proud, his hands were cuffed, his eyes were haunted, and his healthy glow of sunshine a ghostly pall.

She could tell he was scanning the courtroom for her but she sat in the back, afraid to let his eyes find hers.

The prosecuting attorney had a field day, and David was tried for who he was—not for what he might have done. Tom was put on a pedestal and pictured as a defenseless model citizen. What hypocrites, she thought. When he was alive, his children were shunned and called "half-breeds."

The defense? There was none. Had there been time to get a lawyer from South Carolina, David might have had a chance, but there'd been no time. And would David have risked letting the people at home find out what he'd done?

Why, oh why, hadn't she helped him escape?

She'd hired the only lawyer in town who would take the case and, as she'd expected, he charged triple his usual fee. David was on trial for his life yet being represented by a lawyer who couldn't care less whether he lived or died. And his representation proved it.

Witnesses? The sheriff testified that when he arrived, David still held the knife in his hand, that blood dripped from the knife, that David was covered with blood, and that David cheerfully boasted that he'd just killed "another damn Yankee abolitionist."

David looked down and shook his head.

Lily bit her quivering lip.

When the prosecutor called her name, David's head popped up, his face even whiter than before and his eyes wide in disbelief. Again he searched the courtroom for her.

Even as she swore to tell the truth and nothing but the truth, she still debated about what she was going to say and what she wanted the end result to be. Avoiding David's gaze, she said her name and gave her occupation as owner of a sporting house then almost joined the nervous laughs and snickers that filled the room. Could there be a better scandal? A madam named Lily, a customer killed by another customer who was a rich soldier/slave owner?

"Is the man who killed Tom Baker in this courtroom?"

"Yes."

"Will you point to him please."

Lily closed her eyes then pointed a shaky finger at David.

"The defendant?"

She nodded.

"Out loud, please."

"Yes."

The room crackled with excitement. David stared at Lily then closed his eyes and bowed his head. Lily felt her heart crack.

"Please tell the court what happened on the morning of December 7."

She wrung her hands and looked at the jury, at the judge, at the spectators, anywhere but at David. *Forgive me, love, forgive me. But you can't have my child. She's all I have of you, all I'll ever have.* "I'd just come downstairs and wondered where everyone was then walked out to the glen. Tom was with the children. Dav . . . the defendant arrived and the two men began fighting."

"What provoked the fight?"

She breathed deeply. "I don't know."

"Was the defendant's background part of the argument?"

"What do you mean?"

"Didn't the deceased refer to the defendant as a slave owner and didn't that cause the argument? Didn't the defendant pull his knife and," the man lurched forward for dramatic effect. "thrust it into Mr. Baker's chest?" The crowd reacted.

Against her better judgment, Lily looked at David as she answered. "No . . . yes . . ."

"Which is it, Miss Morgan?"

"Yes, Tom called him a slaver but Dav . . ." *David or Grace, David or Grace. He'll take her from you . . . You're killing him . . . Mary Anne . . .* Hang him because he loves another woman?

She coughed and sat up straight, raising her chin. "Tom started the fight . . ." The courtroom silent, she dared look at David again. He was staring at her through cold eyes, his chin resting on steepled fingers.

"But who drew the first weapon?"

Her head hurt, throbbed, felt like it was cracking apart. She looked around the room at the blurred faces. She'd never had such a headache. What should she do? What words should she use?

"Who, Miss Morgan? Who drew the first weapon?"

I can't lose Grace. I can't. *Please forgive me, David.* "The defendant."

Gasps and loud murmurs. A banging gavel.

"I rest my case."

She tried to keep her eyes off David but couldn't. But, oh, how she wished she had. His face was red, his eyes full, his shoulders drooped. She'd just as good as killed Tom and now she'd killed David too.

Oh my God, what have I done?

The defense attorney timidly cross examined the sheriff and used Lily for nothing more than crowd-pleasing titillation.

"Was the defendant one of your lovers?"

"He was a client."

"Of long standing?"

"What do you mean?"

"Had he been there before?"

"Yes, but . . ."

"You like male attention, don't you, Miss Morgan?"

"Objection!"

"Sustained."

"Let me rephrase that. Were you the cause of the fight between the defendant and the deceased that morning?"

"I don't think so."

"Really? Two lovers in the same room . . . that would create quite a bit of tension I should think. Didn't you pit the two men against each other?"

"The men were clients and clients know they have no claim on me or any of the other women."

"But that doesn't stop it from happening, does it? And, really Miss Morgan, they were more than mere clients, weren't they?"

She evaded the question and he went on to another. "With whom did you have sexual relations the night before Mr. Baker's death?"

What was he doing? How did this help David? Or was he more clever than she'd thought? Was he trying to frame *her* for Tom's murder?

"No one."

"Don't perjure yourself, Miss Morgan. We know that the defendant arrived at your house that night and remained until morning. So I'll ask you again, with whom did you have relations the night before the murder?"

"The defendant."

"And the next morning was when the fight occurred, correct?"

"Yes."

"Did you have relations with Mr. Baker after you had relations with the defendant?"

Did he know these things or was he just guessing? "No."

"Again, Miss Morgan, if you're not truthful with us, I'll have to ask our friendly prosecutor to arrest you for perjury." He got so close that his breath fell on her face. "And it would be a shame for a pretty lady like you to spend time in jail. So I'll ask again. Did you have relations with Mr. Baker after you had relations with the defendant?"

"Yes."

The crowd went crazy. Lily heard whispers of "trollop" and saw the judgmental nodding of prim heads. The judge pounded until a semblance of order returned.

Again she avoided David's eyes.

The attorney smiled wickedly. "You're a busy woman, aren't you, Miss Morgan?"

David jumped up. His eyes were black, his hands were fists, his lips quivered. The judge was having an increasingly hard time keeping the room under control and he pointed at David. "Sit down, sir."

"I . . ."

"Just a rhetorical question, Miss Morgan." The attorney paced back and forth then stopped again. "When the defendant returned that morning, were you and the deceased locked in an embrace?"

"No!"

"But you let the defendant know that you'd just shared your bed with another man, didn't you?"

"What does any of this . . . ?"

"I have no other questions for this witness." The man had barely returned to his table when he added, "The defense rests."

Lily looked at David who stared at her numbly. *Let's run out of here, David. Let's go get Grace and run off somewhere.* She stepped down and walked through the gawking crowd to a corner seat in the back of the room then stared down the eyeballers until they grew bored and turned around.

David didn't testify. What could he say that would help? He was too honorable to bring Grace's name into the case, probably the only point that might have gained his freedom. Should she tell them about Grace? Would it make a difference?

The jury was out only long enough to vote, not even long enough for the room to clear of the spectators enjoying the juicy gossip. After all, how often did a case like this come along? How often could the "good" citizens of Louisville legitimize their voyeurism?

And why pretend they didn't know the verdict? Why pretend they had to give it any thought? Even had the defense had a case and David a good lawyer, the verdict would likely have been the same.

Which was, of course, guilty. The sentence was, of course, that David "be hanged by the neck until dead" the next morning at six o'clock.

CHAPTER 14

Lily remained in her seat with her eyes down until the courtroom was empty, until everyone had had their fill of staring at her. She almost laughed because those few who didn't stare were clients. But she knew the score. She'd learned it the day the police raided Mama Rose's, the day that her virginity—and childhood—were stolen.

Because of the craned necks and ladies' hats, Lily hadn't seen David when the verdict was announced or when he was taken out. But she could see him in her mind. She could see his face, his gentle loving face now etched with grief, just as plainly as if he were standing in front of her. Through her tears she could see him so clearly that she felt she could touch him.

How she loved him. How the very thought of him filled her with both complete delight and total despair. Filled her. She sat there with her eyes closed, his face in her mind, when she realized that by the same time tomorrow, he would be dead.

David dead.

Her eyes popped open. No! What had she done? *I'm sorry David, so sorry. I love you, love you . . .*

When she was sure that her shaky legs wouldn't betray her, she stood up and went home.

Then found TJ sitting at the kitchen table.

"Thanks for watching the girls. Are they upstairs?"

He nodded. "What happened?"

She couldn't speak.

"They found him guilty, didn't they?"

Tears rushed down her cheeks and she could only nod.

"What happened?"

Lily shook her head and shrugged her shoulders.

"Did you try to help him?"

"It's so complicated, TJ, so very complicated."

"But I thought you loved him. How could you let someone hang, especially someone you love? Even I couldn't have testified against him and it's his fault my dad is dead."

Lily grimaced at his words as she paced around the room. There *was* one thing she could do, one way she could—hopefully—free David. But freeing David meant she might lose Grace, and she'd be right back where she was before the trial. She paced a moment longer then realized she had no choice. She couldn't let David die, never. She hated him for the things he'd done and if he tried to take Grace ......*she'd* kill him and gladly rot in jail or hang if he tried to do that, but better she fall off the face of the earth than lose Grace—or David. And losing them both? Breath left her body even thinking of such a horrific life.

She rushed to a drawer for pencil and paper and wrote furiously. "TJ, please take this note to the judge. He's likely to be in the bar but go wherever you have to until you find him, okay? And hurry, please hurry. This note could keep David alive."

The young man nodded, took the note, then rushed out the door.

TJ was shaking her shoulder. "Why don't you go upstairs and take a nap?"

Lily had fallen asleep at the table, her head on crossed arms. In addition to the persistent headache, she now had a stiff back. "Thanks, sweetie." She looked around and panicked. "Where's Gracie?"

"Upstairs. I'll watch them."

"You're such a good boy. I appreciate you so much." But she had barely made it to her feet before her eyes widened. "What happened? Did you find the judge? Did you give him the note?"

The boy almost laughed at Lily's panic. He'd never seen her eyes so wide. He smiled as he patted her shoulder. "He's free."

"What?" She grabbed his hand.

"He's free. He won't hang."

She grabbed the young man's shoulders. "Really? What happened?"

"You were right; the judge *was* in the bar. What was in that note? As soon as I gave it to him, his face got really red and he said words I can't repeat then he stomped out the door."

Lily laughed and plopped down on a chair. She didn't think she'd ever felt such relief. "Let's just say that I reminded him of something in his past that he probably wouldn't want his wife to know about. But how do you know that David is free?"

"Because I followed him to his office and waited until he wrote something then took it to the jailer. He got really tired of me hanging around so he showed me what he wrote then said, "Okay, kid, tell that . . . I don't like what he called you, Lily . . ."

She smiled and patted his shoulder. "I can imagine, TJ. Don't worry about it."

"Tell her that the scumbag will be free by sometime tonight. As I left the room, I heard him mumble something about it being fine with him, that he didn't care one way or another and he was just glad to get rid of the whole mess.

"Lily . . . I don't understand something. Why didn't you help him before?"

"He wants to take Grace from me." She said the words without thinking then felt the fear in them return.

"He's Gracie's dad?" He shook his head and smiled. "I kinda wondered. They do look alike, don't they?"

She nodded then squeezed his hand. "Don't tell her, TJ. She doesn't know."

"Why not?"

"I just don't think it's time and it could be hurtful to many people."

"Well, I think she should know. Everyone should have a dad."

Lily looked closely at the red and puffy face. This poor boy, this fine young man, should have been receiving comfort instead of straightening out the messes that the adults around him had made.

But David would live!

And despite her fears about Gracie, her body cried out for rest. Besides, David's close call with death and disgrace surely must have dampened his desire to take her. Surely he was already on his way home.

"I think I'll take that nap, TJ."

When she woke again, it was dark. The headache was finally gone and she even had an appetite, the first since Tom . . . Oh, Tom . . . She allowed herself to remember him as she checked on Gracie who was sleeping soundly. Sweet TJ had put both girls to bed, secured the house, then gone to bed himself. The house was quiet, closed for the day in honor of Tom's funeral. Tomorrow life would resume and the house would be full of laughter once again.

She tiptoed downstairs to the kitchen and foraged for a snack, finally settling on a biscuit and coffee. As she sat at the table and ate, her mind was far away—on Tom and his sweet smile, comforting bear-like arms, warm eyes—and so caught up in reverie that she jumped when someone knocked on the door.

She pulled back the curtain and peered into the darkness, felt her stomach roll, then looked again. Surely her mind was playing tricks. Hesitantly, she opened the door.

He came in without being asked, walked to the table and stared at it, then tapped on it with his knuckles and looked at her, his eyes cold. "Are you going to leave the door open?"

As if simple-minded, she looked at the door then shut it and cautiously stepped around him to the other side of the table.

They both stood with hands on chair backs and stared at each other.

David broke the silence by pulling out one of the chairs then sitting down and calmly tapping the table with his fingertips. Without looking at her, he spoke. "Why?"

She'd not realized that she'd been holding her breath until she tried to speak. "I had to." She pulled out a chair and sat down then silently urged him to look at her. "I had to, don't you see?"

His eyes finally met hers. "Send a man to the gallows? No, I don't see."

"You were going to take Gracie from me. I couldn't let that happen."

His chin raised. "You would have let me hang?"

She started crying. "I'm sorry, David. I'm so sorry. But I had to. I couldn't let you take her from me." She pulled out her handkerchief but knew it was useless. She felt weak and vulnerable, drawn and quartered, pulled apart piece by piece. She'd gone through hell and could fight no longer. She looked down at the table and let the tears fall on folded hands. "Please don't take her. Please. She's all I have."

He reached across the table and wove his fingers with hers. Startled, her eyes widened as they met his. What was happening?

His voice was as warm as his strong hands. "I'm sorry I scared you. I didn't mean to."

Lily felt her heart swell. How could this be happening? Surely she was dreaming. How could he be apologizing after she'd almost caused him to hang?

"Is TJ awake? I'd like to thank him."

Lily realized that David had no idea how he'd been freed. Should she tell him? What difference did it make? "No. Maybe you could come back in the morning, although you're probably anxious to get back home to your family and the convention." The feel of his hands and the warmth of his voice made her dizzy. And his eyes . . . she felt she was drowning in them.

"There's time." He walked around the table, his eyes never leaving hers.

She was excited by his nearness but also afraid. Would he hurt her? His demeanor was loving but was there a cauldron of hate boiling inside? She could only watch and hold her breath. When he stood behind her and put his hands on her neck, she jumped, but he held her down and began massaging her shoulders. His very presence confused her, and now this affection . . . But her body and soul were weary and they quickly succumbed to his strong fingers.

Just as she felt herself floating into unconsciousness, David put his hands on her face and found her mouth with his. His hands and mouth explored her neck then moved to her breasts making Lily sigh and pull him close. She clung to him, wove her fingers though his hair, moaned his name. Was this really happening? Once again tears fell down her cheeks but now they were tears of gratitude and joy—David was going to live. David was loving her.

As their tongues met again, David's hands traveled under her skirt and up her legs. His eyes glistened and his breathing accelerated so that he could barely speak. "Upstairs, Lily. Please."

"Yes, sweetheart." But when she stood, her legs gave way and she fell into his arms. He carried her up the stairs and they fell together on the bed.

How could things change so completely so quickly? But it didn't matter. David was going to live. David was here.

That's all that mattered, all that would ever matter.

CHAPTER 15

Lily smiled wickedly, her eyes still closed to savor the moment. Just how many times had they made love last night? She couldn't remember. Yet she couldn't think of a more beautiful way to start the day than to love him again. As she inhaled their smell that permeated the room, she stretched languidly and smiled again at the idea of waking up with him, of him being the first thing she would see. To think that yesterday their lives had been so hellish . . . How could things change so drastically?

Her arms reached for him as her eyes opened. "Good morn . . . David?" She sat up. "David?" Fear gutted her stomach as she wrapped her nakedness in a robe and tiptoed downstairs. "David?" There was no sign of him. No sign of him anywhere. She ran to the front window and tore open the curtains. His horse was gone. She held her stomach with one hand and clasped her mouth with the other.

Grace!

Lily ran to her daughter's room and threw open the door. "Gracie?" But the room was silent, the bed empty. Except for $50 and a note in her lover's handwriting: "I'm doing what's best for our daughter."

Her wail brought TJ and Ruthie running into the room, but all she could do was thrust David's note into TJ's hand before falling onto Grace's bed. She smelled the sweetness of her child and sobbed. Sobbed because her baby was gone, sobbed because she'd been made a fool by the man she loved. He'd even left money! Lily picked up the coins and threw them at the wall then held Gracie's pillow to her face.

"I'll stay with her, Ruthie. You go make some coffee." After Ruthie left the room, TJ put his arm around Lily's shoulders. "Shh, Lily. You'll get her back. Besides, you know she's okay."

She sniffed and nodded. "But he can't get away with it, TJ. I won't let him."

He patted her arm.

Although her first instinct was to either call the sheriff or leave immediately for South Carolina, Lily knew that TJ and Ruthie had been through too much for her to leave them now or put them through more crises. And, as TJ had said, she knew Grace was okay. She knew David would take care of her. There was even a weak part of her that wanted to see father and daughter together again. She'd fantasized about it so often.

She also knew that David would be kind and loving toward their daughter, even give his life for her if necessary. Hadn't he proved that already? Chances were good that he was taking her to his mother's house, for no matter how saintly his Mary Anne might be, Lily doubted that even she would welcome her husband's bastard—although the vision of him saying, "Look honey, I've brought you my whore's daughter to raise" was an amusing one.

No, Lily wasn't worried about Grace's safety.

She was insulted and hurt.

And she was worried that Grace wouldn't want to come back.

She sniffed and wiped her nose. "You're right about him taking care of her, TJ, but I can't let him get away with taking her. As soon as I get someone to watch the business, I will go after him." Her eyes narrowed. "I will get my daughter back."

Her demeanor frightened TJ. "Are you okay, Lily?"

She smiled. "Yes, TJ, I'm fine. I'll have to be gone for awhile but I will return. Have no doubt about that. The four of us *will* be a family again."

As Lily continued to devise a plan to get her daughter back and look for someone to run the business in her absence, she couldn't help but wonder: Could she even get to South Carolina? How did a citizen of the United States get to the country of South Carolina? How sad to think of any state as enemy territory.

Louisville had turned into a giant military camp and there were soldiers everywhere, reminding Lily of Gladys and Stella. What had become of all those ladies, she wondered as she had so many times. One thing was for sure, if they weren't in prison, they were bound to be having the times of their lives and making a lot of money.

Yes, war was good for prostitutes and Lily's business boomed. But soldiers are a rowdy bunch, as are most young people when away from home and filled with liquor, and there were many nights she longed for quieter times. All those young men, boys really, so anxious to lose their virginity but usually so drunk that they didn't accomplish their goal or didn't remember doing so. Either way it was good for business because even those who accomplished their goal did so quickly, thus giving Lily's business an astounding turnaround rate.

But each time she saw an especially shy soldier, one who was so drunk he could barely stand yet still a gentleman, she thought of David on that first night . . .

Then quickly pushed the thought out of her mind. He was the enemy, she told herself again and again.

Lily soon hired Sarah Gunther to run the business and prepared to go after Grace. She'd still not developed a plan but she had more than enough "dirt" on David to blackmail him into returning their daughter. After all, it had worked to gain his freedom, hadn't it? And though her skin crawled at the idea of treating David in such a way, he'd brought her to it, and she'd make sure he learned never to humiliate her again.

How had she ever thought he loved her? But even that last night he'd seemed so loving, had seemed so genuine . . .

As she boarded the train for Bowling Green, she was thankful for the many miles ahead in hopes she could formulate a better plan—or at least gather her courage.

The clicking of the wheels on the tracks brought back memories of her escape from Lexington and she gathered courage from it, saw it as proof that she could do anything. It had been fun to dress as a boy, act like a boy, listen to "unladylike" conversations, and observe men when they were being themselves and not sizing her up as a potential bed partner.

Dressed as herself, Lily always drew male stares, and she always knew what was behind them. But she'd always liked men and the attention they gave her. And except for the heartache that David had caused—heartache that she blamed herself for allowing—she'd always found men intriguing and appealing. The smells of cigars, brandy, and cologne were aphrodisiacs to her—and the train was full of those smells.

But there were also smells not so appealing, and when she felt sure that the train's smoke wouldn't blow in her face, she poked her head out the window and inhaled the smells and sights of winter's cleansing. The bright blue sky and bright sun combined with the chill made Lily feel clean, healthy, and strong. And she needed her strength for what lay ahead.

Lily leaned back and closed her eyes. Where was Gracie? Probably with David's mother, but what explanation had he given? Did he visit her? Did she know he was her father? Was she frightened?

"Lily!"

She looked up to see one of the last people on earth she wanted to see. "Saul! How good to see you."

"May I sit with you?"

"Of course."

"I hope I didn't interrupt the dream you were having." He eyed her wickedly then lit his cigar and took a puff.

"Not at all. How have you been?"

"Just fine. I've been taking care of some business and am on my way back home. You?"

Since she did not want to make a long journey with anyone, especially Saul, she needed to discover his plans then change hers if necessary. "Just doing some business in Bowling Green."

"Business, huh?" He whispered in her ear. "A lucky man." His eyes examined her. "Lucky man, indeed."

"Well, thank you, but it's not that kind of business."

He nodded and winked, a smirk on his face. "Of course." He puffed on his cigar then turned to face her. "I am sorry I haven't been to see you. I've been a very busy man but I have thought about you many times." His blue eyes glittered. "May I say that you're even more beautiful than before?"

"Yes, you may, and thank you. It has been a long time. How's that shy friend of yours?"

His eyes darkened. "Evans? I avoid him as much as possible."

"And why's that? You seemed such good friends. You certainly spent a lot on his graduation present. What happened, didn't he appreciate it? Should I be offended?"

He laughed. "I can't imagine that." He shook his head and grew solemn. "He's a strange duck, very strange."

She laughed flirtatiously. "What do you mean by that? He seemed normal enough to me, though quite innocent."

"Well, he's certainly not innocent anymore. His fourth kid's on the way." Saul puffed on his cigar again and she saw a growing anger. "He treats his wife like she was made of glass, like she was a queen. When they're together, he watches over her and . . ."

Lily felt sick. The last thing she wanted to hear was how much David adored Mary Anne.

"What's wrong? You look like you've seen a ghost."

She waved a gloved hand in front of her face. "Just the close quarters. I'll be okay. Please, go on."

"Well, he doesn't know the first thing about commanding men. I mean, he knows his strategy but he's so nice to them. He says he wants their respect, not just their compliance. What a fool. He doesn't seem to know that he has to be forceful. We will be in war soon, you know."

Lily shivered at the idea and didn't want to discuss it. "Have you seen him lately?"

"As I said, I try to avoid his company, but I did see him several weeks ago. He was telling everyone about his forthcoming child and his new assignment—and it was impossible to tell of which he was most proud. The man has dreams of glory, of forming a special regiment." Saul stared into space as he continued. "And he's so selfish, so wrapped up in his own world that he can't see how Mary Anne suffers in his absence. He doesn't care that his glory-seeking keeps them apart and her lonely." Saul almost bit his cigar in half. "Yet she says nothing against him, speaks of him as if he were a god, welcomes him home with open arms . . ." He seemed to return to the present. "Yeh, he really has grandiose plans. Thinks he's going somewhere, always has."

"Really?" *He's your enemy, Lily. Why do you care about him?* But she missed him dreadfully and word of him, even though painful, made her feel his presence somehow.

"You know," Saul puffed his cigar and Lily watched the smoke waft in jagged waves as he waved his hand for emphasis. ". . . he always thought he was better than me." He chuckled devilishly. "That's why I got him drunk that night and brought him to your place. Mr. Perfect wouldn't dare drink or visit such places and I knew it. I knew it would shame him. But I'm not at all surprised he went and stayed the night."

"And why is that?"

"Oh, you know the type, not nearly as good as they pretend to be. I mean, there's got to be something underneath waiting to explode." He laughed out loud. "Either that or he's just as boring as he seems."

She laughed and pretended to enjoy his joke. "So, what did he have to say for himself afterward? Did he brag about his bedroom prowess?"

"Well, I didn't see him for some time afterward, but he'd certainly changed—and not for the better. At least before, even with all his lofty ambitions and superior attitude, he'd had a sense of humor, but after that night he'd even lost that. I guess his conscience got to him." Under his breath, he added, "Guess my plan worked," then chuckled wickedly. "So . . . how was the little general?"

Lily forced a giggle as she formed her thoughts. The truth, Saul? David's the best lover I've ever had. No, she couldn't tell the truth, but neither did she want to truly insult David, especially with an obvious rival, but it did feel good to vent some of her frustration. She batted her eyes and played the siren's role. "Well, let's just say it took him a while to get going."

"Ha! I could have guessed. You know, sometimes I wonder whose sons those are that Mary Anne keeps having."

"What?" Her heart and stomach fluttered.

"Oh, there's no doubt they're his. Mary Anne's too dedicated to him. I've never seen two people so close."

The butterflies died. "So . . . what's this remarkable woman like?" Please tell me something bad about her. Lily was quite sick of the saintly Mary Anne.

"Oh, she's a beauty. Smart, talented, and from a good family. Her father's highly regarded and quite an important man. Getting such a father-in-law couldn't have hurt Evans's career plans."

"Ah . . . so it was a marriage of convenience?"

He grimaced. "No . . . they really do love each other, but it can't hurt, can it? I mean the man had to get loans to get that school going."

They really do love each other reverberated in her head and she turned her face away to hide threatening tears. *Damn you, David Evans.*

Before too long the train pulled into the Bowling Green Station for a short stop. Hoping the break would separate her from Saul, Lily visited the privy then headed back toward the train. But she'd barely moved two feet when a very tall, very lean gentleman in a dark blue uniform approached her, kissed her hand, and introduced himself, though his name meant nothing to her and she forgot it immediately.

"I couldn't help but notice your fellow passenger. You two seem to be old friends."

Lily kept her distance. "I know the gentleman—as an acquaintance."

He smiled and took her arm, encouraging her to walk with him as he spoke in a hushed but urgent tone. "Please pretend we're old friends. When Mr. Dundee approaches, slap my face as if I've offended you. Can you do that?"

"What?" She pulled away thinking the man a deviate.

"Just walk with me and I'll explain."

They walked away from the others then stopped. "Did you know that Mr. Dundee is one of the rebel traitors?"

"I know he's from the South. Why?"

"May I ask your feelings about the rebellion?"

She eyed him before speaking. Was this a trap? "I hate to see young men killed but I'm against slavery."

He smiled and nodded. "Your great beauty and charm turned every man's head on that train. I'm sure that happens everywhere you go."

She smiled and enjoyed his words, especially after hearing about St. Mary Anne. "Thank you, but . . ."

"And men enjoy talking to you, don't they? They find you easy to talk to, I mean."

She grew wary and feared arrest. "Why do you ask such questions?"

"Because I think by using your natural attributes you could do your country a vast amount of good."

"In what capacity?"

"Let's just say that it would help the Union if you continued the trip with Mr. Dundee. He seems more than willing to tell you about conditions in the South, about friends in high places, about troop movements. Do you understand?"

"Yes, I believe I do. And just what do I do with such information?"

"You'll find out after you contact Chester Biggs in Nashville."

"I'm not going to Nashville."

"It's for the cause." He nodded toward Saul. "And that's one of your friend's stops."

Suddenly she'd found the solution to all her problems. Although she found the idea of war abhorrent, if it was coming, why not take advantage of it? David was so high and mighty. He had everything. Why not use this debacle as a means to punish him, lower his station? She wanted him to hurt as much as she hurt. The more she thought about it, the more she liked the idea. She could hurt David, get her daughter back, help free the slaves, and restore her country—all at the same time.

"I don't relish a lengthy trip with Mr. Dundee but suppose I can manage, though it will be an effort."

He laughed. "I thought so. Well, I think it's about time for you to be insulted at my ungentlemanly advances. Wait until Mr. Dundee's watching, then slap me."

"I really can't . . ."

"It's for your country. By the way, you'll find Chester Biggs at the Wells Fargo office."

They continued to chit-chat until Saul approached. Lily forced a frown then slapped the uniformed gentleman so hard that she left a print, much to her regret, although the surprise in the man's eyes was almost comical.

"Is this man accosting you, Lily?"

She quickly grabbed Saul's arm and led him away. "He won't again." Turning on her charm, she cooed, "Saul, I've changed my plans and I've so enjoyed your company, will I be too much of a burden if I continue my journey with you?"

Saul stood taller and smiled arrogantly. "Not at all. I'll enjoy your company as long as I can."

CHAPTER 16

The large man's eyes glittered as he gave Lily an appreciative nod. "I'm sure you'll be of great help to us."

"I hope so." Lily extended a hand to shake his. "I never gave my name. I'm . . ."

"No!" He said emphatically as he held up his hands. He smiled then walked behind his desk and flipped through stacks of papers. "Let's see now. . . where did I put that?"

Not words of confidence, Lily thought as she inwardly laughed at his vanity—holding his eyeglasses rather than putting them on—for spectacles certainly wouldn't have made a difference in the appearance of homely Mr. Biggs. Poor man, thought Lily, that he should worry about his appearance when he had such important business to carry out. But she was flattered that he should worry about his looks in her presence, although she'd always had that affect on men and would have worried at its absence. How fun this male-female game.

How fun it used to be.

Handsome he wasn't, but Lily found him interesting to look at with his bristling walrus mustache and twinkling blue eyes that peeked out from bushy graying brows. "Ah, found it." He scanned a long list then looked at her. "Number 63. How's that?"

"I guess it's okay. Is that who I am now?"

"Yes ma'am. We're still getting off the ground, you understand, but since you've already made a good contact, we want you to get started." His eyes were stern. "This means you'll be working on your own. Does that scare you?"

"Should it?"

His smile returned. "I thought as much. Oh, we'll try to contact you somewhere along the way, and I think you're intelligent enough to recognize who's 'safe,' but for now just continue your journey with Mr. Dundee." He walked to the front of the desk and sat on its corner. His eyes twinkled again as he tapped the eyeglasses on his knee. "I understand Mr. Dundee wants to make a name for himself and is quite a braggart. Those kind love an audience." He nodded and Lily saw the familiar gleam of desire as he looked her over head to toe. "Yes, I think this will work out beautifully."

"Well, I can certainly listen but how do I get the information to you?"

"Just keep mental notes—mental notes—write nothing down. I can't stress that strongly enough. The last thing you want is for one of the traitors to find evidence on your person. I'll have someone meet you in Charleston." He tapped his glasses on the desk. "You'll find friends everywhere. Like I said, we're still getting started and, I'll be honest with you, I'm not sure exactly how we'll operate. But I assure you that you'll get paid for your services."

"I'm not doing this for money."

"You have personal reasons?"

"Yes, several."

"Then I must warn you to keep a cool head." He looked quite grave. "Or you might lose it. For all practical purposes, you are on your own."

Lily and Saul's train pulled into Charleston on a day brilliant with sunlight and streets full of deafening bands, flushed faces, and smiling mouths. Men slapped each other's backs, women twirled parasols, children squealed, and strangers danced with one another. All the cacophony of revelry. In the midst of the brouhaha, Lily and Saul got separated. When they found each other again, they were both laughing, caught up in the excitement.

Lily grabbed Saul's arm. "What's going on?"

"We turned back a Union ship!"

"What? Has the war started?" Lily felt her stomach flip-flop.

"Well, not officially, but who knows? Probably soon now." He took her arm and they walked to the battery and looked out toward Ft. Sumter. Saul put one arm around Lily's shoulders and pointed toward the fort on the island. "There it is, Lil. That's where the Yankees have taken up residency. First ole' Lincoln puts troops near us then has the audacity to send a supply ship." He squeezed her then wrapped both arms around her and smiled. "They thought they'd sneak in at night, thinking we wouldn't know a thing about it, but we found out and our cadets saw them and gave 'em what for. Isn't it grand, Lil?" He kissed her and swung her around.

She shook her head, dumbfounded. What made men enjoy war? What made them find glory in killing each other? But it wasn't just men, was it? She'd seen and heard many women speak out for war in voices as strong or stronger than the men, women whose formerly timid voices now rose in anger either demanding an end to slavery or demanding its continuation. And

Lily had to admit that she wasn't immune. Why did she find a man in uniform so attractive?

As they walked to the hotel, Lily nervously wondered how her relationship with Saul would develop. She didn't like the idea of sleeping with him, but she certainly couldn't spend a lot of time with him and not sleep with him. She'd never been a "girlfriend" in a "normal" relationship. What did Saul expect? Did he expect to pay her? She hoped not.

"I hope we can get a room," Saul said as he led her through the exuberant crowds and into the Mills House where Lily felt her stomach tumble. Wasn't this David's favorite hotel? Her heart beat rapidly as she looked for him while Saul paid for a room and signed the register. When he turned to her, he put his hands on her arms and Lily saw the eagerness in his face and heard it in his voice. "I hate to leave you right away but . . ."

She smiled. "Why don't you go on? I know you're anxious to see what's going on military-wise. I'll walk around town a bit then come back here."

"You're wonderful, Lily!" He kissed her then ran out the door.

So much commotion! So much activity! And though the reason—war—created morbid participants of them all, Lily found herself swept up in the excitement. Something was happening, good or bad, something was changing. And isn't change always frightening and exhilarating at the same time?

She made her way through the milling throng, searching the faces for the one she so longed, yet feared, to see. Surely he was there. But she also peered into every face and listened to every utterance in hopes of picking up information, though she quickly dismissed most of the chatter as gossip. Who would be the next Mr. Biggs and how would she know him? She wandered down Meeting Street and admired the churches and halls—all the places that David had described—and was almost run over by a small brass band carrying a banner that read "Independence."

She stepped out of the way and joined the spectators, taking little notice of those around her until the tall man next to her leaned down and whispered in her ear. Startled at first, she remembered her job and quickly assumed the pretense of being a fellow spectator sharing the moment's enthusiasm. As the man whispered names, Lily put them to the band's tune. The names he gave were of rebel commanders so she would better know how to distinguish idle chatter from important information. The rest of the message was to continue her charade with Saul.

Although they were both tired, Saul begged Lily to go out that night to dine with friends. As usual, she expected—and received—the attention of the males in the party, but she was surprised at how good it made her feel to see how Saul beamed as he introduced her. And though she enjoyed outshining the other women, as she always did, she found it humorous that her priorities had changed, that now she paid much more attention to what the men said to each other than the flattering words they said to her.

The evening was magical—a restaurant full of lights, laughter, music, and good food. And Saul was entertaining, smart and well-educated, and Lily was honored at the confidences he shared with her.

As they took a break from dancing, Lily enjoyed watching the swirling glamour in front of her, the glorious gowns and magnificent uniforms, the spinning and twirling of handsome heads. The town was celebrating and feeling quite cocky. Their mindset was even published in the local paper: Charleston had started the second American Revolution! Between traveling, dancing, and drinking way too much champagne, Lily was giddy and eagerly joined in the celebrating going on around her.

"Guess who I ran into today?"

Lily giggled as Saul's distorted image and voice came through the liquored fog.

He laughed and nudged her. "Lily?"

"I'm sorry. Did you say something?" The dancers held her attention.

"I said, guess who I ran into today?"

"Who?"

"Your novice."

"Who?" She still wasn't paying attention.

He leaned close and whispered in her ear. "Evans."

Her hand stopped tapping and her heart stopped beating. "Where?" She scanned the room.

"Not here. At least I haven't seen him here tonight. He doesn't often come to these affairs without his precious Mary Anne and she's at home. He's in town recruiting—as I am." He swirled his brandy then took a drink. "Unfortunately, we'll be seeing a lot of each other."

Suddenly the dancers became a tangled mass of color and the music the drumming of her heart. *Calm down, Lily. Remember why you're here.* She took a deep sobering breath. "Really?"

"Yes, I'm sorry to say. I just hope we're not thrown into the same battles. I'd not feel safe if I were him."

His laugh sent a chill through her. Surely he wouldn't purposely hurt David? But what did she care? David had Grace. David was the enemy. "Do you think you will? Be thrown into the same battles, I mean."

"Probably so." His hostile eyes faced the dancers.

"So." She reached across the table and touched his arm. "How's it going . . . the recruiting?"

"Very well. But that's to be expected after a victory. Three other states have already seceded and we expect a lot more soon. If we get enough of them on our side, I think we've got a good chance of proving something."

"And just what is that exactly?"

He looked at her oddly. "That we can take care of ourselves, of course. That we don't want or need help from the Feds."

She itched to argue with him, to question his views on slavery, but thought better of it. At least for the time being. The night had been glorious and the band was striking up "Dixie." A roar rumbled through the crowd and everyone stood to sing.

After bidding his friends good night, Saul and Lily walked to the hotel, Lily feeling regal with a handsome soldier at her side and his cape draped over her shoulders. She looked up into the purple velvet sky with its canopy of blinking stars and thought of how exciting the night had been and how much she enjoyed this part of her new persona.

And her worries about sleeping with Saul proved unfounded. Much to her relief, he had reserved just one room, and much to her surprise, their lovemaking came easily and was even adventurous and fun.

But the mention of David had dampened the evening and after Saul fell asleep, Lily could think of nothing but the possibility of seeing David the next day. Yes, she wanted her daughter. Yes, she wanted to help defeat the rebels. And yes, she wanted to hurt David for making a fool of her—and she assured herself that she'd meet those goals—but she couldn't help herself when it came to David. The very idea of seeing him made her blush, made her want to run instead of walk, made her heart beat so fast she felt she'd pass out.

She also couldn't wait to see the look on his face when he saw her!

When Saul left the next morning, Lily promised that she'd meet him for lunch then spent the entire morning preparing herself. After changing clothes a dozen times, she decided on a pale blue dress that was snug in all the right places and as low cut in front as polite society allowed. She pinched her cheeks and bit her lips, lavished jasmine on all her pulse points, and made sure the hair by her cheeks fell in bouncy ringlets.

She admired her reflection in the mirror and saw a deep blush rise on her cheeks at the thought of seeing David. Did she hope to tempt him? Of course.

But did she think she could?

The coquettish smile left her face. "Damn you, David Evans. I'll make you want me. I'll make you suffer then I'll hurt you, toss you aside as you did me. I'll have the last laugh."

She picked up a picnic lunch from the hotel's restaurant and wove through the hubbub that was downtown Charleston. Again the brass band almost ran over her but this time she followed it to the city hall then raced up several steps to better scan the hundreds of heads. All the uniforms caused her to think again of Gladys and Stella, but a waving arm caught her attention and she waved back, then made her way through the crowd.

She'd never seen Saul smile so broadly as he grabbed her and kissed her quick and full on the mouth. "I'm so happy to see you! Please forgive me, Lily, but I must be honest and tell you how eager I am for the men to see us together. See all the eyes on you?" Lily looked around as he escorted her through the mob. "Do you mind terribly if I show you off?"

"I'd be offended if you didn't." She returned his smile and realized that her feelings for him were changing.

"Let's sit over here." He led her away from the bustle of the streets to a small rise and began spreading out a blanket under the trees. "I came prepared." He made an exaggerated bow. "Have a seat, my lady."

She curtsied. "Thank you, sir."

As she unpacked the lunch, she playfully pretended that she'd prepared it. But when they ate, they ate quietly and comfortably, as a couple who'd shared hundreds of meals together. Afterward, Saul stretched out and watched Lily throw leftover bread at the seagulls. "Isn't the weather perfect?" She wrapped her arms across her chest and twirled around.

He was lying on his side, propped up on an elbow, smiling. "Yes, it's nice now, but it will be miserable in a couple of months."

"Really?"

Lily sat down and leaned against the tree. Saul put his head in her lap and looked up at her. As she touched the blond waves that fell in his face, she realized that she'd never seen him so relaxed—and felt pangs of regret.

"It's the humidity you know. Unless you're right on the water it's quite oppressive. And the mosquitoes . . . miserable. That's one of the reasons I moved north."

"That's where the school is, isn't it?"

His eyes clouded. "Yes."

She touched his arm. "I'm sorry, Saul. I'm just trying to familiarize myself with your background. I didn't mean to upset you."

He kissed her hand. "That's okay." He raised his eyes to meet hers. "Are you really? Trying to learn about me, I mean? I didn't realize you cared so much."

How could she lie to him? But she was getting better at lying, wasn't she? But she didn't like it, not at all. It was one thing to lie to a man about his prowess in bed if it made him feel good, but she'd gone way past that. "Well, I didn't used to."

He tenderly wove his fingers with hers. "I'm glad you do now. Isn't it funny that we met again and how things have changed between us? I would have never expected this to happen."

"Neither would I." She smiled for him. "But I'm glad it did."

They kissed tenderly then he sat up and pulled her close. "Oh, Lily." He was kissing her neck. "I wish we could go back to the hotel right now, right this minute." He pulled away and scanned her face. "You're so pretty." He touched her cheek with his fingertips. "So very pretty."

"I'm flattered you think so."

"Well, you know it's true." He stood up and stretched then offered his hand to her. "I wish I didn't have to get back so soon."

"Me too." She took his hand and stood up then put the lunch remains in the basket while Saul folded the blanket. He took the basket then her hand and they walked back to the hall.

"I wish you'd let me walk you back to the hotel. I do have that much time."

"I know, but I want to enjoy the excitement, wander down by the water, see the sights. Besides, what else do I have to do?"

Saul kissed her hands then her mouth. "I was much better at this before I met you, you know."

"Better at what?"

"Working. Now it's not only torture getting out of bed but it's torture leaving the room, leaving you." He kissed her again. "And it's torture leaving you now. My only consolation is knowing that you'll be waiting for me." His eyes and voice were sober. "I don't think I'll ever tire of being with you."

Lily held back tears of guilt as she nodded and kissed his lips then watched his blond head disappear into the crowd. Oh, Saul, I'm using you, she thought, using you to get information about your army, using you to see David. In all her days of servicing men Lily had never felt so cheap.

But, as usual, the very thought of David made her heart beat so fast that she felt her face redden. *Damn you for letting him affect you this way! He loves another woman. He stole your child.* She took a deep breath and turned her head from side to side and toward every dark head, of which there were hundreds. Where was he?

"What are you doing here?" The voice was cold, despotic, offensive.

CHAPTER 17

Her heart leapt but she forced a disgusted expression and answered coolly. "I don't think what I do and where I go is any of your business." She enjoyed his shocked reaction and knew he'd probably expected a sad and penitent female ready to beg for her daughter, but she wasn't about to give him the satisfaction.

Scoring the tiny victory helped maintain her resolve and she raised her chin. "I think the more appropriate question is where's my daughter?"

"From what I've seen the past hour, you don't care a thing about your daughter."

She slapped his face. "How dare you!"

He touched his cheek and looked around.

"What's wrong, Mr. Evans?" She laughed sarcastically. "I doubt that anyone's seen you get slapped before." She folded her arms across her chest. "My, my, what will people think?"

His eyes squinted black in anger. "At the risk of another slap, you must see how your behavior is anything but that of a grieving mother."

She wanted to scratch his eyes out but struggled to keep her voice low. "You have no idea what a grieving mother looks like, you bastard. I came down here to get my child—and I will. Where's your commanding officer, David? He might be interested in a charge of kidnapping. Oh, and there's that murder in Kentucky . . ."

"You wouldn't."

"I don't think you know me well enough to know what I'd do. I'm a tigress whose cub has been stolen from her den. The law of the jungle, Mr. Evans. I should be killing you at this moment."

"But you won't." He raised his chin.

"And just why not?"

"Because I do know you."

She laughed. "I wouldn't be so sure."

"Why have you become involved with Dundee?"

"If you know me so well, why do you ask?" She smiled at his irritation. "Besides, I thought you two were good friends. After all, it was he who . . ."

He yanked on her arm and led her to a white wrought-iron bench under a tree and almost pushed her down. Lily glared at him as she rubbed her arm but relished the guilty and disturbed look on his face. "Not that it's any of your business, but it just happens that Saul and I became reacquainted on our trip down here and are now very good friends." She stared at him. "He doesn't know about Grace."

David seemed relieved for a moment before his brows furrowed again and his eyes showed vulnerability. "How can you, Lily? Him, I mean."

She had to turn away to keep from weakening. "What's wrong with him? I find him extremely handsome and virile."

"You do?"

"Yes, I do. Besides, Mr. Evans, my personal life is of no concern to you. The only thing we have to discuss is Grace, and on that I want to make one thing perfectly clear . . . If I had any doubt as to her safety and well-being, I would have called the sheriff the day you left. But I think I know where she is and believe that you love her and won't harm her. Believe me, if I thought you'd harm one hair on her head, I'd make your life hell—and don't think I wouldn't."

He nodded and whispered. "She's fine. I see her as often as I can."

Lily softened at thoughts of her child. "Is she okay? Is she scared? Does she wonder where I am?"

His hands reached for her but he pulled them back and looked down at the ground. "Yes, she's fine, really. She was scared at first, and I'm sorry for that, but she's very happy now, though, of course, she misses you and asks about you every day."

"Does she know who you are? Have you told Mary Anne?"

He shook his head.

"Then what have you told Grace? What are your plans for her?" Her temper was rising as it did only around him so she looked away and took a deep breath then fixed her eyes on his. "How can she feel secure when she's a stranger in a house full of strangers?" Lily was shaking. "You think I don't care about her . . . how dare you! You don't know . . ." She calmed a little and whispered, "You don't know."

"Of course she was scared at first but I told her I was taking her to visit my mother and she perked up. I couldn't tell her that my mother was her grandmother, of course, but I told her that she could call her that." He smiled. "She got pretty excited about having a grandmother, cousins, aunts and uncles." Again his hands reached toward her but again he stopped himself. "She's being taken care of, Lily. My mother adores her."

Lily wondered what he'd told his mother and what the woman's reaction had been. She must have been horrified at her angelic son bringing home a bastard child, but there was no way the woman could have denied that the child was his. Lily was relieved to know that Grace was being loved and cared for, but why did the idea of her child being happy somewhere else, with someone else, scare her? She was fighting tears and clinching her fists. "I'm sure she does and I'm happy . . . but I'm her mother."

A search of his face revealed no hope of changing his mind and panic rose in her stomach until she thought she'd be sick right there on the street. David saw it and whispered, "Here," as he handed her his handkerchief and grazed her cheek with his hand. "I'll be right back."

Tears flowed down her cheeks, tears caused by David's concern, by the smell of him, by the way his fingers had felt on her cheek . . . She inhaled the scent of his handkerchief and cried even harder.

In moments he was helping her sip water from a tin cup. "Better?" He wiped a drop of water from her lips with his finger.

She nodded and thanked him as she handed him the cup. Their fingers touched.

He sat beside her then, their faces only inches apart, and Lily hated her arms for wanting to hold him, her lips for wanting to kiss him, her body for wanting his to become part of it.

"I'm truly sorry, Lily, but can't you see that I can give her what you can't?"

"No, I can't see that at all." She held out her fingers as she listed reasons. "First, she's my daughter and I'm her mother. A little girl needs her mother. Second, you people own slaves and I don't want her reared to approve such barbarity. And third . . ." She lowered her voice to a whisper and spoke smugly, "when your little uprising is put down, you and yours may not be so well off anymore. You might actually have to mingle with the rest of us.

"If you're lucky to stay alive, you won't be able to work all those acres without free help, if you still have your acres." She raised her chin. "Which I doubt you will because Uncle Sam will likely want some revenge and repayment for this little exhibition. Do you remember your history, David? Do you remember a little thing called the French Revolution? I believe a lot of wealthy people lost their heads over that one."

His eyes stared into hers throughout her explanation then he looked around. When he spoke, his voice was so low that she could barely hear him. "I think you might watch your words around here. We happen to believe that we'll win this 'little uprising' or we wouldn't pursue it. As to the rest of your tirade, I'll leave it right now." His eyes continued to bore into hers. "Although I find several things quite curious."

"And what are they?"

"One is how you lash at me with such venom. Usually such hostility is coupled with passion of some sort . . ."

Lily struggled to shield the feelings she knew he sought in her eyes.

"But whatever your reasons for such personal animosity, I'm particularly curious to find you here with a Confederate officer. Aren't you being a hypocrite?" His eyes remained fixed. "Or is money more important to you than loyalty?"

How she hated the smugness on his face, the seductive smile on his lips. How she wanted to slap him again. How she wanted to tell him exactly why she was with Saul, how she was working to destroy him—David Evans—and all he stood for.

But personal vanity wasn't important anymore, and Lily knew that she needed to recover the situation and maintain her ruse, so she lifted her chin high and stared into his eyes. "It's not always about money, Mr. Evans." She stood up and he did the same. She straightened her dress and tried to be nonchalant before looking at him and batting her eyes. "Some men are worth lowering one's political beliefs . . . for free I might add."

She'd never seen such surprise in his face and, relishing her victory, she tossed her head and spoke coyly. "I've changed, David. I'm with Saul because I want to be." She batted her eyes again. "My only payment is his superior company."

"Well." He straightened his uniform. "I suppose there's no more to be said then, is there? You're obviously happy with your new . . . beau and plan to deceive him as to your true feelings, even though he'll be risking his life for what he believes. But, why Saul instead of someone else?"

"David." She put a fingertip to his lips and laughed seductively. "How can you be so naive? Saul has everything I want. He's handsome, brave, wealthy . . . uhm . . . yes, he can keep me quite happy for quite some time. Deceive him? Saul and I don't talk politics." She smiled wickedly. "Actually, Saul and I don't talk much at all." She was winning and couldn't stop herself. "Besides, if I'm down here, I can see Grace."

"No!"

"No? And just how will you stop me? Or do you plantation owners post guards at your front doors?" She laughed haughtily. "Come to think of it, that's probably true, isn't it? Tell me, how do you sleep at night? Don't you worry that your slaves will murder you in your sleep?" She turned from him then looked back again. "Don't worry, *General*, I won't upset your perfect little family life. Not yet, anyway." The look on his face was priceless and Lily couldn't resist another jab. "By the way, does your wife know of your trial and jail time?"

His face blanched.

"And another thing," she threw fifty dollars at his feet, "my child cannot be bought and sold—or are you into white slavery now too?"

She'd won and saw her victory in his face.

But why wasn't it sweet? And why were tears falling down her cheeks as she ran away?

CHAPTER 18

Lily returned to Louisville to check on TJ and Ruthie and found the ease with which she crossed the borders almost comical. "Almost" because the fact that men thought women too dim-witted to pose any threat wasn't comical at all, and she added women's rights to her list of causes. If slaves could be freed, why couldn't women?

And though she hated the label of "campfollower," she traveled with Saul to get information. When she hung onto Saul's shoulder and pretended to be in a romantic stupor, or when she poured drinks at officers' meetings, the men spoke freely. And since all men enjoy being flattered by a beautiful woman, Lily found it easy to get them to answer questions. How ignorant they were.

So far, Chester Biggs was very happy.

And Saul was a constant source of information, especially about David, because his envy of the man caused him to keep constant tabs on him. In battle and around his peers, Saul was confident and strong, but the private man had insecurities and fears that could be calmed only by Lily and she soon learned how to play her role in his life. Sit passively while he paced and ranted, comfort him, watch him sleep, then make love to him when he woke. After all, she was an expert at making men feel better, wasn't she?

As she'd always suspected, being a "wife" wasn't much different than being a prostitute.

Saul's best days were when David was out of his sight, which usually meant that David was home on leave, but those were the days and nights when Lily went mad envisioning David making love to Mary Anne.

And though she hated herself for it, she savored every scrap of news about David, every tidbit of gossip. She saw him at officers' meetings and ran into him fairly often, but they were never alone and their words never went beyond formal greetings. Even so, she lived for those moments although she always felt frustrated afterward. But what did she expect?

Besides, wasn't she supposed to hate him?

Why did she keep forgetting that?

Lily's wartime travels with Saul began when they boarded the train in Charleston and went to Richmond, a city Lily liked immediately. It had everything—good restaurants, hotels, and stores. And since it had recently become the capital of the Confederacy, it was not only an exciting place to be, but an invaluable place for information.

A particularly popular place to hear news was the Spotswood Hotel, and Lily and Saul were having lunch there one afternoon when hearty male voices filled the lobby and they turned to see David surrounded by several men patting him on the back. Saul tensed, but Lily flushed at the sight of David's handsome face and broad grin, and she found it hard to take her eyes off of him—until he saw her. The smile left his face and she turned away.

And braved up to meet him.

He approached their table and nodded. "Dundee. Miss Morgan."

Saul's knuckles turned white as his fingers tightened around his dinner napkin. He barely nodded as he muttered, "Evans."

But Lily forced her brightest smile. "What's the happy occasion?"

"I . . . my wife . . . I just found out I have another son."

Her heart wrenched but her practiced smile remained. "Oh? So, how many have you sired now, Mr. Evans?" She looked at his broad shoulders then his neck and saw the three stars. She dared not linger on any part of him. "Excuse me. Colonel Evans."

"Four."

She wanted to wretch, she wanted to scream.

But she calmly reached across the table and squeezed Saul's hand. "Isn't that nice, Saul?"

"Yes. Congratulations."

"Thank you. Excuse me." He bowed then walked away.

The tension radiated from Saul's body and Lily found herself oddly thankful to have him to worry about. She covered his hand with hers and whispered, "I wish I could kiss you right now, put my arms around you, hold you . . ."

He kissed her hands and she dared look again toward the lobby and saw that David was watching. She neither smiled nor scowled, just looked into his eyes before very purposely turning toward Saul. The next time she looked, he was gone.

The opposing armies fought their first battle about ninety miles north of Richmond at a junction called Manassas and a river called Bull Run. Although it was a success for the South, Saul was irate because President Davis wrote glowing reports about David. "No one knows him the way I do," he said one night. "His men love him, the other generals love him . . . My God, the man's really licking all the right boots."

Lily watched him pace and waited for him to stop, but that night was different. That night he fell on his knees in front of her, grabbed her hands and kissed them. She saw tears running down his cheeks. "Marry me, Lil. Please?"

"Marry?" He'd just spoken the very last words she had expected to hear.

"Yes, please marry me."

"Why, Saul? Why bother marrying me? I'll stay with you."

"But don't you see, I want you—us—to be legitimate."

"So you'll get promoted? So you'll have a wife—like he does? Is this because of the attention he was getting at the Spotswood?"

"I admit that's part of it, but we've always been honest with each other. You know how I feel about you and how much I need you."

"Yes." She stroked his hair and looked into his blue eyes. "I do know. I also know you don't love me."

"But I do." He smiled brightly. "I really do."

She shook her head.

"No, really. The time we've spent together has made me feel something I can't explain." He kissed her hands again.

"But what of the talk? What of the other men who've known me?"

"They'll know better than to speak ill of my wife."

His eyes shone and Lily saw a vulnerable child who had slowly but surely attached itself to her heart, and though she wanted to say yes, she knew that they were a disaster waiting to happen. Her history and their feelings about David, not to mention her deception, were lit fuses waiting to go off. But it was wartime, and in wartime people live for the moment, and getting married seemed a nice thing to do at least once in a lifetime.

Lily looked into his shining blue eyes and caressed his cheek. "I must tell you about three people who are more important to me than anyone, and if you still want me after I tell you, then I'll be proud to marry you."

Saul was excited about the children and his enthusiasm regarding their marriage was charming and he spoke of nothing else to everyone the next day. As Lily watched his excitement, she prayed that he would never learn of her love for David or of Grace's paternity, for she truly believed he'd kill David if he did.

He was anxious to make their union legal, so as soon as the army moved to Fairfax Courthouse in late July, Lily put together a gown and veil and they got married then celebrated with dancing to the camp's band. After the newlyweds danced several dances together, they both danced with others, and Lily was proud to see that her new husband's face was never without a grin.

They were both taking a break, and Lily was talking to another officer's wife when suddenly David was in front of her, bowing, and offering his hand as he requested a dance. Her heart fluttered at the thought of being in his arms, but she knew that his very touch would make her feelings for him obvious to everyone. No, it was much too dangerous.

Damn this weakness.

Waving her fan furiously, she avoided his gaze, fixing her eyes across the improvised dance floor at Saul instead. "I'm sorry, Colonel, but I'm truly exhausted." Saul was laughing heartily, probably at a good joke that he'd tell her later. She smiled at the times they'd laughed together. His memory for jokes astounded her.

But David remained fixed in place, his eyes on her.

"Oh, Lily," one of the other wives spoke up, "you've danced with every other officer. Don't exclude poor Colonel Evans. He's so lonely without that lovely wife of his, aren't you Colonel?"

David nodded politely but kept his eyes on Lily. And though she winced inwardly at the mention of Mary Anne, she delighted in his determination to dance with her.

"You're right, Miranda, of course." Even as she put her arm through his, she continued to avoid his eyes. "I meant no offense, Colonel."

And though she tingled when their hands touched, she maintained her cool persona. And though they kept a more than safe distance between them, David's eyes penetrated hers and forced them to lock with his.

"Why?"

"Why what?"

"You don't love him."

"How do you know?" Lily looked at Saul and gave him a smile. Through gritted teeth, she whispered, "Smile, pretend you're having a good time."

He ignored her. "Because I know you. I'm right, aren't I?"

"That's a personal and offensive question and absolutely none of your business." She continued to smile as if she and David were discussing pleasantries. "Besides, I would think a man with a wife and four children would be much too busy to concern himself with the affairs of others."

"Does he know about Grace?"

"Yes."

His eyes widened and she laughed wickedly. "He doesn't know that she's yours if that's what you mean. Why should I let that be held against her? Besides, she deserves a father who can acknowledge her publicly. You can't do that, can you? And I think Saul will make a very good father, and I think Grace will adore him. You may have her now, Colonel Evans, but we'll have her—*soon*." She dropped his hand and went to her new husband.

She stared at David's dumbfounded expression as she kissed Saul's cheek and whispered, "You're right, sweetheart. He *is* a bore. I'd much rather dance with you."

CHAPTER 19

The war raged on. By the winter of 1861-62, most people agreed that it would linger, that neither side would earn the quick victory they'd expected. The North even feared that the South might actually be able to win—an unthinkable idea before.

Now that marriage had made Saul more secure, Lily no longer had to travel with him or wait for him at the hotel, so she helped out in the hospitals. The horrors there were already infamous, but until she'd seen it for herself, Lily had no idea just how horrible, how sickening. The wailing and moaning; the putrid smells of blood, dead bodies, and fouled bed linen; the pathetic sight of destroyed bodies and minds. But she learned the first day that you had to cope if you were to be of any use. A helpless fainting female was only in the way.

And she wanted to help, felt compelled to help, because she felt that she was the cause of some of it. She also knew that she could learn even more information there, information she hoped would restore the Union sooner and end the bloodletting.

Many of the men weren't men at all, but boys—sweet young boys who should have been home helping on the farm, skinny-dipping in the local creek, courting a sweetheart . . . But no matter the age, they all needed a hand to hold and a female voice to comfort them. Lily wrote countless letters, gave countless farewell kisses, listened to countless farewell prayers, and felt far too many hands grow still and cold.

She also continued to run into David from time to time, but she always walked away feeling sad and out of sorts. It was so hard to be near him and not touch him. And since his brown eyes usually looked right through her, she feared that he'd lost all feeling for her. Like Saul, David was a different person when Saul and Lily weren't around, and Lily constantly heard of "Evans's broad smile" and "Evan's optimism." She knew that smile. She'd seen it aimed at her. She knew just how powerful it could be, and she missed it.

By winter they were housed in log cabins in Camp Pettus close to the city of Centreville. Since Manassas, they'd seen only slight skirmishes and picket duty. Life was peaceful and seemed more of a camping trip than war—until news that Union forces had invaded the South Carolina islands made Lily crazy with worry. Somehow she must find a way to speak to David alone. Surely he knew how things were back home.

It was common for officers to linger over brandy and cigars after their meetings, and though some opted for their cabins and sleep, David and Saul always stayed. Neither dared miss some tiny piece of information or gossip that the other was privy to.

But one night Lily purposely kept David's coffee cup filled so nature would force him outside, then smiled at her plan's success when he hurriedly exited and headed for the bushes.

Her touch so surprised him that his sword was half drawn when he spun around. Expelling his caught breath, he put his hands on her shoulders and shook her. "Don't ever sneak up on me like that!" He took a deep breath. "My gosh, Lily, I could have hurt you."

His hands remained on her shoulders, his eyes remained locked with hers, his breath touched her face . . .

"I'm sorry but I have to speak to you about Gracie."

He pulled her farther from the cabin, into the trees and out of the full moon's glaring light. The night was freezing cold and they shivered as they spoke, their breath wisps of life in the filtered moonlight. "What about her?"

"What about her? I heard the Yankees are in South Carolina! David, what's happening?"

He nodded as his eyes searched their surroundings. "I know." He rubbed her shoulders briskly then folded his arms across his chest. "I've asked that my regiment be sent there but my request was denied."

Damn his army. "But Gracie, David, Gracie."

"She's okay. I'm sure she's okay."

"But how can you be so sure? Have you heard something?"

He looked into her eyes. "I know you probably won't believe me, but my mother loves Grace just as much as she loves the boys. She won't let any harm come to her." He warmed her hands with his. "I'm leaving for home the day after tomorrow and I'll check on her."

She stared at their hands, at how easily he took them into his, and her heart lightened. But what had he just said? She struggled to stop the quivering in her voice. "You're going home? To your mother's . . . or . . . ?"

"Actually, Mother has moved inland. That's why I know Grace is okay. The Yankees just took the islands."

"Where? When were you going to tell me?"

He shrugged his shoulders. "To Columbia. I couldn't see what difference it made."

"What if I'd wanted to see her?"

He frowned.

"How unfair of you to keep us apart. She'll think I've deserted her."

He nodded and looked ashamed. "You're right and I know Grace would love to see you." Suddenly he smiled, his eyes bright from the moonlight that shone through the tree branches. "Why don't you come with me? We couldn't leave here together but we could meet in Richmond."

"Oh, David!" She squeezed his hands and they both looked down at the union then back into each other's eyes. Their breathing accelerated and suddenly it wasn't cold at all. "Could we really . . . ?" She shook her head. "No. It wouldn't work. You know it wouldn't work. What would your family think? What would you tell them?"

"Actually, my mother arranged everything when I first took Grace down there."

"Really?" She frowned.

"Now, Lil, don't get mad. Let me explain."

She held her tongue and listened obediently as he described the scenario. Lily was a very distant cousin, a grieving widow who'd left her daughter with Mrs. Evans while she took care of her husband's business matters. Since her husband had done a poor job with their finances, the business matters would take longer than expected, so Grace would be staying longer than originally planned.

In other words, Lily was a poor relation.

They'd thought of everything. Mrs. Evans "allowed" Grace to call her "Nana" just like the other grandchildren so the "poor child" would feel comfortable and not "different," and David and his siblings were all "aunts and uncles." The story was told to everyone. According to David, only he and his mother knew the truth.

But Lily knew better. Only a blind person couldn't see David's relationship with Grace. Lily laughed to herself. Even a blind person would pick up on the similarities the two shared. She smiled, too, at the great lengths to which the rich went to take care of their reputation.

"What are you thinking?" His brows furrowed.

She maintained her secret smile. "Nothing."

"Why don't I believe that?"

She shrugged.

A knowing twinkle sparkled in his eyes and Lily could tell he wanted to say more, but loud voices and the stomping of booted feet caught their attention. He squeezed her hands, said, "I'll see you in Richmond," then rushed away.

Lily quickly exited the woods and walked briskly back to the officers' meeting. She was shaking, shivering, fantasizing . . . A trip with David! And she would soon see her baby! She felt radiant and thought surely she outshone the moon. But how could she explain such happiness to Saul? More importantly, how could she get away?

"What are you doing out here?" Saul put his arms around her waist and nuzzled her neck.

"Just getting some fresh air." She squeezed him and added, "And waiting for you."

"Well, I'm glad our meeting ended early then." He looked up at the sky. "It is a beautiful night, isn't it?"

She nodded and pulled at him. "Yes, but it is cold. Why don't we go back to our cabin so we can keep each other warm?"

As they loved each other that night, Lily's mind was a million miles away. Yes, she'd grown to love Saul in a very special way, but she couldn't quit thinking of traveling with David, of being alone with him. When she closed her eyes, she could still feel his breath on her face, his hands on her hands. But then she remembered that David was going home to Mary Anne, and her rapture turned to tears.

"What's wrong?" Saul was on his side facing her, stroking and kissing her chest and arms in the sweet way he did after lovemaking.

"I miss my daughter, Saul. I think I'll go crazy if I don't see her soon and with the Yankees in South Carolina . . ."

"She's fine, Lil. They'll never reach Columbia."

Among the lies that Lily had told Saul was that Grace was in Columbia. She couldn't have told him the truth or he might have connected her to David. Mrs. Evans's move to Columbia actually worked to her advantage.

Saul playfully grabbed her hair and pulled her lips to his. "I tell you what, why don't you visit her? I'd go with you but can't get away right now and I know you've been bored."

"Really?" She sat up.

"I'll go crazy without you, but I'll manage for a while—just a short while you understand." His eyes explored her face and he smiled. "You've made me so happy, Lil. How can I not let you go see your daughter? Besides, you can prepare her for her new father because next time I want to go with you."

"Of course. Oh, Saul, thank you."

Lily made the rest of that night extra special by loving Saul in all the ways he enjoyed. And the next morning she wasn't shy about embracing him in front of everyone. Even as the wagon pulled away, she turned and blew kisses.

111

CHAPTER 20

The Richmond train stations bustled night and day. Since Lily had left a day before David, she had many long hours to spend on the hard depot benches eating cold sandwiches and drinking watered-down lemonade and stale coffee sold at outrageous prices by train butches.

But he should be there any time now . . .

She'd fallen into yet another boredom-induced sleep when yet another train whistle woke her. Every muscle in her body complained when she stood and stretched, but being with David was worth any inconvenience or discomfort, and she anxiously peered into the rising steam. Lily had seen so many handsome men in gray that she had become excited then disappointed time and time again, but still she scanned the passengers as one after another stepped down onto the rickety wooden steps.

Was that him? She strained her eyes as a handsome soldier, resplendent in his dark gray uniform, stepped down and looked around while shielding his eyes from the sun and steam. Lily's heart leapt. It was David! It was him, really him! She ran in his direction then stopped short of seeming too anxious.

But his broad smile let her know that he was glad to see her too, and he put a hand on her elbow and led her inside the depot. "I'm sorry we couldn't coordinate our plans so you'd know when I was coming."

She nodded and felt warm and secure, as if the two of them had been enveloped into a cocoon, as if everyone else had disappeared. There were no voices, no shouts, no train whistles, no shoving, no one else in the world. Surely she'd drown in those eyes, those velvet brown eyes that meant everything.

But someone bumped her and Lily fell into David's arms where, for another glorious moment, they touched and their lips were only inches apart. David looked at her mouth and hesitated before speaking. "Wait here." He walked to the ticket counter then returned. "I've arranged passage on the next train." They sat down. "By the way, I managed to get a sleeping car. I thought it would be more private and comfortable."

How could this be happening? Sleeping car? Private? Was this really David uttering these glorious words? The vision of them making love for days and nights, of no one but the two of them cramped into a tiny room squeezed together with no place to go . . . Lily blushed from the thoughts.

"All aboard!"

And her heart thumped in anticipation as she followed David eagerly and obediently— ignoring the loud voices, crying babies, and bodies of every size and description—until he finally stopped and opened the door to a car with several short black curtains on each side.

"What's this?"

People's backsides filled the aisle as they pulled back curtains and stuffed in their belongings.

"It's the sleeping car." They maneuvered around the odd assorted passengers until David pulled back one of the curtains to expose a single narrow wooden bench. "Here, I think this is it."

"This?"

He nodded casually. "Not much for the extra money I admit, but at least it will give you some privacy and you can stretch out."

"Me?"

He nodded then saw her frown. "I thought you'd appreciate it."

Lily plopped down and wanted to cry. There was no blanket, no pillow, nothing but a worn wooden bench and a musty black curtain. But she wouldn't have cared about blankets and pillows if David shared the space with her. It was him she wanted, only him. And though she was furious, she knew she should never have let herself fantasize about being alone with him on a romantic journey. That wasn't the purpose of the trip and he'd said nothing to encourage such an idea. But Lily was disappointed, so very disappointed. She wanted him to want her as much as she wanted him. She wanted him to find a way for them to be alone together. She wanted him to squeeze into the tiny space with her and shut the curtain. Shut them away from the world.

But he seemed to have no such thoughts or desires. "What's the matter?"

"Nothing."

She refused to make eye contact so he shrugged and nodded toward the car's entrance. "Let's go find a seat."

"No."

"No?" He looked perplexed. "Then what do you want to do?"

I want to slap you and your self control. She shrugged.

"I think you'd be more comfortable out there until night but it's your choice." He walked out.

113

Lily scooted against the wall of the tiny berth, snapped the curtain shut, and cried.

But soon he was back. "Lil . . ."

Deliriously happy, she pulled at him and found his mouth. At last they were together, touching, holding . . . "Oh, David. I knew you'd come back . . ."

"No, Lily." He was leaving again.

She pulled on him. "David, no. Don't leave, not again."

"Lily, wake up!"

Someone was shaking her and her dream was fading even as she grasped at it and slapped at the intruder. "Leave me alone. David's here."

But the dream disappeared and she woke feeling empty and sad until she saw David. "You are here. It wasn't a dream." She wrapped her arms around his neck and pulled him downward until their lips met.

But David removed her arms from his neck and stood up. "Yes, Lil, it was a dream."

She slapped at him.

"Hey! What's that for? I came to get you for dinner. We'll be stopping soon and they don't allow much time." He stood up and straightened his uniform. "I'll wait for you outside."

She watched him walk out then held her stomach and lay down. Memories of the dream, especially of his lips on hers, confused her and she wanted to cry but couldn't for the anger. Had he really kissed her or just in the dream? Damn him. Well, she'd not let him humiliate her like that again. She pulled herself out of the cramped berth then straightened her dress and hair—paying particular attention to the curls by her cheeks.

And though it was almost freezing outside, it felt good to be on solid ground, and by the time Lily filled her lungs with the invigorating air and took in the sunset, her anger had subsided. Besides, David was approaching. As he handed her a cup of coffee and a sandwich, she pointed to the sky. "Look at the sunset, David. Isn't it glorious?"

"We don't have much time."

All business, all dignity. Lily made a face as she followed him to a bench. Without uttering a word, he unwrapped his sandwich and began to eat. She watched him for a moment, annoyed at his one-track mind, then unwrapped her sandwich and took a bite. She'd not realized how hungry she was and found the dry fried-egg sandwich and lukewarm stale coffee better than expected.

Suddenly she felt mischievous, childlike, frisky; and she wanted a playmate. She leaned toward David and commented on fellow passengers. No response. Like a child, she asked multitudes of questions. No response. He obviously didn't want to play. She hated being ignored and hated his stuffy demeanor. Desperate for his attention, she leaned toward his sandwich so that her head was between the sandwich and his mouth.

His response was cold and irritable. "What are you doing?"

She sat back up and grinned. "I just wanted to see what was so fascinating about that sandwich, Grumpy."

He frowned.

"What's wrong with you?"

Silence.

"How dumb of me not to think that traveling together would be a problem for you. I can't believe you even suggested it." She whispered in his ear. "Well, you'd better go hibernate then, Mr. Mouse. Heaven forbid that the same man who can lead men into battle is scared of a little gossip. Besides, we're cousins, remember?"

Fury blackened his eyes as he wadded the brown paper around the remaining piece of sandwich and stood up. He started to speak but clamped his mouth shut and spun around and stomped back to the dining station to return the metal cups.

"All aboard!"

She looked up at his formidable presence as he spoke in a monotone. "We have a lot of miles to cover together. First you pout when I pay extra for a sleeping berth then you ridicule me and attempt to humiliate me in public. Is this to be your attitude for the duration?"

"You pompous . . ." Now she stomped away, just dramatically enough to turn a few heads. Damn him. How could he find it so easy to be together but not touch? How could he stand being cousins?

She pranced back to the depressing wooden slat, yanked the curtain closed, and plopped against the wall. Damn the man.

But as the train lurched forward and the familiar rocking motion began again, Lily smiled. He couldn't hold out indefinitely. Tonight he would succumb to the swaying of the train and the cold night air that begged for intimacy.

Yes. He'd be begging for her before the night was over.

CHAPTER 21

But he didn't.

But what did she expect? He was trying to be faithful to his wife and protect his reputation. And, grudgingly, she not only respected him for it but knew she should be doing the same. She, too, had a spouse who deserved fidelity.

But when she was around David she forgot about Saul.

When she was around David, she forgot about everyone and everything.

Behave, Lily. He's not your husband and you're not his wife. His friend is all you can ever be.

The idea broke her heart but she'd do whatever she had to to be with him.

Knowing that they would stop soon for breakfast, Lily primped as best she could then walked through the train until she found him.

There he was . . . an older version of the sleepy boy she'd fallen in love with. He was slumped in his seat, a little disheveled from sleep, his hair mussed . . . *Be strong, Lily, be strong.* He was in the aisle seat and leaning toward the aisle so she was able to kneel beside him and touch his arm, their faces only inches apart. Could she steal a kiss? Dare she? She settled for the feel of his uniform under her fingertips as she patted, squeezed, and rubbed his arm.

"David," she whispered then watched his brown lashes flutter open, watched him focus his eyes. Oh, the memories of that night so long ago . . . She continued to whisper, "We'll be stopping soon," and continued to rub his arm and take advantage of their nearness. "I'm sorry about last night."

He blinked several times then looked into her eyes and smiled sweetly. Touching the curl by her cheek, he softly said, "Forget it."

"May I buy you breakfast?"

"Sure."

His twinkling eyes made her catch her breath and when she brushed the hair off his forehead, he caught her hand and held it, held it close to his lips, then let it go.

As soon as they were off the train, David left to take care of personal needs while Lily hurried to the refreshment salon, found a table, and ordered coffee and doughnuts. It was so much fun to order for two, and the picture of she and David as a couple took over as it had so many times. She wiped away the beginning of tears and tried to shake away the melancholia.

"Good morning." He was chipper, his eyes and smile bright.

His friend. That's all you can ever be.

"Good morning." She purposely avoided his eyes, appearing fascinated with stirring black coffee. "I hope this is okay."

"It's more than okay. Thank you."

She felt his eyes on her, even as he unfolded his napkin and placed it on his lap.

"Are you okay?"

"Yes, why?"

He ladled spoonful after spoonful of sugar into his coffee then stirred it. "You seem a little upset. Did you sleep well?"

She nodded then dared look at him. His elbows were on the table, his dark eyes looking over steepled fingers that rubbed his lips.

"And you?"

He laughed. "Fine—under the circumstances."

Silent, they picked at their food.

"Aren't you hungry?"

She didn't answer.

He reached across the table. "Lil?"

She refused to look at him.

"What's wrong?"

"Nothing." She bit her lip and forced a smile. "I'm sorry. I'm fine, just fine." She took a deep breath and forced another smile. "Let's go outside, shall we?" When he hesitated, she patted his hand. "That's okay. I understand. I won't jeopardize your reputation. I'll go by myself."

But he was at her side before she'd made it out the door. "Lily?"

"Yes?"

"Nothing." He studied her eyes then put his hand on her elbow and led her outside.

Much to Lily's surprise and great delight, David suddenly relaxed. He didn't touch her but neither did he keep a careful distance, even after they boarded the train and sat together. For once he seemed to just *be*.

It was fun not to be Lily and David, two people married to others with so much heartache between them, but to be Flora and David—two people who'd just met, two people with an obvious attraction who flirted as they exchanged information about themselves.

117

Lily had never seen David so talkative and she wallowed in the way his eyes lit up when he described tormenting his sisters or some of the pranks he and Jonathan had played at school. And he seemed equally captivated by her imitations of Gladys and Stella, looking into her eyes and laughing full and deep. They even teased each other's laughs, full hearty laughs they'd not heard much in their times together. "Now I'll always be self conscious," Lily said as she slapped him playfully on the shoulder.

"Well, I can't help it if you snort when you laugh." His eyes delved into hers. "I don't believe it, your face is turning red." He leaned toward her.

She made a face. "Well, at least I've never eaten so much fried chicken that I threw up or tried my big brother's snuff after given strict instructions not to!"

"I knew that would come back to haunt me, but I didn't think it would be within minutes. But aren't you the one who got caught in a tree overnight because the local boys had your pantalettes and waited for you to come down to get them?" He bumped her shoulder with his.

"Well, I can't wait to taste these Kiss Cakes you rave so about. You do have a sweet tooth, don't you Colonel?"

"Yes, ma'am, I admit it." His eyes twinkled. "That's why I'm so sweet."

"And modest too."

Lily learned that he was good at chess, archery, fencing, and shooting. He adored horses and dogs. He loved to sing, especially church hymns, and adored dancing. So well rounded, she thought, but rich young people are taught these things to make them successful and . . . marriageable to the right people.

But David seemed equally impressed with her talents, especially her business sense. She noticed how mesmerized he was when she described business dealings and investments she'd made. He also seemed impressed (impressed because she was a prostitute and should be stupid? Lily chose not to believe that's what he was thinking.) with her other talents. She was also good at chess and archery, and they vowed to compete some day. Who had taught her so much, he wondered, then realized it may have been one of the many men she'd been with, men he chose to forget. The idea of her being with other men made him sick. All of these moments and memories made Lily's love for David grow even deeper, made her image of him even higher, and made her wish even harder that this was their everyday relationship.

Eventually the two tired from talking and laughing and the click-clack of the train put them to sleep. Lily's head fell against the windowpane, David's fell against her shoulder.

When she woke, he was staring at her. "Hi."

"Hi." She felt herself blush. "How long have you been watching me?"

"Long enough."

"What? To see me drool?"

He touched her lips with a fingertip and whispered, "I've never seen you drool but I wouldn't mind if you did." He smiled. "Do you?" He straightened up in his seat but continued to look at her, a sly smile on his face.

"Of course not." She turned away and took a deep breath then started kneading her neck.

"Here, let me."

What had gotten into him? Why was he being so affectionate? What miracle had made them an ordinary couple for the past several hours? But Lily didn't care, didn't care at all, and gladly turned around so he could massage her neck. As her body relaxed from his magic fingers, she sighed and whispered, "That feels wonderful."

"Does it?" His breath was on her neck and she shivered then turned to find his lips in front of hers, his eyes delving into hers . . .

"David Evans! Is that you?"

They jerked around like guilty children.

"It is you. I thought so." A matronly yellow-haired woman stood next to David, her large bosom almost bumping his face with each rock of the train. Lily wanted to laugh at the scenario, especially the expression on David's face. He attempted to stand as his gentlemanly code required, but the woman's proximity made it impossible and she even patted his shoulder indicating that he shouldn't. "I saw that lovely wife of yours the other day. She's at her father's now in Columbia. But you knew that of course." The woman laughed, her bosom bouncing ever closer to David's face. "Your poor mother has moved there too." She laughed again. "But you knew that too, I'm sure." Her hands fluttered like a disoriented bat.

But her words made Lily's blood boil and it was suddenly very clear why David hadn't volunteered the information about his mother's move. Mary Anne, too, had moved, and now she was in close proximity to Mrs. Evans—and Grace. Not a state apart as when Mary Anne was in the northern part of the state.

David added very little to the conversation but had very little chance, for the woman jumped from one tidbit to another without stopping. But women know women, and Lily knew that the woman was waiting for David to introduce his mysterious female traveling companion. This old family "friend" was giving Lily the once over and mentally preparing her report to everyone she knew—especially Mary Anne.

"Since David's forgotten his manners, I'll introduce myself." Lily extended her arm across David's chest. "I'm his cousin, Lily Morgan." Out of the corner of her eye Lily could see David's astonishment and she wanted to laugh, but instead acted as if their being together was an everyday—and very innocent—occurrence.

"I'm sorry." David gave Lily an odd look. "Cousin Lily, this is one of our dear friends, Mrs. Crowley."

The woman smiled apprehensively and fidgeted with her shawl. "Who are your parents, dear? I don't recall any Morgans in this area." She eyed Lily suspiciously and looked at her ring finger. "Or is Morgan your married name?"

"Yes," Lily bowed her head and solemnly said, "but my husband and parents are deceased and my relationship to the Evanses is quite distant. I'm not from South Carolina." She gave her most innocent smile.

"I am sorry, my dear, but you're not wearing black so the deaths aren't recent?"

"A few years."

"Well, I'm still sorry for your loss." She clucked and shook her head. "I'm also sorry that you're seeing our beautiful country at such a horrible time. Please don't judge it from current appearances. Land sakes, no. Of course, you can't even visit the islands with those damnable Yankees there. No. Life's not at all what it used to be." She again adjusted her shawl across her large chest. "But you come back after these no-account Yankees leave and you'll see why so many families have been here for generations, won't she, David?"

"Yes, ma'am."

"Ah, yes." Her eyes drifted toward the ceiling in memories then returned to Lily. "So, is this just a family visit?"

"My daughter is staying with Mrs. Evans."

The woman nodded then her eyes widened. "Yes, of course. . ." She stared at Lily. "Excuse me, dear, but that child looks nothing like you. Of course, you look nothing like that family at all, but your daughter looks just like . . ." She eyeballed David and her face grew sober, "like you, David!" She chuckled but her scrutiny continued. "Uhm . . . yes, remarkable . . . She looks exactly like you."

Lily couldn't decide whether to cringe with fright or laugh out loud and she dared not look at David. Finally, she said that yes, they'd noticed the resemblance and wasn't it interesting.

"Yes, well . . . It's so sad that her father won't be around to watch her grow up."

"Yes, ma'am."

She nodded and stared at the "cousins" again then took a deep breath. "Well, my feet are killing me so I'd better get back to my seat." She patted David's shoulder. "I hope you both have a nice visit and do give your family my regards, David. It was very nice meeting you, Mrs. Morgan."

"My pleasure."

David released a long-held breath and fell back into his seat as Lily covered her mouth to muffle giggles.

"What's so funny?"

"What's so funny? Don't you see?"

"No, I'm sorry, I don't. I found that encounter completely unsettling."

"But you said that this was all planned. You expected people to see us. Didn't I play my part well?"

He frowned.

"Besides, I'm the one who should be upset."

"Why?"

"How can you even ask? First you didn't bother to tell me that my daughter had moved and now I find out that your wife has moved too—near *my* daughter. How many other secrets about *my* daughter are you keeping?"

He hissed under his breath. "*My* daughter. She's my daughter too."

"But you can't claim her, can you?"

His eyes squinted and blackened.

"Next stop, Wilmington!"

"That's our stop."

They gathered their things and stepped off the train. Still fuming, Lily headed toward the depot but saw David heading elsewhere. Dumbfounded, she silently let him help her into a carriage then stared at him in wonder as they took off.

CHAPTER 22

As they sat in the inn's cozy crowded restaurant, Lily looked around for prying eyes then finally broke the uneasy silence. "Aren't you afraid we'll run into someone else?"

"Now who's the fearful mouse?" He speared a potato chunk and popped it in his mouth then chewed as he looked at her over steepled fingers, his eyes sparkling.

Thankfully, David was quick to forgive and forget, and though Lily wasn't normally the same way, time with him was too precious to waste quarreling, too intoxicating to even eat. "So, you're no longer upset about our run-in with Mrs. Crowley?" She imitated his steepled fingers and looked into his eyes.

He wiped his mouth with the corner of his napkin then shook his head and returned to his thoughtful pose. "I can't explain it, Lily, but the way you handled her . . ." He smiled wickedly. "You did that very well . . ."

He was being uncharacteristically calm and seductive, and though Lily was aroused by the devilish manner, she found it unsettling.

"Don't you see? Without realizing it, Mrs. Crowley's made it easier for us. We've passed the first test. If we can convince Crowley, we can . . ." The smile dropped from his face and all light left his eyes as his head bowed and he lay the fork beside his plate. Without looking up, he whispered, "I just wanted to be with you, Lily, and this was the only way I could think of to do it." He raised his eyes slowly. "There, I've said it. Now you know of my weak moral character, my . . ." He stood so quickly that the table shook and the dishes rattled. As other customers looked their way, David kept his eyes down and put money beside his plate then whispered, "I'm not fit for you or Mary Anne. Excuse me." He walked away.

Lily was on her feet instantly.

When she caught up with him, he was outside sitting on a porch bench, his hair blowing in the cold winter wind, his tear-filled brown eyes staring at nothing.

She sat next to him and lightly touched his arm. "Oh, David, don't you know that this is what I've been hoping for? But you turn hot and cold and make me crazy." She saw his fingers tighten into fists and she curled her fingers over them. "David."

Their eyes met and he whispered, "I can't . . . I shouldn't . . ."

"Shh, I know, I know." She looked into his glistening eyes and put a finger to his lips. "And we won't if you don't want to. I'll be your cousin."

He pursed his lips and turned away as he shook his head. "But that's not . . . I'm so selfish, so . . . We should have gone on and not stopped here. Mary Anne will want to know why we got off the train, why we made a detour to some obscure town . . .What is she to think?"

"I don't give a damn what she thinks."

He looked at her, disgusted. "That's obvious."

Griting her teeth, Lily spoke as calmly as she could. "Number one, I doubt that she's the delicate hot-house flower you make her out to be. Number two, just tell her that this side trip was my idea, that I begged you to take me and you were just too nice to refuse. There's bound to be some reason I'd want to visit this place." She smiled and touched his cheek. "Everyone knows you're a soft touch."

He studied her. "Don't you understand? I owe her better than this. She's already had to take on more responsibility than I ever wanted her to. She's raising four boys on her own."

She jumped up. "Damn you, David Evans! Why do you do this to us?" Customers studied the irritated redhead as they entered and exited the restaurant. Lily feigned a smile and sat back down and spoke in a whisper. "We've been through this so many times. If you don't want to hurt your precious saintly Mary Anne, don't, but make up your mind!" She stood again and headed toward the street, thankful to hear his footsteps close behind.

She turned toward him. "As for having four children, maybe you should learn to keep your pants on!"

His eyes, dark at her admonition, suddenly widened and his jaw fell open. "What did you say?"

The expression on his face was priceless and Lily could barely speak for laughing. "You heard me."

"Did I?" He shook his head and smiled. "I swear I never know what you'll say next." Her giggles were contagious and soon they were both laughing. "Really, Lily, I do wish you'd speak your mind." He was trying to stop laughing but not having much luck.

She batted her eyes. "Are you sure?"

"No!" He held one of his hands on his stomach while he waved with the other and shook his head. When he was finally able to speak, he took one of her hands and rubbed the top of it with his thumb then spoke through happy tears. "You're amazing, absolutely amazing."

Lily pulled her hand from his and wrapped her fingers around her arms. Trying to get warm. Trying to keep from holding him. "I know you worry about her but she has her family, doesn't she?"

He nodded. "She's always been her father's pet so he's more than happy to have her back home, and her mother's wild about the boys. Mary Anne idolizes her father as I idolized mine. It's almost funny," he said quietly, thoughtfully, "I grew up trying to be like my father and now I'm trying to be like hers." He coughed and blinked. "But I can never be as grand as either of them and I'm scared I'll let her down."

Lily touched his cheek lightly with her fingertips. "She couldn't get any better than you, David, and I'm sure she thinks so too." The temperatures were dropping as they stood in the middle of the street. Lily pulled her shawl tighter around her shoulders and shivered.

His eyes turned hopeful, childlike. "Do you think so? Do you really?"

She looked at his lips and stuttered, "Of course I do," then quickly looked away. "I appreciate the trip but it's obviously not been a good idea."

His brows furrowed.

"You said you planned this so we could be together," she allowed her eyes to examine his face, "and you don't know how much that means to me, but it's not going to work. We talk so much about Mary Anne that we tend to forget that I, too, have a spouse."

He pursed his lips. "It's not the same."

"You . . . How stupid of me. How could I presume that my husband could possibly be as important as your wife."

He clinched his jaw.

Lily took a deep breath and held her arms tightly against her chest. "Whatever your opinion of my husband, you must realize that he is a very real threat to you. I know you don't want to hurt Mary Anne, but Saul could—and would—take great pleasure in ruining you. Earlier you said that we'd 'passed the first test,' but that's only because Mary Anne believes I'm a cousin coming to see my daughter. I don't think Saul would believe that, do you?"

David pounded his fist in the air. "What have I done?"

"I tell you what, you get on the first train to Columbia and I'll catch another . . . to Richmond." Lily let the wind blow away her tears. "I just won't see Grace. Saul won't know the difference."

"No!" He caressed her cheeks with shaky hands and teased her curls then whispered, "Oh, Lily, don't you see? I want to be with you. I want my family to meet you. I want you to see my home. Don't you see? I want you near *me*, near everything that's dear to me."

Lily felt his words pour over her and knew she'd cling to them for the rest of her life, for they were probably the closest to a declaration of love that she'd ever hear from him. As she studied his face and touched his cheek, she wondered how two such strong people could be so weak when together.

But they couldn't afford to be. One of them had to be strong. He had been on the train. Now it was her turn. She couldn't let him lose what he'd worked so hard to get. He didn't deserve to sacrifice everything because of Saul's cruel graduation present.

She looked at the face she adored and whispered, "It can't happen, David. I can't go with you."

He lowered his head in defeat. "Grace is expecting you."

"What? Why didn't you say that before?"

Both of his hands formed fists. "Because I want you to go for me, to be with me!"

She wanted to throw herself in his arms and declare her love but instead spoke quietly. "Then I'll go with you—for Grace's sake. But we're cousins, nothing more."

They walked silently to her room.

David unlocked the door then spoke coldly, "So, you're going only because of Grace?"

"Don't, David." The hurt in his face weakened her resolve and her voice quivered, "We . . . you can't afford to take any more chances."

He closed his eyes and nodded then touched the ringlet by her cheek and let his finger graze her lips. Lily closed her eyes and soon felt the familiar soft mouth that matched hers so perfectly. But she opened her eyes and whispered, "Good night," and closed the door before she could change her mind.

CHAPTER 23

The next morning Lily walked to the dining room. She'd cried all night and knew her face looked puffy, but as always she was anxious to see David. Surely they could finish the trip together without touching. They could, couldn't they?

But the very thought of giving up David felt like a million pin pricks, and even as she ordered coffee and a roll, her hands shook and her stomach churned, and she knew she wouldn't be able to eat.

She looked out the window at the lightly falling snow and thought of how contradictory their relationship had always been, how she'd spent half of her time hating him. Then she smiled. No, she'd never hated him. She'd been hurt, angry, and jealous, but she'd never hated him. She sniffed back tears and tried to remember why she was spying. David owns slaves. David has Grace. But it didn't matter.

"May I join you?"

She looked up and into David's brown eyes. "Of course."

He also ordered coffee and a roll then said, "I don't know why I ordered that. I know I won't be able to eat it."

She laughed quietly. "I was just thinking the same thing." She sipped her coffee and let her eyes gaze on him. His uniform was immaculate as always but tiny facial cuts revealed shaving mishaps and shadows under his eyes revealed a sleepless night. Then there was that lock of hair that just wouldn't quite stay in place—that little boy inside him who refused to be polished and dignified, refused to be a part of the military persona. She smiled at him. "Do I look as awful as you do?"

He smiled and his eyes sparkled. "Of course not. You could never look awful." He thanked the waiter for his coffee then began adding sugar. Without looking up, he spoke, "I know you're watching me. Stop it."

She smiled broadly. "Yes, sir! But really David, that can't be healthy."

"I know. Mauma Hattie and Mary . . . fuss at me all the time about it."

Mary Anne.

Lily winced and looked down. Her hands were shaking and her cup rattled on its saucer. She quickly put her hands in her lap. "So . . . when does our coach leave?"

He set his cup down and warmed his hands around it as he looked out the window. "I'd not planned to leave today." He looked into her eyes. "But I guess we might as well. Since there's no longer a reason to stay."

She was dying to know what his original plans had been and fought to keep from asking, from taking back last night's words of determination. And since she knew that that was exactly what she would say, she said nothing. And dug her fingernails into her palms.

They lingered over several cups of coffee and attempts at polite conversation until David suggested they take a stroll. "I promise to keep my distance," he whispered as he pulled out her chair.

Although aware of the stares they were receiving, Lily savored their walk and simple conversation. But soon an uneasy silence made them all too aware that their attempt at a platonic relationship wasn't working. They could neither be together nor apart. Was this what hell would be? Being together but not being able to touch?

Of course it wasn't hell. Any moment with David was better than any moment with anyone else, but being with him and not with him was excruciating.

They still weren't hungry when they returned to the dining room for lunch. Both were anxious and ill-at-ease, and it seemed that David put even more sugar than usual in his coffee. Lily smiled and nodded toward his cup. "What are you going to do when you run out of that—and everything else?"

His eyes darted around and he whispered. "You really must watch your words. In case you're unaware of it, there are spies everywhere—on both sides. In fact, a female spy was brought to my tent the other day."

Lily panicked but outwardly remained nonchalant. "Really?"

He nodded then leaned forward and spoke softly. "She was posing as a man in an attempt to infiltrate our unit." He leaned back in his chair.

"How intriguing . . ." She sat up very straight. "I could pass for a man, don't you think?"

His eyes grew wide then he laughed and shook his head. "Not in a million years."

Happy to hear him laugh, Lily fluttered her lashes and smiled, enjoying the way he gazed upon her.

"Seriously, Lily." He sipped his coffee then leaned across the table again. "You must be careful with your words. I know you like to goad me, but someone else might have you arrested."

She shuddered. "What did you do to her, the spy?"

He shrugged his shoulders and spoke casually, matter-of-factly. "Had her arrested, of course."

"Of course." They stared at each other as Lily studied him. Yes, he would do that. Would he arrest her too? She shuddered again and looked away.

After a few more moments of uneasy silence, Lily leaned across the table and whispered. "I've been wanting to ask you . . ." She looked into his handsome face and gentle eyes that watched her every movement. Dare she continue? "You lead your men in prayer, you read the Bible, you're such a fine and good man—how can you possibly justify owning slaves?"

He shook his head and looked around them. "Do you really want to speak of this here and now?"

"Yes."

Their faces were only inches apart and Lily could see his growing impatience. She hadn't meant to upset him but couldn't forgo an opportunity to change his views. Besides, at least they were talking. She couldn't stand the way they'd been all morning. She reached out a hand and left her palm open as she whispered. "Seriously, David, how can a Christian man justify slavery?"

He inhaled deeply then sighed. "There have always been slaves, Lily. It's a part of human existence. Our slaves are Christians, churchgoing Christians. If we hadn't taught them and provided churches for them, they'd be heathens. And what would they do without us to feed and clothe them?" He shook his head again then sipped his coffee. "You don't understand what all is involved."

"I hope you don't mean I don't understand because I'm a woman."

"Not necessarily."

Her eyes narrowed. "I'd think twice before even thinking that, Mr. Evans. You know that I understand business so just admit it. You must have labor to plant and harvest your crops and what's better than free labor?"

"Quite the opposite. We spend a fortune on our people. My mother spends more time making sure they're fed, clothed, and doctored than she ever spent on us."

"Doesn't that seem odd to you, that because your mother took care of them, she had to have them take care of her children? Wouldn't it make more sense for mothers to take care of their own children?"

Grimacing, he leaned back in his chair and tapped a finger on the lip of his cup as he stared at her. "It's always been like this. Why should a centralized government be able to change it, be able to tell each state what to do? That's not the way this country was founded. That's what we're fighting for."

Lily shook her head. "But don't you see, the government can't sit back and ignore the mistreatment of its people." He must see, he must. Lily loved him too much to see him continue such a barbaric practice.

His eyes were downcast and he nervously turned his cup around in its saucer. "But . . ." he looked at her, "what would they do, where would they go? They don't know any other life."

"They're people, David. They'd do as most people do. They just need the education and the freedom to try. You do see them as people, don't you? You do believe that God created them as He did you and me?"

He continued to shake his head and his brow remained furrowed. "I've not given it any thought, but now that you've asked, yes, I do see differences. Surely even you will agree to that? As for education and freedom, I don't agree. They're like children."

"I agree that we're different in color and some features, but that's all. And that's no different than you and me being different because of our hair color or eye color. Do you honestly think that Mauma Hattie and the other servants at your home are less intelligent than you or me? Do you honestly think that they're incapable of taking care of themselves? For heaven sake, David, Mauma Hattie probably had more to do with your rearing than your own mother. If she's good enough, smart enough, capable enough, for your mother to put her in charge of her own children, how can she not be equal? Can you really think of her as less a person than anyone else?"

He shook his head and whispered. "Of course not." He tapped the coffee cup with his fingertips again then sighed.

Although she was happy that she'd made him think, Lily hated to see him so sad, and she longed to hold him. But this was their lot, wasn't it? They didn't have the luxury of being a couple, of being able to disagree then console and comfort.

David coughed. "I'm really not hungry and you don't appear to be either. Shall we take our leave?"

She nodded, uncomfortable with the look of irritation and vexation that she saw on his face. Had she finally overstepped her bounds?

He silently escorted her to her room, gave her a curt nod, then walked away.

Lily shut the door then fell on the bed and cried herself to sleep.

CHAPTER 24

Then woke to light tapping on the door and David's voice. She was dazed and disoriented and her hair was loose from its pins, but the urgency of his voice kept her from primping.

As soon as she opened the door, he walked in and led her to the room's small balcony. "Look, Lil. Isn't it glorious?"

"Oh, David . . ." Lily marveled at the breathtaking sight of sparkling snow.

But her attention was diverted by the feel of his eyes on her face and his hand on hers, and for one moonlit moment she pretended that they were all alone in the world, cushioned and protected in nature's downy white quilt.

If only she could make time stand still.

And though his breath on her neck made her shiver, his words broke her reverie. "After I take you to my mother's house, I have to leave." He turned her toward him and raised her chin. "I'll be gone a few days then come back with . . ."

Lily nodded as sobs came up from deep within. "It's too hard, David, too damn hard."

He pulled her head to his chest. "I know." He wiped her face with his handkerchief and they looked at each other for several silent seconds.

"I thought you were angry with me."

"No, not angry." He looked at her face, touched her hair. "More than anyone I've ever known, you're able to put ideas into words that make me think. You make some things hard to ignore."

She felt his breathing accelerate as he put his fingers through her hair and pulled her face to his, her mouth to his. They leaned back against the wall, their bodies pressing together as their kisses grew harder.

"No, David, we can't." She pushed on his chest.

His voice was gravelly as his mouth trailed down her neck. "Please don't turn me away, Lil. Please let me love you."

They woke several times during the night—to reassure each other that they were really there, to make love. And each time they fell back to sleep, their arms and legs tangled together.

Touching, always touching.

She looked down at him and traced his lips then kissed them and lightly bit his bottom lip. "I love your face . . . even the mustache."

"Finally. Since you hadn't said anything I was afraid you didn't." He smiled meekly then added. "I thought it would command respect."

"Ah." She playfully tugged on the small beard. "But I'm not sure about this."

His lips turned down into a pout. "You don't like it? But it's what all the generals are wearing this war."

"Really?" She continued to trace his features with a fingertip. "I seem to remember seeing a much fuller version. Let's see . . . several come to mind . . . Lee, Jackson, Longstreet, Stuart . . . So, are you planning to let yours grow? Will that assure promotions?"

He pretended to touch a full beard. "Yes, I think so. Wouldn't you like it really long and bushy?" Lily shook her head emphatically and David chuckled.

Her shining eyes held his gaze as her fingers and mouth followed the growth pattern of his hair from his chest to below his belly, and for a few moments he was still, his eyes closed, his fingers tangled in her hair. But soon his breathing accelerated and he pulled her mouth to his and loved her again then held her as they slept.

Was it love? Did David love her? Or was his passion caused by the guilt, the forbidden? Lily wanted to believe he loved her but until he said the words, she would always doubt.

But didn't it mean something that his lovemaking didn't stop after he was spent? If he just wanted her body or the excitement of the forbidden, would he continue to touch her, smile when he saw their limbs tangled together, gaze at her face, kiss her lips, trace her features with his fingertips, kiss her tears?

As the small carriage bumped along, Lily looked up at the moss-covered trees that canopied the roads and let herself be lulled by David's accent, by the fondness with which he described his boyhood years. ". . . and in the summer we move closer to the water to get away from the heat and mosquitoes."

"Yes. Saul told me that the humidity can be unbearable and . . ."

The chaise stopped short and David turned to her. "How could you marry him, Lily? Him of all people? How could you?"

Lily was startled at the sudden outburst, the anger in his voice, the trembling of his hands, and she reached for him. "David?"

But he pulled away and scowled.

"How can you speak of whom I should marry—and what's wrong with Saul?"

"What's wrong with him?" His face was red, his speech stammered. "He's just . . . I just can't believe you married him."

"Well, I think I'm lucky to be married to him. He's handsome, hard working, kind, gentle, ambitious . . . a lot like you, don't you think? Besides, you have a family. Should Saul and I be deprived of one? Do we deserve less?"

He took a deep breath and looked away. When he turned back, he was a little calmer, his voice quieter. "No, of course not." He shook his head. "You just don't understand."

"I guess I don't. Why don't you explain it to me?"

Silence.

"You're selfish, you know that? It's okay for you to have money, children . . . and a spouse, but not for Saul, not for me."

"You know that's not true. You know I want the best for you, but I can't stand the idea of you . . . of him . . ." He pursed his lips and curled his fingers into fists then jerked back around in his seat and angrily shook the reins.

They had silently passed field after field yet seen few people when suddenly there were rows of humble white-washed homes with dark-skinned children running in the yards. Lily felt David watching her—daring her to comment? Worried that she'd argue with his family?

Again, the shay jerked to a halt.

"Okay. Out with it."

She smiled innocently. "Out with what?"

"You know what. Get it out of your system."

She laughed. "Why? Is your conscience bothering you?"

"No. Just . . . please don't raise the issue while we're here, okay?"

He exaggerated a pitiful pose and Lily laughed even harder then kissed his pouting bottom lip. "Okay, I promise I won't embarrass you. Are you happy now?"

He grinned then flicked the reins.

Her head against his shoulder, Lily dozed with a contentment she rarely felt. But all too soon David was whispering, "Almost there," and Lily woke to see that night had fallen. Their precious time together was almost over.

They turned onto a path of white crushed shells bordered by magnolia trees and huge oaks, and in moments there appeared an enormous green-roofed two-story frame home, more wide than tall, with wide wooden steps that lead to a wraparound veranda lit by the hazy light of oil lamps.

"You people are amazing," Lily whispered as they neared the front drive.

David's pursed lips and exasperation returned. "What's that mean?"

"You're so accustomed to all this. What are you going to do when it disappears?"

"That's why we're fighting, so it won't disappear."

She looked at him and stifled the words she wanted to scream. "I'm sorry. This isn't the right time."

He gave her a stony look then urged the horse with another slap of the reins.

"Hey, if you're mad at me, take it out on me, not a defenseless animal."

With a shake of his head and a smirk on his face, he looked at her and muttered, "If only I could."

"I heard that!" She laughed again then gazed at his profile and fought back tears.

She missed him already.

CHAPTER 25

As they came to a stop, Lily felt her stomach knot at the reality of meeting David's mother, his brother and sisters, his children . . . Mary Anne. Why had she come?

"George! How are you?"

"Just fine, Master David. It's sure good to see you."

"You too." David patted the man's shoulder then helped Lily out of the shay. "This is Lily, Grace's mother."

The man tipped his hat and Lily felt a familial warmth.

"Fish! Momma!"

"Gracie, my baby!"

Her brown eyes wide in excitement, Gracie ran out of the massive front doors and into her mother's arms. As Lily pulled her close, she looked up to see David embrace his mother.

But Grace's embrace was quick and she quickly pulled away from Lily and ran to David. "Fish, Fish! I knew you'd come back!" She ran into the strong arms that closed lovingly around her, and Lily watched as David and his daughter embraced. From the relief on David's face she realized that he, too, had been worried about the child's safety but hadn't let on. And was it her imagination or did Grace seem happier to see her father than her mother whom she hadn't seen in a month or more? Lily felt a knot in her stomach but tried to quell it. *Don't ask for trouble.*

When he finally stood, his face glowed as he took his mother's hand and led her to Lily. After kissing his mother's hand, he patted it. "Mother, this is Lily." His smile was broad and Lily was thrilled that he introduced her with such pride.

The tall imposing image of gray was shattered by a bright genuine smile as Mrs. Evans clasped her guest's hand warmly. "Welcome to our home."

As Lily blinked away tears of gratitude at the woman's welcome, she heard another voice coming toward them. "Is that my boy?"

"Yes, ma'am, it sure is!" David's eyes twinkled as he wrapped his arms around the black woman who embraced him, tears of joy streaming down her round cheeks.

"How are you, child?" She put her hands on each side of his face and examined him. "Are you well?"

He put his hands on hers. "Yes, Mauma Hattie, I'm very well." He looked down at Grace. "Thank you for taking such good care of Gracie."

As Lily observed her daughter standing between David and Mauma Hattie, she realized just how spoiled the little girl was, how much attention she demanded. She had always exaggerated her expressions, had always displayed her every emotion dramatically, but was she really spoiled or was her grabbing for love and attention a trait she'd inherited from her parents? Was the passion Lily and David shared so strong that it had passed down to their daughter?

Mauma Hattie held Grace's hand and patted it. "This darlin's been after me every minute, 'When are Fish and Momma going to be here?' I swear if you hadn't arrived today, I'd have come lookin' for ya'!" Lily saw how comfortable the three were together and how obvious it was that they adored each other.

As Lily watched the reunion, David's mother whispered, "I'm glad to meet you, Lily. I'm sorry you've suffered so, but you can't imagine how much joy that little girl has brought to me."

"Oh, I think I can. It's the joy I feel every time I think of her." Lily almost choked at how her daughter had slighted her.

The older woman nodded. "And their bond grows tighter and stronger with his every visit. I don't think I've ever seen two people more alike—the same mannerisms, facial expressions . . ." She clasped her hands under her bosom. "But it's dangerous. You know that, don't you?"

Lily nodded. "It's obvious that Grace is happy here. How long did it take her to adjust? I worried that she felt I'd deserted her. I tried to get here as soon as I could. I do plan to take her back, you know."

Mrs. Evans's eyes widened then she calmed and did her lips tremble? She looked directly into Lily's eyes as she spoke. "Actually, she cried for a few days. . . . She wanted her mother, of course, and continually asked when you'd be here or when David would take her home. . . . But every time David was here she blossomed and it really wasn't long before she fit right in. She has really brought the sunshine back to this home, I can tell you." She clasped and unclasped her hands. "We would really hate to lose her . . . not now. We can give her the best of everything, Lily."

Lily felt her temper rise and started to respond as her feelings dictated, but she took a deep breath and calmed down. Forcing a smile (and a mental note to find a way to take Grace back with her), Lily was about to speak when Mrs. Evans spoke.

"I assume David told you how you'll be introduced to everyone?"

Lily smiled inwardly at all the simultaneous deceptions: Mrs. Evans, Lily, and David fooling friends and family; David and Lily fooling Mary Anne and Saul; everyone fooling little Grace; Lily fooling them all . . . What was that saying about tangled webs? "Yes, ma'am. I'm a long-lost cousin, right?"

She nodded. "We had to tell everyone that you're related because Gracie had to be a blood relation. The unnerving resemblance is unexplainable otherwise." She spoke quietly, her eyes never leaving her son. "It's just that David was such a good boy, the model child. Once he made his mind up about something, he stuck to it. But you know, even though I took such pride in his extraordinary goodness, I wondered how he could maintain such high goals for himself." She shook her head. "He was an exceptional child and is now an exceptional man. That's why this transgression surprised me so, yet . . ." She smiled as she admired her son.

Lily remembered the train and David's tales of all the typically boyish pranks he'd pulled. "You're not really surprised?"

"Not really. I guess I expected some indiscretion somewhere along the way. In fact, I know this sounds absurd, but I've actually hoped to see some flaw in his character."

Lily was dumbfounded.

"Yes, I know how awful that sounds, but . . ." She took a handkerchief from her sleeve and quickly dabbed her eyes then returned the piece of lace. "It's because I feared he was perfect, you see, and the perfect ones seem to . . . die young . . . and with this war . . ." She pushed out the last words quickly as if distancing herself from their destructive power then shrugged her shoulders. "Such a silly notion, I know, and it's unforgivable of me to find comfort in my son transgressing God's laws, but David rushed into marriage like he did every other aspect of his life."

She continued. "He was so guilt-ridden and apologetic when he brought Grace. He didn't expect understanding from his siblings but he did from me, so I'm the only one who knows the truth. I shudder to think of how his father would have reacted . . . I was never able to punish David and, thankfully, he never needed much correction." She looked at Lily. "But I did remind him of the very real pain this will cause if the truth is discovered. I did remind him of the moral implications." She looked directly into Lily's eyes. "It is all in the past, isn't it?"

Lily turned from the piercing eyes.

"That's what I feared." She sighed. "Oh, my dear, you must . . ."

"Lily! Come here!"

Lily smiled at the sight of David's grin, at his eager motioning for her to join them. Grace barely looked at her mother, her attention given to her father, holding his hand and gazing up at him. Lily's attempt to take her daughter's hand was rejected, and again her heart tore. Again she wished she hadn't come.

David beamed. "Lily, this is Mauma Hattie. She's another of my favorite ladies."

Lily extended her free hand. "I'm very glad to meet you, Mauma Hattie."

But the woman ignored Lily's hand and hugged her instead. "And I you, dear. I've heard so much about you, so much." She looked at Grace then David. With a twinkle in her eyes, she added, "I see your beauty everyday in these two." She patted Lily's hand. "I'll get refreshments." She touched David's cheek then winked at him and left.

David and Lily smiled timidly at each other, their eyes locked until Grace began whining and pulling at David's hand." "Fish, I'm mad at you!"

David knelt in front of her, her hand still in his. "Hey, that's no way for my favorite girl to talk. How can you be mad at me?"

"Because you didn't bring me anything."

"Gracie! What have I always told you?"

She frowned and rolled her eyes. "To like people for themselves."

"That's right."

"But, you like presents, too, and you always said that if someone gives you something, you should act surprised and thank them."

As Lily felt her face redden, she saw how much Gracie enjoyed the laughs from David and his mother, and she touched her daughter's nose playfully. "I think we're going to have a little talk, young lady" then felt herself react to the look her daughter gave her.

"Besides, who says I *didn't* bring you something?"

Gracie clapped her hands and squealed.

David kissed the top of her head as he stood. "You go inside with Nana, okay?"

She nodded emphatically, grabbed her grandmother's hand, and skipped into the house.

Alone for a moment, Lily and David smiled at each other and he put his hand on her elbow. "Happy?"

"Yes. No." She shook away tears and forced a smile. "Fish?"

He made a face and pinched her. She squealed and he whispered, "You'd better go inside before you get us in trouble."

As they got comfortable in the parlor and waited for David, Lily felt a familiar twinge of worry. It was sadly obvious that Grace now considered this her home. She was content and happy and obviously well cared for. She wasn't even close to thin and her clothes were of the finest quality. Her hair shone and was tied with satin ribbons. Yes, she seemed to belong with these people. Was Lily to lose not only the man she loved but her daughter too?

She was deep in thought when the sight of Mauma Hattie and the other household servants reminded her that her need to see Grace and spend time with David was preventing her from the important commitment she'd made to her country. How could she take Grace back to Kentucky and continue her job? She'd lose so much time, and she wouldn't be with Grace anyhow, not if she kept her commitment to the Union and to herself. Why shouldn't Grace stay here?

Or was she making excuses because she feared that her daughter wouldn't want to return? That her daughter now believed that this was her home. *Because I'll never get her back anyway.* Lily bit her lip.

But just when such thoughts began to crystallize, David walked in the room and made everything but him meaningless.

"Let's see . . . is there a little girl in here who wants a present?"

Grace jumped up and threw her arms around his legs. "Me, Fish, me!"

He pretended to ignore her and walked to his mother. "Here's one." He handed her a small wrapped present and kissed her cheek.

"That's not a little girl, Fish, that's Nana!"

Everyone laughed as David pretended to ignore her. He walked to Lily and handed her a tiny box wrapped in white silk and tied with red velvet ribbon. "For you," he whispered.

Lily felt his fingers purposely touch hers and felt the heat in his eyes. The room was suddenly very warm and uncomfortably quiet.

Until Grace spoke. "Say 'thank you', Momma."

"What?" Lily pulled her eyes from David's and looked at her daughter then blinked rapidly and looked back at David who now smiled mischievously. "Thank you, sir."

His smile broadened. "You're welcome." He turned from her and clapped his hands. "I guess that's all the presents."

Grace's bottom lip stuck out and she whimpered.

"What's my favorite girl upset about?"

"You don't have a present for me!"

"Really? Well, let me think . . ."

His mother spoke. "David, quit torturing the child."

"Yes, I remember there is something else. I'll be right back."

Grace stood in the middle of the room and watched the door, leaning on one leg than the other as she twirled her hair and bit her bottom lip. Lily and Mrs. Evans looked at the child's apprehensive brown eyes and furrowed brows then exchanged knowing smiles, and Lily knew that the woman was seeing David as a five-year-old with just such an expression.

When the sound of David's boots filled the hallway, Grace clapped. When she saw the size of the box with its huge pink ribbon, she squealed.

David knelt in front of her. "It's heavy, so I'll hold it while you take off the lid."

Grace looked into her father's eyes then anxiously untied the ribbon. As soon as the ribbon fell off, the eager brown, black, and white head of a puppy popped up and Grace's eyes widened and filled with tears. She gently took the animal out of the box and clasped it to her chest though it wiggled to get down. "Oh, Fish, I love him. He's the best present ever." She hugged the dog again then kissed David's cheek. "I love you, Fish, I love you."

"And I love you, sweetheart."

As David took his daughter in his arms, Lily looked up to see Mauma Hattie standing in the doorway. She, too, had tears in her eyes as she walked to Lily's side and patted her shoulder. Under her breath, she said, "That's the sweetest and saddest thing I've ever seen."

You don't know how sad, Lily thought.

CHAPTER 26

After blinking away tears, David stood up and looked at Lily, his mother, and Mauma Hattie then said, "I think she likes him."

Now I'll never get her back. I'm jealous of my own daughter and of the man I love. Lily continued to feel her only "hold" on David slipping out of her grasp. Worse was the feel of losing her daughter to him, for he was never hers and Grace was all Lily had ever accomplished that made her proud.

Everyone watched Grace try to hold onto the squirming animal until she finally gave up and sat down on the floor and freed him. He immediately pawed at her, nudged her with his nose, and generally checked her out then licked her with approval. Grace was enchanted and in a world of her own.

David watched her for a moment then looked at Mauma Hattie. "Don't think I forgot you." The woman giggled as he handed her a long narrow box tied with yellow and blue ribbons. When she took out the red parasol, she grew quiet and seemed capable only of kissing David's cheek.

Mrs. Evans spoke. "Have you two had your supper?"

David and Lily exchanged smiles as both silently remembered that afternoon.

David pulled the shay into a secluded spot by a small creek and they made love—slowly—conscious of each word, movement, caress—until release left them giddy and tired, but with voracious appetites. Lily took a drumstick out of the lunch basket and they shared it, watching each other's mouths move in rhythm, watching each other's tongues lick greasy lips . . .

And his words, "I love being with you, love the way I feel when I'm with you" gave her renewed hope that he loved her, loved her. And, as always, she wondered—if he didn't love her—why he always seemed so comfortable and natural with her.

He held her in his arms and whispered, "It feels like Eden, doesn't it?"

She couldn't speak.

He touched her hair, stared into her eyes. "If only . . ."

She blinked away tears and whispered, "I know."

They stood to leave and David pulled her to him again and whispered in her ear, "But it's a nice idea, don't you think? Just the two of us wandering naked in our own world?"

"Son?"

"What?" David tore his eyes from Lily's and looked at his mother.

"I asked if you'd had supper."

He cleared his throat and his face reddened behind a guilty smile. "Yes, ma'am, we ate earlier." He wrapped his arm around Mauma Hattie's shoulders and his eyes twinkled as he spoke. "But I'd sure like some Kiss Cakes."

She pinched his cheeks. "You knew your Mauma Hattie would make 'em for you, didn't you, baby?"

He grinned bashfully. "I hoped you would."

On her way out the door, Mauma Hattie whispered to Lily, "Never once saw that boy turn down Kiss Cakes."

When she returned with a tray of goodies, Grace jumped up and clapped her hands and David almost did the same. Lily smiled at the sight of their expressions, at their love of sweets, at their joyous warmth.

Mrs. Evans poured tea and everyone took a cup and at least one of Mauma Hattie's famed cookies. Lily bit into the puffy morsel and immediately realized why David enjoyed them so. They were almost air, baked meringue, nothing but egg whites and sugar. As she watched him talk animatedly to his mother and spoon sugar into his tea, she laughed quietly to herself, especially when she saw the disturbed look on his mother's face as the woman said, "Son, are you still using so much sugar?"

When he saw that Lily was also observing his habit, he pouted playfully. "Why does everyone want to deny me my one vice?"

But he heard his words and blushed.

"What's a vice, Fish?"

The three adults looked at each other and laughed uncomfortably.

As Lily sipped her tea, she looked at her surroundings. The dying fire's light sparkled on the highly polished rosewood tea table and its sterling service. Family members stared at her through oval glass frames on the walls while military statuettes stood proudly on either side of the mantel clock. A collection of porcelain roses filled a corner etagere.

She felt herself grow sleepy then realized that the room was silent except for Grace's hushed tones and the puppy's nips and chirps. When she set her cup on the tea table and looked up at David, she saw that he was staring at her. Nervously, she looked for his mother then realized that the woman had left them alone. Alone with her family. *Her* family. She absorbed the moment and let herself be lost in David's eyes. *Can you read my mind, David? I love you.*

"Momma!" Grace was standing in front of her, her hands on her mother's cheeks, her voice irritated and demanding, her eyebrows furrowed. "Momma!"

"What?" Lily took the small hands and kissed them. "Yes, baby? I'm sorry, Momma was deep in thought." She glanced at David then blushed at his devilish smile.

Grace plopped down. "How long are you going to stay?"

"I don't know, honey."

David stood and took off his coat then carefully laid it across the back of a chair and walked to Lily and Grace. Kneeling down on one knee, he took one of Grace's hands. "Your momma's going to be here for a week or so, sweetie, but I've got to leave in the morning." Her face darkened. "But I'll be back in a few days with the boys."

In the morning . . . Lily's eyes darkened as Grace's lit up. "I can show them Rebel."

"Who's Rebel?"

"My puppy. I named him that because I heard somebody call you that. Are you a rebel, Fish? I don't know what it means but I like the sound of it."

Lily shook her head and David leaned toward her and whispered in her ear, "Like father, like daughter," then grinned, his eyes sparkling. "I think that's a grand name, Gracie." He nudged Lily. "What do you think?"

His nearness made her light headed. His face was so close that she could feel his breath, and with his sleeves rolled up and the neck of his shirt unbuttoned, Lily felt herself weaken. She slapped him playfully then let her hand linger on his strong arm with its soft brown hair as she eyed him wickedly. "So, you and a dog have the same name." She grinned and popped one of his suspenders.

"You . . ." He tickled her and she squealed then saw her daughter watching them, her eyes dark. Lily shook her head and gave him a playful frown.

Reluctantly, David stood up, but he kept his eyes on Lily's.

"The boys are coming!"

Their moment of family was over. Grace had brought them back to reality. David's eyes softened as he knelt in front of Lily again and whispered, "I'm sorry."

She touched his hand and nodded then turned toward her daughter and forced a smile. "So, you like those guys, huh?"

"Oh, yes. They're so cute and I can make them laugh! Aunt Mary Anne even lets me hold Luke. He's the baby."

Aunt Mary Anne.

What was she thinking coming here? What made her think she could see David with Mary Anne? See him with his children? And now Grace was a part of this family. How on earth would she be able to get through this visit?

She felt stifled and panicky, and she wanted to run far and quickly away. She was an outsider here. She didn't belong. Her own daughter belonged but she didn't.

David saw her anxiety and took charge. "Gracie, I think Rebel needs some fresh air before you two go to bed. Why don't you take him outside and show him to George."

"Okay!" She bounced off the couch and ran out of the room, the pup half in and half out of her arms.

They watched her run off then Lily laughed as she spoke. "When did you get the pup? He wasn't with us on our trip, was he?"

"I had George get him while I was gone. Cute, huh?"

She nodded. "What kind of dog is it? I don't believe I've ever seen one before. I hope it's a strong breed."

"It's a beagle. They've been in England for a long time but are just coming over here. Gracie may have one of the first ones."

"You shouldn't spend that kind of money on her."

His face glowed but his eyes were distant. "But I need to, Lil." He sat beside her and took her hand. "But don't worry about the pup. I took Grace's spirit into account when I chose him." His eyes twinkled as he kissed her hand.

They laughed quietly but Lily looked at him and shivered.

He held her hands as he spoke. "I know this is hard for you." He looked into her eyes as he kissed her hands.

"No, you have no idea. You have everything, everything . . . even my daughter. You have no idea . . ." She looked toward the ceiling but couldn't stop the tears. "Oh, my God, David, you will never know . . ."

He put his arms around her and shushed her as he patted her back. But his hands soon moved to her face and in seconds their mouths and tongues were loving each other while David's hands caressed her breasts and his lips moved down her neck.

"This will *not* happen in my house."

They jumped apart and David leapt to his feet.

Mrs. Evans walked toward them. "What if the child had been with me? Or one of the servants? I will not have Grace confused or the servants given fuel for gossip. Do you both understand?"

They nodded.

"I'm so sorry, Mrs. Evans. I never meant to disgrace your home or abuse your hospitality."

"Mother . . ."

"Am I going to have to watch the two of you like you're cats in heat? No. I think you're both more responsible than that. And you, David, you have too much to lose. I sympathize with the feelings you two share but you mustn't act on them. You know that, don't you?" She put a hand to her face and shook her head. "What were you thinking to travel together? What's wrong with you, David? I raised you better than this. I will not allow our family to be ridiculed. If it weren't for the child, I'd ask you to leave, Lily."

Lily nodded, feeling the daggers in her heart. Not her and Grace, just her....

David walked to his mother and hugged her. "I'm sorry." His arm was around her shoulders as he looked at Lily. "We . . ."

She raised a hand. "I don't want to hear it." Her handkerchief to her lips, she touched her son with shaky fingers. "Please, son, don't throw it all away. Please." The formidable woman suddenly appeared fragile and tiny as her son embraced her again, and Lily could see the pain in both sets of eyes, the strain in both faces. But the woman quickly regained her dignity and stood on her own. "You are going home tomorrow, aren't you? And staying a few days?"

David nodded as he knelt again in front of Lily, taking her hands in his and trying to make her smile. "Just think, with me gone, you'll have Grace all to yourself." He squeezed her hands and saw tears drop. "Except for Rebel, of course."

She nodded.

"Well, you'd better get some sleep then. I'll make sure Mauma Hattie has something for you to eat before you go."

Still watching Lily, David stood and walked to his mother and kissed her cheek then whispered, "I'll go say good night to Grace."

"No. I'll go get her." She looked at the two of them as she shut the door. "Say your good nights. Quickly."

They sat on the sofa, their hands locked together. "Oh, Lily . . ." He freed a hand and touched the curl by her cheek. She closed her eyes and willed his mouth to meet hers then fell into a blissful fog when it did. They held each other tightly as their mouths opened again and again in a search for satisfaction they couldn't, wouldn't, find.

And all too soon Mrs. Evans's voice filled the hallway and they hesitantly pulled away from each other. Lily touched David's lips with a fingertip then pulled it away when the door opened.

CHAPTER 27

The time with Grace was fun and lively, but Lily thought of David every minute. And though Mrs. Evans gave her many hours alone with her daughter, Lily found the times shared with Mrs. Evans and Mauma Hattie just as enjoyable—actually more so. It broke her heart to accept it, but she had lost the special bond she'd once shared with her precious daughter.

"Why does she call him Fish?"

It was a brisk sunny day. Lily and Mrs. Evans sat in white wicker rockers in an ornate gazebo sipping tea out of dainty cups. It was mid-afternoon and Grace was just yards away swinging on a rope swing and playing with Rebel. Her youthful squeals broke Lily's heart when they used to bring her her greatest joy.

Mrs. Evans smiled as she thought about her youngest son. "When David was a little boy, he would follow his father around almost constantly, begging him to take him fishing, saying, 'Fish, Daddy, fish' until Mr. Evans gave in and took him." She smiled. "How he loved to go fishing and how his little face glowed when his father took him." She blinked rapidly. "But Mr. Evans was a very busy man and often ignored little David." She swallowed hard and her voice cracked. "And there were many times that David's brother or one of the servants would find him sitting all by himself in the boat sobbing his tiny heart out. It was such a heartbreaking sight that whoever found him usually took him fishing."

She sniffed and looked pensive. "But, of course, it wasn't the fishing that little David wanted as much as it was a chance to be with his father. He adored the man." She shook her head and began rocking her chair. "His siblings call him 'Fish' to taunt him and he's always hated it until little Grace overheard Richard say it and picked it up." She smiled sweetly. "Now David loves the name—but only from her. He can't stand it when one of his boys copies her and says it. He does so love being called 'Papa'." She looked out at

Grace. "How thrilled he would be to hear her call him that." She sighed. "But since that's not possible, he lights up every time he hears her say 'Fish'. That will have to do."

She turned in her chair to face Lily. "I know you don't want to hear this again, but I feel I must repeat it. David cannot be hurt by this. I probably shouldn't say this, but I know he loves you . . ."

Lily's mouth fell open as a warmth shot through her body. Had she heard correctly?

" . . . but he loves Mary Anne too and she's his wife. I don't know how he divides his affections. I don't know how it's even possible. Maybe it's like the love a parent has for more than one child, but when he first met Mary Anne he beamed for weeks. I'd never seen him so happy, and I remember him telling me that he'd found the perfect wife. We rarely saw him after that because he was either at his school or with her. He's probably told you that we thought them too young to marry, but they seemed so determined that we capitulated."

She was quiet and seemed deep in thought. "All his life he'd been so carefree, even with all his serious plans, then he graduated and seemed to change overnight. Meeting Mary Anne seemed to make him happy again for awhile, but by the time they were engaged, he'd grown serious again, almost desperate to make her happy. He bends over backwards for her." She shook her head and frowned. "Much too much in my opinion, almost as if he's trying to prove to everyone that their marriage was right." She looked directly into Lily's eyes. "Or as if he's trying to appease a guilty conscience."

Lily lowered her eyes but the woman's touch made her look up. "Dear Lily, I'm saying these things only to prepare you for their arrival together. Mary Anne adores David and is quick to display affection and I fear you're going to be hurt. Do you think you can manage?"

Lily kept a tight hold on the woman's hand but ignored her question. She didn't want to think of Mary Anne's love for David, all she wanted was to hear the words, *I know he loves you.* "Mrs. Evans, I can't tell you how much your kindness has meant to me and I may have no right to ask this, but how do you know that David loves me? He's never said the words."

"And he may never do so." She squeezed Lily's hand again. "Oh my dear, he shouldn't. What good would it do?" She shook her head. "I knew I shouldn't have told you. Don't you see how dwelling on such thoughts will only make your pain harder to bear? I pity the heartache you and my son share, I truly do, but I cannot condone your relationship. I believe that marriage is a sacred bond that mustn't be broken. So does David." She patted Lily's hand. "In our family, we believe that a person's word is his bond and mustn't be severed. David's given his word to Mary Anne and God. He mustn't declare his feelings for you and he must work to overcome them."

Lily nodded and attempted to speak while damming a flood of tears. "Then why are you so kind to Grace and me? Why do you allow me to stay in your home?" Lily worried that her tears would upset Grace but once the tears began, she couldn't stop them. Her chest heaved with convulsive sobs and she felt the ground opening beneath her. And she wished it would, wished it would swallow her so she wouldn't have to hurt this much ever again.

"Oh my dear. Isn't that obvious?" She nodded at Grace. "As much as you love my son and that darling girl, I love my son and his children. I hurt when he hurts, when they hurt. I don't know what to say to you, Lily. I'm sorry for your situation." She looked away wistfully. "And I know how easy he is to love." She patted Lily's hand. "I am sorry for you. I can tell you love him very much."

Lily nodded as tears rushed down her cheeks. "Yes. I've tried not to but it's impossible."

Mrs. Evans sighed and nodded toward Grace. "And now you never will. But we all have burdens to bear. I'm sorry my son is yours."

"Mommy?" Grace was touching Lily's face. "What's wrong, Mommy?" She looked at her grandmother. "What's wrong, Nana? What's wrong with Mommy?"

Lily wrapped her arms around her daughter and pulled her close, smelled the sunshine in her hair, felt the soft innocence. Perhaps she'd just felt self-pity before. Perhaps her daughter did miss her, did still love her. "Mommy's okay, darling." Lily sniffed and wiped her nose then took a deep breath. "I've just missed you so much." She hugged her even tighter and consciously memorized the moment.

Grace pushed strands of hair from Lily's face then kissed each of her cheeks. "That's how Fish says princes kiss their princesses." She stood back and smiled.

"Oh?"

"Uh-huh. That's how he kisses me sometimes."

"Do you love Fish, Momma?"

"What do you mean?"

"Well, I remember when he visited us and . . ." Her voice rose in excitement as she recalled the event. "Remember? I got to eat birthday cake for breakfast because he did. It was both our birthdays, remember? Then he came back the next day and he and Tom got so mad at each other . . ." Her brows furrowed and her voice trailed off into childish elaboration.

The two women looked at each other. How could David have thought a small child could keep quiet about what she'd seen? Obviously he'd not thought it through when he'd taken his daughter.

"Tom never came back, did he?" The child's lower lip stuck out and her big brown eyes filled with tears.

Lily pulled Grace onto her lap. "Tom's fine, sweetheart, but Momma doesn't like to remember those couple of days because—except for your birthday—they weren't very happy ones. Fish doesn't want to remember them either. Do you think you can forget them too?"

She was shaking her head and pulling away. "But I liked them, Momma. It was the first time I saw Fish. Remember? I made Ruthie jealous because I saw the handsome soldier before she did." She turned to her grandmother and grinned. "Ruthie didn't get cake for breakfast either, just me and Fish."

"I tell you what . . . don't forget them but keep them here," Lily touched the child's chest, "inside your heart. Those days will be ours alone—yours, mine, and Fish's. I'm not asking you to lie, Grace, just don't tell anyone about Fish coming to our house. Do you think you can do that?"

Her dramatic nodding made her curls bounce.

"Good." Lily hugged her tightly and kissed her cheek, then lost her happiness when Grace stretched her legs to the ground and returned to her play.

Mrs. Evans had lost all color. "Oh, my heavens. I fear there's a lot my son has hidden from me."

Lily nodded and thought: *And you wouldn't want to hear about it.*

"I'd not thought about what she's seen and heard."

Lily smiled wanly. "I guess we're at her mercy."

When would Grace innocently mention the incident to Mary Anne or her children? The matriarch shook her head and sat back in her rocker. Lily saw the woman bite her bottom lip and thought of all the times she'd seen David and Grace do the same. *Oh, David, we've made quite a mess.*

Voices penetrated the afternoon breeze and Grace ran toward the front of the house. Mrs. Evans looked at Lily. "I think they're here."

Lily panicked. Her mouth went dry, her stomach churned, and her eyes filled with tears again. Could she do this? Why hadn't she left? But it was too late. *You've been through worse than this, Lily.* But had she? Had she really?

Mrs. Evans helped her stand and the strong arm around her waist gave Lily some courage, as did her words, "You'll be fine, girl. Stand tall. You're Grace's mother. Be proud."

Lily kept telling herself that she was a strong woman, that she'd been on her own since she was thirteen. She even ran her own business.

But she wasn't prepared for Mary Anne.

She wasn't prepared for the way the petite woman floated across the lawn, her skirts billowing gracefully behind her as she followed two little boys who came giggling and running around the house. She wasn't prepared for the silky voice that rippled through the rowdy noise of children.

"Mother Evans!" With her white arms stretched out in greeting, Mary Ann resembled an angel flying through the air.

Lily stared at the hair that was black as night, eyes that were almost the same, and a face as perfectly proportioned as any she had ever seen—even down to that perfect rosebud mouth. As the knot in her stomach tightened, she remembered David's description and how it had broken her heart. And she remembered the intimacy that had followed.

But it was when the smell of jasmine filled the air that Lily felt her newly fortified defenses crumble. He likes jasmine. Had he been thinking of Mary Anne?

"How are you, dear?" Mrs. Evans greeted Mary Anne with a warm embrace then knelt down to greet her grandsons who rushed her skirts.

Mary Anne stuck a hand toward Lily. "I'm Mary Anne, David's wife."

David's wife. Lily swallowed hard and accepted Mary Anne's hand, noticing that it was small and dainty in size but surprisingly red and rough.

"I'm Lily . . . Morgan."

Mary Anne looked curiously at Lily as she pulled her shawl tighter around her shoulders. "I'm glad to meet you." She finally broke her stare and looked out at the lawn where the boys were playing with Grace and Rebel.

Lily followed her gaze and watched Rebel jumping and barking, obviously relishing the attention. Like his owner, Lily thought. And its owner's parents?

"She's a beautiful child."

"What?" Lily realized that Mary Anne had spoken again. "Oh, thank you."

Again Mary Anne watched Grace. "And she so obviously takes after the Evanses. Exactly how are you related?"

"I'm a distant cousin, very distant. I only discovered our relationship recently. I think I'm from the only clan that didn't come to South Carolina." Lily laughed nervously.

Mary Anne nodded as she continued to stare at Lily. "I so wanted a girl this last time and I know David did too." She sighed. "But he said it was just as well that we had boys because a war was no atmosphere in which to rear a daughter. And we do so love our little boys." Her attention turned again to the children.

Had David really made such a statement? Lily found it odd. Yet it sounded like something he would say to make Mary Anne feel better, and it was obvious he wanted a daughter by the way he adored Grace, and for a moment Lily reveled in the knowledge that she had a part of David that Mary Anne didn't.

But it was a part he couldn't claim.

And a part she no longer had either. David couldn't claim her, but he had her. Lily could claim her but . . .

149

And David's comment was so like what a man would say, not realizing that war hurts sons more than daughters, not realizing that a mother's heart is wrenched asunder each time a son is taken from her. No, David wouldn't understand. But Mary Anne's adoration of her sons was apparent and Lily knew how desperately she would hurt if she lost them. Was any cause truly that worthy?

And what of David? Lily had heard many Southern women say that they'd rather be widows than shamed by husbands who wouldn't fight. Did Mary Anne feel that way? And Mrs. Evans? Was the "Glorious Cause" worth the lives of either of her sons? Lily shuddered. David was so loved by so many. What a chasm of heartache his death would cause.

She shook the gloomy thought out of her head. "Well, Gracie certainly adores them."

"Yes. And they play so well together. Cousins are good to have, don't you think?"

Lily nodded but wasn't really listening. She was looking for David.

And there he was, coming around the corner, carrying a baby with one arm and assisting a toddler with the other. Lily felt her heart stop.

Damn her adoration of this man, another woman's husband.

The elder Mrs. Evans rushed out to meet her son and grandsons, Mary Anne right behind her. Lily stayed at the gazebo and watched, and noticed that both women kissed David before taking a child. What had his mother said? *"And I know how easy he is to love."*

David reluctantly released his youngest children. "Don't go far with those guys. I want to spend time with them too."

"Fish!"

"Papa!"

Instantly attacked by the three older children and the puppy, David picked up each child and swung them around causing squeals of delight. As she watched, Lily knew that this was the life David should lead—and it didn't include her. No matter how she daydreamed about it and wished for it, this wasn't her family and never would be. If it weren't for David's blood running through Grace's veins, Lily would be an outcast to this family, lower than an outcast. And even though they loved Grace, how would they feel if they knew how David and Lily had met, if they knew what Lily was?

She hated herself for pretending to be someone she wasn't. She hated herself for devouring the kindness and acceptance as fast as it was offered. She hated herself because she enjoyed it, wanted it, would miss it.

But mostly she hated herself for loving another woman's husband.

As she watched David with his children, Lily found it hard to believe that he could cheat on this wonderful family. Why had he? Was she foolish to think he loved her or was she just a handy substitute who wore the same fragrance? Was he really as noble as she thought or as low as they come?

As she wallowed in self-pity, David came toward her, children hanging on both of his legs, the pup barking. Taking off his coat as he approached, he handed it to Lily and purposely touched her hand. Although laughing with happy exhaustion, his eyes met hers and he whispered, "Are you okay?"

Her smile was sweet, her voice was low. "Go to hell."

CHAPTER 28

His eyes darkened and his brows knitted. "What? What's wrong?"

The children whined for his attention as they clung to his legs.

"Lily? Please."

"Your family's waiting for you."

Both Mary Anne and Mrs. Evans were watching so David quickly resumed his play with the children though his smile wasn't as broad as before.

As Lily watched him walk away, she lifted his jacket to her nose and smelled it then hugged it to her stomach as she sat down on the steps to watch him. He tickled one child then another while encouraging Rebel to run after each one. Although she would never admit it to him, Lily knew that David had been right to bring Grace to this happy home. He gave her the same attention and love he gave the boys and his very presence made Grace's eyes glow just as it did Lily's. Yes, her daughter was happy here. Would Lily be able to take her from this family?

"I'll take that."

"What?"

Mary Anne was reaching for David's coat. "I said I'll take that. He's always handing me his coat."

"I don't mind."

"But I'm his wife and expect to be a pack mule. It was rude of him to expect you to do the same."

Lily watched the coat slip from her fingers to Mary Anne's.

David's wife took the coat then hooked her arm through Lily's. "Let's go inside. It's getting a little chilly for the babies and they're getting hungry."

"Mommy, Mommy, look!"

David was holding Grace on his shoulders. He was smiling but looked tired and Lily walked toward them. "I think you're overtaxing your fa . . . uncle, Gracie, and you're a little big to expect him to carry you around."

"Aw, Momma!"

David was helping her down. "Actually, Gracie, I am getting a little tired. Fish is getting old."

"Even though your birthday's the same as mine, you're a lot older than me, right?"

The panic on David's face gave Lily devilish delight as she knelt in front of her daughter. "Remember what Momma asked you not to talk about this afternoon?"

"Uh-huh." She nodded emphatically. "But I didn't say anything about him eating my birthday cake."

Lily dared look into David's panic-stricken eyes and whispered as she stood up, "What did I tell you about keeping those pants buttoned?" She smiled at Mary Anne who'd joined them. "I was just convincing Grace to give your husband a rest."

Mary Anne smiled and patted David's shoulder then used her fingers to get grass out of his hair before playfully touching his lips. Her love for him was painfully obvious, as was her hold on him. Did she suspect anything?

Lily wondered what affection he would be showing his wife if his mistress weren't there, and she loved him for caring enough to abstain for her sake.

But the sight of them together caused Lily to tremble and look toward the elder Mrs. Evans for courage. Through a haze of tears she saw the woman's sad smile and found herself fortified. Blinking away tears and standing a little taller, Lily took her daughter's hand. "Come on, sweetie. I think you could use a bath before dinner."

David's siblings and their spouses laughed easily and loved playing games and singing. They were fun and friendly and Lily enjoyed them all. And she found it both amusing and disconcerting how their eyes darted back and forth between her, David, and Grace as they searched for traces of Lily in Grace—and found none.

Except for the vile crime of owning slaves (for which Lily would not excuse them), she could find no fault in any of them, though she tried desperately. Why weren't they cruel to their slaves? Why weren't they pompous and boring? She wanted to leave the Evans home with a feeling of self-righteousness. She also wanted to feel justified in memorizing conversations that she would later pass on to Chester Biggs.

She searched especially hard for flaws in Mary Anne. Oh, the woman talked and laughed a bit too much and was a little bossy, but she didn't gossip or mistreat her children, and her love for David and his family was genuine. More than anything, Lily was surprised at the woman's ceaseless energy and constant activity. Why, Lily wondered, did David worry so much about her?

153

This was no shy wallflower but a determined and intelligent woman as capable as any man of running a home.

She was especially busy around David and even through her envy, Lily found his effect on women quite comical. Mary Anne, his mother, Grace, Mauma Hattie, the other female servants, his sisters—all women fawned over him. No wonder he'd chosen the military—it was his only way of getting away from all the female attention. But it was obvious that he loved it and he flirted shamelessly with them all.

It was also obvious that he adored Mary Anne, albeit almost reverently. She made him laugh. She made everyone laugh. And when David's sister played the piano, Mary Anne sang and she sang flawlessly. She was as close to perfection as a human being could be. She and David did, indeed, make a perfect couple.

So why did he cheat? Lily asked herself that question again and again.

Especially at night when visions of David loving Mary Anne tortured her and she cried as she beat her pillow and cursed him, all the while swearing that she would quit loving him yet knowing she never could.

She did her best to avoid being alone with him, even avoided eye contact when they were in the same room. But, somehow, one evening found them in the parlor alone except for the children.

Dominated by a large picture window that faced the gardens, the room was the favorite of the family. Mahogany and damask overstuffed chairs and sofas were arranged in small groups, tapestries covered the walls, and a piano filled one corner. There were several tables for playing cards and even a telescope for viewing the stars.

David and Lily were watching the children from sofas on either side of the carpet in front of the fireplace when the children abruptly ran off and the room was suddenly silent. Lily knew she should leave, told herself to leave, but she didn't. She picked up a magazine and pretended to read it.

David stood and paced then returned to the sofa.

Lily knew he was watching her.

"Are you okay?"

"Yes." She spoke casually and turned pages.

"I've wanted to talk to you—alone."

She looked at him, her eyes wide. "I can't believe you've even considered it."

"Of course I have."

She gave him a defiant look. "Why?"

The poor man didn't know that Lily's "why" was an all-encompassing female "why." Why do you cheat on your wife when she's so perfect? Why do you take such chances? Tell me, David. I need to know.

But he, of course, didn't know the meaning behind her "why?"

"After your suggestion the day I returned as to where I should go, I've been more than a bit curious about the reason for such hostility. I'm worried about you."

She shrugged. "No need." With feigned concentration on the magazine, she added, "I believe you have more than enough to command your worries."

"I know this has been hard on you, and . . ."

"What's been hard on Lily? Family?" Richard chuckled as he sat down beside Lily, crossing his long legs and taking care that his cigar smoke wafted away from her face. "Family can be quite tedious."

She looked at him and smiled. "But yours is so friendly." She liked this man, really liked him. His darkly tanned skin barely covered a frame so tall that he seemed to fold and unfold when sitting and standing. His hair was darker than David's, black with gray, and his face was long where David's was round. He had bright green eyes that flashed when he chuckled, which was often, and he was always dressed in an almost foppish manner. Even his uniforms were adorned somehow—a plume in the hat, a stickpin in his collar.

"What do you mean 'yours'? You're part of this group, Lily—though you may not want to be." He laughed again then nodded toward David. "I know why he's apologizing. It's for boring you to death, right?"

She and David were staring at each other.

When they didn't laugh, Richard tried again. "What have you said to offend our cousin, David? Or should I call you Fish?" He grinned. "You know he detested that name before Gracie came along."

Mention of Grace got her attention and Lily smiled.

Richard raised an eyebrow and took a puff off his cigar. "That little girl of yours has charmed the socks off of everyone around here. When this war is over and things get back to normal, she'll be the belle of all the balls. Our mother will see to that." He puffed on the cigar again then looked at them and frowned. "My, but you two are stimulating conversationalists." He winked at Lily. "I know what will get little brother's dander up." He stretched one arm on the back of the sofa. "Tell me Colonel, I've heard rumors that Longstreet wants you to replace Jones but Davis is being contrary. Is that true?"

Richard was right, for David's demeanor changed instantly. His hands formed fists and his eyes squinted, but he took a calming breath before he spoke. "Yes. Longstreet and Davis are in some sort of political struggle, something to do with Bragg. Anyhow, Old Pete told me that he told Davis I was the best colonel in the army and had the best regiment."

Richard was smiling and winked at Lily again. "He's right, of course."

"Of course." She smiled at David.

Richard stood and laughed as he looked down at her. "My brother's a proud man, Lily. I don't know if you've noticed that."

She was still looking at David and, despite her determination to hate him, her pride in him won out and she smiled and said, "I'm sure he has a right to be."

The smile David returned was so warm and appreciative that Richard's eyes widened and his brows rose as he looked at each of them. "Oh, I agree. He's good. I hate to add to that ego of yours, little brother, but if Davis would listen to you and Longstreet, we'd have this thing won in proper time."

David and Lily continued to stare at each other as if the only people in the room.

Richard coughed and spoke louder. "But I am beginning to wonder about his motives. Can you believe it, cousin, that he actually talks of abolishing slavery?"

"What?" Lily looked up at Richard. Had she heard him correctly? Could it be true? She looked at David, at his downcast eyes and reddened face. *Oh, David, you have been listening to me, hearing me!* Lily felt her heart would burst from the joy of it and she wanted to throw her arms around him, kiss him, thank him.

"I see that got your attention." Richard laughed but Lily sensed he wasn't happy, that he was hiding his anger at David's changing beliefs. "Absurd, isn't it? He says it's inevitable anyway, but I don't know who he thinks will work that land for him for what he can afford to pay. He's not exactly bringing in a bundle at that school. I've spoken to him on numerous occasions. We even got into a bit of a row the first time."

Lily stared at David and walked toward him as if drawn. "Actually, Richard, I think he's right." She stopped in the middle of the carpet, in front of the fireplace where Richard was standing. David was standing just a few feet away, his eyes locked with hers, and Lily had to stop herself from throwing her arms around him.

"You can't be serious."

Lily continued to look into David's eyes as she spoke. "Yes, I am. I know it's not a popular opinion and I've hesitated to say anything, but . . ." She knew David worried about her words, ". . . I am against slavery." She looked at Richard and turned on her charm. "But you're fighting for more than that, aren't you?"

He coughed, looked at David, then flicked cigar ashes in the fireplace. "Of course." His eyes darkened. "You're not the one putting such ideas in his head, are you?"

She felt her face turn red and she stammered, "I doubt it, though he does know of my feelings."

"Well," Richard cleared his throat, "this is certainly interesting and quite unexpected. Who'd have thought we'd have abolitionists in the family?" He barely hid his anger when he spoke again. "All I can say is that it's a good thing Father's not around to hear of it."

David stared at Lily as he spoke. "Father always said I walked a different path from the rest of the family." He blinked rapidly and Lily saw him struggle. "I was never quite what he expected." He looked at Richard. "A bit of a disappointment."

Richard put his arm around his brother's shoulders. "Now, now, let's not get melancholy." His arm still around David's shoulders, he smiled radiantly at Lily. "We have a beautiful guest to entertain."

David looked at her and smiled sheepishly. "Yes, we certainly do." Again, his eyes locked with hers.

After clapping his hands and saying, "That's better," Richard again saw the tension between his brother and Lily. "Am I missing out on something here?"

They jumped nervously and David answered. "I'm sorry, brother, did you say something?"

"Well, obviously nothing important." He waved a hand toward each of them, the cigar smoke forming waves in the air. "What's the secret between you two?"

The moment passed and Lily and David giggled and David slapped Richard on the back. "Nothing, big brother. Just a secret between cousins."

"But *I'm* a cousin." Richard exaggerated a pout and they all laughed.

"Did you learn that face from Gracie?" Lily was laughing so hard she hurt.

He continued his charade and nodded in Gracie's exaggerated manner.

"Stop it, Richard! Please!" She was holding her stomach.

He grabbed her hands and twirled her around. "I certainly didn't know we had any cousins this pretty, did you little brother?"

"No, I surely didn't."

The twinkle in David's eyes made her weak. He was carefree and full of mirth, the way he'd been on the train, and Lily wanted the moment to last forever. They continued to look at each other and the room became suddenly quiet.

"Well." Richard broke the silence as he walked to the fireplace and tapped his cigar ashes over the pit. "Have you heard from Buford?"

"What? Oh, yes. He's been recuperating in Charleston and we'd planned to meet in town tomorrow and make the return trip together." David looked at Lily. "But my plans have changed and I won't be able to. I've already left a message for him at the hotel."

Richard followed David's eyes as Lily did her best to cover the anguish she felt. "So Lily has to make the journey by herself?"

CHAPTER 29

"Yes, I'm afraid so." His brows furrowed as he looked at her. "I'm sorry."

Lily blinked rapidly and shrugged. "Actually, this might work out for the best. I can get some shopping done."

Richard smiled and his eyes twinkled. "And you ladies do like your shopping."

"Did I hear that someone's going shopping? What a luxury." Mary Anne floated in the room and wrapped her arms around David's waist then looked up into his eyes. "I wondered where you'd gotten off to."

Feeling her face blanch and her legs shake, Lily quickly sat down on the sofa.

Richard walked to her side. "I was telling Dave that Lily's probably appreciative of the reprieve from his company on the return trip so she can buy some pretty garments in our fair capital." He looked at Lily and winked. "I dare say the men in town are in for a treat."

David glowered.

Lily stood and took Richard's arm then smiled up at him as she spoke to David. "Cousin, you didn't tell me your brother was such a flirt."

"I never knew he was." David's voice was flat, cold, angry.

"What's wrong, little brother? You appear a bit perturbed."

"Nothing. Not a thing."

"He gets grumpy when he's tired." Mary Anne pulled him closer and kissed his cheek. "Did I hear correctly? I knew we had to bid brother good bye in the morning, but you're leaving us too, cousin?"

"Yes." Lily forced forced herself to look directly at David. "I'm sorry we won't be keeping each other company, but I hope you have a safe journey."

"You too."

"And I too, wish you a safe journey." Mary Anne released David's arm long enough to kiss Lily's cheek. "You too, brother." She kissed Richard's cheek then tugged at David. "Let's go to bed, sweetheart."

"You're right, Miss Mary Anne, I think it's time we all slumbered." Richard offered Lily his arm. "May I escort you, cousin?"

"Certainly."

As Lily and Richard took the grand staircase from the cozy parlor to the long hallway of bedrooms, Lily found out where, when, and how several regiments were moving, even their numbers. She also learned that David was going back to Virginia.

"All kidding aside, David truly is a special one." They were standing outside Lily's door. "I honestly believe we'd win this thing if he were in charge. He gets so excited, you know, about anything that appears promising." He shook his head. "But he's going to have a tough time getting the promotions he deserves." He frowned. "I'm afraid he's in for some disappointments. You can't get ahead when your biggest supporter butts heads with the president." He put his hands on Lily's shoulders. "I'm sorry, my dear, to bore you with all this war talk, and I'm sorry we're going in different directions tomorrow else I would take great delight in escorting you in my brother's absence." He kissed her cheek and smiled. "Good night."

"Yes, that would have been nice for me too, but I've had such a nice visit." She stood on tiptoe to kiss his cheek. "Thank you."

The house bustled with good bye preparations. Richard was going south to Charleston and Lily was going north—alone. David had to be back at camp soon and had seemed so anxious to see Jonathan that Lily wondered what was important enough to change his plans.

She spent most of the night watching Grace sleep, weeping silently so as not to wake her. *Oh my precious little girl. I'm going to miss you so very much.* As Lily watched her, she thought, as she always did, of David—the fluttering lashes and furrowed brow—and today she was leaving both of them at the same time. Yes, she'd planned to take Gracie with her but . . .

Although it was barely daylight, Lily tiptoed down to Mauma Hattie's room and tapped on the door. "Mauma Hattie? Am I disturbing you?"

The woman opened the door and grinned. "No, child, never." She motioned for Lily to sit at a small table then gave her a cup and poured tea out of a kettle from the fireplace. "It's been such a joy having that child of yours here."

"That's one of the reasons I wanted to talk to you before I left. I want to thank you for treating her so kindly, for taking such good care of her. As much as I miss her, I see that this family is good for her."

Mauma Hattie sat down. "Well, how could I do less for my baby's baby?"

Lily looked into the twinkling eyes. "You know?"

She laughed. "How could anyone not know? I've never seen two people so much alike in this world, and since I raised that sweet boy, I remember him at her age." She shook her head. "It's uncanny, it surely is."

"But . . . what about Mary Anne?"

"That's the sad part of it, now isn't it? None of us wants to hurt that sweet lady or those darling baby boys, no ma'am. Hurtin' her would be hurtin' Master David's reputation, and I'd go to my death protecting him." She sipped her tea. "I doubt that the Lord looks kindly on what the two of you have done, but that little girl is surely a gift from God. There's nothing else that sweet child could be."

Lily put her hands on those of the other woman. "Thank you, Mauma Hattie, thank you. I never meant to hurt anyone, but David and I met before he met Mary Anne. I know he loves her so I don't know why he came back after he met her. I want to think he loves me, but . . ." The woman was nodding and smiling and Lily felt a surge of hope. She squeezed the woman's hands, "Does he, Mauma Hattie, does he?"

"Now, now, that's not something we should talk about." Her eyes twinkled again and she held up a coin. "Have you ever noticed that there are two different pictures on a coin but they go together and can't be separated? There's folks like that." She laughed and put the coin in her apron. "'Course you know he's a soulful man, a Godly man, and never had a tolerance for weakness in anyone, 'specially hisself, so he'll punish hisself for wrongs long after our Lord's forgiven him—and he'll be a varmint for any poor soul around him. He's talked to me, you know."

Lily's mouth dropped open. "About us?"

She nodded. "Came to me with tears in those precious eyes telling me of what a sinner he is. I tell him again and again that the Lord forgives him but he can't believe it." She stood up and set their cups on a small sideboard then wiped her hands on her apron and sat back down. "'Course he keeps sinnin', don't he, and the Lord don't look kindly on that."

Lily reached across and touched the woman's arm. "It's so hard, Mauma Hattie. I love him so much. Why does the Lord test us so?"

"Now you're askin' a question even Mauma Hattie can't answer." She laughed. "But Master David's a good man and I'll never quit askin' the Lord to settle his soul and give him peace."

Lily shuddered and looked down. "There's no way either of us will have earthly peace."

The gentle woman put her arm around Lily's shoulders. "Now, girl, don't talk like that. Don't get woeful like that handsome boy. None of us knows what the good Lord has in store. Why, who'd have known that Master David would want to give me my freedom?"

"What?" Lily hugged the large woman. "Really? When?"

"Just the other day." She looked upward and smiled at the recollection. "He came in real quiet-like," she looked at Lily, "kinda like he did as a child when he tried to sneak in here to get cookies after his momma'd told him 'no'." She laughed and folded her arms across her chest. "I started to scold him, tease him you know, but I saw tears in his eyes. 'What's wrong, baby?' I asked him, but he just hugged me real tight then whispered, 'I'm sorry'. 'Sorry for what?' I asked him. He looked so sad and his voice was so shaky that he could barely talk. I was gettin' real worried about him when he finally said, 'for us keeping you a slave'."

Lily gasped. He'd spoken to Richard *and* Mauma Hattie.

Mauma Hattie nodded. "I tell you I was surely surprised and asked him what brought on such thoughts. I mean, he's fighting a war to keep my people as slaves and even though I knew he loved me and was a good master, he's never shown any feelings toward freeing us. Anyhow, he can't give me my freedom 'cuz he don't own me—I belong to his mama—but he says he's goin' to talk to her about it. I did ask him where he'd gotten such a notion." She smiled knowingly at Lily. "Want to know what he said?"

Lily nodded, feeling so happy inside that she felt she'd burst.

"He said, 'Someone once asked me how I could love you so much and put so much faith in you yet think you weren't my equal. I gave it a lot of thought and tried to justify everything I'd been taught, but I couldn't. You are every bit my equal if not better'. That's what he said, Miss Lily, on my honor." She put her hand on her chest. "I don't suppose you'd know where he got such ideas or who that 'someone' might be?"

Lily smiled.

"I thought so." She gave Lily a bear hug. "Thank you, darlin', thank you for making my boy a better man."

"Is he the one who gave you the money?"

She nodded. "When I told him how much I loved his wanting to free me, I told him that even if his mama gave me my freedom, I wouldn't leave her, that Mauma Hattie has nowhere to go. I told him that if I was young and pretty I might fly off and try my wings but I'm too old and set in my ways now." She winked. "I did tell him, though, that I wouldn't mind knowing I'm free and I wouldn't mind having a few coins to buy pretty things with. That's when he laughed and gave me some money, includin' the coin I showed you.

"'Besides,' I told him, 'how could Mauma Hattie go off and leave her baby Grace?'" She shook her head and smiled. "I wouldn't leave that baby, no ma'am."

"That's another thing I want to ask you about . . ." Lily found tears in her eyes once again. "Grace . . . she seems a stranger to me now. I've missed her so very much yet she almost ignores me. I want to take her home and was planning to today but now . . ."

Mauma Hattie nodded. "I feared as much for you. You know as well as anyone," she winked at Lily, "probably more, how that man can wrap himself around your heart. Your little lady isn't any different and he's a daddy to her, even if she doesn't know he's her real daddy. You've heard of daddy's girls?

Lily nodded.

"Well, that little girl is one of them. They're so very much alike that there's no way they could not grow such strong attachments to each other." The woman rocked a few moments. Lily could tell she was thinking. "As for taking her, I know you want her but why not leave her here for now? She's living a good life and truly happy here. Why not come back when this ole' war is over? I understand you have a husband to take care of?"

Lily nodded and hesitantly began, "And I'm working . . . I'm trying . . ."

"I think I know what you're doing, and it's a good thing."

After a light tapping, the door opened. "Mauma Hattie, have you seen . . . Lily . . ."

The old woman shook her head as she patted David's cheek, her words still aimed at Lily. "You leave things here the way they are, okay? I'll make sure *no one* forgets you." Mauma Hattie winked at them then nodded. "You two better make those good byes real quick." She walked out the door.

He took her hands in his. "I've been looking for you." His brows furrowed as he nodded toward where Mauma Hattie had stood. "What was that all about?"

Lily shook her head and drank in his words and the tortured expression on his face. "Nothing. You've been looking for me?"

"Yes." He put her hands to his mouth and ran his lips over them. "I'm sorry about the trip."

"I know."

"I thought you'd be mad. Aren't you going to ask why I can't go with you?"

She shrugged. "It doesn't matter, does it?"

"I guess not." He put his hands on her cheeks and kissed her quickly but sweetly. "I'll see you soon."

"No, David. It ends today, right now. Mary Anne deserves better. Saul deserves better."

"No! Please don't say that."

"Fish!" Grace appeared at the door with her hands on her hips then shook a finger at David. "Aunt Mary Anne's looking for you."

"Thanks, sweetie," he said though his eyes never left Lily's face. "Think about what you're saying," he whispered as he touched her elbow on his way out of the room, Grace on his heels.

Lily watched the two of them leave then blinked away tears and composed herself, but as she walked to the dining room, she wondered how she'd be able to face David over breakfast. She stopped outside the dining room doors and took several deep breaths to help control her tears. At least, she told herself, everyone will assume that her tears are for Grace, and many of them would be.

But just as she was about to open the doors, she heard voices inside.

"I'm sorry, sweetheart. I know you wanted to see Jonathan, but one more day will mean so much to me." Mary Anne was crying. "I'm so afraid each time you leave that you won't come back."

"I know and I'm so sorry, but don't worry about me. I love you and the boys too much to let anything happen. I owe you and the boys as much as I can possibly give you. Now, Mary Anne, don't frown. I didn't mean 'owe', you know I want to be with you."

"Sometimes I wonder. I see it, David. I see that little thrill in your eyes when you think of battle strategies and giving orders. I knew you wanted all this when we married but . . . and I know you can't help the fact we're at war." Their voices muffled and Lily pictured Mary Anne putting her head on David's chest, David stroking her hair. "It was just so pleasant before."

"Yes, it was."

The silence made Lily shudder as she knew that they were probably kissing. Did he rub Mary Anne's lips and hands with his thumb as he did hers? Did he weave his fingers through her hair when the pins were out and it flowed over her pillow? Did he tickle her with his beard, nibble her with his teeth? Did he smile at their legs when they were tangled together? Lily knew that most people's lovemaking habits were the same with every partner, but *she'd* taught David and felt sick at the thought of him loving Mary Anne the same ways he loved her, the same ways that she'd taught him. But surely there was something, no matter how slight, that he did differently with her. She had to be special somehow.

But even as she longed for such a difference, she cursed herself for wanting it and cursed herself for making vows to forget this man then breaking those vows. Yet even as she stood at that doorway, she made the vow again.

Then took another deep breath, blinked away tears, pinched her cheeks, and knocked on the door.

CHAPTER 30

Lily found Columbia a beautiful and charming city and wished she had someone— David, of course—to show her around, but she managed to see much of the city and do a lot of shopping. And she bought something for everyone—Grace, Ruthie, TJ, Sarah—and of course, Saul. She even bought something to send Mrs. Evans and Mauma Hattie. She felt so close to both women and was truly sorry to bring them such pain.

She had so many good memories of her visit—of Mauma Hattie and Mrs. Evans speaking of David's love for her, of Mauma Hattie and Richard speaking of David's new views on slavery. Such memories filled her mind to such distraction that she exited one of the stores and bumped into a passing stranger. Packages flew into the air then toppled to the ground but the gentleman immediately helped her recover them as she delivered profuse apologies.

"Think nothing of it. A gentleman never minds running into a lovely lady." He tipped his hat and Lily took a good look at the immaculate gray uniform, the reddish hair and beard, the warm smile and twinkling gray eyes, eyes that were even with hers because the man was about her height. "On second thought, I'll carry these," he said as he proceeded to take back the packages. Dumbfounded, she let him as he added, ". . . since we're going to the same destination for lunch, are we not?"

Her eyes were wide.

"I assure you I'm not a rake or scoundrel, but it is noon and you've helped me work up an appetite."

She liked him immediately and had never felt safer with anyone, safe from harm and heartache. "I'd love to, sir. Although I should be treating you."

"Nonsense. Here let me." He took the remaining packages then laughed when he tried to extend a hand for her to shake. "I am sorry. Let me introduce myself. Jonathan Buford."

Almost choking, Lily stammered, "Jona . . .?"

"Oh, my. Has my reputation preceded me?" He chuckled. "Although to my knowledge, I don't have one. I'm quite a blank slate. How do you know of me?"

"I . . . I just came back from visiting the Evans family and Dav . . . they speak very highly of you."

"Oh my yes, the Evanses are the best of folks. Dave and I have been best friends since our academy days. How is he?"

"Yes, they're very nice people. Da . . . he seemed all right." As they walked, Lily found herself hanging onto every word and realizing that she would never rid herself of David Evans. They found a table at the Congaree Hotel and ordered.

"Actually, it's odd that you and I should run into each other today because Dave and I had a meeting planned but he telegrammed that he couldn't make it. I'm very disappointed about that, but we'll see each other in Richmond soon."

"Yes, he told me. Richmond?"

"Yes. He hopes to raise a special regiment and is going to the capital to submit his application."

"He's very ambitious, isn't he?"

Jonathan laughed. "Oh, my, yes! I don't know how well you know him or how much of his past you know, but he and I opened our own military academy. I'm not praising myself, you understand, because it was Dave's idea. I would never have had such grandiose plans at such a young age, but once Dave puts his mind to something, no one or nothing can deter him." He smiled and took a sip of coffee. "Have you known the family long?" Before she could answer, he shook his head and extended his hand across the table. "I am sorry, but I failed to get your name."

Lily met his hand with hers. "I'm sorry. How rude of me. I'm Lily Dundee, but please call me Lily."

The man's eyes widened. "Lily Dundee?"

She laughed nervously. "Now it seems my reputation's preceded me. Have you heard *my* name before?"

His eyes examined her face as their meals were set in front of them. He thanked the waiter then nodded and smiled. "Yes, I most certainly have. Dave's spoken of you." He was suddenly very still.

What had David said? Surely he hadn't . . . "He has?"

"Yes. You're the beautiful wife of Saul Dundee, correct?"

"Well, I'm Saul's wife. Do you know him?"

He nodded. "He went to school with us."

"May I be so bold as to ask why he and David don't get along?"

165

Jonathan's head reared back in robust laughter. "I'm not laughing at you, my dear, but at the delightfully polite and understated manner in which you asked such a formidable and complicated question. That David Evans and Saul Dundee 'don't get along' is putting their childish but very antagonistic—and very real—feud very politely, very politely indeed."

He shook his head then continued. "I think if my friend has any flaws, they are ambition and pride, both which allow this idiocy to continue. I enjoyed Dundee's fellowship at school and I don't know what caused this feud, but whatever it was is kept actively alive by them both. And, I'm sorry to say, the feud seems to have gotten even worse since the war started and that's not healthy for anyone.

"So, in answer to your very polite inquiry—no, I can't tell you because I don't know. I have my suspicions—though I'll not speculate—but Dave's been very hush-hush about this." He sipped his coffee then proceeded to cut his steak.

Lily nodded and tried to eat but couldn't. Her stomach was in knots.

"Not hungry?"

"No, and I'm truly sorry. It's a lovely meal."

He didn't push her, either to eat or talk about herself, but continued to eat in his easy carefree manner that Lily had already grown to admire and enjoy. "But you're not in a hurry to leave?" His fork was in mid-use, his eyebrows raised.

"Oh, no. I'm enjoying myself too much to leave."

"Good, good." As he chewed, his eyes grew serious, as if in deep concentration. "How is Dundee these days?"

"Quite well when I left him."

"Good." He swallowed. "Dave tells me he's quite a changed man since you wed."

She smiled. "Yes, I think he is. I'd like to think I've mellowed him somewhat, but I guess it's the security of marriage."

"Ah, marriage . . ."

"Are you married, Mr. Buford?"

"No, not yet. You see," he smiled, "I'm not in as big a hurry as Dave. Oh, I expect to marry someday, probably to some fat wealthy widow with six children." He laughed again. "You know, David's rush into marriage broke many a heart."

The knots in her stomach tightened. How many other women had there been? Perhaps Lily hadn't been the first after all. "Really?"

"Oh, yes. He's such a good-looking man—and so tall." He laughed at himself. "I can't imagine what you ladies see in tall, good-looking men."

She blushed and looked down at the table.

"The truth is, Mrs. Dundee, I've always envied Dave but always loved him too much to resent what nature bestowed. Besides, he's not vain." He seemed to be thinking and added quickly, "Not too much anyway. Proud, yes, but not about his looks." He laughed quietly, still remembering, his eyes twinkling. "Yes, the ladies adored him—and he liked them too, still does." He nodded as he smiled. "Yes, there's a side of Dave that most people would never suspect."

Lily was dying to know more but knew it was inappropriate to seem too anxious. "When did he have time? He married so young."

"Boys will be boys and we attended many dances and parties. He was a shameless flirt." He saw the surprise on her face and laughed. "Yes, I know it's hard to believe. He seems so shy, but that's also attractive to you ladies, isn't it? Much like this tall thing." His expression was devilish.

Lily shrugged and smiled.

"Ah, don't want to give away any female secrets? I understand. Well, as I said, Dave was quite the flirt all through school, but right after graduation he disappeared for a few days and came back a changed man. He'd always been a little temperamental and sensitive but suddenly he became distant and much too solemn. I've always wondered what happened." He looked at Lily—searching for answers?—then shrugged his shoulders. "Thankfully, a few months later he met Mary Anne and perked up. From outward appearances, he was the old Dave again, the happy David we'd all loved. But I say 'outwardly' because I still saw something uneasy and anxious in him, as if the outward happiness was an act, as if he were trying to convince everyone—especially himself. When the families set their minds against the match, Dave was furious. Everyone, of course, thought it was because he loved Mary Anne so much, and he did—does—love her, but I saw something suspicious under all his bluster."

Jonathan took a deep breath and a sip of water then continued. "Anyhow, after the families relented, the couple became engaged and Dave disappeared again." Jonathan laughed quietly as he searched Lily's eyes. "I just realized that I'm gossiping about my dearest friend to someone I just met. What makes me think you want to know these things and that it's not gossip between us?"

Lily felt herself redden again and smiled halfheartedly. "Because we both care about him?"

He nodded and continued to hold her gaze as he spoke. "Well . . . when he returned this time, I realized that the dour changes would be permanent. His ambition and drive became frenzied and his attentiveness to Mary Anne almost stifling."

"You don't know what happened?"

"I have my suspicions."

"But you don't want to speculate?"

He laughed. "Oh, Mrs. Dundee. I do like your style."

She'd rarely felt so comfortable with anyone. "Has he always been so . . . regimented, so . . ."

Jonathan continued to chuckle. "I think you're asking—and again most politely—if David's always led such an exemplary life." He smiled when she nodded. "I'm often asked that about him. Some people admire his high standards and others think he's a self-righteous bore. Well, the answer is yes and no. He's always held high standards for himself—I tease him that Evans children are breastfed milk and morals—but, believe it or not, he's had to work at it.

"In fact, during our first years at the academy his language was less than angelic." He laughed at the shock on her face. "Yes ma'am, the archangel David used profanity. But before you lose your faith, I must tell you that from the very day he vowed to discontinue the habit, such words have not passed his lips."

But Lily knew better and blushed remembering the times she'd made David so angry that he'd broken that vow.

Jonathan's eyes twinkled. "At least, not to my knowledge." He looked at her for another second or two then took and expelled a deep breath. "So, you can see that I observe my friend objectively yet still love him although I admit that some aspects of his character are hard to accept." He saw her surprise. "Yes, I admit that it's hard to spend time with someone so driven to perfection. So driven, in fact, that when he acts against his better judgment, his eyes glisten. Strangest thing. From guilt or excitement I don't know, but I discovered that about him back in our first years of school together."

All those times she'd seen his eyes glisten . . . She looked up to see Jonathan examining her face. He nodded. "I, too, strive to be a better person but not with the same zeal that drives him. My goodness, I even enjoy an occasional mint julep but alcohol's never touched our friend's lips."

Her giggle made him laugh and he leaned back in his chair. "I'm beginning to think there may be many things about my old friend that I don't know." At seeing her panic, he reached across the table and patted her hand. "Don't worry, my dear. You and I are two friends sharing loving memories of a third friend and nothing we say will leave this table.

"But, seriously, I worry about him. He's always been in too much of a hurry. I don't know how many times I've told him to slow down and enjoy himself. My goodness, he has four children already!"

Lily looked down at her lap.

He wiped his mouth and became very still. "I hope you'll forgive me for staring at you so often during our meal, but I'm quite enchanted with you." He patted her hand again and looked into her eyes when she looked up. "Don't worry. I'm not making advances, though I might were you not married and . . . but Dave has spoken so often of you. . . ."

Her hand jumped involuntarily and they both looked at it then Jonathan smiled and looked at her intently as he'd done several times, as though he were trying to tell her something. When she opened her mouth to speak, he nodded. "Yes, many times."

Her heart raced. "Really?"

He nodded and smiled sweetly. "Let's just say that you're held in very high esteem by our friend, very high."

She was desperate to hear more, but when she opened her mouth to speak, Jonathan interrupted. "I think we've said enough, don't you?" He stood and pulled out her chair then put money on the table. "If you'll permit me, I'll escort you, and your parcels, to the . . .?"

"Train station."

"Train station it is."

Lily was so confused and jittery that she heard little of the small talk they shared on their walk. Jonathan helped her get settled on the train then kissed her hand. She kissed his cheek. "Thank you . . . for everything."

"You're most welcome. I look forward to seeing you again—and we will, I assure you."

"I'm glad, very glad." She squeezed his hand and kissed his cheek again.

He walked away and she fell back into her seat totally confused. So much had happened on the trip, so many winks, stares, smiles, unfinished sentences . . . and then there were those glorious moments with David before they reached his mother's home.

But there had also been reprimands and reminders that David loved Mary Anne. And, of course, there were the very real physical signs of love between David and Mary Anne. Lily shivered and bit her lip. And what about her own vows to stop loving him?

CHAPTER 31

The wagon had barely stopped before Saul's hands were on her waist lifting her in the air and twirling her around. "Did you miss me?"

She touched his face and hair and was almost blinded by his smile. "Of course I did! Did you miss me?"

"Did I?" He picked her up again and kissed her hard on the lips. "You have no idea! Oh, Lily, I'm so glad you're back, so glad. I don't think I could have lasted another day without you. I don't think I'll ever let you leave me again. But you must be tired. Come."

As they walked to their tent, the men greeted her with broad smiles, a few even told her how much Saul had missed her. "They're glad you're back too, Lil. I'm afraid I became a bear again." They'd barely shut the tent's flap when he pulled her close to him. "You're the only person who can calm me." He kissed her lips. "Are you *too* tired?"

She shook her head.

"Good." His kisses trailed down her neck and she eagerly opened herself to him, releasing the frustration built up from the days of seeing David with Mary Anne and from the excruciating nights of knowing that they were making love.

Camp life soon became routine again as Lily's jobs of getting information and being a wife resumed. And while she told herself that making the return trip without David had given her time to garner strength to put him out of her life, it took only one glimpse of him to sap that strength and weaken any resolve. Even the simple act of pouring his coffee at officers' meetings was almost more than she could stand. To be so close to him, see his eyes, hear his voice, feel his wool uniform brush against her arm . . .

But since his return, his demeanor had been unsettling and he seemed to avoid her. Had Mary Anne found out about them? Was Grace okay? Such scenarios kept her so preoccupied that one afternoon, as she had in Columbia, she wasn't watching where she was going and bumped into him.

And couldn't move.

She stared up into his eyes and he stared down into hers. She looked down to see his hands on her arms and a glimpse of his shirt exposed by the unbuttoned coat. As she looked back into his eyes and felt his fingers tighten on her arms, camp noises interrupted and they pulled apart and hurriedly went separate ways.

But she couldn't bear to see him go. "Wait!"

He turned around.

"May I walk with you? Just a little way?"

He looked around then nodded.

They walked in silence for a few minutes until she could stand it no longer. "Is Grace okay?"

He stopped and looked puzzled. "Yes, why?"

"Good." She touched her chest and expelled a sigh of relief. "You've just looked so sad since you got back."

He shrugged his shoulders and they continued to walk, finally stopping in a small grove. Suddenly self-conscious, Lily looked around and realized that spring was with them again, that the seasons refused to stop because of war. She saw how the white flowers of the dogwoods and the dark leaves of the birch shimmied in the peaceful breeze. When she looked again at David, she could tell he'd been watching her.

She touched his arm. "Tell me." She squeezed his arm then sat down on a log. "Please."

"There's nothing to tell."

She watched him pace and found his distraction unnerving. He seemed unsure about where he was or what he should do and it was so unlike him. As was his appearance. Although Lily preferred him this way—the hair mussed from nervous fingers, the unbuttoned coat hanging open, the boots scuffed—he was far from the usually immaculate Colonel Evans, and she was disturbed by such uncharacteristic behavior.

And she couldn't stand his indifferent attitude towards her.

After a moment, he broke a small twig off a dogwood and began twisting it as he put a booted foot beside her on the log and leaned on his knee. His voice was almost a whisper, almost a thought spoken aloud. "I've just become a little discouraged lately." He shrugged his shoulders. "But it happens. It's politics and, sadly, part of the job." He continued to twist the tiny branch, a distant look in his eyes.

Lily looked up at him then reached her hand to touch his leg but pulled it back. "I'm sorry, truly I am. Is it the special regiment?"

He nodded.

"I'm sorry, David. I know it's important to you."

"Thank you."

"Is everything okay at home?"

"What?" He looked down at her but there was no smile. "Yes. It was when I left."

"Good." She stood up and brushed her skirt. "I guess I'd better go. Saul will be looking for me."

David seemed to study her but said nothing, showed no response.

She had to make him respond to her. "For some odd reason he's jealous of you, you know."

But his eyes remained blank and cold as they looked into hers. "But there's no reason for him to be, is there?"

She felt she'd been stabbed, but then her last words at his mother's had been about ending their relationship, hadn't they? "No, absolutely none." She searched his eyes for the sweetness she'd seen so often but found none. "You will let me know if there's news of Grace?"

"Of course."

He nodded his good bye then handed her something and walked away.

Lily looked into her hand and saw a tiny white flower clinging to a weak and fragile twig.

Soon it was the middle of April and they were preparing to enter Richmond. The men put on their best uniforms before entering the city because they were usually met by large crowds, and this time was no exception.

When Lily helped Saul dress that morning, he swore that by the next parade he'd be wearing a general's uniform, and with each item of clothing he put on, he elaborated on the differences. Although Lily couldn't imagine that he could be handsomer and thought the differences he described sounded minuscule, she knew they were very significant to him. As she watched him straighten his sash and give his boots one last wipe, she thought of David, of the times she'd seen him agonize over the same details, and she knew that he, too, was thinking of those significant uniform differences in his desire to be a general.

"I can't tell you how handsome you look. You must be the best looking officer in the Confederacy."

He continued to primp, adjusting his saber and sash once again, until he finally seemed satisfied and smiled nervously. "What do you think?"

"I just told you." She stood on tiptoe and kissed him. "But I'll gladly tell you again. My husband is the best looking officer in the Confederate army."

"Oh, Lily, you don't mean it."

"But I do."

His eyes shone with pride and Lily hoped that he believed her, that he would enjoy this day, that he would maintain his confidence around the other officers, particularly David.

David. Lily summoned all her courage and resolve in preparation for seeing him, for in her mind he was the best looking officer in any army. But she couldn't give Saul any reason for doubt. She was his wife. David had his own, and Saul deserved her lauds, not David.

People lined up five-to-ten deep all along the street all day long. As the men marched, the bands played and the sun shone as if God did, indeed, think The Glorious Cause a worthy one. Ladies raced into the lines handing out violets, jonquils, and daffodils, sending the men away with signs of spring in their forage caps and jacket lapels. Many of the men blew kisses and even more received them. Prostitutes waved hankies and threw flowers out their windows, and Lily thought of the ladies from Lexington and wondered where they were.

All of the men looked marvelous that day but the officers were truly splendid. Wearing their gray frock coats with elaborate braiding and shiny buttons, bright sashes, and glistening scabbards, they towered above the crowd on majestic horses. Lily gave Saul her brightest smile but saw trouble in his face. When she saw David atop the beautiful Samson she felt her heart leap inside her chest and she bit her lip to stop tears of love and pride. And how handsome and happy he looked! What had happened to cause such a smile? Had his fortunes turned since she saw him last?

She went to their room at the Spotswood Hotel and prepared herself for another outburst.

"Damn him!"

She put her hands on Saul's face and kissed him then busied her hands untying his sash. But when she reached the buttons on his coat, he jerked away and plopped down on the bed. Lily gave up and sat down beside him. "What happened?"

He jumped up and began pacing. "That little . . . Napoleon. That's who he thinks he is." He stopped in front of her, his face red. "He actually got permission to organize a special regiment."

"I thought that was turned down."

He shook his head. "Well, he applied again and got it, and guess what he calls it? Evans's Sharpshooters! Of all the conceited, vain . . ."

No wonder David had looked so happy.

Lily patted the bed and Saul sat down. She massaged his shoulders and kissed his neck then whispered in his ear, "I've sent for a hot bath."

"Lily . . ." He pulled her into his arms. "I haven't told you everything."

"Oh?"

"We're leaving tomorrow." He held her hands.

"Tomorrow? Where? When will you be back?" She swallowed. "I guess you never know about that."

"No. We're going to Yorktown to stop McClellan's advance. We can't let him reach Richmond."

"No, of course not." She threw her arms around him and fought the fear bubbling inside. Was David going too? "Oh, Saul." She touched his lips, "Please be careful. Don't let your anger get you hurt."

He kissed her hands. "Okay. But just for you."

That night she loved Saul in all the ways he liked in hopes of restoring his confidence. And while the march out of town was as jubilant as the previous day's entry—flags and flowers—this time there were also tears and lingering hugs. Lily strained her neck and eyes in search of David then felt her pulse race when she saw him, but her heart broke to see her husband force a smile in her direction, and she worried for his safety.

She couldn't bear to go back to her room and the hospital was quiet so she decided to treat herself to lunch at the hotel's outdoor cafe. While waiting for her order, she enjoyed the early spring sun and the diversion of people-watching.

She'd just thanked the waiter and took her first sip of tea when she realized someone was speaking to her.

An elegant woman with a parasol spoke again. "May I share your table?"

"Of course."

"I'm Sarah Biggs. Is your husband one of our illustrious men in gray?"

"Yes." Lily eyed her suspiciously.

"How wonderful. Mine is beside himself with grief because he's too old."

"Really?"

"Yes, he's sixty-three." Her look was penetrating.

"Ah, yes, well that's too bad."

"Yes, he's particularly upset that he can't help stop McClellan."

"Oh?"

She nodded then thanked the waiter after he set her cup of tea down in front of her. "I hope you don't think me forward. I ordered when I walked in."

"No, of course not." Lily's appetite was gone, her day ruined.

The woman sipped her tea and smiled as she nodded at two officers who tipped their hats as they walked by. "These young officers are so handsome and dynamic, don't you think? So many of them putting themselves in harm's way in hopes of glory and promotions. My, but they are dashing."

"Yes, they are, quite dashing."

Lily watched the woman sip her tea and wondered who she was and where she was from. Pink ribbons woven in her blonde hair brought out the pink in her complexion. Was her southern accent real or well rehearsed?

"Tell me . . . is your husband on his way to stop that horrid little man?"

"Yes." Although she continued telling herself that it was for the better good, Lily was finding it harder and harder to give information that she knew would kill the boys and men she'd gotten to know, information that might kill Saul—or David. These were no longer rebels or traitors to her but travelers on the long treks from one camp to another, helpmates who'd chopped her firewood, homesick men who'd confessed their love to sweethearts in letters that she'd written for them, lonely men who'd thanked her for coffee and danced with her. Had she not been so sure that what she was doing was right . . . She was doing right, wasn't she?

"I've heard so many names bantered about . . . Johnston, Hill, Longstreet, Magruder . . . Yorktown, Williamsburg . . . I've also heard that there's a new regiment, the Evans Sharpshooters. Another man's attempt at glory, don't you think?"

Lily's insides were churning. She wanted to scratch the woman's eyes out. She wanted to slap her and say that David Evans was the bravest most honorable man, but she couldn't. Forcing a smile, she said, "I suppose so, but their colonel is quite . . . "

"Quite what?"

"Handsome."

The woman raised her chin and eyed Lily curiously. "Really? Is that all you know about him?"

"Yes."

"Well, you must have a very understanding husband, Mrs. Dundee, to have the courage to voice such an opinion of another man . . . and one of whom your husband's not particularly fond if I've heard correctly."

Lily should have known that they would know all about her. How stupid of her to think otherwise. "Well, Mrs. Biggs, many of these men *are* quite good-looking, don't you think?"

"Yes. Of course." She sipped her tea then glanced around. "I suppose I must leave you for now." She extended a gloved hand and Lily shook it, feeling a bulky piece of paper as she did. "But with a little something you might find interesting."

The woman smiled demurely and walked away, and Lily quickly opened her palm and saw a folded envelope addressed in David's handwriting. She immediately paid for her uneaten lunch and rushed to her room—then read through tears.

Dearest Mary Anne,

I've missed you so much lately, more than usual, which is constant. I hope you and the boys are well and managing. Forgive me for not being there. War politics is so discouraging that I find myself getting depressed then try to remember what's important is staying safe so I can return to you and the boys. Kiss them for me. God keep you until we meet again.

Yours until death, David.

Lily put the letter to her lips and kissed it, smearing the ink with her tears. If only Mary Anne's name wasn't on it, she could pretend he'd sent it to her.

She didn't know who she despised the most at that moment, but decided it was probably Biggs and the smug woman he'd sent today. They knew that David's words of love to his wife would keep Lily angry.

And keep her working for the Union.

CHAPTER 32

Within weeks the city was in panic and rumors flew that Richmond would be trapped by McClellan from the south and McDowell from the north. Even President Davis had moved his family and the Confederate archives to North Carolina. And the men? Rumors flew regarding them too—they were all safe, all killed . . . but if McClellan's army was truly on its way to Richmond, did that mean that he'd destroyed all Confederate forces sent to stop him? After all the jokes Lily had heard about McClellan's indecisiveness, she found it hard to believe that he could accomplish such a victory, but who knew?

They finally heard that the men were on their way home, that both sides claimed victory at Williamsburg, that losses were low and morale was high. Reports also described their journey back as a miserable one: heavy rains, mud several feet deep, low rations. Lily's nurturing nature longed to warm and comfort David but her spiteful jealous nature wanted to laugh in his face. After all, he enjoyed "playing" army, didn't he? Well, the mud comes with the glory.

She worked with the other women to prepare for the homecoming by baking breads and sweets, rolling bandages, and making beds. When everything was ready, they waited.

One afternoon she was fluffing a pillow in an attempt to quell her nervous fears when cold hands covered her eyes and warm breath fell on the back of her neck. She touched the hands and coyly asked that the person identify himself.

"You better know your husband's hands!" Saul picked her up and laughed as he swung her around.

She was so relieved to see him safe that she circled his neck with her arms and kissed his mouth then looked him over. "Are you okay?"

"Yes, my darling. Oh Lily, I've missed you so much!" He squeezed her.

"And I you." Lily remembered Biggs and realized just how very glad she was to see that Saul was safe. She returned his squeeze then leaned her head on his chest. "Very much."

He whispered in her ear. "And I'm starving for you. You smell so good, I could eat you alive."

"Well, I have been cooking for a week." She smiled wickedly.

He grabbed her hand and almost ran to the hotel.

Their lovemaking was fun, adventuresome, and quite romantic, and afterward Saul slept peacefully and soundly. She looked at him and was thankful that his life had been spared—but what of David?

The next morning she almost ran to the hospital and didn't rest until she heard that David was safe, but the news so relieved her that she had to find an isolated spot to release tears of joy.

"What's wrong?"

"David?!"

He was kneeling in front of her.

She was giddy with relief. "Nothing! Absolutely nothing's wrong. Not now." Her arms desperately longed to circle his neck and they ached their disapproval when she wouldn't let them. She peered into his eyes and scanned his face, his neck, his body. "You're okay? Truly okay?"

He smiled. "Yes. I'm fine, quite whole."

"I heard such awful rumors . . ." She shook her head. "Horrid, horrid rumors. Someone said you were shot, that you made yourself vulnerable to enemy fire until . . ." She covered her eyes with her hands and started crying again.

He laughed and briefly touched her knee. "Lily," he whispered, "I'm okay. But I am flattered to think you'd worry about me."

She couldn't believe her ears and frowned as she raised her face to his. "Flattered? You're flattered that I worry about you?"

He stood and laughed again. "Oh, Lily, don't you know that the bullet hasn't been made that can kill me?"

She slapped him and ran out the door.

She was pacing the small hotel room when Saul returned that night, his face as red with anger as hers. "Damn him! Damn him!"

How could she bear another of Saul's outbursts? She was so filled with her own anger that there was no room for his, but she took deep breaths and sat down then waited for him to speak. He continued to pace and mutter under his breath until the words forced themselves out of his mouth, but even then he was so exasperated that he started and stopped several times before he could connect a full sentence.

He finally stopped moving and stood with one hand on his hip and the other running through his hair. "That . . . you should hear the stories I'm hearing, Lil! The brave Evans, the great Evans, the heroic Evans . . . It's only sheer luck that he's alive! What they're calling bravery was stupidity that happened to work out well. Had luck not been on his side, he and most of his men would be dead right now. He's so damned anxious for those stars that he flaunts himself to the enemy like a cat with all nine lives left."

He looked weary as he knelt in front of her and she knew he was wearing down, that his tirade was almost finished. She brushed his hair away from his face then kissed his lips as he whispered in a worn-out voice, "I swear, Lil, if he becomes a general before I do . . ."

She pulled his head to her chest but he chuckled eerily and she pushed him away. His eyes and grin were almost demonic. "He almost got it, though."

"What do you mean?"

"Twice actually. Two of his men were killed right in front of him. He was missed by just a few feet both times."

So the rumors she'd heard were true. David's cocky words echoed loudly in her ears and her rage at him returned. How dare he challenge God like that?

"You can't seriously wish him harm?"

"Why not?"

"Because you're on the same side. I think you tend to forget that. And even if you weren't, how can you really wish harm on another human being?"

He stood motionless, staring at her. "This is war, Lily. We kill each other."

"Don't patronize me, Saul. When are you going to get over this obsession you have with David?"

"David? David? Aside from helping him lose his virginity, just how well do you know our esteemed colonel? I didn't realize you two were chums."

"Good grief, Saul. It's the man's name." She was shaking inside. "We've been through this before and it's becoming much too tiresome."

He wasn't accustomed to being questioned and her counter-attack surprised him. For once he was speechless.

She walked to the bed and lay down. "I'm sorry, Saul, I don't feel well."

Expecting an attack of self-pity, she was surprised to get sympathy. He sat down on the bed and stroked her hair. "I'm sorry, Lil. You've always been so patient with me. I've taken you for granted, haven't I?" She opened one eye and nodded then smiled. He smiled back. "That's my Lil. Never afraid to tell me the truth, are you?"

Truth? No, Saul, I've deceived you from the first moment. "I just want to make you happy, Saul." She touched his cheek. "But I can't right now."

"I'm sorry. I'd leave you alone but we're leaving early in the morning. Please let me hold you."

Lily saw tears in his eyes as she stroked his cheek. "Of course." She kissed his lips and pulled his arms around her, but though Saul fell asleep almost immediately, Lily slept barely at all. David was almost killed . . . twice. *The bullet hasn't been made that can kill me.*

CHAPTER 33

By the middle of May, Saul and David were both on their way east. And though Lily spent much of her time at the hospital, the exhaustive work could no longer keep the nightmares at bay—the haunting and all too lifelike images that taunted her every night.

David lies in a pool of blood, his brown eyes stare blankly at the sky. Saul lies next to him, his body torn apart. When Lily cries, they jump up, point at her, call her traitor and whore. David cries out, but for Mary Anne, not Lily. They jeer and taunt her without moving their mouths because their mouths have been shot away.

And when she wakes, her heart is beating so loudly that she hears it in her ears. Her gown is soaked with sweat, her face puffy from tears, her stomach upset.

Were her messages to Biggs, at this very moment, killing her husband and the man she loved more than her own soul?

The town and hospital were quiet—the proverbial lull before the storm?

The heat and mugginess weighed on her spirits without relief and she envied the men in their shirts and pants. Earlier in the summer she'd given up several of her petticoats and pretended it was for the war effort. Each day she remembered the carefree clothing she'd once worn and found her heavy long skirts more and more of a nuisance.

The men were still close enough to Richmond that Lily heard fairly current and accurate reports, but she also became more and more uneasy—as if it were only a matter of time—and they heard so many rumors . . .

Then it all changed.

It was mid-afternoon and Lily sat in her room patting her face with a wet cloth and watching the street below while dreading another night of nightmares. But just as the lethargic afternoon caused her eyelids to droop, the street came alive.

"Wounded!"

"Troops coming!"

Her heart in her stomach, she ran to the hospital and found it already so crowded that there was barely room to turn around. The front doors banged open as stretchers made deposits then exited empty and blood-soaked only to return again and again. Moans. Screams. Blood. So hot. So hard to breath. The ceaseless sweltering stickiness . . .

She took a deep breath and got to work, all the while searching each litter for the faces she prayed she wouldn't find. *Please let them be okay.* But then she learned that every home in Richmond was filling with wounded and realized that David or Saul could be hurt, could be within reach, and she wouldn't know.

When she found men from David's regiment, she questioned them. As far as they knew, David was okay, but their descriptions of his close calls made her feel faint. How could so much grape and ball fly so close to him yet leave him intact? Was it possible? No, until she saw him with her own eyes, she feared the worst.

In the meantime, she cared for all the men but gave David's special attention—bought them food from the street vendors, slipped money in their pockets. And what pitiful shape they were in—and not just from battle—but from a lack of food and supplies. Many were barefoot and all wore uniforms pathetically torn and piecemeal.

She was sitting with one of them, listening to his memories and holding his hand, when he fell silent and she knew that he'd just died. She kissed his soft cheek then found a corner in which to cry.

"That's her, General. She's been leaving us money and buying us fruit 'n' sandwiches. Ain't she purty?"

"Yes, Corporal, she's very pretty."

As she had so often, Lily was dreaming that David was there, a dream so real that she could hear him and felt she could reach out and touch him.

"Lily?" He touched her cheek with his hand, his warm calloused firm hand.

Oh please, let this dream go on forever. But she woke, hesitantly and regretfully, then saw him and realized that it *had* been his hand on her face. He was there, right there. She threw her arms around his neck and cried.

"Shh. I know, I know," he said as he patted her back.

Lily quickly pulled away and swabbed at tears then laughed as she spoke to the young man watching them. "I'm sorry. I've just been a little weary and Colonel—General?—Evans is an old friend." She looked at David. "Please forgive me." She touched her hair. "And forgive the way I look."

His sad eyes stared at her as he whispered, "I think you look beautiful."

David promised his men that he'd return to check on them, bade them good bye, then turned to Lily. "Mrs. Dundee, may I have a word with you?"

They walked a few feet then stopped. "Thank you for helping my men. They speak highly of you."

"It's my pleasure." As Lily looked at him, her heart broke. His eyes were red, his cheeks sunken and tear stained. His uniform was splotched with smoke, ripped from shells, splattered with blood. His boots were filthy and his face smudged with smoke and dirt. He seemed in a daze and wrung his hat in his hands as he looked around the room. Had he finally endured too much? He looked much too tired and haggard for someone only twenty-six years old.

You wanted responsibility. You rushed headlong into a family and career. See, David, this is what you have. Is it what you want? "You need to rest. Sit here and let me get you something to eat and drink."

He sat down but shook his head. "No. I don't need anything."

She knelt in front of him but when she touched his cheek, his eyes flashed at her with so much venom that she was barely able to stand and make her legs take her outside.

She stood on the hospital's front steps trying to calm herself and stop shaking, but the foul heavy air and a chest full of heartache made it impossible. This awful stench! This awful war! Would there ever be fresh air again? Lily closed her eyes and tried to remember the sweet smells of rain, magnolia, jasmine . . . jasmine . . . Mary Anne . . . She turned her eyes to the sky and allowed the tears to flow.

"Lily?"

She kept her gaze on the dusty street. She was so hurt, so very hurt, that she no longer cared that he saw her filthy with stringy hair and bloodstained clothing, that he saw tears flow down her dirty cheeks. Why should she care what he thought anyway? She'd been such a fool. He didn't love her. He never had. She bit her lip to keep from screaming out her rage at the constant trembling in her heart that wouldn't go away and the hopelessness of it. She refused to look at him and tried to quiet the shaking by hugging herself. "You should be resting."

"Lily, don't . . . I'm sorry, I . . ."

She turned to face him, determined to give him a piece of her mind. But her eyes saw such grief in his face that she took his hand and led him to an empty supply room, turned over two crates for them to sit on, then pulled him into her arms. He heaved and shuddered as he released guttural heart-wrenching sobs. He tried to speak but choked on words about death and lost friends. "I recruited most of them, promised them glory." He looked at her, his face wet. "Lily, there were a thousand of us in April. There are only 150 left! Young Carter . . ."

"Your aide? Jeffrey?" She knew that David was particularly fond of his new aide, the son of a friend, a boy of only seventeen.

He nodded and the tears flowed even heavier. "He's dead, Lil." His eyes widened as he relived the event. "His legs were blown off! Blown off! What have I done? How am I going to tell his family?" Disbelief and panic filled his eyes and voice. His hands shook.

Again she pulled him to her chest and rocked him, soothed him, cried with him. But she said nothing. What could she say? It's not your fault, it's the war were wartime words that had grown tired and useless.

At first he clung to her so tightly that she could barely breathe, but as he calmed and grew quiet, she felt his arms loosen their hold and she dreaded the moment that he would pull away. With his head still at her chest, he rubbed her back and she hoped he would kiss her, confide in her awhile longer, but he pulled away and looked at her. She couldn't read his thoughts and he didn't voice them.

He sniffed and wiped his face with his handkerchief as he stood up. "I'm sorry." He blinked rapidly and coughed as he straightened his uniform. First attempts at speaking were hoarse but he finally succeeded. "I should never have broken down like that. It's not your place to listen to my problems and I beg your forgiveness for imposing on you. It was inexcusable and I'm truly sorry."

"Damn you David Evans, damn you to hell!" She slapped his cheek then ran out of the room.

CHAPTER 34

Lily was so full of her own anger when Saul finally came home that she wasn't sure how much comfort she could give, and he needed comfort, needed it desperately. As he held her in his arms, he spoke in a wavering voice, "Oh, Lil. It was awful, so awful."

Although Lily felt her energy being sucked out of her by the constant sights, sounds, and smells of the hospital, the nightmares, the heat and humidity, and the endless worrying about David and Saul, she helped him to the bed then knelt in front of him. Placing one hand on his knee and the other on his cheek, she whispered, "Do you want to talk about it?"

"Bodies everywhere. Oh, Lil, it was sickening. We even lost Johnston."

"Oh, no!"

"He's not dead but he's been replaced with Lee."

"You're not confident with Lee?"

"Oh, he's a good man, I suppose." Saul looked at Lily almost pitifully and whispered. "I guess you've heard that Evans got his promotion."

The young corporal *had* called him "General," hadn't he? That was the first she'd heard of it. So David finally had his promotion yet he'd been grief-stricken instead of exuberant. And why hadn't he told her? And why wasn't Saul storming around the room? But she knew why. The hellish battles had taken their toll. "You'll be promoted soon. You know you will."

He shook his head. "I don't know. And sometimes it doesn't matter. Sometimes all of it, everything, seems so useless."

She helped him undress then bathed him with a warm cloth and tucked him into bed. While she watched him sleep, she recalled the words he'd spoken that evening, words of doubt, words that other men were probably pondering. What had they gotten themselves into? Did The Glorious Cause have a chance? She'd heard Saul mumble such thoughts before, often to himself, and she realized that as this war dragged on, he'd need her more than ever.

185

David certainly didn't. David had his promotion. David had Mary Anne.

But still she wondered. Of whom did David dream at night? Did the image of Lily sleeping with Saul torture him as much as the image of him with Mary Anne tortured her? She kept remembering how he had looked that afternoon, how good it had felt to hold him, how hurt she was from his comment that it wasn't her place to comfort him.

But he was right, wasn't he?

Finding sleep impossible, Lily eased out of bed and sat at the dresser then studied her reflection in the mirror. Yes, they were there—the same signs of aging that she'd seen on the faces of the men she loved. But it wasn't the passing years that were leaving their imprints, it was the worry, grief, guilt . . . She dressed quietly then crept downstairs.

The high humidity kept the smells of smoke and blood alive in the air and slapped at her like a wet woolen blanket. Would it ever rain? And how could the moon be so full and the sky so tranquil while men killed each other?

"Hi, Doc."

The old man was reading so she knew better than to expect a response. Everyone knew that once Doc got his nose in a book—which he did every time he sat down—that his ears and mind were closed for anything but his patients. It was his way of blocking out the horrors of his occupation. Lily looked at the title: *Moby Dick*. He'd probably read it five times yet his eyes traveled the black words as intently as if he'd never seen them before. She smiled as he tugged at his white beard.

She tiptoed past him to the alcove where the books were kept and reached for *Ivanhoe* then changed her mind. Sir Walter Scott's romantic images of war had already done too much damage to these men, convincing them that war was righteous and chivalrous, so she chose instead, *The Scarlett Letter*—an appropriate choice?—then walked quietly down one of the aisles. But the sight of all the indentations in all the sheets where all the limbs should have been made her decide that perhaps this wasn't a good night for her to be there, and she headed back to the front door. Her head was pounding and her mind a thousand miles away. If only she could sleep. That's what she needed.

What she didn't need was to bump into David.

His eyes were tired, confused, irritated, but they looked into hers before he turned and walked away.

She wanted to shout at him, run after him, pound on him. How he enraged her! Now she'd never be able to sleep. She stomped back to the hotel then tiptoed up the stairs and opened the door.

"Where have you been?"

"To the hospital."

"Really?"

"Yes." Lily began unbuttoning her dress as she walked to the wash basin and patted tepid water on her face, neck, arms, and upper chest. "Why aren't you asleep?"

"That's what you hoped, right?"

In addition to being hot and tired and angry, she now had a full-blown headache, and listening to Saul rant was the very last thing she felt like doing. She turned to him, hands on hips. "Okay Saul, what's wrong this time?"

"That's not the voice of a loving wife, now is it?" He towered over her, his face red even in the dim light. "I saw you out there—with him."

He referred to David as if his name were a dirty word. "Who?"

"You know who. Evans." He stomped around the room until someone downstairs beat the ceiling. Saul just stomped harder and shouted, "Go to hell!"

"Saul!" Lily touched his shoulder but he pushed her away.

"I guess an ordinary colonel isn't good enough for you anymore."

"Saul, please don't. You're disappointed and tired. Go back to sleep." She plopped on the bed and began removing her stockings. "Cut the man some slack, for heaven's sake, he just lost most of his men."

"And how do you know that?"

"I work in the hospital. I've seen them come in." She was so tired of listening to his tirades and playing the helpmate that she exploded. "I even saw him there today. Yes, him, your nemesis, that evil, power-hungry, glory-seeking rival of yours. And you know what he was doing? He was crying! Crying, Saul. I don't know why you two hate each other but, my God, there's so much more going on here than just the two of you . . ." She shook her head and began putting her clothes back on.

"Where are you going?"

"Anywhere but here."

"NO! You're not tramping out in the middle of the night."

She sat back on the bed, too tired to speak.

"Evans was crying, huh?" Saul was rubbing his chin and smiling and Lily longed to retrieve the words she'd thrown out in anger. "The great little general crying?" He turned his attention back to her. "So, you admit you saw him?"

"Yes."

"Have you two been meeting behind my back?"

"Sure, Saul, while his men were getting killed, he was back here with me. How absurd! Besides, you know how devoted he is to his wife." Even spoken in anger, the truth hurt, for Lily wanted Saul's accusations to be true, wished they were true. Again, she began to undress. Her head was pounding and all she wanted was sleep.

He paced the small room. "I'm sorry, Lil, but it drives me crazy to know that Evans has had you."

"But it was your doing."

"Don't you think I know that? That's one of the reasons it drives me insane. I just get so tired of his pompous attitude and sometimes wish I could tell everyone about how drunk he was that night, about where he spent that night."

"But you can't, can you? You can't tell them who got him drunk and why. You can't explain me, can you?"

"No."

"Are you sorry you married me, Saul? You must have thought about what your family will think when the war's over and you have to take me home. You have, haven't you?"

"I'd be lying if I said I haven't, but there's no reason anyone should know about your past and, no, I'm not sorry I married you." He grabbed her by the shoulders and kissed her then looked into her eyes. "But you've never told me . . . how was he?"

Lily shook her head. "He was a virgin, Saul. How do you think he was? Please stop this." She tugged on his hand. "Come. Sit."

When he rested his head in her lap, she toyed with his hair. "Feel better?"

He nodded and she felt him relax.

"You're in too dangerous a business to let yourself get upset over something or someone you can't control. I don't want you to get hurt because your mind is elsewhere." He was asleep.

Well, Lily, you settled him down again. But how long can you keep the truth from him?

Lily spent more and more time at the hospital and as many hours as possible with David's troops. She played cards with them, combed their hair, massaged their shoulders and weakened limbs, listened to them, prayed with them, held their hands. She rejoiced in every improvement and inhaled their praising words about David. They loved him, looked up to him, were proud to serve with him; and Lily took every word and put it in her heart. No, she wasn't his wife, but his wife wasn't there. Besides, she thought, I bore his first child. I loved him first.

She continued to buy fruit and sandwiches for the men and found their childish delight worth every penny. Except for her own children, what better use for the money could there be?

Or was she doing penance?

Thoughts of money made her think of going back to Louisville to check on the kids and the business. She'd never trusted Sarah completely—a frightening thought since she'd left her independence in the woman's hands.

As for TJ and Ruthie, Lily knew they'd be okay. She knew the ladies would watch over them and knew that TJ was mature enough to take care of them. But she missed them and was afraid they felt abandoned.

The idea of returning to Kentucky began to dominate her thoughts. But what about Grace? And Saul? And David? No, she couldn't worry about David. He had Mary Anne for that. Isn't that what he was telling her that day? *It's not your place to listen to my problems* . . . Those words reverberated inside her head and made her crazy.

Especially when she learned that he was back in South Carolina. The thought of him being so close to Grace and Mary Anne made her livid. Hadn't those romantic days and nights together meant anything to him? Couldn't he at least have told her that he was going so she could have sent a present for Grace?

No, this trip was a final gesture, his way of saying it was over. Whatever they had had—if anything—was over. And she knew he was right.

CHAPTER 35

She was at the hospital talking to one of David's men, wiping his brow and holding his hand, when a shadow fell over them.

"General!" The boy saluted.

"Jackson." David returned the salute then sat down on the bed, his smile bright. "How're you doing?"

"Gettin' better, sir. Mrs. Dundee's feeding me real well."

David nodded solemnly toward Lily. "Mrs. Dundee."

She returned his polite nod then turned to leave but his fingers grabbed her arm. "Wait. Please."

How dare he make her wait, make her obey his command as if she were one of his men?

After a few minutes of talking to the young private, David stood up, told the young man good bye, then turned to Lily. "Thank you for waiting, Mrs. Dundee. May I speak to you outside?"

When they reached the outside steps, Lily took a deep breath and rubbed the back of her neck. "This heat is damnable." She felt him watching her.

"Yes, but a nice sunset's beginning."

She shrugged.

"Do you remember the one we saw at the train station?" He slapped his cap against his thigh.

How dare he! Well, she wasn't about to give him the satisfaction of reminiscing about "good old times" as if those times had been casual outings, as if he could act hot and cold, as if he could recall their times together when it was convenient for him to do so then expect her to respond as if her feelings didn't count, as if all the words spoken since the trip hadn't been spoken. No, as far as she was concerned, she and David Evans had nothing to talk about except his troops and the welfare of their daughter. She folded her arms across her chest and turned toward him. "Why did you need to speak to me, General?"

"I just wanted to see how you are."

"I'm tired, General. I'm disgusted with this damned heat and this damned war. How about yourself?"

He bit his lip and Lily could tell he wanted to laugh. He wouldn't dare!

"Oh, I'm okay." He pointed to the sky. "And the weather's about to break. See the clouds? We'll have rain tonight."

He was looking at her with his adorable little-boy look that made her helpless—and mad at herself—but she was determined to resist his charms. She glared at him, her arms still firmly against her chest. Damn him with that sweet smile and vulnerable brown eyes. Don't give him an inch, Lily, not one inch! The sun beat down relentlessly and she couldn't imagine his prediction coming true though she prayed it would. She looked at the sky and stretched her arms then wiped the back of her neck again.

"Do you have time for something to drink?"

"No."

His hand reached toward her then dropped to his side.

She spoke in a monotone. "Is Gracie okay?"

He smiled gently and nodded. "Yes, she's fine."

She longed to talk to him, to find out news about Gracie, but what if Saul showed up? He would start a commotion that wouldn't be good for anyone, especially the careers of these two, though she cared less and less about that. She looked around. "I . . ."

"Are you worried about Dundee?"

"Just about the scene he might cause. You two are really something, you know. If I didn't know better, I'd swear a woman was involved." His face went pale. "Or is there?"

"I'd rather not talk about it."

Lily felt a sinking in her stomach. "Is it Mary Anne?"

He wrung his cap in his hands. "I don't want to talk about it." His voice tempered somewhat. "I'll tell you someday, perhaps."

"Of course, *Master* Evans. We talk when *you* want to, that's the way it works, isn't it? Only on *your* schedule, when *you're* ready, when it's what *you* want to talk about, and even then it might not be my place to help you, or it might be an imposition on me. I'm supposed to know when and how to react. I'm sorry, General, I'm just a lowly civilian silly female and can't comprehend it all."

His eyes were wide as he shook his head. "If I live to be a thousand, I'll never understand half of what women say."

"Don't you dare lump me with other women!"

"Okay!" He held his hands up in self defense. "If I live to be a thousand, I'll never understand half of what *you* say." He shuffled his feet and fidgeted with his cap. "I've been concerned about the last times we've talked. You've told me to go to hell and slapped me and I don't . . . "

"Your ego hurt, General? Well not all of us are impressed by those gold stars and willing to accept our assigned niche in your life."

He shook his head. "Okay, Lily. I don't know why you're upset when it seems I'm the one who should be, but I can see when I'm not wanted." He plopped his hat on his head and walked away.

Damn him!

She stomped back to the hotel, stopped at the front desk to order bath water sent to her room, then stomped up the stairs. The door was barely shut before her dress was in a heap on the floor. This heat, this damned relentless heat . . . She leaned over the wash basin and poured lukewarm water from the pitcher over her head then fought the temptation to throw the vessel across the room. What she really wanted to do was throw it at David. To aggravate things further, she couldn't get a decent lather. "Damn, damn, damn!" She dug her nails into her scalp.

Lightly tapped knuckles on the door were followed by a weak, "Bath, ma'am."

"Damn!" With water streaming down her face, arms, back, and chest, Lily tripped over her dress as she stomped to the door.

Those poor children! Four young black boys cowered in the doorway, their shaking buckets of water almost spilling into the hallway at the sight of a half dressed, half lathered, dripping cursing woman. Lily attempted to apologize for her rudeness as they poured the water into the tub but they kept their eyes downcast and their voices silent. As they left the room, one reached into his pocket and extracted a note which he gave to her. She generously tipped all four of them then shut the door.

The note was from Saul. He wouldn't be back that night. No explanation.

Sweet relief.

As she piled her wet hair on top of her head, Lily looked forward to an evening without Saul's tirades. Perhaps she'd take a walk outside. Perhaps have a late dinner at the outdoor cafe. Hopefully, it would rain and cleanse them all . . . Eagerly, she took off her underthings then eased into the hot water. The heat from the water combined with her wet hair cooled her, and she felt comfortable for the first time in weeks, and soon she was dozing.

Until someone knocked on the door.

"Damn . . . Who is it?"

"A message, ma'am."

"Just slip it under the door, please."

"Yes ma'am."

But her reverie was broken, the water had turned cold, and the envelope beckoned. Who? Why? She could stand the suspense no longer. Still dripping, she picked up the envelope. David's handwriting . . . *One of my men has asked to see you. Please come to the hospital tonight at eight o'clock—D*

CHAPTER 36

Her hands shook and her entire body trembled but she managed to get dressed and do something with her hair, first styling curls at her cheeks then combing them out. She picked up the bottle of jasmine perfume then chastised herself for keeping it. She hadn't worn it since that first day in Columbia and those memories now flooded back . . . Mary Anne floating like an angel, Mary Anne touching David's lips, Mary Anne smelling of jasmine . . . . *How stupid can you be, Lily? When will you realize that you're just a handy substitute?*

Well, of one thing she'd be sure—David would never again find his wife's scent on her. She tossed the bottle in the trash then generously splashed the scent of gardenia on her neck, shoulders, and arms.

As she pinched her cheeks and bit her lips, she heard the almost foreign sounds of thunder and rain, and she smiled. David was right again.

She knew she shouldn't be so giddy about seeing him, but knowing that he wanted to see her—combined with the bath and refreshing rain—made her feel feminine and pretty; and it had been a very long time since she'd felt that way.

Besides, she knew she'd never turn down a chance to see David.

She accepted her weakness as she took a last glance at her reflection, curled the hair by her cheeks, grabbed a shawl to cover her head, and ran to the hospital.

She tiptoed into the sleeping building. "Hi, Doc. Quiet night?" She peaked over his shoulder at *The Last of the Mohicans* then patted him and eagerly headed toward the ward full of South Carolinians. She walked by each bed, nodded and smiled at those still awake, but saw no sign of David. As she headed outside, she berated herself for being so foolish to think that David really wanted to see her. But why the note?

But it was impossible to be angry on such a night, for the rain—though short-lived—had washed the world and left behind an arena full of sparkling diamonds powdered with stardust. Yes, this night was too magical to go indoors and besides, hadn't she promised herself an evening out?

She breathed deeply and walked briskly to the cafe then sat at a corner table, ordered dinner, and began watching couples stroll by—heads and hands touching, voices whispering.

How many of these men would survive the war? How much of this city would survive? It was sad knowing that these very streets and buildings that now seemed like home would likely be destroyed. It was just a matter of time. It had to happen. The South couldn't win. What were they thinking to even try? How many people would die before the madness ended?

She sighed and sipped her coffee.

"I see you got my note."

Lily looked up and into the brown eyes that never failed to weaken her, and though her blood rushed wildly through her body, she pretended he meant nothing. And nothing's what she said.

"May I join you?"

"Suit yourself."

"Here's your dinner, ma'am. May I help you, General?" The waiter was a very young boy and Lily stifled a snicker at his fawning attitude toward David.

Hungry when she sat down, Lily now wondered if she could eat with David so near.

"I'll have what the lady's having."

"Yes, sir!"

She tried to avoid his gaze but felt his eyes on her face.

"Please talk to me, Lil. I've been worried about you."

She finally looked at him. "Why should you worry about me?"

"Why must you be so stubborn?"

She glared at him and started to get up, but he grabbed her hand and she sat back down then both of them looked around to see if they'd attracted attention. David whispered, "Please stay and hear me out and answer some questions for me. I seem to be upsetting you but I honestly don't know how or why. Like the times you slapped me. What's going on?"

"You'd as good as dismissed me. Should I have stayed around for another insult?"

"Dismissed you? Insult? What do you mean? How did I dismiss you?"

"You said it wasn't my responsibility, my place . . ."

"It wasn't, isn't."

"That's why I slapped you."

He shook his head. "I don't understand. I was apologizing for making you listen, for making you see me in such an undignified condition. I was embarrassed, Lil. Surely you knew that, didn't you? I assumed the slap was for that, though I certainly didn't understand it."

"Your opinion of me is awfully low if you'd think that."

"That's why it didn't make sense. I've always felt that you . . .that I . . .that you were . . ."

Say it, David! Say the words!

But the waiter returned with David's dinner. "Anything else I can get you, General?"

"No, thank you."

Again she stifled a chuckle at the boy's enthusiasm and obvious awe of David.

"You find something amusing?"

"'Yes, sir!' 'May I help you, General?' My, but those stars on your collar certainly do get the attention. That poor boy almost tripped over his own feet just walking over here."

David smiled in the silly way he did too rarely. "Well, some people have the proper respect." He was adding sugar to his coffee. "Stop it."

She laughed. "Stop what, General?"

He stirred in the sugar then looked at her. "Stop grimacing. Just because I like a little sugar in my coffee . . ."

"A little?"

He crinkled his nose.

"So attractive!"

He laughed and her heart somersaulted.

"I guess congratulations are in order. You're finally a general . . . my, my. So, tell me, does all the power make you happy? Is it like you always dreamed it would be?"

He bit his bottom lip and she saw the twinkle in his eyes. "I suppose I could accept that insincere congratulatory message or take issue with it, but I'll choose to do the former since it's much too beautiful a night to argue." He took a bite of steak then set his elbows on the table and steepled his fingers as he chewed, his eyes staring into hers. "Besides, I think you enjoy tormenting me."

"Perhaps." She took a small bite of potato but found it hard to swallow.

He pointed toward her plate with his fork. "I know an awful lot of men who'd do almost anything for that."

"I know and I'm sorry. Perhaps you can take it with you?"

"And have them fight over it?" He smiled and shook his head as he took another bite.

How lucky for men, thought Lily, that they neither lose their appetites nor gain weight. She looked at him, studied him, then spoke quietly. "Ever since we returned from Columbia, I've wanted to thank you for what you told Richard about freeing the slaves."

He looked around self-consciously and she could see his face redden even in the evening's dim light. "Well . . ."

She found his discomfort charming and left him to find the words.

He shrugged and nervously touched his coffee cup. "I've been doing some thinking."

She smiled. "And?"

He cleared his throat. "Well . . . I've decided that you're probably right."

"About what?"

He gave her an annoyed look then smiled. "You know."

"Yes, I do know, because I also spoke to Mauma Hattie about it."

"You did?"

She nodded and smiled. "May I thank you for that also?"

"I guess but why are you thanking *me*?"

"For listening to me, for hearing me." She waited for his eyes to meet hers. "For being the man I always knew you to be." She watched him pick at the food with his fork and could tell he was uncomfortable. "Are you finding it difficult to fight now that you've changed your mind?"

He shrugged his shoulders. "A little, but we're not just fighting for that, Lil. I've told you that before. We're fighting to keep the government out of our hair. Longstreet once said that we should have freed the slaves then declared war. I think he's right." His voice cracked and Lily saw his struggle. "I don't know if you can understand, but our land is who we are. My family's been there for generations and I assumed that we would always be there."

He reached a hand across the table and Lily put hers inside and they both looked at the union as he continued. "It's something that can't be put into words. The land owns us, Lily, it's a part of us." His eyes searched the sky. "When you ride into the fields, oversee the planting, watch it grow . . . even the sound of the workers in the fields . . . These are me. The land is where I came from, who I am. Even though I'm a soldier, it's still part of me."

"But is your life and what you love worth their freedom and their lives?"

His eyes widened and he stared at her then looked down at their hands and squeezed hers before releasing it. "I . . . I don't know anymore."

As she looked across the table at his eyes so deep in thought, she saw the insecure little boy who was always so eager to please his family, and she knew that he was struggling to reconcile all he'd ever known with what she truly believed he now knew was right, that even though he was a general, a husband, and a father, he was still growing and maturing.

Besides, he didn't have much choice. David and his family would never again live as they had before the war, and she felt sorry for the little boy with memories of a carefree childhood,   and she was sorry that those memories would now be tainted.

He cleared his throat. "Well . . . we really shouldn't be speaking of such matters. Not here, not now." He looked around but they were the only two customers.

"I am sorry for you and your family, David, truly sorry for the hardships you'll have to endure." Lily dared touch his hand which still lay in the middle of the table. "You believe me, don't you?"

"Yes."

She pulled her hand away and tried to lighten the conversation. "The way I look at all this is that our country is still maturing, like a child torn between childhood and adulthood." She laughed. "Or to put it another way, the country is wet hair and we're combing out the tangles."

His eyes sparkled. "Will I be admonished if I say that that was a very female metaphor? Clever, but female."

"I guess not. *This* time."

His eyes examined her face. "You're a very wise woman. Do you know that? Actually, next to my mother and Mauma Hattie, you're the wisest woman I've ever known."

Lily felt her face redden. "I'm flattered, genuinely. Especially coming from a gallant officer like yourself."

He grimaced. "More false praise?"

"Oh, no."

Their eyes met and remained locked as the waiter refilled their coffees, took their plates, and told them that the restaurant would soon close. The city's lights were going out one by one and soon the street lamps were dimmed.

"David, why did you want to see me tonight?"

CHAPTER 37

He looked down at the table. "I told you." He traced the pattern on the tablecloth. "Our last meetings haven't been, should I dare say, satisfactory." He smiled sweetly. "And I wanted to find out what I've done to upset you so much."

She sighed. "Oh, David, it's just too complicated."

He looked confused. "But if you won't tell me, how can I keep from hurting you again?"

She laughed quietly. "Oh, that's simple." She looked directly into his eyes. "You can't."

He scanned her face, his brows knitted in confusion. "You frighten me."

"I'm sorry. That's not my intent."

He seemed flustered and unsure what to say or do. "I just want to talk to you, to see how you've been, how you are. I . . ." He looked into her eyes and grabbed her hands. His voice cracked. "I've missed you."

What could she say? How could she hold onto this precious moment? But a distant raised voice broke their reverie and they laughed nervously and released their hands.

"If you wanted to see me, why didn't you take me with you to South Carolina? How could you go without me? At the very least you could have told me you were going so I could have sent along a present for Grace. Why, David?"

He nodded his head even as she spoke. "I'm sorry, very sorry, and I understand why you're upset." He looked at the lip of his coffee cup and tapped it with a finger then looked back at her. "I was scared to take you, Lil . . . scared. It seemed too chancy." He held her eyes. "But please know how much you were missed."

"Really? Did Gracie really miss me?" How sad that she no longer knew if her own daughter loved her.

He interrupted. "By me, Lil, by me."

What was he trying to say?

"Everyone asked about you."

"Even Gracie? Does she miss me? Oh, tell me about her, please."

Her voice was so desperate and now that he thought about it, Gracie never talked about her anymore, did she? But he would never break her heart by telling her. "Of course she misses you and asks about you all the time." Lily's relieved smile wrenched his heart, and David made a mental note to talk to Gracie about her mother. "She's getting so tall, too tall for me to pick up." He pretended to pout. "I miss that."

"I'm surprised she doesn't still expect it."

He laughed quietly and nodded his head.

"But you still have the boys."

"Yes, but they're growing up quickly too. Besides . . ." He looked at the coffee cup and traced its shape with the fingers of one hand, ". . . a girl's different." His fingers continued to touch the mug but his eyes rose to meet Lily's.

She returned his smile then nervously studied the table—her hands wrapped around a warm ceramic mug with its chipped lip, David's finger slightly curled in a mug handle while his other hand lay flat on the table top, its fingers stretching dangerously out toward hers.

"Lily."

She looked up. "Yes?"

"Do you . . . "

She watched his fingers tap the table, watched his dark eyebrows knit together in frustration, watched his eyes glisten. *Say it, David, say it!* She was scared to move, scared that any word or movement would stop whatever it was he had to say.

"Never mind."

The waiter approached and David coughed nervously.

"More coffee, General? Ma'am?"

They both stuttered "yes" then watched intently as the hot beverage was poured. When the young man walked away, David smiled nervously. "I hope I'm not causing a problem for you . . . meeting you here."

"You wanted to discuss your men, didn't you?"

He smiled with relief. "Yes."

As she looked at his face, she felt a smile coming from deep inside, a smile that forced its way to the surface, a smile that said I adore you, David Evans and nothing will ever cure that.

"What?"

She didn't realize she'd been staring. "I'm sorry, what did you say?"

"Nothing. It's just the look on your face. It was so . . ."

"What?"

"Nothing. I just liked it, that's all." He poured sugar and stirred while they both smiled. "I really do appreciate all you're doing for my men." He sipped his coffee. "They sing your praises every time I walk in—you have the prettiest handwriting and the sweetest voice, you're patient, understanding, gentle, smart . . ."

"I try to help them, that's all. And I think you're exaggerating."

"Not a bit."

"Well, then I must have angel's wings and a halo." She touched the lip of her coffee cup then looked at him. "And we both know that's not true."

His expression was serious and his eyes penetrating. "That depends. I think they're right on target."

"David, I've never pretended to be anything other than what I am."

"Don't, Lily. When will you leave your past behind you?"

"Because it's not past. I still own the business and have no plans to sell it."

"I was wondering how you could afford to do so much for the men. Can you?"

"Right now I can. Actually, I've been thinking of returning to Kentucky to check on TJ and Ruthie—and the business."

"Well, from a business standpoint, it's a wise idea and I think a pass from Dundee could get you through the lines easy enough, but . . ."

"What?"

"If anyone finds out what your business is, it won't look good for him."

She nodded. "I haven't decided anyway, but I do worry about the kids and the business."

"How long were you planning to keep it? I thought that since you married . . ."

She shook her head vehemently. "No, I'll never sell it. It's my independence, my security. It's all I have." She looked into his eyes. *Tell me you want me to sell it, that you want to take care of me.*

But he didn't say the words. He couldn't. Even if he weren't married, Lily knew that she was better off financially than David and probably always would be. She knew that he and Mary Anne were having trouble paying their bills and that he worried about their future if the South lost the war. She knew all these things. She knew he couldn't take care of her.

She just wanted him to say he wished he could.

"Well, I certainly understand that." He leaned back in his chair. "You're amazing."

"You think so?"

"Yes. I admire your self-sufficiency." He tapped his cup with the spoon. *clink, clink, clink* "I wish Mary Anne were more . . ." His eyes stared into the distance. *clink clink*

Lily stiffened. Did he realize he was speaking out loud?

clink, clink "She's so very dependent on me. Now that the school's closed there's no money coming in and the creditors are demanding payment. The boys need discipline and new clothes, the servants . . ." *clink, clink, clink*

How could he speak to her of Mary Anne?

clink, clink, clink

Lily reached across the table and put her hand on his.

Silence.

He immediately looked into her eyes and his fingers closed over hers. "I'm sorry." She tried to pull her hand away but he held it firmly. "I said I'm sorry."

"Yes, as am I."

He seemed hurt. "Are you? Are you, really?"

What did he mean? Lily pulled her hand from his grasp. "Anyhow, I can't afford to lose my business although I do worry about how it's being run in my absence." She watched his expression as she added, "I've also thought about staying there."

His eyes widened. "Why? What about m . . . Gracie? Dundee?"

She shrugged then eyed him pointedly. "I'd take Gracie back with me." Would just saying the words make it happen? Would Grace ever live with her again?

His eyes widened even more than before. "No!"

Lily quickly continued, "As for Saul . . ."

"What?"

"Nothing."

Other patrons had come and gone and they were alone again. How did David expect the evening to end? Did he know that Saul was gone for the night? Lily tingled at the idea of their making love but doubted that it would happen—and knew it shouldn't. Did he even want to? "So . . . how did the recruiting go when you went home? Any success?"

"Yes."

"You don't sound excited."

He shrugged his shoulders and cupped his hands around the coffee mug. "It's not as it used to be. I can't . . . don't have the same enthusiasm."

She saw his anguish and longed to comfort him.

"It's not the same. I know now that I'm asking men to die." He shook his head then looked at her, his eyes red. "Oh, Lil, it's so horrible . . ."

She reached for him and he clasped his hands around hers.

"I know I should have known what to expect when all this started, but I'd never experienced battle before." He squeezed her fingers. "But even in its horror, there's something about it that's exciting, challenging, addictive . . ." He saw her disgust and held onto her hands when she tried to pull them away. "Please hear me. I certainly don't enjoy the killing but I do enjoy the planning and the strategy, and there is a thrill of anticipation before the battle starts." He unclasped his fingers from hers then touched hers delicately, as if examining them, and the feel made her crazy. He stopped and looked at her. "I'm a soldier, Lil. That's all I was ever meant to do."

"Then what will you do when it's over?"

He sighed. "I'm surprised you even asked."

"Why?"

"According to you, I'll either be in prison or hanged as a traitor."

She grabbed his hands. "No, David! Don't even say it."

"Hey." He touched the curl by her cheek and laughed quietly. "I was just echoing your sentiments." He pulled back his hand as the waiter approached.

"I'm sorry, sir, ma'am, but I need to take your cups." David paid the boy and included a generous tip. "Thank you, General!" His stuttering awe of David was adorable. "Actually, sir, you can stay as long as you want. I just can't serve you anymore."

A melancholy look filled David's eyes as he looked at Lily. "We have to go anyhow."

"Good night then." As the boy walked away, Lily wondered if he would save the coins he'd been given in case David became famous.

She started to stand but David pulled her hand. "Just a few more minutes?"

"What . . ."

"Doc knows we both care about my men. He'll tell people . . ."

"David . . ."

"I know, Lil, but . . ."

She sat back down but neither of them spoke as they watched his thumb rub the top of her hand. Such a familiar habit, such a warm feeling. Those fingers . . . Lovers are such fools, Lily thought. Why does every part of your lover's body seem magical and special when they're really quite ordinary? David's fingers were average in size and shape, but Lily found the callouses and chewed fingernails perfect and knew that she would always judge all men's hands by his. As she watched the stroking that both relaxed and excited her, she longed to kiss his hands, suck his fingers, feel his fingers stroke her skin . . .

But then she wondered as she had before . . . Did he hold Mary Anne's hand like this? Suddenly she felt weepy and pulled at her hand.

But he held it fast. "What is it? What's wrong?"

"I need to go."

"Yes, I know, but something's bothering you. Please tell me what it is."

"No, I'd rather not." She jerked her hand free then stood and turned to go.

"Lil?" He grabbed her arm.

As Lily looked at the fingers clasped around her arm, she scanned the barren street and dark windows and felt a chill. How many eyes had observed them tonight? How long would it take for someone to tell Saul about his wife and the general?

David released her arm and nodded and they walked the few steps to the hotel's entrance. "Where's your hus . . . Dundee?"

"I don't know. I received a message that he'd be gone all night but there was no mention of his whereabouts."

The night was dark, even the moon was hidden by clouds, and quiet, so quiet. When David whispered, she had to lean close to hear. "We're leaving in a few days."

"Oh?" She smelled him—the intoxicating combination of fresh air, cologne, soap, wool, and even sweat that was his scent, that was him, and she felt lightheaded.

His eyes examined her face and he, too, took a deep breath. "Gardenia?"

She nodded.

"I like it."

"Better than jasmine?"

He shrugged his shoulders. "They're both nice." He took another deep breath then smiled. "Very nice." His eyes fell to her lips and he licked his own then stammered. "We're heading north again, back toward Manassas Junction."

She spoke but her eyes were on his lips. "How long will you be gone?"

"I don't know." His lips moved closer and closer. "Lily?"

"Uhm?" She felt drunk from his very presence.

Suddenly he whisked her into the alley and pushed her against the hotel's rough brick wall. His mouth covered hers as his hands lifted her skirts. "Lil, oh Lil . . . "

Her body responded until her eyes opened and saw the filth, her nose opened and smelled the stench. "No!" She pushed him away. "No, David. It can't be like this. I won't . . ." She looked around at the dank alleyway. "I may be a whore but I refuse to be a common slut." Her lips tingled with the taste and feel of him and she trembled from the conflicting emotions jostling inside her. Who was she fooling? She wanted him so desperately that she would have wallowed in the filth just to be with him. Thankfully, she still had some pride left, paltry though it was.

"No, Lil, no." David held her tight. "It's not like that at all. I'd never do that to you. I'm sorry, so sorry. Forgive me, please. I just need you and want you so desperately." His lips brushed her hair then he pulled away and looked into her eyes. "I'll never do it again. Can you forgive me?" He outlined her features with a shaky finger. "I just want you so much, so very much . . ." His mouth covered hers again but he quickly pulled away. "You do forgive me, don't you? I couldn't stand it if you didn't."

She nodded as she stared at him, memorized every inch of him. How she loved him. How she ached for wanting him. She licked her lips and tasted him.

"Will I see you at the hospital tomorrow?"

"Yes."

His smile was sad as he kissed her hands then released them. "Good night, then."

CHAPTER 38

Lily barely slept that night. She was too full of the feel, sight, and smell of David and so eager to see him the next morning that she got up at the crack of dawn, primped just enough, smiled as she splashed on gardenia cologne, then almost ran to the hospital.

David was already there.

It was so hard to pretend indifference when all she wanted to do was throw her arms around him, love him, laugh with him, make him smile. Memories of loving him became so vivid in her mind that she couldn't quit smiling then wondered if people who saw her didn't think her demented.

He was sitting on a chair next to the bed of one of Lily's pet patients, a boy named Daniel who couldn't have been older than fifteen. "There she is, General, our angel!"

David's eyes twinkled as he stood and kissed her hand. "Good morning, Mrs. Dundee."

"Good morning, General Evans." Lily sat down on the boy's bed as David sat again in the chair. "And good morning to you, Daniel. How're you feeling today? Very good from what I observed." She felt David's eyes on her.

"Fine. I'll be out of here today." He smiled at David. "Just in time to go with the general."

Lily felt like she'd been hit in the stomach and glowered at David. "You can't possibly be planning to leave today, can you? And take him? He's just now feeling better."

"But that's what soldiers do when they recover, go back into battle. He's lucky he can."

"Yes, ma'am. I'm a lucky one." He looked around the room then back at Lily and whispered. "There's so many who'll never fight again, won't even leave here in one piece."

"Well," she blinked nervously and shook her head, "I'm afraid I don't see returning to battle as good news." She patted the boy's hand. "Don't you want to stay here a few more days?"

He grinned and blushed. "No, ma'am, but I'm sure gonna miss you."

Lily whispered, "And I'll miss you" as she looked at the boy's rough red hands with nails that were probably clean for the first time in his life, then looked at David. Threatening tears made her stand. "Excuse me, gentlemen." She directed a forced smile at Daniel. "Take care of yourself." She kissed the boy's cheek then walked away, walked as fast as she could into the open air then stood on the steps and hugged her arms as she cried.

"Mrs. Dundee?"

She swiped at tears. "Yes?"

"Mrs. Biggs told me that you and she got along splendidly."

Not now, go away. "Yes."

"Will you walk with me a few minutes?"

Lily nodded and they walked as if going to the hotel. The man smiled a lot and she finally recognized him as someone she'd seen at the hospital. He spoke quietly. "If someone approaches, we're talking about patients and supplies, okay?"

"Yes, of course."

"Jackson's already in Gordonsville and we hear Longstreet's preparing to help out. Has your friend, General Evans, said anything to you about it?"

She looked back at the hospital and saw David standing on the steps watching her. *Oh, Dear God, what should I say?* She quickly turned away from David's gaze and hastily reminded herself of her priorities—slaves on the auction block, David's love for Mary Anne, Grace, saving the Union. "They're leaving for Manassas in the next couple of days." She added some vague troop numbers and current locations.

He handed her a note then whispered, "Your general's coming this way, so smile." Suddenly the man raised his voice and startled Lily with his obvious change in demeanor. "Why, thank you, Mrs. Dundee. I told him you'd know." He greeted David then returned to the hospital.

"Who was that?"

She looked at David then at the ground. "No one. I mean he's just someone from the hospital."

"He gave you something."

"Just a letter from one of the patients."

"Why did you run out like that?"

She stared into his eyes. "How can you not know? You two spoke of going back to battle as something to look forward to. Daniel just recovered from being wounded and you'd have him get hurt again, or worse. And he's just a boy. You look at this as a game."

He slapped his thigh with his cap and spoke roughly. "Don't ever say that! Ever! You know better."

Her head dropped.

He tried to get her to look at him but she wouldn't even though his voice was soft and intimate. "You do know, better than anyone."

She nodded.

He laughed quietly. "We're standing in the middle of the street again."

She laughed nervously and raised her eyes to his. "Then we must not be doing anything wrong. Lovers don't normally have their rendezvous on the street for everyone to see."

Lovers. Why had she used that word?

But he didn't look away, didn't seem shocked or embarrassed. "I have to get back to camp. I'll be back the day after tomorrow to sign my men out and get them to the train. I'll look for you here." He nodded toward the hospital. "I hope I'll see you."

She looked into his eyes. "Then you will."

His broad smile made her feel like a princess with her handsome knight standing tall in front of her, a look of love on his face. He has to feel some love for me, just has to, she thought. If only he could kiss me right here in front of the entire town and yell his good byes to me, but she was happy with the satisfactory words they'd shared, the warm smiles she'd received. They would have to hold her until she saw him again.

At least she thought so at the time.

She watched him walk away then almost ran to the hotel, eager yet frightened to read the letter Biggs had given her. But as soon as she looked at the delicate handwriting, she began to shake and could barely open the envelope.

My Dearest,

I'm still enjoying the euphoria of being a general's wife and have told everyone I see. I'm so anxious to show you off and am thrilled to write that I'll be able to do just that in October if you can come home. That's when our old chums, Dick and Marjorie, are finally getting married. The nuptials will be in Charleston so I dream every night about the balls and festivities.

The boys are growing like weeds and seem to be a size larger every day. Thankfully, I'll always be able to pass Richie's clothes (when they're not full of holes!) down to his brothers, but it's keeping him clothed that's the hardship. It seems I do nothing but sew. They miss you terribly and have taken to playing soldier. Richie is, of course, a general. I sewed gold stars on one of his shirt collars and now it's the only garment he wants to wear! I fear another generation of soldiers.

I hate to bother you with upsetting words, dearest, but please find a way to keep these dreadful collectors away. They plague me at least once a week and I fear our Negroes will have to be sold.

On that subject, I'm most distraught at the rumors of servants killing their masters during the night. You know I feel safe with our people but fear they may get ideas. I know Susan Baker now fears hers since she was silly enough to teach them to read. I warned her at the time that it would make them restless.

We so enjoyed your last visit but wish it could have lasted longer. Your mother cried and cried when you left, more than she's ever cried before. And though you think our premonitions silly, she and I fear something will happen to you. Always at her side, little Grace comforted her. I know the girl's your pet, dear, and I know you say it's foolish of me, but I do bear some envy at the close relationship you and your mother have with her. After all, though Grace is a beautiful sweet child, she's not your mother's grandchild as are our children. If the boys didn't adore her, I fear they'd be jealous. I still can't get over her resemblance to you and would be suspicious if I didn't know you better. I know we've discussed this before, but you must understand how my silly female brain wanders when you're not here to reassure me.

My father is as proud of you as I am and brags of your bravery to all his friends. And wouldn't your father be proud? We follow the footsteps of great men.

Do take care and think of me every moment as I do you.

—*Mary Anne*

As Lily finished reading, she realized she was holding her breath. She stared at the dainty paper and beautiful script then noticed a crude and quickly scrawled note on the envelope: "Provide more information. Husbands hate alley cats."

She felt sick. Not only were David's letters to and from Mary Anne intercepted, Lily's every movement was known. She shuddered. These people had powers that went beyond what she thought possible. Damn them! She paced with the letter clinched in hand. She knew her mission was for the good of the nation but she wanted to stop. She couldn't stand hurting these men any longer. Kentucky was beginning to sound like her only option. But would she be allowed to get there?

And what of Mary Anne's letter? That she loved David was obvious, but Lily had just seen a side of her that conflicted with her perfect image. She obviously saw slaves as inferior and loved the society that wealth brings. But Mary Anne, like David, had known no other life. What on earth will she do when her world falls apart? And her words proved, once again, how much pressure David was under.

CHAPTER 39

Saul came home that night.

"What have you been doing while I've been gone? Have you missed me?"

"Of course I've missed you," she lied. "The temperatures have lowered a bit, we've had some breezes, and it's not been so sticky."

"I appreciate the weather report, but how have *you* been?"

"Fine. I've kept busy at the hospital and taken some walks. What about you?"

"Busy. We're heading out again, you know."

"Really? Where to this time?"

"Back north. Seems Pope's visiting Northern Virginia and Lee's ready for him to go home."

"That's very clever, Colonel Dundee, comparing Pope to bad company."

"Like it, do you?"

Lily was undressing for bed and sat down at the dresser to brush her hair. Saul took the brush from her hand and proceeded to do the job. "Am I pulling too hard?"

"No, not at all." The mirror reflected his masked anger.

"So . . ." He brushed harder and harder until her neck hurt with the downward strokes, but she said nothing. ". . . you've been busy, have you?"

"Yes." She watched his eyes in the mirror.

"Seen any old friends?"

She spun around and grabbed the brush. "Saul, if you have something on your mind, say it." She stood up and walked to the bed, but just as she pulled the covers back, he grabbed her upper arms.

"Evans has been here, hasn't he?"

"What do you mean?"

"I mean I saw the two of you together." He released her so hard that she fell on the bed.

She laughed as she pulled the covers to her chin. "I thought you were trying to win those gold stars. Are you telling me that you stayed here to spy on me instead? Believe me, if I were so inclined, I'd find a way to do it whether you were here or not. You need not pretend you're gone." Her insides were jelly. What did he know? What had he seen? She kept seeing the words: "Husbands hate alley cats."

"If you were so inclined? My God, the two of you were practically mating in the middle of the street today. How can you be so stupid, so brazen?" He laughed. "But I keep forgetting, you're a whore, aren't you?"

Lily closed her eyes and took deep breaths. "Yes, Saul, that's right. I'm a whore." She turned onto her side and closed her eyes. "Good night."

But as she reached to lower the lamp's wick, he grabbed her arm. "So, you admit you were with him?"

She shook off his hand. "I admit nothing. I deny nothing. If you're so insecure that you disregard your duty in order to spy on me, it's no wonder that you've not received that promotion you covet so dearly."

He yanked her out of the covers, his hold burning her wrists.

"Let go of me, Saul. Now."

"How could you? With him of all people?"

"For heaven sake, we talked about his men. Let me go!"

He dropped his hold again. "All those cow eyes were about his men?" He ran his fingers through his blond hair and paced. "Damn it, Lily, how does that make me look?"

She walked to the wash bowl and soaked her wrists. "I'm sorry, but I don't spend every minute of the day worrying about how things will affect you. Maybe I should, but I don't. Maybe you should just trust me."

"But I can't, not as long as he's around. All his life he's had everything he's ever wanted but I'll be damned if he gets you too!"

"Gets me? I am not a piece of property. If he *gets* me, it's because I choose him." She saw his face redden and his mouth fall open and quickly added, "but I chose you. Besides, as you've said so often, he's married, so there's nothing to discuss."

Saul sat on the bed, his shoulders sagging, and she pulled his head to her chest. "Forget him, Saul, forget everyone. If you're leaving again so soon, let's not waste time talking of anyone else." He raised his face and she kissed his lips, kissed them hard, then pushed her body into his, encouraged his hands to explore her and release her desire for David.

And he clung to her after lovemaking, kept his legs and arms wrapped around her. She didn't know whether to pity his need for her or hate him for hanging on so tightly.

David was leaving the hospital when she arrived.

211

The place was chaotic with men being discharged and saying their good byes, many of them leaving behind items to be sent home—just in case. Letters, locks of hair, jewelry, pictures, Bibles. Lily was flattered at the hugs and kisses given her and she felt privileged to have known these men, privileged to have helped them. But she also felt guilty, for hadn't she been responsible for getting them injured?

She loved watching David with his men and saw that he was, indeed, a natural leader. He was patient with them, understanding of their need to say good bye to friends, yet firm enough to get them to their destination on time. They respected him, that was easy to see, and Lily felt honored to know him, particularly honored to have loved him—and been loved by him?

But he was leaving when she arrived.

"I couldn't get away."

"I know." They were surrounded and separated by bodies that interrupted and bumped them. Lily and David stretched their necks to look over and between bobbing heads. "I'm sorry we can't . . ."

"I know. I am too. I'm sorry I couldn't get here earlier. I wanted to. I . . ."

Bumping, shoving, yelling. They hollered above the voices, peered around the bodies.

"But you got here before I left. I was hoping you would. I wanted to tell you . . ."

"What?"

All of the men seemed to be ready at the same time and David shouted, "I'm sorry, Lil, I've got to go."

He raised his arm so she could better see him amid the throng and she stuck her hand through the crowd and stretched her fingers until she felt his fingertips.

But it was just an instant and he was gone.

The days and nights rolled into weeks. The hospital was almost empty but everyone knew a battle was being fought, about to be fought, had been fought—they never knew exactly—and they never knew when patients would arrive, or how many, so every waiting moment was used for preparation. The women washed and ironed sheets and pillow cases, aired pillows and blankets, washed down cots and beds, mopped floors, rolled bandages, and stocked shelves with the few remaining medicines.

By the end of August, they heard frightening rumors about officers wounded and killed, about the Confederates driving the Yankees off Chinn Ridge leaving Federal bodies everywhere. But of David Lily heard nothing.

By September 3, every hospital and home was filled with wounded.

How could she have forgotten how hellish it was? Screams of men in agony, some pleading for medication, some pleading to die. Screams of men begging Doc not to cut. But cut he did, again and again, and soon the garbage cans were full of arms and legs. Blood was everywhere. Great pools on the ground, splatters on clothing, sticky dried pieces in hair. Yet in all the melee, all Lily could think of was David. Where was he? How was he? And her anxiety only worsened with each conflicting report. He was shot but alive. He wasn't even wounded. So far there were no rumors of his death.

She listened for news and pestered Doc every time she saw him. One afternoon he was washing the blood off his hands and about to take his first break in more than twenty-four hours when she asked him again.

"Young lady, you've got to leave me alone about that young man. I'm too busy and have too many other men to worry about. But since I'm fussing at you, let me say that I've seen the two of you together and I don't like what I see, not one bit, and I think you're headin' for trouble, the both of ya'. I'm sure I don't need to remind you that you're both married to other people and the damage you could do to your husband and his wife can hurt a body just as sure as bullets—and leave much deeper wounds." He saw her shame and tears. "Now, now, don't cry. I like you, girl, like you very much, and I don't know your history with this fine man, but I'm tired and you've pestered me about young Evans once too many times. I just felt I had to say something because the feelings you have for each other are painfully obvious to everyone and it's just a matter of time before some real trouble comes from it."

She patted his arm. "Thank you, Doc."

"For what, girl? I wouldn't think you'd be thanking me."

"For caring." She started to walk away but stopped and turned around. "Doc?"

"Yes."

"I love him."

He patted her shoulder. "I know darlin', I know. And I've seen too many a lovesick boy not to recognize that he loves you too. I'm sorry for you both, truly I am." He winked. "I'll let you know if I hear of him."

She kissed his cheek. "Thank you."

"Now help these other poor boys." He grinned slyly. "They might not be as handsome as your general but they need and deserve attention too."

Had Doc said that David loved her? David's mother had said it. Jonathan and Mauma Hattie had hinted at it; and now Doc. Surely they couldn't all be wrong. Surely David loved her—at least a little.

But the rest of Doc's message was also familiar and broke her heart. No one had to tell her how much damage her love for David could cause. Not only could it damage forever the hearts of Mary Anne and Saul, it could ruin David's career chances both now and after the war. Yes, she knew these things, always had, but how could she help what her heart felt?

CHAPTER 40

"Lily!"

She ran toward Doc's voice then saw him nod toward the corner.

David's face was ashen and his brows knitted in pain as he moaned in his sleep. Lily saw that his chest and left arm were covered in bandages and that he squinted and grunted with each breath. Doc came over and whispered, "He lost a lot of blood but he'll live. He's a lucky boy."

"What happened?"

"Got shot, pure and simple. Looks like a ball entered his arm and went through his chest." The white-haired man shook his head and tugged at his beard. "It always amazes me how men can get shot so many times and survive or have bullets rip hats or clothing but not skin. He should be dead but he'll be fine." He continued looking at David and nodding. "This one's been shot at before and the way he leads his men, he'll be shot at again." He saw her horror. "He's a soldier, girl. Some are born to it and this is one. He hates it and loves it but would be lost doing anything else." He looked her in the eye and added with a slight smile, "Kinda like the women in his life, I'd say."

Lily smiled faintly.

He watched her face as he added, "You know he'll be going home to recuperate."

She felt a lump in her throat and nodded. "Of course." But she hated the idea of Mary Anne nursing him back to health. Lily wanted to take care of him, feed him, change his bandages, help him exercise his arm, watch him get well . . . Tears welled in her eyes as she imagined performing wifely duties for him, and her heart broke.

Doc patted her shoulder then bent down and whispered, "Don't tire him and don't spend all your time with him. Remember his reputation."

Lily nodded again, her eyes still on David. *Open your eyes, David. Tell me you love me and won't get yourself killed, and I'll be able to live while you're with Mary Anne.*

Finally, the dark lashes fluttered open and he saw her and smiled, then winced.

"Don't push yourself. Keep your eyes closed if it's more comfortable." She found a wet cloth and patted his forehead, his cheeks, his lips.

He smiled again and she knew he was asleep.

Oh my dearest darling, how I love you. Quietly and hesitantly, Lily left David to check on the other men, but she listened for any sound from him. Like a mother hears her own child's cry above all others, she could distinguish David's moans above those of every other man in the large room, and she tended the others quickly so she could return to his side.

And there she sat all night.

Somewhere in the dark morning hours, she woke and found him watching her, a pained smile on his lips. She touched his brow with her hand and found it cool. "You're going to be fine."

He nodded then winced.

"Hurts?"

"Yeh." She wet his dry lips with a wet cloth and he whispered, "Thank you."

"Are you feeling any better?"

When he nodded, he winced again and Lily laughed then saw his brows furrow. She touched his cheek. "I'm not laughing at your pain, swee . . . David." He raised his brows and she looked away.

"Lil?" His voice was hoarse.

"Shh. Don't tire yourself."

"Thank you."

"For what?"

"Staying with me."

"You're welcome." She smiled at his slurred voice and droopy eyelids then dared let her fingers touch his face and trace his mouth, his nose, his eyes . . . Every fiber in her wanted to kiss him but she knew eyes were everywhere and she forced her fingers to leave his face.

Again she checked on the other men but quickly returned to David's side in time to help him eat some breakfast. As she spooned watery oatmeal into his mouth, she remembered the times she'd fed their daughter and was grateful to have this time with him—one more moment of feeling like family that she would cherish. He didn't eat much and she could see that the effort tired him.

While he slept, she bathed his face and neck and the little bit of chest that wasn't swathed in bandages. Although his eyes remained closed, she could tell when he woke and she took comfort in his peaceful demeanor. When she washed his right hand, his fingers curled around hers in a weak embrace and his eyes opened. "Feels good," he whispered.

"I'm glad." She gazed into his eyes and was encouraged by the length of time he stayed awake and the way he looked at her. "I think you're getting better."

He nodded. "You."

"What?"

His mouth was still cottony and his voice weak so she leaned down to hear him. "Because of you."

The breath that came with his words excited her. But, oh, how hard it was to be so near him and not caress him. She could barely stand it. Dare she kiss him? Was it desire she saw in his eyes too? But when she looked to see if anyone was watching, she saw Doc approaching. As she stood, she was glad to see the disappointment in David's eyes.

The old man was shaking his head and about to speak when Lily said, "I know, Doc, I know," and walked away.

But the next morning she found an empty bed and felt her heart stop. "There you are."

She turned to see David and her heart pumped again.

"I thought you'd forgotten me."

"Should you be up and walking around?" She reached toward him, putting a hand on his right arm.

He laughed softly. "I'm fine, trying to build up my strength. I've got a long ride in front of me."

She searched his eyes. Why did he speak of home to her? How could he not know how such words hurt?

"You can help me back to bed. I think I've done enough for awhile."

She savored the feel of his weight and the wifely feel of making him comfortable in his sick bed. But he'd talked of going home and Lily's feelings were hurt, her voice cold. "Better?"

He smiled boyishly and nodded.

"Good." She turned to walk away.

"Why are you rushing off?"

"There are other men who need attention more than you."

His dark brows knitted in confusion. "Lil?"

Of course he had no idea how badly his casual words of home had hurt her. Lily had spent enough time with men to know that they speak in plain language with no hidden meaning, blunt and to the point. But his words had reminded her, once again, that it was Mary Anne's duty—and privilege—to care for him. It was his wife's place, not Saul's wife's place.

To fight back tears, she looked at the ceiling and around the room, then felt her stomach lurch. The man who'd posed as Biggs was across the room watching her with David. Now at the mercy of the man she loved *and* her tormenter, Lily obediently sat down and attempted to appear normal.

When she looked up again, Biggs was gone, and she shuddered at his almost unearthly ability to appear and disappear then saw David watching her, an odd curiosity on his face. He reached for her but winced. "Move your chair over here." He nodded toward the right side of his bed.

"I don't think I should."

"Please."

As soon as she moved the chair and sat down, David took her hand and squeezed it then began rubbing it with his thumb. Lily was nervous, scared, felt on display, but their hands were hidden from anyone who wasn't standing right by them. But she could feel eyes on them—Doc's eyes, Biggs's eyes—then looked down at their hands and felt like she was in the middle of a tornado. Would she ever know peace again?

"You're so quiet and distant. Please tell me what's wrong."

She laughed and he smiled but looked puzzled.

"Saul said you sent the Feds running."

"Saul?"

"Yes, Saul. You know, my husband."

He squeezed her hand. "Yes, I know he's your husband."

"He came home quite bolstered from the victory, quite elated and full of vigor." She chose her words deliberately and watched David's eyes darken. "I'm sure his promotion will be soon now. He certainly deserves it, don't you think?"

His thumb stopped its rubbing motion. "Of course."

"But he's already left again. He said they're going to Maryland. Why, David? I thought the idea was to get them to leave you . . . us . . . alone."

"Why not? This last battle was a huge success. If we have another, it's almost certain that Great Britain will recognize us as a country. If that happens, the Yanks are bound to stop this thing. Besides, we want to get the fighting out of Virginia during harvest, and just think of all the men in Maryland who'll join us!" He grinned broadly. "We've already surprised everyone. No one expected us to win any battles, much less the number we have." He rested his head on his pillow and looked up at the ceiling and smiled. "Oh, Lily, now they see that we're not a bunch of crazy hayseeds."

Lily looked at the handsome face, the elegant profile, the brown eyes glistening with boyish hope, and she wanted to cry. So sweet, so gallant, and though she was relieved that he wouldn't be fighting for several months, she worried about Saul and shuddered.

David turned toward her, wincing as he did, and she jumped up to help him maneuver. He said thank you, then inhaled and smiled. "I've never smelled a gardenia so sweet."

"So," Lily took a deep breath, "you're going home to recuperate."

Taken aback, he wet his lips and looked away. "Yes."

CHAPTER 41

Her voice cracked. "How long will you be gone?"

"I'm not sure. A few months I imagine."

She remembered Mary Anne's letter and the October wedding in Charleston and was sickened by images of Mary Anne with David. Images of David in his general's uniform with Mary Anne showing him off like a prized pet. Images of them together, at night, alone.

"What are you thinking?"

"Just wishing I could go with you . . . so I could see Grace."

He nodded. "Yes, it would be nice . . . for you to see her, I mean."

"You're leaving . . . ?"

"The day after tomorrow."

"Is Mary Anne still in Columbia?"

"No, she's back at school." His eyes blinked rapidly. "Perhaps we could . . ."

"Go as far as Columbia together?"

They looked into each other's faces for answers, solutions, approval. Dare they plot such a thing? If she stopped in Columbia and he went on . . .

"It's been so long since I've seen Gracie."

David smiled and Lily saw an eagerness in his face that renewed her hopes that there was, indeed, a place in his heart for her, that she wasn't just a substitute for Mary Anne. He squeezed her hand.

"Mrs. Dundee, I think our young general needs his rest, don't you?"

Lily knew she looked guilty. She certainly felt it. David released her hand and she stood up, aware that Doc had seen their hands, aware of the man's concern for them. Lily knew that had she and David not been married to other people, Doc would have greeted their love with hosannas and hallelujahs. She dared look at David and saw the same feelings on his face that she knew were on hers.

Doc shook his head. "I don't know about you two. Go on, girl, get."

She looked at David.

"For heaven's sake, don't you two know what chances you're taking?"

As Lily walked away, she heard Doc's hushed words and knew he was admonishing David as he had her. But the idea that David's love for her was obvious . . . Love? Was it love? She hugged the words to her heart as she greeted the other men. And the idea of traveling with him! All she could think of was being alone with him—and of seeing Grace. Why not? She had a right to see her daughter, didn't she? They'd traveled together before, hadn't they?

But her euphoria was doused on her way home.

"We really need more information, Mrs. Dundee. If things don't go well for us, they don't go well with you. Do you understand?"

She nodded.

"I'd hate to see what an ugly mess your affair with the general would stir up, wouldn't you? Do you really want your daughter to learn that her mother's a common whore and her father is her favorite 'uncle'?" The man faked a shudder. "It's amazing how a beautiful woman can cause a man, even one as dedicated to advancing his career as Evans, to forget his priorities, isn't it? And you are a beautiful woman, Mrs. Dundee. Your husband already suspects your affair with the esteemed general, doesn't he? Wouldn't it be sad if your husband accidentally shot your lover? Such accidents do happen, don't they, Mrs. Dundee? All those little boys without a father, a fine career destroyed, a grieving widow ashamed to show her face . . . My, my, Mrs. Dundee, you're a very destructive force."

"Why are you doing this to me? I've been helping you. I want your . . . our side to win."

"I'm not so sure anymore. Like your general, I think your priorities are askew. Sexual attraction is a very powerful force. It's destroyed more than one good man in history, men much stronger than your general."

"What do you want?"

"You know what we want. We have reason to believe that the traitors are preparing to invade the Union and we want to know when and where, numbers, dates. You know what to give us." He inched closer and whispered, "Just give us something important and soon. Very soon, Mrs. Dundee." He started to walk away then turned around. "I'd hate to see your general get a sudden infection and take a turn for the worse or have an accident on his way home." His smile was so wicked that Lily felt ill. "Good day."

She stood in the middle of the street, too dazed to move, too frightened to think clearly. What could she do? She was trapped and David was doomed. Either way she went she hurt him. If her information didn't kill him in battle, her lack of information would kill him anyway. And if Saul found out about them, he might kill him.

Somehow she made it back to her room where she paced, wrung her hands, talked out loud. How could she rid herself of this burden? How could she protect David? There had to be a way. But until she thought of one, she had to give Biggs information.

And that meant she needed to stay with Saul, talk to Saul, listen to Saul, pry Saul's lips for information, perhaps travel with him again? And that meant she couldn't go with David to South Carolina. Tears rolled down her cheeks as she remembered her trip with David. How she'd dreamed of repeating that voyage with him, of caressing him, easing his suffering, helping him on his journey.

"Are you sure you're ready for that trip tomorrow?" She helped him back into bed.

"No," he laughed, "not really." He squeezed her hand. "But you'll be there to help me, so I'll be okay."

She withdrew her hand from his and sat down. "No, David, I won't be with you."

His brown eyes darkened. "Why? I was looking forward . . ."

His words cut into her heart. He wanted her, was looking forward to being with her. "I can't, David, I need to stay here."

"But you were going to see Grace, weren't you?"

"Yes." Grace. When would she ever see her again? "But something's come up."

He turned his face toward the ceiling. "I don't understand, not at all. I can't see what else could be as important as seeing Grace."

"You'll just have to believe me. I want to go, David, you don't know how much."

He grabbed her hand. "Then go with me, Lil. Please."

She shook her head. "I can't."

He dropped her hand. "Well, then."

"David, please."

"Are you here again?"

Lily stood up. "Just leaving, Doc." She looked at David whose face was like a statue sculpted in a permanent gaze at the ceiling. "Good bye, David."

"You okay, girl?" Doc's hand was on her arm, but she just shook her head and walked away.

She returned the next morning but purposely didn't let David see her. She watched as he climbed into the ambulance that would take him to the train station, his pain obvious as he winced with every movement. But were those tears on his cheeks? Lily had to keep herself from running to him. If he hurt this much, he shouldn't go.

"Girl, you beat all for timing."

"I'm sorry, Doc, I didn't want him to see me."

"Well that's quite admirable, but he needed you this morning more than ever. Didn't you hear? One of his best friends was killed."

"Jonathan?"

"No, some boy named Martin. Evans was so distraught that I tried to get him to stay here another day or two but he wouldn't hear of it. Stubborn. He was looking for you."

She looked toward the wagon. "Oh, Doc." She looked at the old man. "I thought it would be easier if I weren't here."

He patted her shoulder. "I know." He turned and walked back into the hospital.

Lily clutched her arms to her chest and tried to stop the trembling as the wagon pulled away. *I'm so sorry, David, so sorry.* How long would it be before she saw him again? He would need at least two months to recuperate. That would mean all of September and October—the month Mary Anne expected to show him off to their friends in Charleston. Would he be up to such a performance? He'd do it, of course. He always did what was expected whether it be a social obligation or military duty.

Though she could barely see through the tears in her eyes, Lily stared at the wagon until it was out of sight then was startled by a voice in her ear.

"I see you made the right decision, Mrs. Dundee."

CHAPTER 42

She tried so hard to forget David, to concentrate on Saul and her duties as both an army wife and Union spy, but she couldn't—and hated herself for it. If she had to fall in love, why did it have to be with someone else's husband? If she had to spy, why did it have to be against the men she loved? Of course, that's why she'd been chosen in the first place, and it hadn't bothered her then because Saul had meant nothing to her and she'd been determined to hurt David. Now there were multitudes of young Confederate men she loved, men she cared for, men who saw her as an angel.

Angel of death?

As when she'd traveled with Saul before, Lily served coffee and brandy at the officers' meetings then lingered to listen. Saul was relaxed in David's absence and obviously happy to have his wife with him again. They made a very happy and attractive couple. And things were good between them, somewhat as they'd been before. Saul was free with his kisses and caresses and Lily accepted them needily, always wondering why she couldn't be content with him.

And Saul had finally gotten his promotion. There was a very small ceremony and Lily was proud to be at his side to see his moment of glory. Silently, she breathed a sigh of relief. Surely now that Saul and David were generals—and equals—they would end their rivalry.

But they didn't.

It was almost the end of November. David had been gone so long that Lily worried that the news she'd been giving Biggs hadn't been enough and Biggs had followed through on his threats. But recently there was talk of his return, that he was in Richmond, then Culpepper, that he was on his way back. She could barely contain her excitement at the thought of seeing him and hearing about Grace. Yes, he'd been with Mary Anne, but he was coming back, and thoughts of seeing him surpassed everything else.

The officers were conducting their nightly meeting over a well-stocked stove when the tent flap opened and David and Jonathan walked in. The smile on Saul's face disappeared immediately.

After David shook hands and received welcomes, he patted his best friend on the back and said, "Gentlemen, I'd like to introduce my good friend, Colonel Jonathan Buford. He's just assumed command of my old regiment." As Saul and Jonathan shook hands, they renewed old ties and congratulated each other. David's congratulations for Saul were almost nonexistent.

The men sat down and Lily walked toward David and Jonathan. "Welcome back, General Evans. Would you like some coffee?"

He answered in a monotone and without looking at her. "Yes, thank you."

Shaking from his rebuff, she almost spilled the coffee and was thankful for Jonathan's presence. "And you, Colonel Buford?"

Jonathan's smile was broad and warm, and a wink accompanied his words. "Actually, Mrs. Dundee, I'd enjoy a brandy."

How genuine this man was, how kind and warm. "I think that can be arranged." His smile was contagious and Lily returned it.

But she couldn't stand David's coldness, and she ran out of the tent as soon as she gave Jonathan his drink. Angry and hurt, she paced, biting her lip and trying to hold back tears. She finally stopped and stood by a small fire to warm her hands and try to calm down. Before too long, the quiet night was filled with male voices, slaps on shoulders, and masculine laughter. Lily turned around. Only two men had exited. David and Jonathan.

Jonathan came straight to Lily and clasped his hands around hers. "My but it's good to see you again, Mrs. Dundee, so very good. I knew we'd meet again but didn't know where or when. Who knew it would be on such a cold night in Fredericksburg after our very pleasant day in Columbia?"

"I thought we'd gotten past formal titles, Colonel Buford."

"So we did, Lily."

"Congratulations on your promotion. Is there a Mrs. Buford to share the excitement yet?"

His eyes twinkled. "Not yet, but I'm working on it."

"Ah? Well, you'll let me know who the lucky lady is when you've found her, won't you?"

"You'll be one of the first." He continued to hold her hands as he glanced at David then winked at her. "I'm quite exhausted, so I'll say good night now."

"Good night." Lily kissed his cheek.

Flames lit David's dark eyes as he watched her from across the fire.

Trembling, Lily held her hands near the flames. She'd noticed during the evening that David favored the wounded arm and seemed stiff. "How are your wounds, General?"

"Fine."

"How's your family?"

"Fine."

"Did you see Gracie?"

"Yes."

"Is she well?"

A faint hint of humanity showed on his face as it never failed to do when he spoke of Grace. "Yes. Very well."

"How I'd love to see her."

He blew on his hands then rubbed them. "Yes, well, I guess that's debatable."

"How dare you. You know I want to see her."

"But not enough to go with me."

"You? Is it always about you?"

"Of course not."

"Well, it certainly seems that way. I'm afraid, General, that you don't always know the full story. There are obligations some of us must keep that prevent us from doing what we want."

"Really?"

"Yes, really."

"Such as a new regard for your husband now that he's a general?"

"That galls you, doesn't it? You can't stand his being equal with you, especially since he's younger. Yes, I'm proud of him. Don't all women want to be escorted by a general, show off a general, parade a general around like a prized pet at weddings in Charleston?"

His eyes widened. "What are you . . . ?"

"Ah, darling. I'm sorry I took so long." Saul wrapped his arms around his wife and pulled her close.

Lily glared at David. "Good night, General."

The next day Lily was hanging out Saul's shirts when an unusually ragged and dirty soldier approached. "Good day, Mrs. Dundee."

"Good day."

He looked around then walked closer and whispered, "Mr. Biggs sent me to thank you for the warm greetings you've been sending."

Lily shuddered.

"He says you're doing a fine job and likes the fact that you're traveling with your husband again." He winked and Lily sickened at his yellow-toothed grin and unwashed hair. "He also says you must be a handful of woman to bed two men in the same camp, and generals yet."

She looked around. "Don't you dare speak to me like that, you . . . I'm doing what Biggs wants, so leave me alone."

"Yeh, just as I thought, you're a real hot one." His lecherous eyes looked at her from head to toe. "These reb generals like to share their women, don't they? Their slave women too, so I hear."

Lily slapped him but his filthy hand tightened around her wrist. "I wouldn't do that again, if I was you. Accidents do happen, you know. I understand you care little for your own old man but quite a bit for the other one. He's been shot before and can be again." He tightened his grip and her wrist burned but she said nothing. "Maybe next time he won't live through it." His greasy face came within inches of hers and he whispered again, "You little slut. Maybe next time I'll ride you and find out what these traitors find so delicious." He licked his lips.

"Say, what's going on here? Who are you, soldier?"

At the sound of Saul's booming voice, the sick little man released her arm and saluted. "Private Holmes, Buford's Regiment, sir."

"And what are you doing here?"

"Just relaying a message, sir, from the colonel."

"Have you done so?"

"Yes, sir."

"Then leave us."

"Yes, sir."

Lily wanted to run into Saul's arms but dared not show her fear, though she trembled and longed for a bath to rid herself of the grime she felt from touching the horrid messenger.

"What's this about?"

"Nothing. He just gave me a message from Jonathan."

"How do you know Buford? I meant to ask you that the first night he arrived in camp. I didn't know you two were acquainted."

"I met him in Columbia. Remember when I visited Grace?" She forced a seductive smile and hoped Saul's interest in Jonathan would take his mind off Biggs. "Remember that nightgown you liked so much?" Saul smiled. "Well, I bumped into him while carrying a lot of packages and he was kind enough to help me with them. He took me to lunch then to the train station. I really like him."

She couldn't believe how stupid this Biggs was to say that he was from Jonathan's regiment, something that could be so easily verified—something Lily was sure Saul would do.

Her days were numbered now, her time growing short. Could she stand prison? Ha. Prison would be nothing compared to the looks of hatred and disgust she would get from Jonathan, Saul, every man she'd gotten to know.

But especially David. How hard those brown eyes would become, how cold. This was the worst thing in David's ethical code, the absolute worst. He would never forgive her. How could she have ever entered into something that would hurt him so? As for her, she could be hanged. But perhaps that would be a blessing, for how could she ever have a moment's peace knowing that David hated her? And what about Gracie?

Lily's mind raced with the enormity of her future as Saul stood there completely ignorant of the enormous turn their lives were taking.

"I find it hard to believe that that piece of filth is in any of our regiments."

"Well, all the men are in pretty sad shape right now."

"Yes, but there's a difference." Saul rubbed his chin and looked away then back. "Something about him bothers me." He patted her arm. "I'll check into it soon. But you appeared a little shaken when I walked up. Are you okay?"

She put her hand on his and realized just how very much he meant to her, how kind he'd been, how much he loved her, and she wanted to confess and throw herself at his mercy, but she knew that nothing she could possibly say would ease the pain that she was about to cause. "Don't worry about me."

He smiled warmly then gently kissed her lips. "But I do, very much." His hands were on her shoulders, his blue eyes looking down into hers.

Lily put her arms around his neck and leaned into his chest. "You're a wonderful man, General Dundee, a kind, handsome, good man, a man I've been very privileged to know. Please don't ever doubt that or forget it." She looked up at him. "Please."

"Lily?" He touched her cheek. "Are you crying?" He pulled her to his chest and held her tight. "That creep did upset you, didn't he? I'll take care of him for you, sweetheart. And soon."

And he didn't waste any time.

CHAPTER 43

As Lily paced inside their tiny tent, she looked at their meager possessions now precious because they represented the months that she and Saul had shared, the months that she had been the wife of a proud officer. Each time she heard a rustling sound she knew it was a guard coming to take her away, for surely Saul would be too hurt to face her. Surely he'd send someone else to arrest her as he loudly claimed that he had had no idea what she'd been doing, that he'd been deceived. It was true, of course, and she wouldn't blame him.

"Lily?"

David? She held her breath and opened the flap of the tent.

His face was grave. "I need to see you. Come with me. Please."

She shivered. His eyes searched hers.

He knew.

She followed him until they stopped in a small secluded thicket of trees. Curling yellow leaves crunched beneath their feet, thin bare dogwoods swayed, and the few remaining birch leaves rustled. David motioned toward an old fallen log. "Sit, please."

She sat then took a deep breath and studied him as he paced, his hands clasped behind his back. *I'm watching you, David Evans. I'm memorizing every line on your still young face. I'm remembering the young virginal face that first taught me I could fall in love, the cruel face that killed Tom in a jealous rage, the noble face that refuses to give in. I shall never forget your face, David, even at its saddest and cruelest, which I fear I'll soon see.*

"I just heard something very disturbing." He stopped pacing and stood in front of her. "Saul asked Jonathan about a private in his regiment, a private who doesn't exist, a private Saul says he found talking, quite suspiciously, to you. Do you know of whom I'm speaking?"

"Yes."

"Who is he?"

"How should I know? All he told me was what Saul reported to Jonathan."

David knelt in front of her and took her hands in his.

She shivered at the feel of him and at the sight of their hands together and she wished, as she always did when she was with David, that she could stop time.

His voice cracked and his eyes moistened. "Tell me the truth, Lily, please."

She closed her eyes tightly then opened them and looked again at their hands then at his face. "What truth, David? What is it you expect me to say? Why are you questioning me?"

"Because I've seen suspicious men with you before and each time it's disturbed me."

"Don't I have a right to speak to whomever I please?"

"Yes, but I know how you feel about saving the Union, freeing the slaves, and . . ." He stood up and paced. "Things look . . . odd . . . including the dubious obligations that kept you from going to South Carolina with me."

"Is that what this is all about? Are you still angry with me for not making that trip with you?"

"Yes, damn it!" He returned to her side and began kissing her hands almost frantically. "I needed you, Lily. I needed you desperately, as much or more than I've ever needed anyone in my life. I needed the comfort and attention that only you can give me. One of my best friends had just died." His eyes were pleading and his face was innocent once again.

"David." She touched his cheek and he kissed her palm. "I wanted to go with you, truly I did. But I couldn't."

He sprang to his feet. "Why not? I don't understand and you won't give me reasons."

She was instantly on her feet shaking a scolding finger at him. "There's more going on than just you, David Evans. Look around you. I'm sorry you were hurting in body and spirit and I wanted to comfort you, truly I did, but . . . damn it, David, you were going home to Mary Anne. How could you even ask me to escort you to your wife? How cruel are you?"

He paced in a circle. "Is that why you didn't go?"

His words finally caught up with her and she reached out a hand toward him and stuttered, "Did . . . did you mean what you just said?"

"What?"

"That only I can give you the comfort and attention you need?"

His voice and eyes grew soft and he took her hands again, tenderly. "Oh Lil, of course I did." They sat down and he pulled her to him, smelled her hair, kissed her hands again and again.

"You don't just mean the sex a whore can provide when your wife's not available?"

"Aw, Lily, please don't . . ."

"I mean it, David."

"No. Never." His mouth moved on hers and she responded pliantly then welcomed the feel of his lips searching her face and neck. He pulled her to his chest and she inhaled him.

"Lil . . . do you love me?"

Her heart raced. Why on earth was he asking that now? If only he knew how long she'd waited to hear those words. But he wasn't declaring his love, he was asking for hers. Did he really love her or just want her declaration like another title in front of his name? Was he testing her loyalty? Worse still, was he wanting her to tell him that he, not Saul, was the better man?

"Lily?" He squeezed her then pushed her away and looked into her downcast eyes. "Do you love me?"

"David . . . I . . ."

His expression went from disbelief to despair to icy indifference in a matter of seconds and he dropped his hands from her shoulders. "I didn't realize the question was such a hard one. I guess after all these years I thought . . . But I guess I was wrong. Forgive me for embarrassing you." He took a deep breath and stood up then straightened his uniform. "Perhaps your judgment of our relationship has always been more accurate than mine after all."

Lily felt sure that she was falling apart, that if she spoke, she'd scream. "What do you mean?"

"I mean that I'm just one of your customers."

She buried her face in her hands. "No, David, no."

He grabbed her hands and looked into her tear-filled eyes. "Then tell me, Lil! Tell me you love me!"

"What purpose would it serve? What good would it do? Why do you torture me with such a question when you're not free?"

"What good would it do?" He ran his fingers through his hair and paced. "What good would it do? My God, Lil." He grabbed her shoulders and shook her. "I'll tell you . . ."

"Get your hands off of her!" Saul pulled David away then hit him. David returned the punch and soon the two men were rolling on the ground as Lily watched, her face wet with tears and her mind reliving that horrible morning when David killed Tom. "Stop, please . . ." She wailed as she watched the cruel expressions smear their handsome faces. "Please stop, please!"

Jonathan flew into the middle of the melee and separated the much larger men. "You two aren't fit to lead anything more than a bunch of thugs!" He kept a hand on each man's chest and continued to push them apart. "Really, gentlemen! You're officers, supposedly above this childish exhibition. Collect yourselves, please." He finally lowered his hands then walked to Lily and put a comforting arm around her shoulders. "Are you all right?" She nodded and he pulled her close in a quick hug. "Now gentlemen—and I use that term hesitantly—what's this all about?"

"This son of a . . ."

Jonathan put up his hand. "Your wife is present, Dundee. Please watch your language."

"Evans can't keep his hands off my wife and I decided that today was the last time he'd ever touch her." Saul's eyes narrowed as he looked at David. "I swear if I ever catch you with your hands on her again, or even catch you alone with her, I'll kill you. My God, you have a houseful of kids and a beautiful wife yet you want mine too. What would Longstreet or your men think if they knew the truth about you, you lecherous hypocrite?"

David lunged toward Saul but Jonathan stepped between them again. "Enough, enough!" He looked at David. "Apologize."

Lily noticed how David nursed his left arm, how he winced with each breath, and she longed to comfort him. But despite his obvious pain, he stood haughtily, his chin raised and his eyes narrowed in defiance.

"I said apologize."

"We're not children, Buford. We're two men settling our differences."

"Differences? Is that what you call this ridiculous competition?" Jonathan shook his head. "You've really changed, old friend. This is not your style of settling an argument and you know you've wronged Mrs. Dundee. If you don't apologize, I might take great delight in delivering you to the guardhouse myself and bringing you up on charges."

"You wouldn't."

"Don't be so sure."

Lily saw the humiliation and embarrassment on David's face and the smugness on Saul's and she wanted to slap them both.

David faced Lily and bowed. "I beg your forgiveness, Mrs. Dundee." He immediately walked away and Lily had to stop herself from running after him. Why couldn't everyone else in the world just disappear and leave David and her alone? She needed him—his body, his touch, his lips . . . Oh, David! Why hadn't she confessed her love for him? Would this scene have ended differently? Would David have declared his love? Was he about to when Saul interrupted? Would she ever know?

Saul moved toward his wife but Jonathan blocked his way.

"What th . . . ?"

"You need to cool down too, Dundee. Give the lady some time to collect herself."

Saul gritted his teeth and his jaw muscles tightened. "Okay." He pointed at Lily. "But don't be too long."

As soon as Saul walked away, Lily fell back onto the log and hugged herself as she rocked and cried. Jonathan sat beside her and whispered calming words as his arm wrapped around her shoulders. "What happened, Lily? What's going on?"

She looked at him, into his sweet kind face. "Everything's so messed up. Everything's so awful. Worse than you can imagine."

"I wouldn't be so sure."

He wiped her face with his handkerchief then handed it to her. Lily turned away and blew her nose.

"I think you're in quite a complicated situation from which you can't escape."

"I didn't mean to love him."

"I know and he didn't mean to love you, but that's the least of it now, isn't it?"

"What do you mean?"

"I mean Private Holmes."

She winced and wondered when his eyes would turn dark and his comfort turn to hate.

"You see, I didn't tell David or Saul, but I've seen this Holmes before. He's not in my regiment or even in the Confederate Army. When David's spoken of you in the past," he nodded at her hopeful expression, " . . . yes, he speaks of you often, almost constantly. You see," he lifted her chin with his thumb and forefinger, "I'm the only person to whom he can confide and he so desperately needed to tell someone, to share his feelings for you with someone. He adores you, Lily. I probably shouldn't tell you that but there it is." She started crying again and he pulled her close and rocked her. "Now, now, that should be good news to you." He looked at her. "But the timing's not right, is it?"

She shook her head and bit her lip.

"No. As I was saying, David's been quite concerned about some suspicious meetings you've had with men he's never seen before. One time he said you met one such man in the middle of the street, that the man passed you a note and quickly walked away when David interrupted you. Who are these men, Lily? Holmes is one, isn't he?"

"How can I tell you something so dreadful, something so awful that you, that everyone, that David . . ." The vision of David's sad face made her break down again. "You'll hate me so . . . I hate myself, but it started with good intentions, honestly it did."

"Shh." He stood up and searched the trees and bushes then sat back down. "I think it's best that we whisper, don't you?"

"You know, don't you?"

"I have my suspicions."

"Then why don't you hate me?"

"I liked you the moment I heard David mention your name. I knew that any lady—and I do mean lady—who could bring such a smile to my friend's face must be a gem. Meeting you only convinced me of it. You're a good person, Lily. If you're guilty of anything, it's loving the wrong man. Not only is he married, but he's serving the wrong army. Am I right?"

She nodded and felt a tiny spark of relief that someone knew the truth. "I'm so sorry, Jonathan. I'm so sorry."

"Are you sorry you did it or sorry you had to?"

"I'm sorry I hurt all of you but I had to. When I was thirteen I saw a girl about my age being mauled by an auctioneer then torn from her mother while both women screamed." Lily covered her ears, surprised that the event could still trigger such strong feelings even now when so much was happening. "It was horrible, just horrible." To her amazement, Jonathan put his arm back around her shoulders. Now that she was confessing, she wanted to say it all. "And I wanted to save our country."

He nodded.

"And . . . I wanted to hurt him!"

"David?"

"Yes. I've never loved anyone else, Jonathan. I can't. He's so deep inside me that I can't breathe without him. Then I had our child and he took her from me . . . I just wanted to hurt him as much as he hurt me, keeps hurting me . . . I hate this hold he has on me and I would rip out my heart if I thought it would make it go away, make it quit hurting. I love him so much, so very much . . ." Lily leaned against Jonathan and released more tears.

"This is dangerous, Lily. You know they can hang you, don't you?"

"Yes, and I'd welcome the peace of death if I knew that Grace, TJ, and Ruthie were safe and cared for. I'd welcome the peace that not loving David would bring me."

"I think we need to find a way to get you back to Kentucky."

"No. I can't."

"Why? You don't *want* to hang, do you?"

"No, but if I run away, they'll . . ."

"There she is." David's arm shook as it pointed at her. "There's the . . . traitor, the spy, the . . . Arrest her!"

The guard gripped her arm so hard she winced, but her eyes were on David whose red swollen eyes and quivering lips would haunt her forever.

Jonathan touched the guard's shoulder. "You don't need to squeeze her arm so tightly soldier. She'll not try to run away." He turned to David and lowered his friend's arm then whispered, "This is wrong, David. You don't know what you're doing."

David's eyes were full of tears, his voice was cracking. "I know very well what I'm doing. She's betrayed me . . . us, all of us." He walked to Lily, his voice and hands trembling as he spoke. "How could you?" He raised his hand to strike her but Jonathan caught it.

As Lily was ushered away, she heard Jonathan whispering to David and before she'd cleared the thicket, she heard David cry out, "Why didn't you stop me?"

CHAPTER 44

"I will see her!" Saul's commanding voice boomed as he forced his way past the guards and into the tent where Lily was being held. He stared at her as he paced then he reached toward her but shook his head and lowered his arms. Again he paced, threading his hair with his fingers, staring at her like she was something disgusting. Barely audible words finally broke through quivering lips. "Lily, please tell me this is all some horrible lie, some sick dream."

She took his hand and tried to calm him. "I'm sorry, but . . ."

"Sorry? Sorry? How could you do this to me, to us? Did you just use me, Lily? Was that all I was to you? Has this been going on since the beginning? How about Evans? What's his part in all this?"

She spoke quietly. "David has nothing to do with any of this."

"David, huh?" The sneer on his face was ugly as he yanked his hand from hers. "You've always been free and easy with his first name, haven't you? I hear he's the one who had you arrested. What happened? Was he tired of you and afraid his wife would find out? Or had you tired of him and hurt his pride? Did he know what you were doing? Who was the best source for information, him or me?"

"I'm sorry, Saul. I don't know what else to say. I believe in the Union and had to stop your barbarous lifestyle."

His eyes widened then darkened. "You didn't seem to mind that lifestyle when it provided jewelry and pretty dresses, when we danced and ate at the nicest restaurants and slept in the nicest hotels. Or was all of that part of your disguise? The charming wife of a Confederate officer . . . Is that all it was? Did you care for me at all?" He breathed deeply and closed his eyes before speaking again, almost pitifully. "Did you ever love me, Lily, or have you always loved him? How long has it been going on?" He looked into her eyes. "From that first night? Did I cause all this? Did I bring you two together? He wasn't the innocent you claim, was he? You toyed with me, made me think you didn't care for him." He paced again, his face red, his fingers clinched then stopped and whispered, "I loved you. I thought we were happy. I thought you loved me. I had visions of our children . . ."

Lily saw tears in his eyes and berated herself as she had so many times. Why, oh why, couldn't she have loved him the way she loved David? "I love you in my own way." Tears blurred her vision.

"As a chump, you mean." He blinked away his tears and threaded his hair with his fingers then his eyes widened and he spoke as if to himself. "Oh my God, what have I done? All the confessions, all the battle plans . . ." Lily saw his temper regaining control as his cruel eyes pierced through her. "You took what I said in confidence and used it against me and my country, my men! You're not only a traitor, you're a murderer!" He held his stomach and glowered at her. "You make me sick!"

He ran out as she called his name.

But what was the use? She could swear she loved him in her own way, that she felt horrible for betraying him, but what good would it serve? Poor Saul. Perhaps he'd gotten the worst of all of this, for she'd not even loved him—not like she loved David, would always love David.

The ruination of two good men. That would be her legacy.

That night she wrote a letter to Grace. She'd always planned to write such a letter, always planned to explain the girl's parentage to her, but she'd hoped it wouldn't be for many years. As she put the words on paper, she thought of Grace's sweet face with her father's loving features then envisioned her as a young woman. The cause of unity and freedom—were they worth all she'd sacrificed, all her daughter would sacrifice? When Grace finds out that her adored Fish is really her father, will she be able to understand why her mother betrayed the cause her father fought for? Although she doubted that Grace would ever forgive her, Lily had to tell her why.

They were preparing to move her to Richmond but that was all she knew. Jonathan felt sure that she'd be held in a private home but Lily was beyond worrying about herself. The well-being of her children and Jonathan—and David—was all that mattered to her.

Jonathan was a faithful dependable friend, and he had been to see her every day even though there were rumors of an impending battle. When he visited on her last day in Fredericksburg, she gave him the letter for Grace. "Don't give it to her until you have to, okay?"

"Of course. Perhaps it won't be necessary."

"I like your optimism but something always told me that I wouldn't be around to explain things to her properly. I just don't want her growing up resentful, choosing a lifestyle that's not in her best interest. David's family has been so good to provide her with the best of everything that if she uses her head, she'll do fine whether I'm around or not."

Jonathan patted her shoulder. "That little girl will be just fine. She's from good stock, very good stock. You and Dave are the best folks I know."

"Oh, Jonathan, I can't tell you how much I appreciate what you've done, what you keep doing. You know, neither David nor Saul will come see me. I was hoping . . . Anyway, I guess I won't see them again except at the trial where I'm sure they'll have plenty to say about me."

"Don't worry about that yet. Things move so slowly that who knows what will happen. I am sorry that Dave hasn't come by. I know this is driving him crazy. Unfortunately, it's affecting the way he treats his men. He's always been so good with them but I'm starting to hear talk of discontent in the ranks, rumors that he's pushing them too hard, handing out severe punishments where he would have gone easy before."

"Jonathan, I need to tell you something but you must promise me that you won't tell David."

"I'll do what I can for you, you know that, but I'm hesitant to make promises."

"Then I'll just say this. Watch over him. He could be in danger."

"Have they threatened you?"

"Not me but David and Gracie. That's why I couldn't quit and why I can't return to Kentucky. I don't care what happens to me, but I can't risk harming either of them."

"My poor girl. I'll do what I can but you must tell the authorities when you get to Richmond."

"No! I can't and you mustn't either. Please."

"Okay, for now." He winked. "I'll watch him for you."

"I feel I'm asking too much of you, but . . . when you have a chance, would you please check on TJ and Ruthie and let them know that I haven't forgotten them, that I still love them?" She pulled a map from her bodice. "Here. This shows where my valuables are hidden in my house. With it you can provide for the kids and Mary Anne, and David's men if there's enough."

"Of course I'll do as you ask, but you need to keep that money for after the war. David can take care of Mary Anne, Grace, and his men."

"No he can't. I know he's in debt and worried about paying off his creditors. We both know that David's an excellent soldier but I'm not sure he's the best bookkeeper and he's much too fond of saying yes instead of no when he's asked for anything. Please?" She touched his hand holding the map. "At least keep it so you can help him after the war . . . if I'm not around. I know you'll help TJ and Ruthie with it. I've never met a man I could trust more."

He smiled and bowed. "A very fine compliment from a very fine lady."

"Time's up, Colonel."

Lily panicked. "Write me, please? And come see me?"

"Of course, I will." He kissed her hand. "And I'll keep you informed about our friend."

"And you'll be careful too, won't you?"

"Yes, ma'am. With a pretty lady to wish me well, how could I not?"

Early the next morning Lily was put in a wagon and taken to the train station. She looked for David but he was nowhere to be found and she wondered what he and Saul were doing. Surely they knew she was leaving.

But what did she expect? Why would either of them ever want to see her again? Jonathan said that David loved her, but love and hate go hand in hand. If he, indeed, had ever loved her, he certainly didn't now.

Just the same, she strained her neck to look out the window even as the train pulled out of the station.

And then she saw him, her handsome soldier, standing on the platform—his arms folded across his chest, his glistening eyes staring into hers—an image that she would carry forever.

He'd come to see her.

The ride was rough, the air stale and smoky, but Lily knew that the trip might be her last taste of freedom so she enjoyed the glories of nature and the little bit of fresh air. Her mind, of course, remained on the vision of David giving her that stoic silent good bye. But there were so many good memories, and soon she was smiling, confident that those memories would get her through whatever lay ahead. She'd have David in her mind and heart forever even if she never saw him again.

But the train pulled into a different station than the one where she'd met David, and after a short wagon ride they stopped at a large three-story building where a female guard said dryly, "Welcome to Castle Thunder."

CHAPTER 45

For the first time Lily was scared. Jonathan had felt sure that she'd be incarcerated in a private home. He'd felt sure that she'd be given humane treatment since she was a woman, but it seemed he was wrong.

She stepped down and out of the wagon then was dragged into a dark building that reeked of human filth and echoed with hacking coughs, fiendish laughs, and rattling moans.

"So this is the little princess, huh?" Sergeant Colson was a massive man whose uniform was two sizes too small and whose large head, thick lips, and bulbous eyes reminded Lily of a frog. As he walked around her, looking her over inch by inch, he chomped on an onion. "Well, I can certainly see why men whispered secrets in your ear, dolly. Yes, I most certainly can." Lily almost gagged when his saliva sprayed her face.

Sweaty lank hair clung to his pock-marked face and the veins in his neck protruded when he spoke. "If I had my way, those damn prissy officers would hang right alongside you. Any man who drops his pants for a pretty face then tells her state secrets is just as guilty as you, honey."

He put a large thick-fingered hand on her shoulder and caressed it. "But they won't get into any trouble at all. No, ma'am. You've used them and they've used you and now you'll hang while they go on to glory and honor, go back home to waiting wives and parades." He laughed and Lily saw the hairs in his copper nose and the rotten teeth in his wide mouth. He took another bite of onion and waved his hand as he spoke to the matron. "Get the whore out of my sight."

Lily shuffled in her shackles as the solid stocky woman pulled her outside then into a second building that was no cleaner than the first. As they walked down the dark halls, Lily wondered if she'd ever grow accustomed to the muck, mold, and mildew, the walls and floors caked with smoke and spit, urine, and feces. The roaches and rats.

At least, she thought, she'd be isolated from all the other prisoners.

But she wasn't.

The dampness and drafts hit her first followed immediately by the hollow feel of the cavernous rectangular room. As she reached the bottom steps she saw about a dozen women staring at her. Women of all shapes and sizes in all forms of dress and undress—standing, reclining, squatting. The matron stopped beside a pile of straw and slapped at a roach then flicked it onto the floor. "Here's your bed."

"Where am I to take care of my personal needs?"

The woman laughed. "Outside in the latrine, where else?" She prodded Lily with a baton. "Not quite what you're used to, is it princess? Lettin' all those generals poke ya' has really done ya' proud." She cackled and walked out of the room.

And Lily was immediately surrounded.

But she held her head high and spoke with courage she didn't have. "Nice place, huh?"

Various women touched her dress and hair while mumbling among themselves as Lily watched them. "Most of us used to look as good as you. Didn't we, ladies?" Heads nodded and voices echoed agreement. The woman extended her hand to Lily. "I'm Alma. So, you're a spy, huh?"

"So they say."

"Well, we're in here for about every reason you can think of, most have to do with men, of course." She laughed. "I hope you took a long look at yourself before you got here because you'll soon look like us. Scary, huh?"

Alma's hair was almost gray even though she was probably Lily's age, and even the youngest-looking woman's appearance was haggard and drab. Lily shuddered. David would never love her in such a state. Looking at the group, she asked, "Why are you here?"

Alma smiled and nodded toward the other women. "For letting the wrong men in our drawers. It's amazing how amiable men are until you're a liability. I mean, they're even willing to pay us until their wives find out. Suddenly we become spies and dangerous to the cause."

"But you're . . ."

"Oh, yes. I'm a Southerner. I even used to be a champion of this pathetic farce."

"What changed your mind?"

"Being thrown in here." Everyone laughed then Alma motioned toward the ceiling.

"And meeting the darkies upstairs. My family didn't have slaves so I'd never had any reason to mingle with them until I got here. You see, the guards don't want the whites and Negroes to mix until it's convenient for them. Suddenly we're all the same and they let us congregate, like outside in that ditch they call a privy.

"I admit I used to think myself better than darkies, but being forced together changed my mind. Well, actually, it was meeting Nellie. She's teaching the others upstairs—and even some of us—how to read and write." Alma shook her head. "That Nellie's the smartest woman I've ever met, white or black. You should have heard the way I used to talk before she got a hold of me." She looked at the other ladies who nodded and laughed.

"Nellie?" Lily gulped. "About 30, huge eyes, bossy?"

"Yep, that's her."

"How can I meet her?" Lily was so excited that she'd forgotten everything about the horrible conditions.

Alma winked. "I'll see to it." She added. "Nellie's something, all right. They keep adding to her time because she won't quit teaching. They even throw her into the hole but it don't—doesn't—stop her. She's a stubborn one, that's for sure."

Lily shook her head and smiled. "Yes, that's Nellie."

That night after the gaslights were extinguished and the room filled with moonlight, Lily thought of David, saw David, and suddenly the roaches and smelly straw bed were gone and she was with him, loving him. As she touched herself, she visualized the two of them in that tacky hotel cuddling and loving as the snow piled high outside, saw them traveling to Columbia, saw them in front of the fire in her apartment, saw them conceiving their child.

She climaxed with tears in her eyes and his name on her lips.

"Lily?"

She sniffed and turned to see Alma.

"Come on."

She followed Alma to a stairway that she'd not seen before and climbed stairs that seemed to go nowhere. Alma knocked quietly on what appeared to be a ceiling.

But the ceiling opened and dark faces looked down on them.

"Where's Nellie?"

The door was pulled aside so Alma could climb in. Lily followed.

A room much more crowded and danker than the one below was filled with dark-skinned females who looked at each other then separated for another to come from behind them.

"Flora? Baby? Is that you?"

"Nellie?" Lily and the woman hugged in the middle of the room. "I can't believe it. I've wondered all these years what happened to you and the other ladies. I never thought I'd see you again." They touched each other's faces in disbelief then said, "Is it really you?" in unison.

"Listen, girl, you best get back downstairs but I'll get in touch with you."

"But I have so much to ask you—Stella, Gladys . . ."

"And I'll answer all your questions. Besides, I have a few of my own to ask you. After all I went through with you, how did you end up here? But we best not take any chances. I'll get in touch with you, don't you think I won't. We just have to be careful." She took Lily's hands again. "I'm so happy to see you little girl." She kissed her cheek. "So happy."

Lily hugged her, tears rolling down her cheeks. "And I you."

Lily learned that she was in a building called Whitlock's Warehouse and that it was one of three that comprised Castle Thunder—a name endowed by the prisoners in reference to their receiving the thunder of the gods—and the place was notorious for its cruelty. Whitlock's and another building, Palmer's Factory, were "wings" of the largest building, Gleanor's Tobacco Factory, and all three were connected by a wooden fence in the front and a brick wall in the back. The back enclosure was the yard where inmates exercised and attended to lavatory needs—all in sight of armed guards atop the walls. It was also the site for executions, which the inmates were forced to watch through their windows.

Lily quickly adjusted to her new life, although she starved several days before she was hungry enough to force down the putrid meat, wormy hard cornbread, and slimy roach-infested soup. And for the first time in her life, she was grateful for long skirts that provided a modicum of privacy when she used the latrine.

The ladies exchanged stories of families and men, of happiness and heartache. Most of them expected to be exchanged soon. "They're not comfortable locking up women," she heard. "And they never execute 'em," she was assured. Lily gleaned hope from their words and fantasized about being with her children again.

Her best times, of course, were with Nellie, and she was glad to learn that the ladies from Mama Rose's place had been spared, and most were still plying their trade in Kentucky. Nellie had been the only one in real danger, mostly as a scapegoat because of her color, and her life was spared only because no one could prove who'd murdered the two policemen. She was, of course, given jail time. When released, she joined an abolitionist group and went south to help newly freed slaves go north.

Lily described her life since that horrible day in Lexington. When she described being a prostitute, Nellie shook her head and frowned. When she spoke of wanting to free the slaves, Nellie nodded with pride and smiled. When she spoke of Grace, Nellie beamed in delight. But when she whispered of her love for David, Nellie shook her head in despair.

CHAPTER 46

It was spring by the time Jonathan found Lily, and even she was surprised at how well she'd accepted her existence. She'd lost so much weight that her monthly bleeding had stopped—a blessing under the circumstances—and she'd become quit proficient at picking lice out of her hair and using the sparingly rationed water and pieces of petticoats for bathing.

She was thrilled when told she had a visitor and taken to a small room with a wooden table and two chairs, but she stifled a laugh when she saw that the little alcove was so clean. To fool visitors?

But nothing else mattered because she had a visitor! Was it possible that David . . .?

When Jonathan walked in, Lily flew into his arms but her eyes searched in vain for David. If our places were reversed, she thought, I would visit him every day.

But then their places weren't similar at all, were they?

"No, Lily, he's not here. I'm sorry."

"I didn't really expect him. Did he know you were coming?"

"Yes."

"And?"

"Oh, Lily, you know how he is. His eyes turned dark and his hands balled into fists like he was going to hit someone."

She nodded and smiled. Yes, she could see him, see him so clearly that she almost reached out to put her hands on his fists to relax them. "But . . .?"

"You don't really expect him to come here, do you? He's already jeopardized his marriage and career. Why do you think he's so frustrated? His loyalties are stretched far too thin. He's pulled in far too many directions. He worries about Mary Anne and the boys, his men and the war, and now you. And the guilt he carries for breaking his marriage vows is killing him. I worry about him, Lily, I really do. He's a very strong man but even strong men have been brought down. Certain Biblical heroes come to mind."

Lily nodded then smiled as she hugged Jonathan again, realizing how much she'd missed the feel and scent of a man. "I'm sorry. I am happy to see you, you know that. I was beginning to think that no one would ever show up." They sat down as Lily continued. "How is David? And Grace? How's Saul? Have you seen TJ and Ruthie yet?"

But he was distracted and shaking his head. "I can't believe they sent you here."

She laughed as she eyeballed the room. "This is plush compared to where I live."

"How can you find humor in such filth?"

She shrugged.

"I've got to get you out of here. There's no reason for you to be treated like this."

"But I'm the lowest of the low, Jonathan, you should know that. This place is for the undesirables and that's me."

"No." He stood. "I won't stand for this. What will the world think if they find out we keep women caged in such a fashion?"

She laughed. "If I didn't know you better, I'd think you cared more about how this looks on the Confederacy than how it affects me."

He sat back down and put his hands over hers on the table. "I'm sorry, my dear. It did sound like that, and I do care about how we're viewed, but of course you're more important."

"Besides, there are other women here. I'm not the only one." Her eyes sparkled. "And guess what? I found Nellie!" She saw his confusion. "She worked in the house where I grew up. She taught me how to read and write." She squeezed his hands. "She saved my life."

Jonathan watched her. "You are amazing."

"Just a survivor."

He smiled. "Have they told you how long you'll be here?"

"No. Until my trial I guess, but I have no idea how long that will be. I've been told that most female prisoners are released or exchanged in six months. I've also heard that they never execute women." She smiled. "You can imagine the relief I felt when I heard that." She looked around again. "I guess I'll just bide my time." Her smile grew broad. "I can't believe that I'll actually be able to return to my babies!"

Jonathan shook his head and smiled slightly. "I do admire your spunk and I'm sure you're right about getting out soon, but I'd hate to see what our friend would do if he saw you in here, probably spirit you away on the mighty Samson."

"Ah, that's a very pleasant picture you paint, Colonel, but I doubt he'll ever want me again, if he ever did."

"If he ever did? My gosh, girl, what does it take to convince you how much that man loves you? This thing has driven him almost crazy. He's not himself at all."

"Tell me about him, Jonathan."

"He's abominable. He never smiles and has no sense of humor. He barks at his men constantly and has focused all his energies on getting promoted, speaks of it night and day. Longstreet's even getting tired of hearing about it." He shook his head again. "I swear, Lily, he's going to alienate the only man who thinks as highly of him as he does himself."

"It's that bad?"

"I'm afraid so. He's always at the lead in all the charges, even when it's not wise, and he always volunteers his men for the most hazardous duty. I'm sorry to say it, but I don't think he thinks of human lives at all anymore, only of how it will look for him."

"That's so unlike David to care only about himself. He's always put the welfare of his men above all else."

"I agree." He stood up and slapped his thigh with his cap. "But I've got to get you out of here."

Lily stood and touched his cheek. "Don't trouble yourself, Jonathan. I'm fine, really."

He furrowed his brows. "I find that hard to believe. I'll see what I can do. In the meantime," he handed her something in a napkin, "eat this. I'll be back as soon as I can and bring you more." He smiled and shook his head. "You're a strong woman, Mrs. Dundee. I admire you even more than before, if that's possible."

"I've told you, Jonathan, the only things that can really hurt me are harm to David and Grace." She kissed his cheek. "And you."

He turned to leave.

"Jonathan?"

He turned around. "Yes?"

"Does he speak of me?"

"All the time. Not in words perhaps, but I see you in his face every day. He may talk promotion, but it's because he's trying to forget you. But it's not working."

"Thank you for everything."

"I'll be back."

Lily pulled back the napkin and saw fresh gingerbread. She pinched off a tiny corner and ate it then gave the remainder to her guard, the very young and bashful Peter Wills from Atlanta. "Thank you, ma'am."

Not only was the boy respectful to her, which she appreciated especially under the circumstances, but he often snuck food to her—edible food.

For Lily was alone now. The other ladies had, indeed, been exchanged or fully released, even Nellie, and she missed all of them and found the large room quite lonely. Peter spent time with her when he could and she found his honesty and good manners charming. Since he couldn't read very well, she often read to him, and they spent many hours playing cards, though he always said, "Hope nobody tells my momma about this."

CHAPTER 47

Lily woke from a deep sleep, then jumped when she saw a strange woman staring down at her. Her heart beat so rapidly that she could barely speak. "Who are you?"

"Some call me Biggs."

Lily shivered and wanted to cry but wouldn't give the woman the satisfaction. "What on earth could you want from me now? I think you can see that I've given all I can, including my freedom."

"But it's not for me, madam, it's for your country." She whispered, "You seem to have a good friend in Colonel Buford."

Lily closed her eyes and felt her body sapped of its only remaining energy. "Please, don't make me hurt yet another good man, not anyone anymore, please."

The woman was oblivious to her begging. "It's not just Buford. With the talkative young private and the other lusting guards, this should be an excellent place to get information, and we expect you to make the most of it." The woman looked at Lily from head to toe then smirked, "Although I can't see why any man would want *you*."

"But everyone knows I'm a spy. Why would Jonathan, or anyone else, say anything around me?"

"Because you won't be that obvious. We don't expect battle plans, just little slip-ups, information about troop movements, that kind of thing." At the sound of footsteps, the woman disappeared as mysteriously as the other Biggs had that day in the hospital, and a shaken Lily was relieved to see Peter. "Colonel Buford's here again, ma'am."

Lily ran into Jonathan's arms the instant the door shut to the tiny room. "What's wrong?"

She clung to him and whispered in his ear, "They've sent another Biggs to get information from me. Oh, Jonathan, they're never going to leave me alone. David won't be safe until I'm dead."

246

"Shh." He patted her as he helped her sit down then whispered in her ear, "Just pass on what I give you, okay?"

She shivered and dried her eyes. "Okay." She bit her lip. "But they also expect me to be friendly with the guards." She looked at him hesitantly.

His eyes darkened. "Well, that won't be necessary. I'll give you enough information." He patted her hands. "Now, let's forget it." He slid a large box across the table to her.

"I was hoping that was for me!" She became a child again as she untied the bow.

"Well, I can't get you moved from here, not yet anyhow. But since you're alone down there—and I dare not see what 'down there' looks like—they've agreed that I can provide some things for you—better food and a few amenities."

She shook her head adamantly. "Not if the money's coming out of your pocket, Colonel Buford."

"That doesn't matter as long as they keep it up. I want reports on how they're treating you, okay?"

"Okay." She quickly lifted the lid then squealed as she pulled out one treasure after another. "Books, pen and paper, a comb, mirror, toothbrush . . . even talcum power and cologne. Oh Jonathan!"

"Notice the fragrance?"

She looked at the bottle and smiled. "Gardenia. How did you know?"

"How do you think?" He touched his nose. "Personal memory . . . and a constant reminder from someone we both know."

"Really?"

He nodded. "Yes, ma'am. And now that you have paper and pen, I expect regular communication from you."

"Of course I'll write to you, probably so often that you'll be sick of hearing from me. Oh, thank you, thank you." She kissed his cheek.

"Well there's no one I'd rather help. Besides, you know every man wants to be a knight in shining armor to a beautiful princess."

As he spoke, Lily shrieked. "Oh, my God!"

"What's wrong?"

She was staring into the mirror. Puffy blood-shot gray-rimmed eyes, ashen pinched face, bristly hair. She turned away from the mirror and her guest. "Don't look at me!"

"Lily?"

She looked in the mirror again and studied the ugly face. How could she have turned into such a wizened hag so quickly? She'd known that her hair was ratted and filthy, that several of her teeth were loose, that her skin was dry, and that her ragged dirty dress was several sizes too big—but she looked far worse than she'd imagined and began to cry.

Jonathan reached across the table. "Please tell me what's wrong."

"No." Her back was to him. "Don't ever look at me again. Had I known I looked this horrid, I never would have agreed to see you."

"Lily . . ."

"Now I'm glad that David hasn't come to see me." She cried harder and her shoulders shook. "He'll never love me now. How could he ever want to put his arms around me?" She looked at the chapped lips and yellow teeth. "How could he ever want to put his mouth on mine?" She pulled the comb through her hair and several of the teeth broke out and she spoke through sobs. "It will be easy for him to forget me now. I'll never be able to compete with the beautiful Mary Anne!" She dropped her head on folded arms on the table and bawled.

And drove herself crazy with images of Mary Anne. Had David been home? Did they still make love? Of course they did. Lily knew that there were wives who avoided sex to avoid more children but she doubted that Mary Anne was one of them. Mary Anne adored David.

But it wasn't her desire for him that disturbed Lily. It was his desire for her.

How such thoughts and visions had tortured her through the years, especially in the past months, but none of it mattered anymore, for David would never love her again. She sniffed and wiped her face with the hanky Jonathan handed her. Hesitantly, she looked into the mirror again. "Jonathan?"

"Yes?"

"Has David been home again?"

He looked at the ceiling and sighed. "Oh Lily, why do you torture yourself?"

She shrugged bony shoulders.

"What can he do? Besides, he was sent home to recruit more men."

"He's killing them off so quickly that he had to go back for more?"

"That's not fair."

"But you said that he was acting recklessly."

"And I shouldn't have spoken so disparagingly about my dearest friend."

"Did he spend much time . . . with her?"

"He was gone about a month."

She felt a giant fist slam into her stomach. "When?"

"February."

Lily immediately counted to nine and wondered if David would have another child in November. If he did, she'd know for sure.

Jonathan looked into Lily's eyes. "He loves Mary Anne. You know that. I've never said he didn't. He's never said he didn't."

Lily nodded as tears trickled down her face. "No, everyone makes sure to tell me that, including him."

"You've always known how important his honor is to him. You've always known he'd never leave her. You have, haven't you?"

She bit her lip and nodded as she watched tears drip onto skeletal fingers.

"What do you expect of him?"

She jumped to her feet. "I don't know!" Her voice choked as she spoke. "I don't know. I just know I cling to every chance to be with him, to tell myself he loves me. I keep hoping something will allow us be together."

"Mary Anne's death perhaps?"

"Please don't say that. Of course not."

"Well, there's nothing we can do about any of this now, is there?"

She shook her head and wiped away tears then held up the broken comb. "Can you get me another?"

"That's my girl. You'll be your ole' gorgeous self in no time.

CHAPTER 48

Jonathan wrote to Lily on a fairly regular basis and visited whenever possible. He also hired a lawyer to represent her. About fifty, Samuel Andrews was tall and lanky with broad shoulders and thinning orange-red hair combed straight back from his forehead. He was so quiet and conservative that Lily wondered how much help he would be.

"Why are you willing to defend me?"

Andrews waited until the question was completely out of her mouth then waited yet another few seconds before answering. "I believe everyone deserves a fair trial."

"But I'm a traitor to your cause."

"That may be, although you're not to announce that in court. You're pleading 'not guilty'."

"How can I?"

"Because it is the prosecutor's job to prove that you are guilty. We are not going to hand him what he wants."

"But why would you, a believer in your cause, want to help me?"

"Why does Buford want to help you?"

Lily shook her head and smiled. "You've got me there. Because he's my friend, I suppose."

"Perhaps it's because we believe you have a right to your beliefs as we believe we have a right to ours. It's what we're fighting for, Mrs. Dundee."

"Please call me Lily. But I spied against your country."

He nodded slowly. She'd never seen a more deliberate individual. "Then I don't need to tell you how important this trial is, do I?"

"But no one hangs women so I'll serve about six months, right?"

She finally saw emotion. Surprise. "Where did you come by your information, madam? Spying is a hanging offense. You do realize that, do you not?"

"But they wouldn't hang a woman." The look in his eyes frightened her. "Would they?"

"With the right jury and a suffering economy, yes, they just might. Braxton Bragg almost did so recently—without a trial. You are fortunate that you were with friends when you were arrested or you might already be dead."

Lily couldn't catch her breath.

"I'm sorry to frighten you but you must know how serious this is. No one wants to hang a woman but that doesn't mean it won't happen. Right now the outlook for acquittal's not good, but they have to show proof of your spying and I'm not sure they can do that. I'm not planning to put you on the stand, so as long as you say nothing, they have to prove their case." He stood up and she followed suit, amazed again at his height.

"Thank you, Mr. Andrews."

He bowed and walked out.

Lily began seeing more executions out her window and hearing more rumors of atrocities in the adjoining prisons, Palmer's and Gleanor's. Men placed in isolated pitch-black cells, men strung up by their thumbs, men shackled to chains night and day, men flogged and even branded. And the prisons grew more and more crowded, even though Lily rarely shared her large space with anyone.

The entire Confederacy—military and civilian—was suffering and Lily worried about Gracie. Was she getting enough to eat? Was she staying well? Lily knew that as long as there was breath in Mrs. Evans's body that Grace would be well cared for, and she thanked God every night for that remarkable woman, but the Union blockade was keeping food and medicine from the South and people were starving and dying from yellow fever.

She also heard that prisoner exchanges had stopped. The latest Union general, Grant, knew that even with thousands of Union soldiers in prison, the North had more manpower. If he kept rebel soldiers behind bars, the South would eventually run out of men.

An entire generation of men lost? Yes, it looked like it might wind up that way.

Although Lily's meals continued, thanks to Jonathan, she wished she could share her good fortune with the other prisoners and often did sneak part of her meals to the few women still upstairs. And Jonathan continued to provide books and newspapers so Lily could keep up with the news, but what she really enjoyed were his letters which she read again and again. Not only were they full of news, but they always included something to make her laugh and often included stories about the different women he met.

But he said little of "our friend" and never spoke of Saul. Lily knew it was to spare her feelings but she so longed for news of them. Jonathan and his men spent a fairly calm winter and early spring near Franklin, Virginia. Conditions were quite nice, he wrote, "though not as palatial as your little place." She laughed at his absurdity then read about officers sleeping in real beds in real houses, of men cultivating gardens and even holding a medieval tournament. "I found one tiny lass who actually looked *up* to me! Now I see the attraction of *Ivanhoe*!" Lily found it easy to visualize the small-framed man wooing the women, but what of David? How many of the local women desired him, spoke to him, flirted with him? Was he flattered? Tempted? And Saul? Saul probably gave into any temptation offered him—and he had a right to. After all, his marriage had been based on deception and he'd been hurt so very cruelly. He deserved so much better.

Jonathan was careful not to say much about battles but Lily read of them in the newspapers he sent. She also knew that even during the winter months when there weren't many battles, there were still skirmishes, and if Biggs was serious about harming David, a bullet could come from anywhere at anytime. What had David said: The bullet hasn't been made that can kill me? She remembered the bravado in his voice and face that day and shuddered at his tempting fate so recklessly.

Biggs was quick to tell her about every near-miss, every "accident" involving David, and though she covered her ears and tried to drown out the words, she heard them, every one of them. Did she know, asked Biggs, that as David looked through his field glasses, a Federal sharpshooter missed him by only a foot? Did she know that as David led a charge, a ball broke the handle of his sword and ricocheted into his belt buckle and flattened the buckle causing David to double over?

Each horrifying word was said with glee even as Lily cried and shook her head. "Please don't hurt him, please!"

"Your loyalties disturb us, Mrs. Dundee. Personally, I'd like to stand each of those pompous generals up against a wall and let each slave have a shot at them. The arrogant bastards should deem themselves lucky to die by the gun of a loyal Federal soldier."

Lily fell onto her cot.

"And let me add, Mrs. Dundee, that your general's wife is with him—even as we speak."

Lily's eyes widened as her heart fell into her stomach and she dared look into the woman's eyes. "What?"

"Yes. It's so nice to see the general with a beautiful woman on his arm, a quite pregnant beautiful woman."

Biggs knew the effect of her words.

Suddenly Lily felt caged, helpless—and furious. Her brain ran in circles as she sniffed back tears then spoke with quiet determination. "If you'll get me out of here, I'll be able to get more information."

The woman smiled. "Ah ha. I thought that would get you back on track. You do see, don't you, that these rich pampered cursed traitors are all alike? Your general used you, Lily, used you to bide time when his wife was unavailable. How could you even think that a man like that would take a whore seriously? Those people are all inbred pompous devils."

"Can you get me out?"

"Don't know about that. How do I know you won't turn on us?"

"Because you know everything and because you've finally proven to me that I've had my loyalties confused by one of those devils. Isn't that the gist of your speech?"

The woman eyed her curiously. "I'll see what I can do. And I'll see what you give me in the meantime to show your sincerity."

And so Lily continued to give information even though she knew that Jonathan was allowing wrong information to get out. All she could see was David with a very pregnant Mary Anne, and once again she wanted to hurt him.

"How could you not tell me?"

"Well, that's some greeting."

Lily paced back and forth in the tiny room then stopped and leaned on the table as she spit out the words, "Mary Anne's pregnant and has been with him in camp!"

Jonathan raised his chin. "Biggs?"

"Yes. But you can't deny it, can you?"

"No."

Her shoulders sagged and she fell onto the chair. "I'd hoped, so desperately hoped, that she was making it up."

"Lily . . ."

She covered her ears. "No. Don't defend him."

"How dare you!"

She'd not thought Jonathan capable of anger and was shocked.

"Yes. I said how dare you." He paced, his face red, the veins in his neck bulging. Finally, he stopped and stared at her. "What do you expect of that man? He's only human, for heaven's sake. He's a man . . . and she's his wife! You'd better accept that. I've tried to comfort you and tell you what you've wanted to hear, but I fear I've done you an injustice. He's married. Mary Anne's his wife. Is that plain enough for you?"

She squinted her eyes shut.

His voice calmer, Jonathan sat down and rapped his knuckles on the table. "I'm sorry, Lily. I'm very sorry for you, but you must forget him as he must forget you. Yes, he loves you, but he's married, and that relationship must take precedence over any feelings you two share. She's his wife and he's her husband in the eyes of God, and they have children and, yes, will be having more. Do you really expect him to have a celibate relationship with his own wife?"

"Yes." She felt weak, helpless, defeated.

"Then you're not the strong intelligent woman I took you for."

She stood and glowered at him. "Maybe I'm not." She started pacing. "I was once, you know—*before* I met him." Her shoulders were squared, her voice haughty. "By the way, how's Saul?"

Jonathan shook his head. "Lily, don't do this. This is how part of this trouble started, remember?"

She pouted and walked away from him then turned back and defiantly folded her arms across her chest.

"Don't use Saul to get back at David. It's not fair."

"Well, it wasn't fair of him to bring David to me that night. David didn't drink and didn't want to visit a whore but Saul forced him into both. If he hadn't, I'd be happy running a very successful business right now."

"And you wouldn't have Grace."

She glared at him.

He held up his hands in truce. "I won't argue with you. I'm just surprised that a woman like you would hold blame for so many years, would hold out hopes for so many years. It's not like you."

"I don't know what I'm 'like' anymore, Colonel Buford."

Neither spoke for a few moments.

"The reports of his almost being shot are true too?"

He nodded.

"It's just a matter of time," she whispered.

Jonathan stood up and turned his cap around in his hands. "I'm taking my leave now. You know how much I care for you, but I won't listen to talk of my best friend's death. You've tired me and," he forced a smile, "I must return to war to relax."

She rushed to him. "I'm sorry, Jonathan. Please don't give up on me."

"I won't, my dear, but you must give less thought to our friend and more to saving your life and beginning a new one. You've got children to rear and a business to run. Concentrate on those things, Lily. Think of what you can do when this war is over."

CHAPTER 49

As Lily paced, she worried about Grace, worried about David, worried about Jonathan and Saul. She also worried about herself—but she was last on her list.

Although visits to the yard had been curtailed due to overcrowding in the other two buildings, Lily was still allowed some time outside and she knew it was because of Jonathan's influence. She also knew it was because of him that she now had a daily ration of water, a decent blanket, and a chamber pot. How little one appreciates life's small "luxuries" until they no longer have them. Lily knew how indebted she was to Jonathan, and she appreciated everything.

Yet she'd repaid his kindness by being an ungrateful brat. Well, no longer. Lily decided to take Jonathan's advice and begin planning for her future. She'd already started working on her appearance and laughed inwardly at just how vain she used to be before David. Although her hair would be permanently streaked with gray, the luster had almost returned and, fortunately, she'd not lost any teeth. Her monthlies had also returned, an inconvenience but a sign of healthy womanhood, and her skin was no longer sallow and waxen.

The Lily of the West was on her way back.

After Jonathan's visit, she'd been furious, furious as only visions of David with Mary Anne could make her. But why did news of them always surprise her? She'd known the truth from the beginning. Mary Anne was David's wife and the mother of his children, and David loved her.

But Lily knew that it was possible to love more than one person. Hadn't she loved Tom and Saul at the same time that she'd loved David? If David had never come into her life, wouldn't she have been happy with either man? Yes. They were kind, loving, everything a woman could want, and she had loved them, still loved them.

But she'd never loved them as she loved David and that's the love she hoped David had for her. *Is it, David? Do you love Mary Anne as I love Tom and Saul and love me as I love you?* Again and again she told herself that if he'd tell her, just once, that this was the love he had for her, she could survive. If he'd tell her, just once, that he suffered without her as she did without him, she could survive. If she could hear these words from his lips, Lily felt that she could get through anything—even life without him.

It had been quite awhile since she'd seen Jonathan, but he continued to write, and Lily read each letter dozens of times. He wrote of his men grumbling about constant marches, about being moved from place to place in anticipation of skirmishes. But he couldn't hide his disappointment about what he feared would lose them the war—politics—and Lily was surprised that he wrote with such candor. Had he forgotten Biggs or was the usually controlled man so frustrated that he had to release the words no matter the consequences?

But then weeks passed without any word and Lily grew anxious. About David and Grace. About Jonathan. About Saul.

And about Mary Anne who was due at any time. How desperately Lily hoped that the woman delivered another son.

There was also news of her trial. The date had been set for the last of April—five months away. Lily immediately sent a letter off to Jonathan, not knowing, of course, if he would get it and even if he did, what could he do? But the absence of his letters frightened her. Was he okay? Was David okay? Was there a reason he hesitated to write?

December arrived and brought endless hours of fantasizing about birthdays and Christmases past and present. What were her loved ones doing right now? Where were they? And dare she dream about future birthdays and Christmases? Would she ever get to share a Christmas with David? Would David ever call his home and hers the same? Would there ever again be a warm cozy kitchen where she could make hot chocolate and bake Christmas cookies with her daughter?

Rations soon grew so sparse that only Jonathan's payments assured that Lily got anything. But she knew it couldn't be helped because conditions grew constantly worse for the entire southern population. As Peter told her, "I saw ladies fightin' over a loaf of bread the other day, ma'am, and I've never seen ladies scream and claw at one another like that. The prisoners in the other buildings think we're cheatin' 'em out of their rations, but there just ain't any. My momma depends on my soldierin' money and I ain't been paid for months now. She's gettin' pretty good at makin' coffee out of parched sweet 'taters, but you know, ma'am, she's gettin' real tired of all the killin' and sufferin'. I've even heard her say that if we're gonna lose, she wishes Jeff Davis would go ahead and surrender before I get sent off and shot."

He shook his head. "But I hates to hear her talk like that. I'm more than ready to go fight with General Lee." He straightened his shoulders and stuck out his chest. "I'm not ready for us to give up yet." His eyes turned sad and vulnerable and Lily saw them glisten with tears. "I'm scared of what'll happen if we lose."

She touched his hand. "It's going to be hard on everyone, Private, but don't grieve your mother by getting yourself killed. This war will be but a brief moment compared to the rest of her life without you. Think of her."

He nodded and she saw his face redden. "I guess you're right, but it don't seem right not to fight."

"I know. I know you men think that that's the best way to prove your manhood, but it's really not. I know a soldier who believes as you do and I'd rather have him alive and whole than dead, even if dying made him a hero."

"Really?"

"Oh, yes."

He shook his head. "I ain't met many women who feel like that, before lately that is, but I forget that you're a Yankee so maybe y'all think differently than we do down here." His brows furrowed.

"What's wrong?"

"I just remembered what you're in here for and I should hate you."

"I guess you should and I wouldn't blame you, but I'm in here because I believe in my cause as much as you believe in yours. I love your people and your country, but I truly believe you're wrong." Lily looked down at the floor and almost whispered, "Some of my best friends happen to be members of your army."

"Besides Colonel Buford? Who might they be?"

She smiled as she pictured David's sweet face. "Oh, I can't tell you, but you've heard of one of them I'm sure." How she longed to tell her secret.

"Private!"

Peter turned toward the voice then back toward Lily. "Guess I'd better go." He stopped after running up several of the stair steps. "I don't hate you, ma'am."

"I'm glad."

He smiled then disappeared.

The next morning her breakfast was served by an older man who said, "That youngster came in early and fixed you something special. Merry Christmas."

"Merry Christmas to you, too, Sergeant, and thank you." That morning Lily enjoyed a decent cup of coffee, a real egg, and a piece of fresh bread. Beside the plate was a note that read, "Merry Christmas. Peter." She ate slowly and smiled as she envisioned the young soldier at home with his family.

The remainder of the day she wrote letters—letters to David that she knew she'd never send and he'd never read, but letters she had to write. Her love for him filled her to overflowing and she felt that she'd drown if she didn't release it somewhere, so she wrote "I love you" again and again, so many times that her hand should have cramped but it didn't. What she wouldn't have given for just one letter from him, one piece of paper that he'd touched, one piece of him that she could touch, kiss, hold to her breast, read again and again.

CHAPTER 50

Lily finally heard from Jonathan in January. He and David were on their way back to Virginia via a furlough in South Carolina. "I'm glad you're still getting food although I know it's scarce. Will see you as soon as possible."

Something was missing. The letter was too brief and impersonal, almost like a telegram, not like Jonathan at all. Perhaps he was still angry with her or had tired of caring for her. Lily vowed that she'd treat him well if she were ever free again, that she'd dig up her hidden fortune and give him a sizable portion. Perhaps he and David could restore their school. That, of course, reminded her of Mary Anne. Could Lily really provide funds to help David and Mary Anne? Who was she fooling? Just as David told her that day that he'd had to buy the puppy for Grace, so would Lily do what it took to make David happy.

The days dragged. She received a few more short notes from Jonathan but sensed that he was sending them to calm her, that he had something important to say that he dared not say through the mail. The feeling grew stronger with each day and each letter, and she felt she'd go crazy waiting for him.

And time passed until it was the day before her trial. How she'd hoped for Jonathan's reassurance, confidence, hand holding.

When she walked into the tiny room, a silent Andrews stood then indicated that she should open the large box on the table. Lily opened it then pulled out a dress that was plain but pretty. Andrews nodded and spoke. "I think there's a card."

Lily found it and smiled at Jonathan's familiar handwriting: "So you'll impress them as much as you have us." Us? Was the dress from him and David? Had David helped pick it out? Did they speak of her? Did they worry about her? She didn't know the answers but held on dearly to the ideas, and she suddenly felt warm and confident as she hugged the dress to her chest.

"From Buford?"

She nodded vigorously, knowing that her cheeks were rosy and her eyes glowing.

"I hate to disturb your obvious elation." He motioned toward the chair and Lily sat down. He sat, pulled his chair close to the table, then folded his hands on the table top. His voice was low, his words deliberate. "Did you hear that the Federals hung a young man recently?"

"Not since last year when they hung that young private." She shuddered. "Awful."

"Yes. Well, they hung another just a few months ago, a seventeen-year-old boy from Little Rock, hung him from a tree on the grounds of his old school then forbade any prayers or funeral services. These two young men, and I stress the word 'young', were offered their freedom if they gave up names but they refused. Their only request was to be shot and that was denied them. I'm telling you this, Lily, because you're being tried at a very bad time. The people in the South are starving and fear they are losing the war. They are prime for retribution and would like nothing better than to get revenge for these two boys—before their ability to take revenge is taken out of their hands."

Lily shuddered again and held her arms against her chest.

"I'm afraid it gets worse. They've decided on a closed courtroom because . . ." He reached across the table and put his hand on her arm, his first sign of affection. ". . . David Evans is the key witness."

She jumped up. "No!" She paced, her mind racing but coming up blank. She couldn't think, couldn't think . . . She hit her head with her hand. Think, Lily, think . . . She turned to Andrews. "Why?"

He looked at her dumbfoundedly. "He's the one who ordered your arrest."

She plopped onto the chair. "Of course. I knew that. How stupid of me to forget."

"Dundee and Buford will also be called to testify against you."

She doubled over and felt sick to her stomach.

"They've all witnessed you passing notes, meeting strangers . . . You even confessed to Buford. It was part of that confession that Evans overheard."

Lily nodded as she held her stomach. "I knew this, knew it . . . How, why, did I forget?" She shook her head. "How silly of me, how . . . Well, I know they can't help it. I know they have to. It will hurt . . ." she held her stomach again, ". . . hurt to hear their words, but this is all my doing."

"Most commendable, Lily, but I don't think you fully understand. You see, one of the reasons your trial was delayed was because they didn't want to hang a woman. The main reason, however, was because they didn't want to ruin the reputations of their officers. Do you understand what I'm saying? I'm saying that now they'll do anything to find you guilty."

She searched his eyes. "Please don't be saying what I think you're saying."

"Anything. They've got to ruin you and don't care who else they ruin to do so."

A wail came from her mouth before she realized it.

"Your husband found some letters that will connect you with Evans in a most damning manner. Do you know the letters I speak of?"

She nodded.

"There's also a Mrs. Crowley who saw the two of you together on the train and a couple of other people who saw the two of you together at some hotel—acting like lovers. I don't think it will come to this, but they've even spoken to Evans's brother who said that the family had been told that you were a long-lost cousin."

She heard his words but her brain didn't comprehend them. She felt like she was falling deeper and deeper into a well while reaching up to him for comprehension, reaching up to him for a way to save David.

"Remember what I said about not wanting to ruin the reputations of their officers? Well Dundee and Evans have created so many mishaps during battle and such havoc with President Davis that Davis is now more than ready to make them sacrificial lambs. They're throwaways. They will never be promoted again and Davis wants them out of his hair. The only reason the court is to be closed is to preserve the dignity of the Confederacy—not of the men involved—maybe before, but not now. The two men obviously hate each other and will do or say anything to damage the other. Your husband is almost eager to give dates and places when he saw you with Evans. As you can well imagine, he's extremely bitter and willing to face further humiliation to destroy Evans."

Her head was swimming and it throbbed with pain.

"You realize, don't you, that the Federals have washed their hands of you and would like nothing better than to see you hang? Not only could that keep you quiet, but they could tarnish the reputations of two Confederate officers AND turn you into a heroine, a martyr. You'll do much more for their cause dead than alive."

She shook her head. It hurt, oh, how it hurt. There were words inside, words screaming to come out, and the only way the pain would stop was to let them out, and without realizing she'd even opened her mouth, Lily blurted, "I'll say or do anything, just don't let this happen."

"Those are noble words, but you can't mean them."

"Yes, I mean them. I know I'll be scared to death and may not die gracefully, but I can't let David and Saul be ruined. The Feds have

261

blackmailed me, Samuel. They've threatened me with the lives of everyone I care about. If this is what they want, then I'll die for them. I still believe in saving the Union and freeing the slaves, so let them make me a martyr." She laughed and shook her head then smiled as she realized her headache was gone. "A martyr is certainly something I never thought I'd be. I've been so many things."

"If they blackmailed you, I could use that as your defense."

"But that wouldn't stop the rest of it, would it?"

"No."

She shrugged. "I think we both know that I'm doomed anyway. I don't think there's anything you could say that would save me, even if David and Saul weren't throwaways, so there's no reason to harm them. No reason for them to even make an appearance." She would never see David again, never . . . How could she die without feeling his arms around her again? How could she die without feeling his lips again? Her eyes filled with tears. "If I plead guilty, will their reputations be saved? I mean, there's no reason for their families to know, is there?"

"No. Believe me, Davis would love to stop this quickly and quietly, and he certainly won't damage the reputations of his officers if he doesn't have to. I fear the war is lost anyhow, so I don't know what will happen to any of us." He looked down at his lap then back at Lily. "They will hang you."

She nodded. "When?"

"Soon. Very soon."

"Ask them to give me two days, please. I've got so many letters to write. Can you find Jonathan? I need him, need to give him letters . . . so many people I need to write to . . . TJ, Ruthie, Mrs. Evans . . . I must explain, beg forgiveness . . . my daughter. . . . " Tears rushed down her cheeks.

"I'll go talk to them." Andrews whispered then silently walked out of the room.

CHAPTER 51

Lily was given two days to write her letters and, hopefully, see Jonathan—and David? Again and again she paced the length of the dark room then sat down with pen and paper. The words burned inside her but she wanted to see these people, touch them, hug them. And she worried. Would David ever claim Grace as his daughter or would the girl grow up feeling like an outsider, the distant cousin whose mother betrayed her country and was hanged? And how could she tell TJ and Ruthie that she couldn't keep her promise to come back? How could they live knowing that their father had been murdered and Lily hanged?

And what could she tell Saul? Was there anything she could say to him? Her heart truly ached for the pain she'd caused him as she fondly remembered him so young and cocky, so brash and sure of himself, so vulnerable and loving.

But, as always, the person who mattered most was David. What would happen to him? Each time she saw his face in her mind she felt sick. How could Mary Anne not learn of all this? My poor soldier. He had so much on such young shoulders. Even if Mary Anne didn't find out about their affair, David would have to live with the constant fear that she might. He'd also have to live with the knowledge that he'd cheated on the fine Mary Anne with a traitorous whore.

She wrote and paced until every letter was written except one.

Dare she write to David? Would he care? Would he want a letter from her? She'd written so many letters to him that she'd not mailed that now when she sat down to write one that she might actually give him, she couldn't think. Should she pour out her heart or simply thank him for his kindness toward Grace? Letter after letter wound up crumpled on the cold floor.

And although there were just two days between life and death, she slept. And dreamed.

David was waving to her while smiling his boyish winning grin and sitting atop his beautiful stallion, Samson. And though he was surrounded by such wild forestation that it was hard to see, she could see him.

She sat on a tree stump and admired him, admired his courage and daring, his handsome face and strong body—he and the animal so perfectly matched with their trim power and vitality . . . As she watched the man she adored, she remembered a message she had to give him.

She walked toward him, calling out the words, "May 6th." He saw her and smiled then called out her name. They moved toward each other, their eyes locked.

Shots flew.

David's eyes widened and his brows furrowed. He stared at her, reached for her, opened his mouth, then fell to the ground.

"No!!!!!!" She ran to him, her arms stretched so far that they hurt from being stretched. They hurt from wanting him. They hurt from missing him. "David! I'm coming, I'm coming." But all she could see was blood oozing from under his still body.

"No!!!!!" Lily sat up screaming, her throat raw and her face wet. David dead . . . No, it was just a dream. She wouldn't accept his death, would never accept his death.

"Guard!" She screamed again and again as she banged on the door until someone finally opened it.

"It's three in the morning. This better be important."

"Please, I need you to check on someone for me."

The old man scratched his head. "Well?"

"I must find out if someone's okay. Longstreet's army . . . Do you know where it is?"

He grunted a laugh. "You think I'd tell you if I did?"

She shook her head. "I don't care where they are. I just need to know if they're okay."

"Ma'am, it's the middle of the night and if the men are in a battle, which they wouldn't be right now, there's a good chance someone's not okay."

Tears fell onto the floor as Lily grabbed the old man. "Please find out." Her head fell to her chest as her hands loosened from the man's jacket. "Please."

"I'll see what I can do."

"Thank you. General Evans. Find out if he's okay."

His brows knitted together but he simply nodded then said, "I'll let you know."

"Bless you." She fell onto her cot and cried herself to sleep.

When she woke the next morning, a solemn Peter was watching her. "Colonel Buford's upstairs to see you, ma'am, so I put your breakfast in the visitor's room."

Memories of the dream returned and Lily's hands shook as she stood on wobbly legs. "Please Peter, did you learn anything?"

"About General Evans, ma'am?"

"Yes."

"He's not dead. They said that's all I could tell you."

"Thank you! Thank you!"

"Is it true, ma'am, about you and the general?"

Lily realized that in her panic she'd given David's name. Had she just ruined his reputation? Would she hang for nothing? She thought too highly of this boy to lie to him but couldn't tell him the absolute truth. "What have you heard?"

"That you two are . . . you know." His eyes misted. "I can't believe the general'd betray us, not him. I mean, you're a beautiful lady, but he wouldn't . . . and he's married and a good Christian man, ain't he?"

"I've known General Evans for many years and respect him more than anyone I've ever met. He's probably one of the bravest and most noble soldiers you have. Don't worry about his loyalty. He would never do anything to betray his country. Yes, he's married and very happily with a beautiful wife and a houseful of children." Lily stroked the young man's youthfully smooth cheek. "Your General Evans is the best of men."

He smiled then grinned. "Boy, am I glad to hear that! I was hearin' stuff about him I sure didn't like, but now that I know the truth, I'll set folks straight. Thank you, ma'am."

Lily looked at the sweet innocent face and thought of David so long ago, but David had never been this young in spirit, never as easy-going. David had had his life planned so far in advance that had it not been for the one deviation—brought about by someone else—he would never have experienced life's little accidents and surprises. She grimaced then smiled. Were she and Grace accidents and surprises?

She entered the small room and eagerly embraced Jonathan then sat down in her chair opposite him at the table.

"It looks like someone's taking care of you." He smiled as he nodded toward the single pink rose on Lily's breakfast tray.

She sniffed the rose. "Yes. Peter's been so helpful and such a good companion. He's brought me a flower every day this week. I've been saving them." She twirled the rose by its stem and thought of the tiny bouquet she'd carry with her to the gallows.

"I'm so sorry I haven't been to see you sooner, my dear, but we've been quite busy. How are you?" He shook his head. "That's a ridiculous question. I'm sorry."

"Actually it's not because, believe it or not, I've had both good and bad moments in just the past twenty-four hours." She took a deep breath then shivered as she recalled the dream. "I had the most awful nightmare early this morning. I dreamed that David . . . I saw him on his horse and he was smiling and feeling so confident. We were smiling at each other and I began walking toward him then . . ." Lily covered her face and shook her head then looked at Jonathan. "He was shot." She stood and paced, her voice cracking as she spoke. "Oh, Jonathan . . . He was on the ground and there was blood . . ." She hugged her arms against her chest. "His eyes were closed . . . those beautiful brown eyes." She closed her eyes and wept openly, her shoulders sagging, her chest heaving.

"When did you have this dream?"

"This morning, why?"

He shook his head. "Because Dave had the same dream."

"Oh, my God, no!"

"I'm sorry, my dear, I shouldn't be telling you this. You just took me by surprise describing such a dream."

"Tell me, Jonathan. Tell me about his dream. When did he have it?"

"On our way back. I remember how shaken he was as he described it to me. He almost spilled his coffee."

Lily shivered again and felt the warmth of new tears on her cheeks.

"He said he felt odd, that he'd had the most realistic and disturbing dream, then described it as you just did."

"Oh, Jonathan." She paced then sat back down. "I'm so scared."

He shook his head and forced a slight smile. "We're being foolish, Lily. I don't believe in premonitions and neither does Dave. Dreams can be bothersome but we shouldn't put more stock in them than that."

"But it bothers you too, doesn't it?"

"Yes, I admit it does, but only because Dave took it so seriously." Jonathan shook his head slowly. "He's also been plagued by that damned wound plus he's had so much on his mind, even more than usual." Jonathan looked preoccupied.

"He's not getting better, is he? I could tell he was in pain that last night." She searched Jonathan's eyes. "But there's something else, isn't there? Some reason your letters have been so short. Something awful has happened, hasn't it?"

Jonathan took her hands in his. "His youngest, Luke, died."

"No! When? How?"

"In September. Yellow fever."

"Oh my God . . . How's David?"

"You can imagine. He felt particularly bad because he couldn't be with Mary Anne when it happened."

Lily closed her eyes and tried to drive away the jealousy that always came with the woman's name. "And because she was pregnant?"

"Yes. She had another boy in November."

"Another boy?"

He nodded. "A quite handsome lad. They named him Joseph."

"Are she and the other boys all right? The fever hasn't harmed them?"

"Mary Anne was sick with it for awhile but is okay now."

"The poor woman."

"She doesn't have everything, does she Lily?"

Lily looked directly into his eyes and didn't blink. "She has David."

He shook his head disgustedly and stood up.

"Where is he?"

A slow smile warmed his face and his eyes twinkled. "In Kentucky."

"What?"

He smiled as he sat back down. "I thought you'd be pleased."

"Kentucky, really? Oh, Jonathan, when?"

"He should be back any time now. You know he's wanted to go check on the kids for many months but there just wasn't time."

"But it's so far out of his way."

"Yes, it is—and in dangerous territory."

Although Lily feared for his safety, she was elated that the man she loved was spending days in the saddle when he was exhausted and in pain—for her. "I can't believe it." She put her hand to her chest. "My heart's beating so fast and hard. Can you hear it?"

He laughed. "No, but I'm glad to make you so happy."

"Oh, yes. I'm happy, very happy. Not only did he do this for me, but he'll bring news of TJ and Ruthie"

"Doesn't that prove something to you?"

She felt lightheaded. "Yes, oh yes. And that means he'll come to see me, won't he? I don't want him to risk his reputation, but . . . he will, won't he? I can't bear the idea of never seeing him again."

"Of course he'll come see you." He touched the curls by her cheeks. "He's wanted to all along. You know that, don't you? He's been so ashamed of himself for not doing so. But you can't blame him. The war's going so poorly, our people are starving, then the new baby, Mary Anne, the creditors breathing down his neck . . . He's got too much on his plate. He's—we're —too young for such hardships." Jonathan shook his head again. "I never thought our lives would be this complicated."

"You didn't count on a war."

"I guess not." He forced a smile. "Certainly creates havoc, doesn't it?"

She smiled and nodded. "How's Saul?"

"Okay. No, actually he's not. Poor guy . . . You know, I've always liked him and hated whatever it is that's between the two of them. He's a good man and a good soldier."

"His men . . . the other officers . . . He's not being ridiculed because of me, is he? I mean, what does everyone think?"

"No one thinks he's to blame or holds him up to ridicule. After all," he smiled, "they all agree you're an enchanting woman. In fact, I find it amusing that even now the men don't hate you. It's as if they don't believe the charges, like they don't think you're . . ."

"Capable? Smart enough? That's what you want to say, isn't it?"

He smiled. "I'm afraid you're right."

She returned his smile. "Well, thank you for admitting it. And it's quite true. I noticed it right away. When all this started—and seemed like a game—I almost laughed at how easily men spoke around me, how little credit they gave me. I was a pretty ornament and that was all. It was almost too easy. At first."

"Yes, I'm sure you're right."

"Andrews has told me that neither David nor Saul will ever get promoted again. Does David know?"

He nodded. "Longstreet finally washed his hands of the situation even though he still thinks Dave's the best commander he has, but Longstreet's involved in his own political battles. As for how Dave's handling it, he's accepting it, that's all. He's tired, Lily, tired and disgusted. He thinks we're losing and blames it on Davis. Then there's the baby . . . and, of course, you."

She nodded. "I want him to care about me, but I don't want to interfere with his safety. He'll forget me, forget this." She looked around. "And he'll be better off with me out of his life. I've been a stone around his neck." She sniffed. "I'm sorry. I cry way too many tears."

"Under the circumstances? I don't think so. And don't think Dave will forget you and be better off without you. I worry that just the opposite will occur."

"Do you really?" She paced a few yards then sat back down. "Oh, Jonathan. You don't know how much I cherish every word about him, but when you tell me he cares for me . . ." She smiled. "I know it's pathetic that his every thought means so much to me, and I don't want him to grieve, yet I do. Isn't that awful and cruel? But that's how I feel. I want him to miss me as much as I've always missed him. I want his heart to feel like it's being ripped apart each time he thinks of me because that's how my heart has felt each time I've lost him."

Jonathan looked down at the floor then back at her. There were tears in his eyes. "He already feels that way and has described it in almost identical words. He's so torn between wanting to be with you and doing right by Mary Anne." A slight smile formed on his lips. "Would you believe that this war is probably saving his sanity? He's scared to death about what he's going to do when it's over."

Lily couldn't believe her ears. Could David really love her as much as she loved him? "But now, after what I've done, how does he feel?"

"Oh, he hates what you've done, but he knows you were doing what you thought was right." He continued. "I can't count the times he's mumbled that he wishes he could hate you and get you out of his heart and mind but can't. You don't know how crazy it made him when you lived with Dundee. I swear, if I thought him capable, I think he would have killed him."

Lily thought of Tom and shuddered.

"Uhm. Something else I don't know about him?" When she opened her mouth, he held up his hands. "No, I don't want to know." He smiled and shook his head. "When will I learn that there are things about him that I will never know?"

Lily smiled mischievously as he shook his head.

"I think you'll also be happy to hear that David's sent papers home to free his slaves, though he's asked them to stay on for Mary Anne's sake until he gets back."

"Really? Oh, Jonathan!" She grabbed Jonathan's hands and squeezed them. "I always knew he was good through and through. I knew he was listening to me!"

Jonathan smiled and was about to speak when the sound of footsteps caused them both to listen. When the door opened, Lily felt her heart stop.

CHAPTER 52

Jonathan walked to his friend and they shook hands then hugged. David winced and Jonathan said, "Sorry old man," then turned toward Lily and said good bye. She kissed his cheek but her eyes were on one person and one person only.

As his were on her as he came nearer and nearer until their faces were only inches apart and she could feel his breath on her lips as he spoke and smell the smoke and fresh air in his hair and clothes.

"Hi."

He was there, really, really there. The nearness of him made her feel faint and she started to back away. But he grabbed her hand and kissed its palm then pulled her even closer until she was pressed against him and his lips were on hers.

They held each other, their hands caressing and traveling on heads and backs, arms and faces, but fear of discovery made them pull away, their breathing hard, their eyes and brains dizzy. They fell into the chairs then laughed nervously and Lily could tell that David was as relieved to see her as she was to see him. With broad grins still on their faces, David began circling the tops of her hands with his thumbs and for a moment they silently savored the sight of their hands locked together.

"I'm so glad you came," she finally whispered.

He started to speak then closed his mouth. When he opened it again, his voice cracked. "I've wanted to, from the beginning . . . I've wanted to very much."

She brought his hand to her lips and kissed it then buried her face in it. "I know."

His eyes looked deeply into hers. "Do you? Do you really?"

She smiled. "Well, not until today when Jonathan told me, but I saw you at the train station," she squeezed his hand, "and it meant so much to me."

He looked away and coughed and she saw tears in his eyes. "It was the very least I could do." He pulled her hand to his lips. "Can you ever forgive me?"

His head was bowed over their hands and she stroked the thick brown hair. "Oh my lo . . . David, there's nothing to forgive. Can you ever forgive me?"

He nodded then pulled her head to his and kissed her, their tears mingling. His arms stroked her arms the best they could across the table.

Suddenly she remembered the dream and shivered.

"What is it?"

"Jonathan told me about your dream."

His eyes widened. "Oh."

She squeezed his hand. "It doesn't mean anything, does it? Dreams are just dreams, aren't they?"

"Of course." He smiled but she could tell it was forced.

"David?"

"Of course, Lily. Dreams are just dreams. Let's talk of something else." He smiled again. "I saw TJ and Ruthie."

"That's right!" She squeezed his hand again then looked deeply into his eyes. "How can I thank you for that? I know you've been through so much and must be exhausted, and you had to go into enemy territory, but it means so much to me that you went, so very much."

He blushed and looked down. "I thought it might." His eyes raised to hers. "But I care about them too. You know that, don't you?"

She nodded. "How are they?"

He sighed and she could see his exhaustion. "They're fine, just fine. TJ's quite a handsome young man." His brows knitted. "Looks like his dad." He seemed to search her eyes but she said nothing. "And Ruthie's becoming a very pretty young lady. They're doing quite well. TJ's a good smithy and expert horseman so he's quit farming and is using the land to raise horses. Ruthie keeps the house, cooks for the ranch hands, and takes in washing."

Lily nodded and smiled.

David nodded too. "Yes, I was worried too, but they've stayed clear of the business. Speaking of which . . . I'm sorry to tell you this, but Sarah's made some changes and claims the place is hers."

"How?"

"I'm not sure. It's something I didn't have time to research. Perhaps after the war, we'll . . ."

But they knew that there would be no "we" after the war.

"So." She took a deep breath and exhaled. "Do the kids think I deserted them?"

He shook his head. "No, not at all. They understand that the war has changed everything and know that you still want to come back." He smiled sheepishly. "They're happy that you're still a Unionist."

She smiled at his admission. "Then they're okay."

His eyes twinkled then he winced.

She reached across the table to touch him. "David?"

"It's just," he laughed halfheartedly, "an old war wound."

"What does the doctor say about it? Did it not heal properly? I wish I could look at it, see if there's anything I could do."

"There's nothing you can do. Please don't worry."

Her eyes darkened. "Damn you, David Evans. Have you learned nothing about me? Didn't that mix-up we had before teach you anything?"

His eyes widened in surprise and he shook his head in confusion.

She touched his face, caressed it, touched his lips with her fingers. "Don't you know that I want to take care of you no matter what the problem? If, God forbid, you lost both your legs, I'd be your legs and gladly fetch things for you for the rest of your life. I'd be your eyes if you were blind. I want to take care of you. Please let me, please."

But still he shook his head. "But I'm the man. I should be caring for you . . . I . . ."

She pulled her hand from his cheek and whispered, "Damn you."

"What?"

"I said damn you! Damn you for wanting to take care of the entire world! Maybe carrying the world on your shoulders is why you're in such pain. Just how much do you think you can handle? No, I take that back. You think you can handle much more than you can, or should. You're only one man, David, and though you're a magnificent honorable man, you're only one." She touched his cheek again and he kissed her palm.

He seemed almost meek as he held her hand and looked down at the union. "Do you mean it, that you want to take care of me?" His eyes lingered on their hands.

"Oh, yes." She watched his eyes.

"It just doesn't seem right."

"I know it doesn't, not to you, but all that matters is that people who care about each other are together." Were her words reminding him of Mary Anne and marriage? Was she convincing him to stay with his wife? She swallowed hard. "You need rest."

He smiled wistfully and whispered, "Yes, well . . ."

"Were you able to rest while you were at home?"

"Some."

"But things are bad there, aren't they?"

"It would break your heart. The people have been turned into scavengers, stealing food from each other. The animals are dying from lack of food, those that haven't been killed or stolen by the Yankees." He shook his head. "Then there's the fever . . ."

She squeezed his hands. "I'm so selfish, David, please forgive me. With so much to say . . . I forgot. . . I'm so sorry." He nodded and she touched his wet cheeks with her fingers. "You've been through so much, too much. I'm so sorry. I just wish I could . . ."

"I know."

"And you . . . have a new son. Congratulations."

He smiled and nodded. "Yes. Joseph Ashley."

"And the other boys, they're okay?"

He nodded.

"And Grace?"

His eyes brightened again. "Yes, she's fine. She and Mother are still eating well, not richly, but well enough. Mother always planned for shortages."

She nodded.

All was silent for a few moments as they leaned on their elbows on the table, their heads touching, their hands clasped together. When Lily could tell that he was falling asleep, she cried. He was so tired and his health was ruined. He was fighting a losing cause and had a family he couldn't support, yet he went long miles out of his way to see the children of a man he'd killed and was now risking his marriage and career to visit her. Her. Lily. A whore. A traitor.

As she touched his cheek with tender fingers, she looked at him. So much on such young shoulders . . . But everything he did made her love him more and he was here now, with her, and all she wanted to do was lie next to him, hold him, comfort him, a need so great that she physically ached. But she'd had such aches before—for both David and Grace. Women, she'd long ago decided, actually feel physical pain when denied the touch of those they love. She traced David's lips with a finger until he woke, then whispered, "You need to leave. Go get some rest."

He shook his head. "No, I don't want to leave . . . I can't . . ."

"I'm glad you feel that way but you must get some rest, unless . . . " She should insist he go but she couldn't, just couldn't. . . . "At least put your head down for a few minutes."

He nodded as he crossed his arms and rested his head on them, mumbling, "I'll just close my eyes for a few minutes."

Lily watched him, listened to him, cried with love for him, touched him.

The next thing she knew, Peter was watching, and Lily quickly jumped to her feet.

"It's time for you to go back, ma'am."

"Yes, of course." She saw the boy's eyes on David. "He's exhausted."

"But . . ."

"We were talking and he fell asleep. I didn't want to disturb him. He's been on the road for days."

"But . . . you were touching him." His eyes widened and his breath came in gasps. "You and him are what people are saying, aren't you?"

"No, Peter. I told you. We're just good friends." Lily reached out her hand to the boy but he backed away. "I was just going to show you that friends can touch. I've touched you before, haven't I? Don't you touch your mother and sister?"

"I guess so, but . . . No, I think maybe it's true what they say about you after all."

She closed her eyes and took a deep breath. "No, Peter. Please. You've been so kind to me and I've so enjoyed our talks." She picked up the jar with the roses. "And see. I'm saving the flowers you've given me."

"What for?"

"I plan to carry them with me. To the gallows."

He winced and Lily knew she'd chosen her words well, but David was starting to stir and she feared he might mumble sleepy words of affection as he'd done in the past. Startled and confused at first, he looked up to see an audience then stood, his pain so obvious that Lily felt it.

Peter stood at attention and saluted.

David returned the salute then looked at Lily. "I'm sorry, Mrs. Dundee. It was rude of me to fall asleep like that."

"No problem, General. You were obviously in need of rest." She looked at Peter then back at David and smiled. "I'm not going anywhere."

But neither man smiled at her attempt at humor.

David's face blanched, and Lily realized that they'd not spoken of her situation. Their eyes locked for a moment then both remembered Peter. "I've been telling this fine young man that you and I are old friends, that I know your pretty wife and handsome children." The words almost choked her. "In fact, Peter, General Evans has a new son."

"Congratulations, sir."

"Thank you, Private."

The boy's excitement reminded Lily of the waiter at the Spotswood. How many years ago that seemed now.

"I'm sorry, sir, but I've got to take Mrs. Dundee back now."

"Of course." David coughed as he straightened his uniform. "Just a few more minutes, Private?"

"Yes, sir." The boy saluted then walked out and closed the door behind him.

David and Lily looked at each other. A few minutes. That's all they had, all they might ever have . . .

They moved quickly together and found satisfaction, but it was a temporary satisfaction only, a momentary remedy, a fleeting saturation that left them wanting more. And even as they clung together still flush with lovemaking and stared into each other's eyes, neither dared voice what they both knew.

True satisfaction was something they would never know.

For them there would never be enough time.

For them there was no future.

They had no tomorrows—no days, weeks, months and years of togetherness.

David caressed her hair, kissed her eyes. "Oh Lil, what you do to me."

She met his lips with hers and whispered, "What General? What do I do to you?"

"I just can't get enough of you."

She pulled away and searched his face. "Truly, David? Do you mean it?"

He nodded slowly as his hands caressed her cheeks. His eyelids were heavy, his voice mellow. "Yes, oh, yes, I mean it. How can you not know it? Look at the chances we're taking."

As she covered his hands with hers, she inhaled the scent of their lovemaking and smiled at the hold they'd always had on each other, and suddenly she startled him with a giggle.

"What?"

"I just remembered your mother calling us cats in heat."

He laughed out loud, rearing his head back, then nodded. "Yes. That was," his face grew red as he remembered, "quite embarrassing, wasn't it?"

She shook her head. "Not completely." She smiled devilishly.

"No?"

"Well, I guess it's easier for me since she's not my mother, and perhaps I shouldn't say it, but I liked someone finding us."

He smiled conspiratorially and touched the tip of her nose. "Lily Morgan, will I always be learning new things about you?"

"I hope so."

He turned serious and took her hands in his. "I like people knowing about us too. I just wish . . ."

She squeezed his hands. "I know, but we don't have to worry about that anymore, do we?"

He grabbed her shoulders and shook her as his brows knitted and his eyes darkened. "Don't say that!"

"David, you're hurting me."

"I'm sorry." His fingers trembled as he touched her face and the curls by her cheeks and his eyes darted all over her body as if searching for something but seeing nothing. "But I can't let you say those things. Shh . . .

Don't say them. You mustn't say them." He avoided eye contact and didn't seem to hear her voice or even know where he was.

"What's wrong?" She put her hands on his cheeks and forced his eyes to stop on hers. "David? David, look at me!"

"What?"

He woke from the trance but wore a pitiful lost look in his eyes that broke her heart.

"Are you okay?"

"What? Yes, yes, I'm okay." He looked around then spoke quietly and rapidly. "I'm getting you out of here."

"No. Don't risk anything. I'm not worth it."

His face was red and his eyes black. "Don't ever say that again! I don't ever want to hear you run yourself down again. Do you hear me?"

His demeanor was so bewildering that she could only nod.

He was restless and frightening. He paced as he muttered to himself then stopped and pulled her to him. "I'll be back. I'm not sure when but be ready to leave." He kissed her mouth forcefully then ran out the door.

As he did, Lily noticed that he no longer winced from his pain. Was his mind so muddled that he no longer felt it? Had he known what he was saying or was he crazy from lack of sleep? From pain? From anxiety and strain? From depression? Was he going to get them both hanged *and* ruin his reputation? Or would he regain his sanity in a few moments and forget what he'd said?

CHAPTER 53

That night Peter delivered Lily's dinner tray and left without speaking. She immediately noticed that there was no rose and realized that the boy had lost faith in her and no longer believed her assertions that she and David weren't lovers.

Lovers. Yes, that's what they were. Whether or not David loved her enough to marry her if he were free, they were lovers. He needed her, wanted her, cared for her. She finally believed it and reveled in the idea. And with only two more days to live, she knew that there was only one more thing that would allow her to die in peace. She wanted, needed, to hear him say the words. *Tell me you love me, David, just once. Say the words and let me die believing that you would have married me if you could. I can pretend that part but I must hear words of love from your lips.*

She ignored her meal and chose, instead, to dream of David. As in so many of her dreams, he seemed to be there with her. So real was the feeling that she thought she heard his voice whisper her name.

"Lily."

"David?" But he was there and she ran to him, held his face between her hands and saw that he was, indeed, sane and rational. "You're okay," she whispered.

He kissed her hands and smiled. "Yes, I'm okay." He kissed her lips quickly then whispered, "Put these on. Hurry!"

She took the garments and held them up. "Whose are these?"

"They're Peter's but don't worry about that. Put them on!"

She moved as quickly as she could but was shaking and scared. "You didn't hurt him, did you?"

"Of course not." He looked around nervously. "Tuck you hair under the hat and keep your eyes down and try not to swing your hips when you walk."

She laughed at the idea that he'd noticed her hips, and when they reached the top of the stairs she easily fell into the walk that she'd used so

many years before, a matter-of-fact no-nonsense step with just a hint of
military bearing. And because she'd spent so much time around military men,
she knew to whom she needed to salute and when and how. Lily's pride in
David surfaced again as she saw how his rank got them through any possible
obstacle—so far.

As they mounted their horses, he whispered, "We can't rush through
town or we'll bring attention to ourselves."

She nodded and they turned toward the outskirts of town and didn't
stop until they were almost to Fredericksburg.

After following the rippling sounds of a creek for awhile, they stopped
on its banks in a heavily wooded spot. When Lily saw how much pain David
was in, she ran to him, helped him off his horse, then helped him sit down
against a tree. As gently as possible, she removed his coat then lowered his
suspenders and unbuttoned his shirt. Though they didn't appear infected, the
old wounds were obviously painful and she kissed them.

And David pulled her to him.

She eagerly met his lips with hers then murmured, "Feel better?"

"Oh, yes ma'am." He chuckled softly then lay her on the ground and
kissed her face and neck as she loved his chest with her mouth and hands.

And though he winced with pain at every movement, he made love to
her and, as always, she felt dizzy at the feel of him inside her, at the feel of his
bare skin against hers, at the feel of his hands and lips exploring her. Their
eyes connected as they caressed each other, savoring and becoming
reacquainted with the feel and tastes they'd been denied for so long.
Afterward they snuggled next to each other and slept.

A slight breeze and the hoot of an owl aroused them around dusk. After
a light supper, David leaned against the tree again and pulled Lily into his
arms. She tingled at the feel of his breath on her neck and the feel of the soft
brown hair on the strong arms that tightened around her.

Regretfully, they left their private heaven the next morning, but even as
they rode, they rode slowly so they could talk, so they could stretch out a
hand to touch one another.

"Peter doesn't know who tied him up. I made sure no one was around
then grabbed him from behind. I knocked him out but all he'll suffer is a
headache. I dragged him to a closet then took off his clothes. He was
probably discovered within hours so don't worry that he's suffocating
somewhere. I wouldn't do that."

"Do you think they'll suspect you?"

He shrugged then winced. "I don't know. The way things have been
going I wouldn't be surprised."

She looked at his face and saw pain not caused by the wound. "Tell me."

He stopped his horse and sighed. "It's my career, Lil. It's pretty much over. I really thought I'd have my own division by now but guess it's not meant to be." He urged the bay forward but slowly. "It's politics, pure and simple. Friends and cronies come first and the war be hanged." They rode in silence a little ways before he added, "I'm hoping I can redeem myself at this next engagement."

Lily felt a familiar fist in her stomach. Why had she thought they were leaving the war behind? "What next engagement? Where are we going?"

"A little ways up here, near an area called the Wilderness."

She shivered.

"The Yankees have crossed the Rapidan and we need to send them back home." He rose up in his saddle and looked in the horizon. "Buford!" Lily knew that David wanted to race toward his friend but his pain wouldn't allow it.

Jonathan caught up with them. "Who's the new private?" He winked at Lily. "I'd give you a hug but dare not, just in case anyone sees us." He reached out a hand and patted her on the shoulder. "I'm sure glad to see you out of that place."

She looked from Jonathan's face to David's and saw the mutual joy. "I'd sure like to give you both a big kiss right now."

"Not a good idea but I'll collect it later if I may."

"Yes sir, you may."

Jonathan looked at David then back at Lily and smiled broadly. "Something tells me that General Evans has already collected his."

David and Lily looked at each other and blushed.

"If you two can take your eyes off of each other, I think we'd better get moving. I found a place for our young private. Follow me."

After winding in and out of thickets, they came upon a tiny white farm house. Lily and Jonathan hurriedly dismounted then helped David get off of Samson and inside and onto the small bed. After helping him get comfortable leaning against the rough wooden headboard, Lily removed his jacket and handed him his canteen. "Okay?"

He winced and nodded.

Jonathan sat down in one of the four straight-backed chairs at the square dark pine sawbuck table, but a restless Lily paced and took inventory of the tiny abode. One room with one hastily made bed, the table and chairs, and a make-shift kitchen—stove, open shelves with chipped blue dishes, and a washtub—under a window with a blue-flowered curtain with ripped hem. It was obvious that the house hadn't been vacant long because the dust wasn't thick. Stairs led to a cellar that she quickly investigated, coming back with the happy announcement that it was well stocked with jars of fruits and vegetables.

"We shouldn't be leaving you here for long and I don't think the battle will get out this far, but you never know. If you hear fighting, get into the cellar. If we don't get back, you're on your own."

David's sleepy eyes popped open. "Don't scare her."

Lily stood beside him, a hand on his shoulder. He kissed it then looked into her eyes. "I'll be back. I promise."

She flinched. "No! Don't ever promise something you can't be sure of. Promises are too sacred."

"You're shaking."

"Yes I am. I'm scared to death. Don't you remember our dream? Oh, David, you're hurt and in severe pain. Can't you sit this one out? I have such a bad feeling about it. Something's wrong. I don't know if it's because of me, if I bring you trouble . . ."

"Damn it, Lily, what did I tell you about that?"

She looked at Jonathan and they laughed while David looked perplexed. Lily caressed his cheek then kissed his lips. "Please tell me I didn't hear that come out of your mouth."

He turned red and looked away for a moment. "I don't know what you're talking about."

"Yes you do, General."

"Come here." He winced but pulled her onto his lap and into his arms.

Jonathan coughed. "I think I'll stroll around outside a bit. If you're going, we need to take off soon."

"Why don't you go on back? I can find my way."

"You're going to need help mounting that beast of yours. I'll be glad to wait."

"I can manage."

Lily was eager to keep him with her. "I can help him."

"Okay. I can see that you two are determined to spend some time together." He grinned. "I can't imagine why."

Lily walked Jonathan to the door and kissed his cheek. "I love you."

"And I you." He hugged her tightly.

"I owe my life to you, both of you." She looked at each of them. "Jonathan, if you hadn't fed me, sent me letters and books . . . and if it weren't for you," she walked back to David and put her fingers through his hair, "I'd be . . ."

"Don't."

"But it's true. I owe you my life, both of you. And I don't see why you've risked so much for me after what I've done. I'm so sorry."

"You believe in what you're fighting for just as we do."

"But what about all the men and boys I killed?"

"It's war, Lily. Our spies killed many of their men. Someday it will all be over and we'll be friends again."

"Do you really think so?"

"I really hope so. What do you think, Buford?"

"I agree. Besides, I want to go to Kentucky and find a girl as pretty as Lily."

David pulled Lily back onto his lap and said, "I got the prettiest, ole' man."

"Yes, well, I'll get the second prettiest then."

Lily stroked David's face and he sucked her finger into his mouth. Their eyes locked.

Jonathan coughed. "Guess I'd better get going. You're coming later then?"

Without looking at his friend, David mumbled, "Sure."

The door closed and Lily leaned into David's chest, tears falling down her cheeks. "Please don't go, David, please."

He patted her, stroked her hair. "I have to." He held her a few inches away so he could look into her eyes then touched the curls by her cheeks as he spoke. "You know I can't run away."

"But you've missed fights before. Men go to sick call, don't they? My gosh, you can barely ride. How are you going to fight? What if you get thrown? I can't bear thinking of what could happen."

"Then don't." He kissed her mouth. "We have something much better that we could do right now. Let's don't waste time."

"You just want me for my body, don't you?"

He was kissing her neck. "Mmm, you bet."

"David!"

"Kiss me, Lily."

He sat on the edge of the bed as Lily stood in front of him between his legs. He held her hips with his hands and nuzzled her stomach then removed her shirt as she lowered his suspenders and removed his. He cupped her naked breasts then loved them with his mouth as Lily wove her fingers through his hair and closed her eyes. He unfastened her pants and pushed them to the floor then nuzzled her stomach again while kneading her hips and buttocks with his hands.

As she stood with her hands on his shoulders, Lily whispered his name again and again and almost burst from wanting to scream that she loved him. He gave every indication that he loved her—why wouldn't he say it? He'd risked everything for her—why wouldn't he say it? But he'd made no promises about the future. He never had.

He never would.

Because there was no future.

Forget it, Lily, forget it.

She felt his fingers, felt his mouth . . . *Tell me you love me, David. Give me that much.*

Damn your pride, Lily, love him. Enjoy him while you can.

But even as she closed her eyes and felt dizzy when his tongue entered her, her tears fell and she pulled away.

David's eyes were glazed, his words slurred. "What's wrong?" He pulled at her.

But she stood back. "Are you okay?"

"Yes, oh yes." He pulled at her again.

"You're not in pain?"

"Yes, I'm in pain but I'm always in pain and it didn't stop us last night or this morning." His mouth returned to her breasts and he murmured, "And it's not going to stop me now."

"No!" She pushed at him as she pulled away again.

He shook his head, frustration and aggravation in his eyes. "Lil . . ."

"Damn you!"

He closed his eyes. "What is it this time?"

"What is it?" She paced the small cabin floor then realized she was naked and grabbed Peter's shirt and put it on then continued to pace as she stared at him. "You don't know, do you? You really don't know." She stood in front of him, her hands on her hips. "No, you don't. You don't know anything about me."

David stretched his arms toward her. "Come here, Lily, please. We don't have much time."

"You still treat me like a whore, David Evans. You know I'll let you do anything to me and like it. You know you can play out your fantasies with me then run home to Mary Anne."

What was she doing? Had this man not just risked his life for her, she'd be dead tomorrow. He'd risked everything, was still risking everything, so what was she doing? Why was she so stupid as to give him an ultimatum when she knew that there was only one choice he could make?

Why was she throwing him away?

Fury shown in his red face and icy quivering voice. "Hand me my shirt, please."

Beg his forgiveness. Stop this craziness before you lose him forever. Take what you can and be grateful for it. How many times have you said you would? But she simply handed him his shirt then watched him struggle to put it on.

Her heart broke as she saw the strain in his eyes, the grimace on his mouth, that mouth that had just given her so much pleasure, that would be giving her pleasure still. He winced again and again as he struggled to stand up. But when she finally reached to help him, he jerked away. When they accidentally made eye contact, his eyes were hostile and cruel.

I'm sorry, David, please forgive me. But she said nothing.

He made it out to Samson but couldn't get on the huge animal. Lily saw his frustration and pain, agony and outrage. Silently she offered her help and silently he accepted. After he mounted, she looked up at him and saw his anguished face. He took a deep breath then quickly looked into her eyes before turning Samson around and racing away.

Lily watched until he was out of sight then fell on the bed and cried. "Damn you, Lily, what have you done?" She beat the bed on which they should have been, could have been, making love then screamed out loud. "Are you happy? Why do you expect more of him? You certainly don't deserve more." What was wrong with her? Why couldn't she forget Mary Anne? Why, why, why?

She paced and cursed herself for losing a chance to be with him. And just when her fury calmed a bit, she remembered the dream . . .

Then ran to the doorway and screamed in the direction he had gone. "I'm sorry, David, I'm so sorry! Be careful, please be careful!" But her screams did nothing more than agitate nearby deer.

Are you happy now? Not only is he going into battle in pain because of his wound, he's going into battle distracted and upset because of you! You won't be happy until he's dead, will you? Since you can't have him all to yourself, you don't want anyone to have him. Deprive his children of their father, his mother of her son, your daughter of her father?

Lily stayed on the porch and cried and paced until it was dark then walked back inside the weather-beaten plank home and lay down. She stared at the cobwebs on the ceiling and remembered the glorious feelings David had stirred in her earlier—then the dark look on his face when he'd left. And though she felt dirty from traveling, dirty from the dried tears that pinched her skin, and dirty from useless vanity, she didn't care.

Until she knew that David was safe, she'd lie there. Why light a fire? Why bathe? Why eat? If David died, she wanted to die too.

CHAPTER 54

The door burst open and sun flooded the room.

Lily jerked upright in the bed then shielded her eyes and peered at the silhouette. Her heart pounded. She'd been caught.

Seeing only one silhouette, she assumed the rest were outside—with a hangman's noose? Wasn't this the morning?

The man came closer.

She breathed in relief. "Oh, Jonathan, it's you." But he was obviously upset and David wasn't with him. . . . No, please God, no . . . "David. Where's David? Please tell me he's okay. I've been scared out of my mind."

His eyes flashed. "And you deserve to be. How dare you send him into battle in such a state? How dare you risk the lives of so many men because your fragile vanity's not constantly reassured and pampered!"

He paced a few steps then glared at her again. "That man risked his reputation, his marriage—his very life—to save you and this is the thanks he gets? I swear, Lily, I think you want to see him dead."

She covered her ears and closed her eyes. "No! Don't say that! You don't know how sorry I am, how upset I've been."

He sat down on the bed and mimicked sarcastically. "Sorry? That makes everything go away, makes everything okay? What happened this time? Did you remember, again, that he's married? It's not like that situation changes from day to day. You knew he was married when he freed you from prison. You knew he was married when you made love to him afterward and all the times before. How do you decide when it's okay to bed a married man?"

She covered her face and cried then sniffed and wiped away the tears. "I know, Jonathan. You're not telling me anything I don't know. Yesterday . . ." She remembered it so clearly that she could almost see David sitting where Jonathan was now. "Oh, it was heavenly . . . then pictures of him with Mary Anne came into my mind. Yes, I know he's married but I try to forget, I want so desperately to forget, and sometimes I can . . . but sometimes I can't."

"Don't you think he goes through the same torture, but even more so? He's cheating on his wife, for heaven's sake. It torments him. I know. I've seen him, heard him. I've watched my best friend turn old from this, listened to him weep with anguish over it. But he can't seem to rid himself of you and that alone makes him feel weak. You have nothing to lose but your pride while he risks everything to be with you, yet you throw it in his face and deny the very love you swear you want from him."

He paced the small room then settled into one of the chairs at the table. With his legs spread apart, he leaned his elbows on his knees and looked at her. "I don't approve of any of this, Lily, you know that. And Dave knows he'll have to make a decision soon, but for now he's got to get through this war and he needs a clear head to do so, even more so with that plaguing wound. That's enough of a distraction to harm him—and the rest of us in turn. You do realize, don't you, that he takes everything into battle with him?"

She nodded. "I wanted to tell him I was sorry yesterday. I wanted to call him back. I think I could forget Mary Anne if only he'd . . . "

"What?"

"Say the words."

"The words?" He looked puzzled.

"Yes. You know what women want. If he loves me as much as you say he does, why won't he tell me so? Why won't he confess his love for me? I don't expect him to leave Mary Anne for me, but sometimes I think I could survive if he'd just say the words. I want to say them so bad that I ache inside."

He shook his head. "Is that what troubles you? Such vanity, Lily, such useless pride. If the words are inside you, why don't you say them?"

"Because that vanity, that pride, is all I have left. If I say the words and he doesn't return them," She shivered. "I couldn't stand it."

Jonathan paced the little room, slapping at cabinet handles and faded curtains. "I'm sorry, but I don't think your pride is important, not now. Perhaps if we weren't at war . . ." He shook his head in disgust as he stared out the kitchen window.

Lily walked to his side and after a few minutes he put an arm around her shoulders and she leaned her head against him.

"This can't possibly be what it looks like."

They turned around.

"David!" Lily wanted to run to him and throw her arms around him but was scared to. He'd been so angry yesterday . . .

"What are you two up to?"

"I thought you might be coming out this way." Jonathan smiled at his friend then kissed Lily's forehead and walked to the door. Playfully jabbing David's shoulder, he said, "You can take it from here, old man."

They were alone.

"You fluster me completely."

Lily looked down at the floor.

"I mean completely. It's an awfully poor general who can't keep his mind on his troops and battle plans."

She could tell he was looking at her but she kept her eyes fixed to the floor.

"Look at me."

She raised her face to meet his then smiled at the sight of him bathed in the rays of sun that fell through the cracks in the ceiling. But his eyes were red and moist and Lily wondered if, again, he was doing something against his better judgment.

His voice cracked. "Please don't ever send me away like that again."

She walked toward him. "Never, David, never again." She stood on tiptoe and kissed each of his eyes then his cheeks before stopping on his mouth. "I'm sorry, so sorry." After kissing his mouth again, she touched it with her finger. "I adore your mouth, did you know that? I love the way it feels, so soft, so . . . Oh David, hold me, please hold me."

He wrapped his arms around her and squeezed until she hurt, until she knew he hurt. But she relished the pain and felt tears running down her cheeks then looked up at him to see the same.

"We're a fine pair, aren't we?"

"Are we a pair, David? Truly?"

He closed his eyes. "Lily, don't, please . . ." He sat her down on the bed then stood in front of her and rubbed the tops of her hands with his thumbs as he looked at them. "I don't have much time but we'll talk if that's what you want to do."

"What do you want to do?"

He sat beside her and caressed her cheeks with his hands as he looked deep into her eyes. "I want to do this." He kissed her mouth then pulled back. "And this." He kissed her eyes then nibbled her ear and neck. "I want to love you, Lily, and I have twenty-four hours to do so. I want to fall asleep with you in my arms and wake up with you in my arms. I want you to be the last thing I see tonight and the first thing I see in the morning. Don't you understand? Don't you get it yet? What do I have to do?"

"Say it."

His dark brows knitted in confusion. "Say it? Say what?"

She shook her head. "Have I been waiting for words you don't even know?" She touched his face and kissed his lips. "I'll make love with you

286

tonight—and every night for the rest of my life if you'll let me—but I want to hear the words."

As he leaned toward her, Lily kept her eyes open so she could see the passion in his brow and the mellow glow in his eyes, but he kissed them closed before moving his lips to her ear. He nibbled the lobe then whispered, "I love you."

She threw her arms around him then pulled away when he yelped in pain. But he was smiling, grinning broadly, and she fluttered her arms like a fledgling bird—not knowing what to do with them but needing to do something.

He grabbed her hands and kissed the palms then looked into her eyes. "Are those the words?"

"Oh, yes, yes!" She couldn't quit smiling, nor did she want to. She knew she'd hear those words for the rest of her life. David was the only one who could give them to her and the only one who could take them away.

"Are you happy now?"

She cupped his face with her hands and kissed his mouth. "I don't think I've ever been so happy."

He wrapped his arms around her and kissed her mouth so hard and long that she felt weak.

"Oh, David, don't ever let me go. Let me stay with you forever."

He put his hands on her shoulders and looked into her eyes. "I love you, Lily. I mean it. And if things weren't so . . . please let's just love each other tonight and leave tomorrow for then. Can we? Can you? I want you so much. I need you so much. Do you understand? I need you. I've always needed you. I feel I'll go crazy without you, but I can't make you any promises, not tonight, perhaps never."

"One?"

"One what? Promise?" He looked uneasy.

"Love me forever."

He looked into her eyes and touched her face then spoke, his voice ragged and deep. "That's an easy one to keep. I can't stop loving you and, believe me, I've tried, tried very hard."

Lily played with his hair then playfully tugged on his beard. "Have you, General? Have you tried not to love me?"

He smiled wistfully as his eyes traveled her face. "Yes. I've tried and tried and tried." He smiled again and she felt she'd melt in the warmth of him.

"I love you, David Evans."

His smile grew wider. "I wondered how long it would take you to say that."

Lily grinned as she jumped off the bed and clapped her hands and twirled around like a child. "I said it, I said it! Oh, it feels so good to say it!"

She cupped his face and kissed his mouth again then touched his mustache with a finger tip. "I've wanted to say those words since the night we met. I've said them inside so many times that just now I didn't even realize I'd said them out loud." She knelt in front of him and kissed his hands. "I'm so happy, David, so happy."

She rested her head on his knees and he stroked her hair then took her hands in his and kissed them. "Lily, where's the ring? I've never seen you wear it. Why?"

She shrugged.

"I chose that ring just for you. You knew that, didn't you? You could tell, couldn't you? It seemed to call my name, your name. Why don't you wear it?"

"I didn't feel right wearing a ring from you."

He lifted her chin. "But don't you see? I wanted to give you something and . . . oh, why must you make everything so difficult?"

Difficult? How could he know how difficult it had been for her to get a ring from him? How could he know how often she'd relived that first day at his mother's when he'd handed her that tiny box. How could he know how she'd held it close throughout the afternoon then opened it when she was alone, christened it with her tears, held it to her lips all night. But she'd never worn it, never even put it on. A ring from David . . . How could he know how often she'd fantasized about him giving her a ring? But in the fantasies he put the ring on her finger, and she had vowed that she'd not wear it before then.

She located her bag and ripped its lining then let the tiny ornament fall out of its hiding place. As she handed it to David, she knelt again in front of him then held her breath and watched as he slid it on her finger, hesitating before covering her thin gold wedding band. "This is a sign of my love for you, Lil, my everlasting love." He kissed her hand then held it as they both looked at the white lily on black opal circled with diamonds. David put his hands on her cheeks and kissed her mouth. "Know that forever. I've always loved you and always will."

"Oh, David . . ."

Their kisses grew impatient and Lily eased the heavy dark gray coat off his shoulders and arms, noticing how he groaned in pain, noticing how even the slightest activity tired him, noticing how ashen his coloring—and she knew she was partly to blame.

But their need to be together was too strong.

She helped him undress, quickly wiggled out of her clothes, then got onto the bed and helped him maneuver until they sat cross-legged facing each other, looking at each other as they had that December night in front of the fire. They smiled and let their fingers and lips tenderly explore each other. When David stroked the insides of her arms with his fingertips then began kissing the same places, Lily closed her eyes and shivered. When he touched the hair around her face and looked into her eyes, he whispered, "You're so beautiful."

Were his tears from guilt? It didn't matter. Not now. She'd never again send him away, never. Their time was too precious.

Lily ran her fingers through the soft brown hair on his chest then moved closer. Their legs overlapped, their chests only inches apart. Lily loved the feel and scent of him. "Those words, David, they mean so much."

He nodded. "I know."

"And it feels so good to say them."

"Oh yes." He sighed then smiled and stroked her face with his fingers. "I'm tired of pretending I don't love you, tired of trying not to love you."

CHAPTER 55

Afterward they lay facing each other, their faces only inches apart. Lily touched his nose, the straight regal nose that his boys had inherited and the only facial feature of his that their daughter had not. "That nose commands respect."

"You think so?"

"Oh yes."

He smiled then frowned. "I'm sorry I can't love you properly."

She laughed. "You couldn't love me any more 'properly'." She took his hand and kissed it then held it against her face. "Any love from you is better than the most athletic from anyone else. Don't you know that?"

He looked sad, insecure, childlike. "Is it, Lily? Am I better than . . . him?"

"How can you even ask?"

"Are you sure? Did you love him?"

"If we had more time together I'd tease you and make you jealous, but since we don't, I'll not give you anything else to worry about. Yes, you're better than him—in every way." She kissed his lips. "Don't you know that I would never have turned to him if I'd had you." He turned his head away but she forced it back with her fingers. "Damn it, David, you married first, not me."

He turned away again.

"I'm sorry, but you know it's true. And I did love Saul, did learn to love him. What's more, he was better to me than I deserved and I'm truly sorry to have hurt him." She saw the handsome blond in her mind and felt tears for him, felt a soft kindness for him, an ache, and she wondered again if David's feelings for Mary Anne were like hers for Saul.

"Help me up, please." Lily helped him sit up. "So, he fooled you too."

"No, he didn't fool me. I fooled him. Or is that just your natural reaction to him? What is it between you two?"

He pursed his lips and refused to make eye contact. "I don't want to talk about it. Let's just say that he didn't warrant your love."

"How you relish this feud! How childish of you to continue it. He certainly did warrant my love. If you only knew. . . ."

"What?"

"That I used him—and not just for physical companionship."

His dark eyes squinted but she maintained the stare. "I was on my way to get Gracie when I ran into Saul on the train. During one of our stops I was approached by a Union officer who encouraged me to stay with Saul, travel with him, use him to get information. I didn't want to but it seemed for the best."

He looked away.

"But Saul had changed and I soon learned to enjoy his company." Lily turned his face back toward her. "Don't you see? Don't you get it yet? I spied to help the Union and free the slaves, but I also spied to hurt you."

He fidgeted as if caged. "Hurt me? Why?"

"Why? Because I hated you for making me weak, for making me fall in love with you, for being married to Mary Anne, for owning slaves, for fighting against my country . . . for taking my child! Aren't those reasons enough? I'd wager your reasons for hating Saul aren't as many or as valid."

He ran his fingers through his hair. "I never dreamed you hated me."

"But I didn't, not really. I hated myself for loving you. I couldn't have you and . . . oh David . . ."

He pulled her to him and kissed her forehead then rocked her. She kissed his chest then pulled away to look into his eyes. "Are you sorry?"

"Sorry?" He smiled wistfully. "I'm sorry we've hurt people, but I could never be sorry I fell in love with you." He rolled onto his side and pulled her into him and cupped a hand around one of her breasts. She snuggled as close to him as possible, wanting every inch of him to touch every inch of her.

When she woke a few hours later, David was still holding her and she smiled through happy tears. He'd told her he loved her . . . that hadn't been a dream, had it? No. These were his arms around her. She kissed his hand then held it against her lips.

Feeling devilishly happy, she began sucking his fingers deeply into her mouth until he chuckled and began nibbling on her neck. "I'm starving."

Lily turned to face him. "For what, General?"

He kissed her nose. "Right now, for food."

She kissed his lips lightly then touched them with her finger before kissing them again. "I'll never tire of you, David Evans."

"Nor I you, Lily Morgan."

"What about Flora Rose?"

He grimaced as he sat up. "Who?"

She fingered the hair on his chest. "That's my real name—if I have a real name."

His brows knitted in confusion. "Now what are you telling me?"

"I just thought you ought to know my real name, at least the name I grew up with, the one Mama Rose gave me. I adopted the name Morgan when I ran away then changed it to Lily when I got to Louisville. I always feared that using my real name might somehow connect me with the raid and murders in Lexington. I probably shouldn't be telling you now." She looked away. "And I'm not sure why I am."

He turned her face back toward him. "Because we don't want any more secrets."

"Oh, David." She threw her arms around him. "No. No more secrets." She leaned away from him and looked at him. "I love you so much." She stroked his cheek and whispered, "I hope you don't tire of me saying it."

He kissed her fingertips. "Never."

"I'll make you something to eat," she said as she stood up. "There was quite a stash in those saddlebags yesterday so there should be enough for a meal or two."

She dressed then retrieved the morsels and set them on the table: salt pork, a couple of handfuls of coffee beans, a small tin of jelly, several pieces of cornbread, and a small bag of oats. "I'll get some water and be right back."

"You wouldn't like to help me get dressed first, would you?"

She grinned as she walked to his side. "Not really." But as she helped him put his arms in his shirt, she fretted. "I don't know how you expect to fight when you can't even dress yourself."

He frowned.

"Okay, okay."

He sat in one of the chairs at the table while Lily walked toward the door, playfully messing his hair on the way. He grinned and handed her the bag of oats. "Give some of this to Samson, will you?"

She kissed his lips. "Gladly. Be right back."

They talked as Lily prepared their meal and she pretended, as she had so many times, that they were an old married couple. They were just so comfortable with each other, always had been. *No, Lily, don't . . .*

When she sat down, he took her hand and began to bless their food.

As she listened to his soft voice and stared at his bowed head, she prayed too. She prayed for the health and safety of this wonderful man. She prayed that he not be punished for loving her but blessed for his innate goodness and desire to be a better person. She thanked God for the feeling of family that David had given her, for their child, and for the words of love that he'd finally confessed. But mostly, she thanked God for letting her be loved by a man who would hold her hand as he blessed their food.

Yes, David had another family and Lily knew he loved them. She knew the relationship she shared with him was sinful and against everything he believed in, but she also knew that David had finally accepted his love for her as something he could no longer fight and something that was . . . meant to be? Did he think that God approved of their relationship? No, she knew he would never think that. But she believed with all her heart that David had finally quit trying to hide from God, that he even asked God to bless them—sinners though they were—

And help them say good bye when the time came.

CHAPTER 56

When he whispered, "Amen," Lily squeezed his hand and kissed him. "I can't possibly tell you how much I love you. If we lived to be a hundred and I told you every hour of every day, it still wouldn't express how I feel."

He kissed her hand and nodded. "I know."

She leaned toward him and put a hand on the back of his neck, touched the hair that fell in thick waves. "It started that first night."

He smiled and nodded again.

"Did you feel it too?"

"That's what scared me."

They were eating, or attempting to eat, but they knew time was short and there was too much to say.

"Did it? Did it really? I know why you came to Polly's the first time, but why the second? You were certainly in love with . . . her by then. You even told me so." Her voice shook. "You still love her, don't you?"

His brows rose in surprise. Their hands were clasped together, his thumbs rubbing the backs of her hands, his eyes watching the effortless movements. "Yes." He held fast to her hands when they attempted escape then tenderly touched the curl by her cheek. "Do you really want to hear this?"

She swallowed hard. "No. Yes." *Please God, don't make this too painful.*

"As you know, when I met you I'd just graduated but I already had my life planned. Jonathan and I were trying to get our school started, which wasn't easy since we were still so young." He looked at her cautiously before continuing. "When I met Mary Anne I knew immediately that she was the woman I wanted to marry. She was perfect." He held tight to Lily's skittish hands. "Surely, I thought—and prayed—surely Mary Anne could make me forget you.

"And I admired her father so much that I thought if she would have me, if she thought me good enough to fill her father's shoes, that someday I might be as great as he. I couldn't believe his daughter wanted to marry me."

He took a deep breath. "So, the plans I'd made were moving along right on schedule if not a little ahead of it." He grew silent and seemed inside himself.

"What, David? What are you thinking?"

He blinked rapidly. "I just realized how quickly things happened." He talked with his hands, something he didn't often do, and she saw the look of amazement in his eyes. "Now that I look back, it seems I set the course and it ran itself. I barely remember some of it happening." He shook his head then took a deep breath and exhaled. "But even with the nonstop work of starting the school, I couldn't forget you, couldn't shake the image of you. And I tried, believe me, I tried."

She grasped his hands and squeezed them.

He looked deep into her eyes and teased the tendril of hair by her cheek. "I sometimes felt in the middle of a whirlwind, but one of my choosing, so I kept going. And, from outward appearances, everything was going just fine. But inwardly I was in turmoil. I had everything I'd ever wanted—why couldn't I forget you? Why wasn't I happy?" He squeezed her hands. "Oh, Lily, somehow you became part of me that first night, even before we'd made love. Everything about you impressed me and everything about you burned in my memory and haunted me wherever I went."

"Are you sure it wasn't just because I was forbidden fruit or your first?"

He looked down at the table, his face guilty like Gracie's when she got into trouble.

Lily felt her throat constrict. She touched his chin and tried to smile but she wanted to scream from the ache in her heart.

"I thought so—hoped so—at first."

She closed her eyes and felt the all too familiar tightening knot in her stomach.

"I must be honest with you. I hoped that's all you were. I wanted so desperately to see you again but kept telling myself 'no,' until I finally justified seeing you by telling myself that I'd built you up in my imagination and seeing you again would convince me that it was really Mary Anne—and only Mary Anne—I loved. Why do you think I always reacted so strongly to your use of the word 'whore'? It's because I used the word myself, to myself. I kept telling myself that that was all you were." He touched her sad features. "Don't you see? I tried to convince myself that's all you were but I couldn't, and each time you used the word it reminded me of how deliberately I tried to smudge your memory." He smiled wistfully. "But it didn't work."

She put a hand on his cheek and he kissed its palm, held it.

"That day I returned, the very moment I saw you in the garden, I knew I'd make love to you again, that I'd cheat on Mary Anne. I knew my feelings were just as I'd feared they were. God forgive me, Lily, after that visit I returned home and entered into a marriage that wasn't fair to any of us. Yes, Mary Anne was still the perfect wife and I loved her, I still love her—as a sweet, gentle helpmate and friend. And when I took my marriage vows, I truly meant to be faithful to her. I knew I owed her the very best I could give, but my best was what I couldn't give. Not only did I love you the way I wanted to love her, I knew I'd never be faithful to her—even if I never saw you again. My heart and mind were with you and always would be. It was all these realizations that woke me that night."

"What night?"

He smiled sarcastically. "Right after the hairbrush toss."

She winced. "Was that when you asked me if I'd cast a spell on you?"

He nodded.

"I always wondered what brought that on."

"I continued to tell myself that what I felt for you was just lust and would burn out, that my feelings weren't the kind needed to maintain a lifelong commitment." His eyes glistened and his voice cracked. "But I knew I was wrong even as I heard the words in my brain. I knew there was something miraculous between you and me that I wouldn't be able to forget, something—God forgive me—I didn't want to forget." He brushed her cheek with his fingertips and whispered, "Something I didn't want to live without."

"Seeing Grace only made our bond stronger. The first time I saw her was almost eerie, but it proved to me that my feelings for you were miraculous. I couldn't believe the way I felt, still feel, about her." He kissed Lily's hand. "Have we known each other in another life, do you think? I'd never believed in such ideas before, but there's something about you that's so very familiar to me." He was searching her eyes.

Lily touched his cheek then kissed his lips. "I don't know. I just know that I've always felt the same way. I was so determined not to fall in love, not to have my life determined by emotions, but the instant I saw you . . . It was almost as if your soul forced itself into mine."

They were silent for a few moments, their hands tightly bound, their eyes locked.

She'd now heard all the words. She now knew that David loved her as she loved him, and every part of her was elated yet melancholy. Had she and David met before? And if they had, how many lifetimes would they have to live before they could be together?

As Lily looked at the handsome face she'd loved all her life, she wanted to capture him somehow, bind him to her and keep him safe forever. But she could think of no way to accomplish that goal and inwardly wept at the futility of it.

"I'm such a hypocrite. I expect so much from my men, so much from everyone, yet I'm so weak."

"No, David. No." She kissed his mouth then nuzzled his neck and slipped her hand inside his shirt and caressed his chest. The feel and smell of him made her dizzy and she fell to her knees on the floor and opened his shirt. She felt powerless and out of control as she breathed in his scent. She kissed and licked his chest then began unbuttoning his pants when he lifted her chin.

"I want to love you, Lil. I want to make love to you."

"Are you sure?"

"As sure as I've been about anything in my life."

Afterward they slept, but David groaned and mumbled as he tossed and turned then suddenly jerked upright, hollering to his young aide. "Carter!" Lily pulled him to her chest and rocked him until he silently cried himself back to sleep. But she kept her arms around him and lay awake holding him, kissing his face, touching his hair, admiring his features in the moonlight, holding his hand and kissing its palm.

And smiling at the memory of their loving words and lovemaking.

Until the face of Mary Anne banished everything wonderful.

Lily buried her face in the palm of David's hand. Harder and harder she pressed into it. Could she smother herself? Could she crush her skull and all the pain inside?

No.

As she held his hand to her face, she wept at her fate. She'd always known that Mary Anne was perfect for David, for the lifestyle he'd always known and the new one he'd planned and worked so hard to achieve. She'd always known that David and Mary Anne had one of the most compatible marriages she had ever seen. They had genuine love and respect for each other and were genuine helpmates. David treated her as neither a breeding mare nor a servant as did so many husbands.

She closed her eyes and new tears warmed her cheeks as she turned her back to him, melded into his body, then pulled his arms tightly around her. As she concentrated on the feel of his chest moving on her back, the sound of his contented breathing, and the wonderfully warm comforting feel of his strong hands that had automatically clasped her breasts, she silently apologized to David, to Mary Anne, to God—for being the cause of damage to this marriage.

But she loved him so much.

But did she love him enough to send him away? Wasn't that the test of true love? She'd tried so many times before, always telling herself that she could—and would—send him away if he'd just tell her he loved her, if he'd just tell her that living without her would be agony.

Well, he'd told her. Could she now fulfill her vow and live without him?

David snuggled even closer and she knew he was awake.

"You have to go back to her. You know that, don't you?"

CHAPTER 57

She felt his forehead fall forward onto her back then felt his breath as he spoke. "Oh, Lily, let's don't talk of that, not now. I don't know. I really don't know."

"Yes, you do. Mary Anne's perfect for you. If it weren't for me, you'd be deliriously happy." She sat up and looked down at him. "Besides, you can't take a whore home to be your wife."

His eyes snapped shut. His brows furrowed.

"You could never have forgotten it, could you?"

"No!"

She winced and bit her lip.

"Are you happy now? Isn't that what you've always expected me to say, what you can't leave alone?" He sat up and ran his fingers through his hair. "You don't know how crazy it's made me knowing you were with Tom, with Saul, with all those other men . . ." He took a deep breath. "But I've tried to forget it, why can't you?"

"Because it's why you can't marry me." She was sobbing then suddenly laughing, her eyes wide and wild. "What am I thinking? You already have a wife. Why do I try to forget that?"

He squeezed her hands. "Please don't do this to us, not now, not today. I won't lie to you." He looked at the ceiling and swallowed before continuing in a raw voice. "I have to go home. The school, my family, the church, the community, the land—what else can I do? What other life is there for me?" He pulled her face to his and kissed her hard, their tears mingling, their cheeks wet. "But it doesn't mean I want to." He mumbled between hard kisses. "God forgive me, I don't want to.

"Our relationship . . . some of the things I've done . . . I so wanted to be a good man. I've prayed for help, for guidance, but my love for you has always overshadowed everything else." He pulled her close and she could feel his chin move as he spoke, his chest move as he breathed. "Don't you see?

You mean everything to me, everything, and it's because you're so precious to me that I don't want to ruin what we have and I would if I stayed with you. I wouldn't be able to live with myself and we'd grow to resent each other." He swallowed hard. "I'd no longer be the man you love and what we have now would die and I couldn't stand that."

Lily nodded as she traced his face with trembling fingers and kissed his features with trembling lips, feeling and memorizing as if she were blind. "Oh, David, how do you continually make me love you more?"

"How? Because you continually make me a better person." She shook her head and he took her hands in his and kissed them. "No, I mean it. If I hadn't met you . . ." He took a deep breath then laughed slightly. "I was so set in my ways, so sure of everything, but now I see more than one side of things, important things." He squeezed her hands. "Because of you I'm more flexible, more understanding, more yielding. All my fine words and ideals . . ." He sighed. "Just arrogant verbiage until I met you. Oh, Lil, you have made me a better person. That, alone, has been a gift, but your love and the unrestrained joy you've given me . . . How can I ever thank you?"

Lily touched the brown hair that fell onto his forehead and examined his face with her eyes. "I hate to even utter such words, but I wish this war would go on forever."

He nodded and his voice wavered. "You don't know how many times I've hoped that somehow we could be together. I had no idea how it could possibly happen but I clung to the dream." He traced her lips with his finger, stared at them as he spoke. "From the moment we first loved I knew we'd have to say good bye," his voice choked, "but I kept hoping . . ." He coughed and cleared his throat as he inched toward the edge of the bed, his stiffness and pain so obvious that Lily's body moved sympathetically with his. "Help me, Lil. Please."

She'd never see him again. He was telling her good bye. The war wasn't yet over but he was leaving her. "Please give us one more day. Please don't put your life in jeopardy this way." She knelt on the floor in front of him and grabbed his hands and kissed his palms then sobbed into them. "Don't leave me, please. Don't make me live without you."

He moved his hands to her shaking shoulders, covered again in army issue, and tried to lighten the mood. "Don't cry, Private."

Lily looked up at him and laughed in spite of herself. "Damn you!"

His eyes widened and he laughed. "Now, now. I'll have you up on charges for such conduct."

She slapped his knee then carefully put her arms around his neck and whispered in his ear, "We could stay in bed all day, General. I'll make you forget your pain. Just today, please?"

He whispered in her ear. "No."

She playfully slapped his shoulder. "You're hateful, Mr. Evans."

He smiled but his voice was serious. "No, Mrs. E . . . I'm a soldier."
His words hung heavy in the air.

After a moment, he whispered, "Help me get dressed."

Reluctantly she got his clothes.

"I love you, Lily. You must remember how much I love you. No matter what happens."

"Please don't talk like that." She tried to avoid his gaze as she buttoned his shirt.

He laughed gently. "I thought you wanted to hear those words."

"Yes, but not. . . ." She looked up at him. "Please don't go, David, please."

"I have to, love. It's my duty."

"Damn your duty." She stomped across the floor to the sink and stared out the window.

David came up behind her and put his arms around her and nuzzled her neck.

Lily sighed as she leaned her head forward to expose her neck and encourage his kisses. This is what it must be like, she thought, to live with him, to cook in the kitchen and have him love on you. She turned into his arms, kissed his neck desperately, yanked his shirt from his pants. "Love me, David, love me."

"No, Lily. There's no time." He kissed her even as he tried to pull away.

"It wouldn't have to take long."

"I know." He kissed her again then grabbed her hands. "But you know it wouldn't be enough." His eyes gazed over her face. "It will never be enough."

She shoved him away and shouted, "And it's all your fault!" Her eyes grew wild and her arms violent as she slapped at him, harder and harder, screaming, crying.

"What . .?" He finally caught her thrashing hands and held them tight. "Lil?"

Crying hysterically, she spit out barely audible words. "Damn you, David Evans, damn you to hell!"

His eyes widened, his brows furrowed. "Lil . . ."

"You met me first! You loved me first! I hate you for marrying her, for making love to her, for having all those children with her!" Her wailing filled the small cabin as she stomped around the room. When she returned to him, she beat his chest again and again. "It's not fair, David, not fair! You say you love me, that you've always loved me, then why? Why couldn't you have married me? Why, David, why?" She stared at him. "It's because you don't mean it, do you? You don't love me, do you? I'm not good enough." She beat his chest again then fell against it, sobbing.

David held her against him until her sobs turned to sniffles.

She finally looked into the brown eyes that looked down at her. "Why'd you do it to us, David, why?" Her voice was weak and desperate as she touched his face then fell again onto his chest.

His face red and wet with tears, David took a deep breath and Lily could hear a moan in his chest before he spoke in a shaky voice. "This is what I meant by my weakness." He wiped her tears with his handkerchief then pulled her back to his chest. "All those lofty words I spouted . . . Look what good they did. Even as they flowed off my tongue I hurt the very people who meant the most to me."

She looked up at him again.

He touched her lips as he looked down into her face. "I could say that we came from different worlds but even that would have been no excuse if I'd been man enough." He frowned. "Perhaps that's why I was so adamant about marrying . . . her. In some childish way I was standing up for myself." His eyes were distant before looking back at her. "Don't you see? Not only was I too weak to marry you when I wanted nothing more in this world, but I was too weak to stay out of your life once I'd chosen another path." He pulled her close. "Can you ever forgive me? I know I don't deserve your forgiveness," he touched the curls by her cheeks, "but I don't deserve your love either."

He kissed her forehead then pulled away and reached for his boots then watched her as she helped him put them on.

But his every move caused a wince or groan and made Lily worry again: how could he possibly protect himself in battle if the simple act of putting on boots caused so much pain?

David kissed each of her shaking fingers then sat down and pulled her onto his lap. "I'm going to miss you . . . so much." His mouth moved hungrily on hers and his trembling fingers touched her face. "I love you Lily Morgan Flora Rose. I love both of you, all of you. Don't ever doubt that, no matter what happens." He clutched her tightly to his chest and whispered in her ear, "I wish I could give you more. I'm sorry, so sorry." He kissed her again. "Just remember that I'll love you for the rest of my life." He urged her off his lap and stood up.

Lily bit her lip to stop tears as she helped him ease his arms into the heavy material, and for a few moments the room was silent but for padded footsteps and hands brushing and smoothing material.

"How do I look?"

She shivered but put a hand on his cheek and kissed his lips. "You are handsome, my darling, the most handsome."

As always, he lapped up the compliment and smiled boyishly, looking adorable and absolutely irresistible. "Help me get on Samson, will you?"

She couldn't speak for a throat full of tears and a stomach full of turning churning wheels. She knew something unspeakable was going to happen to him. He'd been shot at so many times and had tempted fate with that asinine remark. And something weighed on her that she couldn't name, something she needed to tell him. What was it?

But tugging at him and begging him to stay would only make it harder on him. After all the years she'd wanted to be his wife, now was her chance to act the role.

She helped him onto the beautiful animal then whispered in Samson's ear, "Be gentle, okay? You take care of him." She patted the proud face then grabbed the hand that David extended to her. She held it to her lips then looked up at him. "Was it worth it?"

His pain-filled eyes glistened. "Oh, yes, Lil, yes. Loving you has been the best thing in my life." He squeezed her hands. "Besides, we had no choice."

She watched her hands slide out of his as he gave Samson a gentle nudge and the warhorse and its rider turned around and rode away. But they didn't go far before they stopped and looked back. David waved his cap and gave her his brightest smile then rode off. Lily watched until she could see them no longer.

Tears rushed down her cheeks and she cried, sobbed until her stomach hurt. Not only did she instantly miss him and fear for his safety, she remembered what it was she'd needed to tell him.

It was her dream. It was the message she delivered to David in the dream—right before he was shot. May 6th. That's what she'd needed to tell him. Lily fell to her knees.

Today was May 4th.

CHAPTER 58

The life that David had known and so dearly loved ceased to exist April 9, 1865, when General Robert E. Lee signed surrender papers that ended the war. In reality, of course, the life he'd known had ended several years before—the day his family home was overrun by Yankees. But as long as he could fight, David had hopes that the South could win its independence then prove to the world that they weren't monsters, that they were honorable men who could—and would—free their slaves themselves.

But such hopes were dashed when Sherman destroyed Charleston and Columbia in retribution for the state leading the South into war, and Southerners—black and white—began a decades-long fight to survive and rebuild.

But the end of the war was still almost a year away when the war ended for David, when a bullet entered his chest and the nightmare that he and Lily shared came true on May 6, 1864.

Historians call it the Battle of the Wilderness, and that does describe the landscape, but it doesn't describe the horrors that took place there. It should have been called the Battle of Fire and Hell, the Battle of the Inferno, or the Battle of Damnation because the blazing woods and useless deaths and maiming were nothing less than the devil's own.

But, of course, the only one who mattered was David.

He'd left in good spirits that last day, and for that Lily was grateful. According to reports she later heard, he'd been smiling and seemed to overflow with confidence as he cheered his men onward, telling them to remember their wives, sisters, mothers, and sweethearts.

Of whom was he thinking?

When Jonathan came to her that afternoon, his face showed the terror that she'd so dreaded. Time allowed few words and those few were shared on horseback on the way to the field hospital.

"He's bad, Lily, really bad. The ball lodged in his spine and the doctors don't expect him to make it." They stopped their horses and Jonathan took her hand and spoke through barely held sobs, his body shaking. "You must maintain your disguise in there. You can't cry a woman's tears. Do you think you can see him, see him so badly injured, and hide your feelings?"

She took a deep breath then nodded though she wasn't sure, wasn't sure at all. His last wound had never healed completely; just how much damage could his insides sustain? But a horizon filled with dark spiraling smoke got her attention and she screamed.

"The hospital's safe," he said, then added under his breath, "at least it was. Come on."

The hospital was safe from the inferno but it was bedlam inside—a chaotic melee of blackened bodies and screaming men, of harried doctors rushing from one table to another. Thankfully, David had been hurt before the woods caught fire or he might be one of these, Lily thought as she scanned every body in search of the one she loved. But he'd been moved to an isolated area almost immediately by doctors who knew they couldn't help him.

Nothing or no one could have prevented Lily from finding David and going to his side, but when she saw how still he was she had to cover her mouth to restrain choking screams. Suddenly his body twitched, jerked horribly, and again she almost screamed. The spasm lasted but a second but the frightening wincing and grimacing continued on his face for several more. She carefully lifted one of his hands and whispered, "David, can you hear me?" then looked at Jonathan who stood on the other side of his best friend. "What can we do?"

He looked around then whispered through tears. "Nothing."

"My brave soldier," she whispered in his ear. "You've done so much, David. I'm proud of you." She squeezed his hand then looked at Jonathan. "Is he going to make it?"

"I don't know. We can only pray."

"But . . ." She blinked back tears, "will God answer our prayers? What if He's punishing us? Oh Jonathan, David's got to live. Too many people will be hurt if he doesn't." Lily had never felt such pain, such complete agony. *Dear God, let him live, please. I'll stay away from him. Take him from me but not from his children.*

She stayed by his side all day everyday then rode back to the little house each night and slept curled up on the bed that still held David's scent and clutched the pillow on which he'd laid his head. Each night and every minute of each day, she prayed that his life be spared, knowing that she would lose him no matter what, and thoughts of life without him made her writhe and wail until she was sick.

But each morning she resumed her masculine role and returned to the hospital. How cruel it was, though, not to comfort him, hold him, kiss him, but she dared not with all the eyes around. And though his condition changed little, he continued to live, most of the time with a peaceful solemn look of sleep on his face. Occasionally he'd groan, grimace, even move his arms and fingers slightly, and though Lily hated seeing him in pain, she saw any movement as hopeful.

But one morning she couldn't find him and was just about to scream Jonathan's name when a firm hand pulled her out of the tent and away from all the ears. "I've been looking for you."

"Where is he, Jonathan? He's not d . . . he's not, is he? Please don't tell me that."

"No, he's not. But he is being sent home. They now think that he'll live but they can't do anything for him and don't have room to keep him. They also," he put his hands on her shoulders and watched her carefully, "think he'll be more likely to improve if he's with his family."

Once again, Lily felt the familiar fist in her stomach. "Of course."

The time had come.

"It's for the best, isn't it?" Benumbed, she saw through dry eyes and spoke monotonically. "Has he left yet?"

Jonathan shook his head. "I thought I'd take you to see him . . . for the last time."

She closed her eyes and nodded. "Yes, I'd like that."

She spotted Samson immediately, the majestic animal hitched to an ambulance as if standing guard over his master. As Jonathan whispered, "I'll stand guard," Lily climbed into the wagon.

"Oh my darling." Lily picked up one of David's hands, one of the large rough hands that had loved her so many times in so many ways. She held it to her lips and wet it with her tears. "How will I live without you? How can I live without you?" She kissed his mouth then touched the soft lips with her fingers. "There's no way I can touch you enough, no way I can capture the feel of you, and believe me I've tried." She stroked his hair. "How can I accept that this touch will be my last? No, David, no. It's too hard. Help me, please." She kissed his lips again and again, licked them, licked his fingers, touched every feature on his face, smelled his hair, feathered it with her fingers, touched the always uncontrollable waves at the back of his neck.

Tears fell on the bloodstained coat, on the bloodstained shirt, on his bandaged chest. They fell on his pants as she unbuttoned them and slid her hand down his stomach. With her mouth and hands she loved that part of him that had joined them as one, that part of him that had created their child.

With her fingers, palms, lips, cheeks, and tongue, she told each part of him good bye, finally resting her head on his bandaged chest and kissing it as she continued to wet his body with her tears. And like a lost pup or scared child, she whimpered. "Please don't make me live without you, David, because I can't." The tears came harder and she wrapped her arms around his soft middle. "I can't. I can't."

"Lily," Jonathan whispered. "Hurry."

"Okay then." She spoke softly and mechanically as she sniffed, sat up, and carefully dressed him. "I have to go now." She picked up one of his hands and rubbed it against her lips and tasted it with her mouth.

But his fingers twitched and his eyelids fluttered, and the young woman was pulled back to reality. "David?" She watched the beautiful brown lashes. "Look at me, sweetheart, one last time, please."

His brows furrowed and she touched them with her fingertips then caressed his face, letting her thumb graze the dimple in his left cheek. His eyes opened, then shut, then opened again and darted back and forth before settling on her face. His fingers weakly gripped her hand and he opened his mouth. "Lil . . ."

"Yes, darling, yes. I love you, David. I love you. Don't be frightened. You're going to be okay. I have to leave now but you're going home. Won't that be nice? You'll get to see your boys again."

He frowned and his eyes darkened. "No . . . don . . ."

Lily kissed his lips and his eyes, tears streaming down her cheeks and onto his. "Shh, sweetheart."

"Lily!" Jonathan hissed.

"I've got to go now, darling. You will remember that I love you, won't you? You'll soon be well and have a good life." Her voice cracked as she forced herself to leave him.

But she turned back one last time and mingled her tears with his as she gave him a final kiss.

SPRING 1890

Dearest David,

Through the years I've written you so many letters but never mailed them, and I doubt I'll mail this one, but again I must write the words that scream to be said: I love you.

So many people tell me how you're doing and bring me pictures of you and your handsome family. I know you're proud of those tall wonderful sons and you should be.

Can you believe it, David, that we're both grandparents? And haven't we both been blessed? I smile when I think of how we would probably argue as to whose grandchildren are the brightest and best looking.

And what a marvelous grandfather you must make! I know it's hard for you not being able to run with them, but you're able to hold them, read to them, listen to them. You're there and that's all that matters. You've made so much progress, so much more than the doctors expected. You don't know how many times I've wished I could have been there to help you. Would you have let me?

I was so saddened by your mother's death and wish I could have comforted you, but I'm glad Mauma Hattie moved in with you. I know she's helped with your recovery and with all that Mary Anne has had to do. She keeps me informed and tells me that you still eat too many sweets—especially your Kiss Cakes! Do you see me watching you when you add sugar to your coffee?

Jonathan told me that you've given letters to him for Grace and your sons telling them the truth of Grace's parentage, letters that he is to give them upon Mary Anne's death. All of us hope, of course, that that is many, many years away, but I do so hope I can see Grace's face when she finds out. She's always adored you and will be so proud to have you as her father, although I think she already suspects the truth. Since you see her so often, you know how beautiful and flirtatious she is, but I doubt that she'll ever marry. I think that she, like General Lee's daughters, will find it impossible to find a man to equal her father.

But it's so hard for me to see you in her—from that dimple in her left cheek to the way she steeples her fingers when she's deep in thought. I hope Mary Anne doesn't mind Grace's visits because she adores all of you so much that I don't think I could stop her even if I wanted to. And I don't, of course, for being the selfish person that I am, I want my daughter to know her father.

But my selfishness goes deeper than that. I want her to see you because I want the little bit of you that comes back with her. For you see, my love, each time she returns from seeing you, I hug her and imagine I can feel where your arms hugged her. I kiss her cheeks and imagine I can feel where your lips kissed her. See what a silly woman I've become because of you?

Nellie still visits us when she's not at one of her many schools. I can never thank her enough for putting this place in order while I was in prison. To come home in such a rough emotional state and find a clean and profitable hotel already running—you can imagine how thankful I was.

You saw TJ's ranch, and Jonathan's probably told you how we merged the hotel and ranch into a company, but did he tell you what we call the venture? "Triple Star." Do you know why? I think there were three stars on your collar, were there not?

All of us speak of you every day almost as if you're here or have just paid us a visit. I try so hard to sound casual but I doubt that I fool anyone. TJ and Ruthie know the truth, of course, so they know why I speak of you so often and blush at the mention of your name, but we all love reading the letters you send to Grace. I, of course, try to find hidden messages for me—are they there?

By the way, please don't feel bad about taking my money. I didn't want you to know where it came from but had a feeling you'd find out. I know how you feel about men depending on women but you know how guilty I feel about hurting Mary Anne and about what I did during the war. You've certainly depended on her and I demand the same privilege.

Besides, what's happened to the South, particularly South Carolina, has been abominable. You must know, my darling, that my taunting predictions were taunts only, and that I've taken no delight in the cruelty your beloved land has suffered. With your physical condition, you must look past your pride and think of what we both owe your family. Besides, before you were hurt, you were the one who gave and gave and gave. It's time you received, and there are so many of us who want to give to you. I have plenty of money and nothing is more precious to me than family. You are my cousin, are you not?

We all look forward to visits with Jonathan and his wonderful family, but I value my moments alone with him and the news of you that he brings. The poor man—he probably wonders how he became a go-between, but he's the only one, David, who knows of the entire past we share. He's the only one with whom I can truly express my heartache.

And when I tell him how hard it's been for me to live without you, he assures me that you also struggle with living without me, that you get through each day by promising yourself that tomorrow you'll write me, tomorrow you'll come visit me. I, too, make daily promises to myself. Each day I promise that tomorrow I'll visit you, tomorrow I'll get a letter from you. But since I know these things will never happen, I cling to every word I hear about you from others and every word you write in letters to them.

He tells me, too, that you have fits of melancholy during which you remove yourself from everyone and will speak to only him and Mauma Hattie. I know how hard these times must be for Mary Anne, but selfishly I wonder: are you thinking of me? Is it my spirit you're trying to reach? Are those the moments I close my eyes and feel you so near that I can almost touch you? Are those the moments I close my eyes and see you asleep in my bed? See you eating that cold dry sandwich at the train station and being perturbed at me? See you with our daughter and Rebel playing in your mother's yard? Are those the moments I cry your name out loud?

Yes, I'm selfish, and whether Jonathan just tells me what I want to hear or not, I need to hear words of your anguish. I know I should want your happiness, but the ache I bear for you never subsides or gets easier to bear, and because I'm selfish, I need to know that you share this ache. It's not that I want your misery, darling, just that I want you to love me as much as I love you.

I once asked you why you married Mary Anne instead of me, even though I knew the answer, but since all of our lives have been so desperately changed, could you—would you—marry me now if you were free? So many people have moved west to start new lives and your world of genteel living and distinct classes is gone . . . Would I now be acceptable as a mate? Could we move west and start over?

But such thoughts are useless, aren't they?

So I cling to every memory of you, the good and the bad, because every moment with you—even the most painful—was better than any moment with anyone else. I hope God forgives me for saying such a thing because He knows how much I adore my children, but you made my life, David. Sometimes I feel I'll dry up and blow away from the emptiness I feel at not being able to touch you, to smell you, to hear you laugh. Yes, even to hear you scold me.

From the first moment I saw you, you became my life, my only reason to exist, and from that first moment I felt alive only when I was with you. I think so often of that first night . . . You were so drunk and looked so lost. I fell in love the moment you walked in the door, fell even deeper when you made fun of my nose. I've not seen a more handsome man than you in all my life and am not surprised at all to see what a regal looking "older" man you've become. I'm so glad that Mary Anne's good to you because I couldn't stand losing you to someone who didn't appreciate you. You're much too precious.

I cling, desperately cling, to the hope that someday we'll be together even if it's after death, because a lifetime without you is all I can bear, surely all God will make me bear. Do you think, my love, that since Mary Anne has been privileged to be with you on earth that God will allow me to be with you after death?

Oh, David, it just hurts so much.

Well, I'm getting the paper wet and some of the ink's starting to run and I still don't know whether or not I'll give this letter to Jonathan to give you at some later date. I know I would treasure such a letter from you.

Before I close, I must thank you, my darling. Thank you for making me a mother, for making me feel proud, respectable, and treasured. All I am is because of you. And even though I know the ache for you will never go away, I welcome it as a reminder of how I've been blessed because of knowing you. I'm a lucky woman.

But most of all, thank you for loving me and for saying the words that keep me going day after day—and letting me say them to you: I love you. I love you. I love you.

I will always love you.

ABOUT THE AUTHOR

Kathi Jackson writes fiction, nonfiction, and childrens' stories. *Lily's War* is her first published fiction.

Her two published works of nonfiction are *They Called Them Angels: American Military Nurses of World War II*, and *Steven Spielberg: A Biography*. *They Called Them Angels* is also a play.

A native Texan, Jackson now lives in New Mexico.

Made in the USA
Charleston, SC
21 February 2012